Trans-Mississippi Commercial Congress

Official Proceedings of the Seventh Convention

of the Trans-Mississippi Commercial Congress, held at St. Louis, Mo., November 26,

27, 28 and 30, 1894

Trans-Mississippi Commercial Congress

Official Proceedings of the Seventh Convention
of the Trans-Mississippi Commercial Congress, held at St. Louis, Mo., November 26, 27, 28
and 30, 1894

ISBN/EAN: 9783337234935

Printed in Europe, USA, Canada, Australia, Japan

Cover: Foto ©Andreas Hilbeck / pixelio.de

More available books at **www.hansebooks.com**

OF THE

SEVENTH CONVENTION

OF THE

Trans-Mississippi Commercial Congress,

HELD AT

ST. LOUIS, MO.,

NOVEMBER 26, 27, 28 AND 30, 1894.

STENOGRAPHIC REPORT BY
CHARLES FREEMAN JOHNSON,
OFFICIAL REPORTER, SAN FRANCISCO, CALIFORNIA.

ST LOUIS:
E. J. SCHUSTER PRINTING CO.
1894.

Plan of Permanent Organization

As Reported by the Executive Committee, and
Amended and Adopted by the Congress,
St. Louis, November 28th, 1894.

The Trans-Mississippi Commercial Congress shall be governed by the following rules:—

1st. The Congress shall meet at such time as shall be fixed by the Executive Committee, not less frequently than once each year, and at such place as shall be designated by the previous Congress.

2nd. The permanent officers of this Congress shall consist of a President; a Vice-President to be named by each State and Territory; a Secretary; a Treasurer who shall be elected by the Executive Committee, and such assistants to the Secretary as the Executive Committee shall deem necessary; an Executive Committee consisting of two members who shall be selected by the delegations of their respective States and Territories, one of whom shall be elected at each session for a term of two years, except at the present meeting, at which time two shall be elected, one of whom shall serve for one year and one for two years.

The President shall be *ex-officio* member of the Executive Committee.

3d. The election of officers shall take place at eleven a. m. of the second day of the session, previous to which time the Committee on Permanent Organization shall make its report.

4th. The Executive Committee shall select its own chairman, who shall be its executive officer, and who shall have charge of the interests of the Congress between its sessions; arrange all preliminaries for its meetings, and take such steps as the committee may deem proper to bring its action to the attention of the United States Congress and urge the adoption of the measures which this Congress may approve.

The funds of the Congress may be used to defray the necessary expenses thus incurred, provided, however, that in no case shall such expenses be incurred unless the funds are in hand to meet them.

5th. In order to provide for such expenses, the annual dues for membership shall be as follows: from every business organization the sum of ten dollars, which shall entitle it to one delegate, and five dollars for each additional delegate. Any delegate appointed by the Governor of any State or Territory, the Mayor of any city, or the Executive officer or officers of any county shall pay five dollars.

Should the amount thus contributed prove to be more than is needed to defray the legitimate expenses of the Congress, the dues shall be reduced at the next Congress to such sum as may be found adequate to provide for such expenses.

6th. The following shall be the basis of representation: —

The Governor of any State or Territory may appoint ten delegates; the Mayor of each city one delegate, and an additional delegate for each five thousand inhabitants; provided, however, that no city shall have more than ten delegates; each county may appoint one delegate through its Executive officer; every business organization one delegate, and an additional delegate for every fifty members, provided, however, that no such organization shall be entitled to more than ten delegates.

7th. Each delegate present shall be entitled to one vote, provided that no State shall have more than thirty votes.

8th. These rules may be amended by a two-thirds vote of any succeeding Congress.

9th. The Executive Committee shall have power to fill vacancies.

OFFICERS

— OF —

The Trans-Mississippi Commercial Congress,

ELECTED AT ST. LOUIS, NOV., 1894.

President.............................HON. GEO. Q. CANNON, Salt Lake, Utah.
Secretary.............................C. F. WELLER, Omaha, Nebraska.
Assistant Secretary and Treasurer.......W. H. CULMER, Salt Lake, Utah.
Chairman of Executive Committee.......H. R. WHITMORE, St. Louis, Mo.
Secretary of Executive Committee.......W. H. CULMER, Salt Lake, Utah.

VICE-PRESIDENTS AND EXECUTIVE COMMITTEE.

	Vice-President.	*Executive Committee.*
ALASKA	GOV. JAMES SHEAKLEY, Sitka.	J. C. GREEN, Golvin Bay, Alaska, E. O. SYLVESTER, Sitka.
ARIZONA	W. J. CHEYNEY, Tombstone.	T. G. COMSTOCK, Tucson. J. H. VANDERWERKER, Prescott.
ARKANSAS	HON. G. W. SAPPINGTON, Little Rock.	J. T. W. TELLAR, Little Rock. GEORGE SENGLE, Fort Smith.
CALIFORNIA	HON. WM. JOHNSTON, Courtland.	A. E. CASTLE, San Francisco. GEO. W. PARSONS, Los Angeles.
COLORADO	A. C. FISK, Denver.	J. L. JOHNSON, Denver, I. N. STEVENS, Denver.
IDAHO	GEO. M. PARSONS, Boise City.	WALTER HOGE, Paris, FRANK A. FENN, Boise City.
INDIAN TER.	DR. D. M. HAILEY, Krebs.	GIBSON MORGAN, Tahlequah, W. H. WALKER, Purcell.
IOWA	LON BRYSON, Davenport.	BART E. LINEHAN, Dubuque, W. A. KIFER, Sioux City.
KANSAS	HON. L. D. LEWELLING, Wichita.	W. R. SAVAGE, Wellington, W. H. TOOTHAKER, Kansas City,
LOUISIANA	HON. D. M. KILPATRICK, New Orleans.	JOHN VAN DORP, New Orleans, BREEDLOVE SMITH, New Orleans.
MINNESOTA	HON. C. E. FLANDRAN, St. Paul.	DAVID H. GILMORE, Minneapolis. E. C. GRIDLEY, Duluth.
MISSOURI	HON. JNO. L. BITTINGER, St. Joseph.	H. R. WHITMORE, St. Louis, WM. G. BOYD, St. Louis.
MONTANA	HON. JOHN E. RICKARDS, Helena.	THOS. G. MERRILL, Helena, W. A. CLARK, Butte.
NEBRASKA	R. W. RICHARDSON, Omaha.	HON. W. J. BRYAN, Lincoln, HON. L. H. BRADLEY, Omaha.

Vice-President.	Executive Committee.

NEVADA......HON. D. R. COLLINS,   B. F. LEETE, Reno,
               Cherry Creek. CON. A. AHERN, Carson City.

NEW MEXICO.HON. L. BRADFORD PRINCE, T. J. HELM, Santa Fe,
             Santa Fe. L. BRADFORD PRINCE, Santa Fe.

N. DAKOTA...HON. E. C. D. SHORTRIDGE, F. T. WALLACE, Bismarck,
             Bismarck. N. G. LARIMORE, Larimore.

OKLAHOMA...C. G. JONES,   SIDNEY CLARK, Oklahoma City,
           Oklahoma City. O. A. MITSCHER, Oklahoma City.

OREGON ......HON. GEO. P. FRANK, ERNEST P. DOSCH, Portland,
             Portland. M. G. BUTTERFIELD, Portland.

S. DAKOTA....HON. STEPHEN E. WILSON, HON. J. R. BRENNAN, Rapid City,
            Hot Springs. WILLIAM SELBIE, Deadwood.

TEXAS........LEWIS HANCOCK,   THOMAS RANDOLPH, Sherman,
             Austin. THOS. J. BALLINGER, Galveston.

UTAH.........HON. C. C. GOODWIN, HON. L. W. SHURTLEFF, Ogden,
            Salt Lake City. W. H. CULMER, Salt Lake City.

WASH'GT'N...HON. EUGENE SEMPLE, HON. W. C. JONES, Spokane,
             Seattle. A. L. BLACK, New Whatcom.

WYOMING....JAMES TERRILL,   ROBT. FOOTE, SR., Buffalo,
             Sheridan. ELWOOD MEADE, Cheyenne.

ADVISORY COMMITTEE OF EXECUTIVE COMMITTEE.

A. E. CASTLE, San Francisco, California.   A. C. FISK, Denver, Colorado.
W. J. BRYAN, Lincoln, Nebraska.   BART E. LINEHAN, Dubuque, Iowa.
L. B. PRINCE, Santa Fe, New Mexico.

Official Stenographer, CHARLES FREEMAN JOHNSON, San Francisco, Cal.

List of DELEGATES appointed to the St. Louis convention of the TRANS-MISSISSIPPI COMMERCIAL CONGRESS, by Governors, Mayors, County Commissioners or Judges and Commercial Organizations in 24 States and Territories, including Alaska, west of the Mississippi river.

ALASKA.

J. C. Green, Golvine Bay.
J. S. White, 40 mile Creek, Yukon River.

ARIZONA.

Dr. Theodore B. Comstock, Tucson.
F. H. Newell, U. S. Geological Survey, Washington, D. C.
W. J. Cheney, Tombstone.
Brewster Cameron, Tucson.

ARIZONA — *Continued.*

Judge T. H. Bunch, St. John's.
Chas. T. Hayden, Tempe.
H. C. Boone, Phœnix.
Sylvester Watts.
Samuel Ford.

ARKANSAS.

Geo. T. Sparks, Ft. Smith.
Harry E. Kelley, Ft. Smith.
S. P. Day, Ft. Smith.

George Sengel, Ft. Smith.
J. H. Clendening, Ft. Smith.
Henry Strother, Ft. Smith.
James M. Bohart, Bentonville.
A. J. Neimeyer, Gurdon.
S. A. Strauss, Gurdon.
J. R. Best, Gurdon.
L. Werner, Gurdon.
Dr. W. H. Barry, Hot Springs.
W. J. Little, Hot Springs.
Col. Ed. Hogaboom, Hot Springs.
L. H. McGill, Bentonville.
B. D. Williams, Little Rock.
G. R. Brown, Little Rock.
Allan Kennedy, Ft. Smith.
H. L. Monroe, Ft. Smith.
Jesse Taylor, Yellville.
Robt. King, Harrison.
Hon. R. B. Weaver, Rally Hill.
J. A. C. Blackburn, Rogers.
Geo. P. Williams, Ft. Smith.
G. H. Scruton, Ft. Smith.
R. B. Wilson, Ft. Smith.
J. T. W. Tillar, Little Rock.
C. S. Collins, Little Rock.
G. W. Sappington, Little Rock.
Geo. H. Saunders, Little Rock.
A. S. Kilgore, Little Rock.

CALIFORNIA.

J. M. Elliott, Los Angeles.
Hon. John R. Mathews, Los Angeles.
John M. Crawley, Los Angeles.
W. S. Allen, Los Angeles.
A. E. Castle, San Francisco.
T. J. Parsons, San Francisco.
Chas. Freeman Johnson, San Francisco.
Hugh Craig, San Francisco.
Capt. W. L. Merry, San Francisco.
T. W. Van Siecklen, San Francisco.
J. A. Flicher, San Francisco.
Evan J. Coleman, San Francisco.
Will E. Fisher, San Francisco.
Geo. Morrow, San Francisco.
Gen. W. H. Dimond, San Francisco.
J. W. Henderson, Eureka.
A. Berding, Ferndale.
O. H. Spring, Arcata.
J. M. Eddy, Eureka.
Hon. A. Caminetti, San Francisco.
Frank Dalton, San Francisco.

Juda Newman, San Francisco.
Wm. Dusbach, San Francisco.
C. S. Laumeister, San Francisco.
H. Sinsheimer, San Francisco.
Col. A. G. Gassen, San Diego.
M. German, San Diego.
W. E. Howard, San Diego.
Chas. H. Bailey, Los Angeles.
Chas. Green, Los Angeles.
J. H. Allen, Los Angeles.
Thos. R. Francis, Los Angeles.
J. C. Van Blarcom, Los Angeles.
Hon. E. W. Davis, Santa Rosa.
A. P. Roach, Watsonville.
Geo. A. Pippy, San Francisco.
Hon. Wm. Johnston, Courtland.
David Lubin, Sacramento.
Wm. Niles, Los Angeles.
E. S. Heller, San Francisco.
W. E. Howard, San Diego.
Thos. G. Merrill, San Francisco.
Ed. H. Benjamin, San Francisco.
Hugh A. Crawford, San Francisco.
M. J. Donovan, San Francisco.
W. N. Miller, San Francisco.
Robt. Smilie, San Francisco.
John Tuttle, San Francisco.
A. Jackson, San Francisco.
Chas. C. Terrill, San Francisco.
W. A. Kenney, Oakland.
S. B. Boyce, Oakland.
James P. Taylor, Oakland.
E. J. Murphy, Oakland.
Mrs. A. J. Wedderburn, Oakland.
A. J. Wedderburn, Oakland.
Edw. Mallinckrodt, Los Angeles.
James O. Churchill, Los Angeles.
F. W. Schnurte, Los Angeles.
Chas. Clarke, Los Angeles.
Geo. W. Parsons, Los Angeles.
C. H. Smith, Los Angeles.
Chas. M. Park, Los Angeles.
B. G. Farrar, Los Angeles.
Geo. H. Goddard, Los Angeles.
S. W. Fordyce, Los Angeles.
Mrs. H. Z. Roach, Watsonville.
Mrs. E. S. Johnston, Courtland.
John Ringen, San Diego.
A. H. Handlan, Los Angeles.
J. W. Phillips, Los Angeles.
A. C. Stewart, Los Angeles.

COLORADO.

Capt. Geo. W. Thatcher, Aspen.
Hon. R. V. H. Hanson, Denver.
O. D. Banks, Denver.
Hon. Wm. E. Pedrick, Denver.
Hon. John F. Shafroth, Denver.
Col. A. C. Fisk, Denver.
Mrs. G. H..Warren, Denver.
Hon. T. M. Patterson, Denver.
Col. R. E. Goodell, Denver.
Hon. E. A. Smith, Denver.
Hon. I. L. Johnson, Denver.
Miss Phoebe Couzins, Denver.
Geo. F. Currier, Greeley.
J. D. Hooper, Aspen.
Mrs. J. F. Shafroth, Denver.
J. W. Deane, Denver.
I. N. Stevens, Denver.
Mrs. Mary E. Stoddard, Boulder.
C. E. Smith, Colorado Springs.
E. E. Vail, Las Animas.
Jas. W. Twitchell, Montrose.
W. T. McGarvey, Telluride.
M. Finnerty, Denver.
Halsey M. Rhoads, Denver.
Wm. Stoddard, Denver.
M. T. Chestnut, Durango.
G. H. Gem, Durango.
H. T. Cook, Durango.

IDAHO.

C. Bunting, Blackfoot.
Ben Rich, Rexburg.
John Donaldson, St. Anthony.
Wm. Budge, Paris.
W. B. Heyburn, Osborne.
Albert Hagan, Cœur d'Alene City.
C. L. Hetman, Rathdrum.
S. L. Tipton, Boise.
W. G. Barney, Banner.
A. B. Clark, Mountain Home.
Franklin S. Bramwell, St. Anthony.
Richard F. Jardine, Rexburg.
Arthur Budge, Paris.
R. F. Buller, Hailey.

INDIAN TERRITORY.

G. B. Denison, South McAlester.
Fielding Lewis, South McAlester.
James Elliott, South McAlester.
J. S. Truitt, Afton.
John J. Hubbard, Afton.

INDIAN TERRITORY — *Continued.*

Col. H. H. Hubbard, Afton.
Gideon Morgan, Tahlequah.
D. M. Hailey, Krebs.
W. H. Walker, Purcell.

IOWA.

W. P. Brady, Cedar Rapids.
F. W. Faulkes, Cedar Rapids.
Hon. J. M. Terry, Cedar Rapids.
J. P. Melcher, Burlington.
J. W. Murphy, Burlington.
Aug. Schlapp, Burlington.
Isaac J. Dodd, Burlington.
Hon. Albert Head, Des Moines.
Hon. Wm. G. Kent, Ft. Madison.
Carl E. Kuehnle, Denison.
Ira J. Alder, Iowa City.
Hon. Calvin Manning, Ottumwa.
H. E. Hull, Williamsburg.
Chas. L. Gilchrist, Des Moines.
Thos. Arthur, Logan.
Hon. S. F. Smith, Davenport.
Louis Harbach, Des Moines.
W. H. Bowman, Waverly.
Del. C. Huntoon, Dubuque.
A. W. Irwin, Sioux City.
Hon. Wm. Groneweg, Council Bluffs.
M. F. Rohrer, Council Bluffs.
A. C. Graham, Council Bluffs.
W. J. Jameson, Council Bluffs.
John W. Paul, Council Bluffs.
Hon. S. F. Smith, Davenport.
Capt. Lon Bryson, Davenport.
Frank Trimble, Council Bluffs.
J. G. Hutchinson, Ottumwa.
J. M. Gobble, Muscatine.
Chas. P. Birge, Keokuk.
Fred A. Lischer, Davenport.
E. M. Sharon, Davenport.
Henry Vollmer, Davenport.
J. R. Black, Council Bluffs.
Jno. N. Irwin, Keokuk.
Jno. H. Cole, Keokuk.
Hon. Geo. B. Burch, Dubuque.
Franc W. Altman, Dubuque.
P. J. Lee, Dubuque.
D. J. Sullivan, Dubuque.
Jos. Kaufman, Dubuque.
Gen. Jas. B. Weaver, Council Bluffs.
Robt. Hufschmidt, Lansing.
Wm. Quigley, Dubuque.

IOWA — *Continued.*

Bart E. Linehan, Dubuque.
A. P. Gibbs, Dubuque.
E. B. Tucker, Wapello.
W. J. Campbell, Wapello.
Dr. A. C. Roberts, Ft. Madison.
C. L. V. Craft, Ottumwa.
C. C. Cole, Ottumwa.
S. D. Cook, Iowa City.
A. P. McGurk, Davenport.

KANSAS.

A. C. Shinn, Ottawa.
S. I. Hopkins, Ellsworth.
Hon. J. L. Bristow, Ellsworth.
E. R. Moses, Great Bend.
A. E. Agrelius, Lindsberg.
M. B. Tomlin, Goodland.
Geo. R. T. Roberts, Morrill.
W. E. Hutchinson, Hutchinson.
H. F. Sheldon, Ottawa.
C. B. Hoffman, Enterprise.
E. R. Ridgeley, Pittsburg.
Geo. M. Munger, Eureka.
W. R. Savage, Wellington.
J. T. Saunders, Wellington.
S. Crane, Wellington.
W. H. Toothaker, Kansas City.
J. Burleigh Johnson, Topeka.
J. C. Fox, Atchison.
S. H. Fullerton, Atchison.
A. J. Harwi, Atchison.
Bernice Clark, Topeka.
Hon. Geo. T. Anthony, Ottawa.

LOUISIANA.

Hon. D. M. Kilpatrick, New Orleans.
T. J. Woodward, New Orleans.
Albert Baldwin, New Orleans.
Capt. A. A. Woods, New Orleans.
P. M. Schneidau, New Orleans.
Capt. Chas. W. Drown, New Orleans.
James B. Day, New Orleans.
J. M. Sherrouse, New Orleans.
John E. Hall, New Orleans.
John Van Dorp, New Orleans.
Breedlove Smith, New Orleans.
B. D. Wood, New Orleans.
Geo. E. Sears, Jr., New Orleans.
Robt. McMillan, New Orleans.
B. S. Leathers, New Orleans.

MINNESOTA.

Capt. Thomas Sharp, Duluth.
Hon. A. A. Harris, Duluth.
Hon. E. C. Gredley, Duluth.
E. L. Danforth, Minneapolis.
D. R. McGinniss, St. Paul.
C. R. Cooley, Minneapolis.

MISSOURI.
St. Louis.

Wm. G. Boyd.
W. T. Anderson.
D. C. Ball.
Alonzo C. Church.
Seth W. Cobb.
Nathan Cole.
H. G. Craft.
Given Campbell.
D. R. Francis.
Louis Fusz.
H. C. Haarstick.
Fred. Hattersley.
Jerome Hill.
Henry Hitchcock.
Geo. A. Madill.
C. D. LeMure.
F. G. Niedringhaus.
John W. Noble.
Chas. F. Orthwein.
D. P. Rowland.
Web. M. Samuel.
E. O. Stanard.
D. P. Dyer.
Nathan Frank.
H. R. Whitmore.
O. L. Whitelaw.
Geo. D. Barnard.
L. M. Rumsey.
Chas. F. Joy.
Isaac M. Mason.
James F. Coyle.
Louis Glaser.
A. L. Shapleigh.
S. A. Bemis.
John F. Cahill.
James Cox.
Nicholas R. Wall.
Sylvester Waterhouse.
Edgar Miller.
Charles J. Holtcamp.
J. E. McKeighan.
G. W. Brown.

MISSOURI, ST. LOUIS — *Continued.*

J. D. Bascom.
J. C. Williamson.
Gist Blair.
R. S. Brookings.
M. Bernheimer.
T. B. Boyd.
J. G. Butler.
J. B. Case.
W. H. Lee.
L. L. Culver.
Chas. M. Hays.
I. W. Morton.
Geo. W. Parker.
Wm. J. Baker.
Richard Shinnick.
Wm. S. Simpson.
Alex. Niedringhaus.
Richard Walsh.
Henry Fairback.
N. Waldstein.
F. H. Smith.
E. H. Warner.
Geo. T. Parker.
N. H. Foster.
H. N. Davis.
R. E. Lasher.
J. Kaiser.
H. S. Tuttle.
Col. Geo. E. Leighton.
Alvah Mansur.
E. A. Hitchcock.
Chas. Claflin Allen.
R. C. Kerens.
E. C. Simmons.
H. F. Langenberg.
C. H. Smith.
Goodman King.

Kansas City.

H. C. Schwitzgebel.
Walter S. Dickey.
G. M. Sargent.
H. L. Harmon.
A. J. Vanlandingham.
Dr. C. E. Edwords.
Col. J. G. Stowe.
J. C. James.
J. C. Horton.
Max Minter.
Blake L. Woodson.
Frank Cooper.
Hon. W. S. Cowherd.

MISSOURI — *Continued.*

Hon. T. B. Bullene, Kansas City.
Hon. C. F. Moulton, Kansas City.
James C. McGrew, Lexington.
W. A. Dallmeyer, Jefferson City.
J. L. Nichols, Trenton.
David H. Harris, Fulton.
H. W. Salmon, Clinton.
L. H. Murray, Springfield.
M. R. Smith, Farmington.
W. C. Ellison, Maryville.
Joseph S. Rust, Kansas City.
S. B. Cook, Mexico.
Chas. E. Yeater, Sedalia.
John A. Knott, Hannibal.
Sam. C. Henderson, Joplin.
Frank E. Williams, Joplin.
Waller Young, St. Joseph.
Henry Weyman, Joplin.
C. O. Frye, Joplin.
S. I. Smith, Joplin.
W. H. Picker, Joblin.
Thos. F. Lane, Poplar Bluff.
L. J. Albert, Cape Girardeau.
D. A. Glenn, Cape Girardeau.
F. W. Pott, Cape Girardeau.
L. F. Klosterman, Cape Girardeau.
Prof. Courtenay DeKalb, Rolla.
Frank Hill, Carthage.
Albert Cahn, Carthage.
A. W. St. John, Carthage.
Hon. Jno. L. Bittinger, St. Joseph.
Col. John Doniphan, St. Joseph.
R. O. Stauber, St. Joseph.
Hon. Geo. C. Crowther, St. Joseph.
Hon. C. F. Cochran, St. Joseph.
G. W. Samuels, St. Joseph.
Maj. H. H. Harding, Carthage.
Geo. W. Dulaney, Hannibal.
Col. Jno. H. Garth, Hannibal.
Prof. Walter B. Richards, Rolla.
D. D. Duggins, Marshall.
Thos. H. Harvey, Marshall.
R. C. Horne, Marshall.
R. M. Reynolds, Marshall.
Chas. A. Calvird, Clinton.
Sam'l A. Blasland, St. Louis.
Jas. A. Reardon, St. Louis.
J. H. Babcock, Moberly.
C. C. Maclay, Tipton.
A. H. Danforth, Charleston.
Jas. H. Bethune, Charleston.

MISSOURI — *Continued.*

H. R. W. Hartwig, St. Joseph.
R. M. Todd, St. Joseph.
John E. Lonsdale, St. Joseph.
A. Hemming, St. Joseph.
Louis Mutter, St. Joseph.
Joseph Fountain, Carterville.
J. C. Stuart, Webb City.
Jesse A. Zook, Webb City.
H. Snodgrass, Webb City.
Frank Stewart, Oronogo.
L. F. Watson, Oronogo.
W. A. Snodgrass, Oronogo.
P. H. Wise, Moberly.
D. S. Forney, Moberly.
W. C. Van Cleve, Moberly.
H. F. Avery, Clinton.
Hon. Champ Clark, Bowling Green.
E. D. Graham, Mexico.
W. S. Hathaway, Mexico.
J. B. Wolfe, California.
E. D. Anthony, Fredericktown.
G. R. Gillette, Marionville.
J. Reed Miller, Tipton.
F. Seager, Moberly.

MONTANA.

H. I. Wilson, Butte.
Geo. W. Irvin, Butte.
A. F. Bray, Butte.
D. R. Barlow, Butte.
Hon. C. P. Hough, Butte.
Joseph Oker, Marysville.
Sam. Gordon, Miles City.
Lee Mantle, Butte.
S. T. Hauser, Helena.
Paris Gibson, Great Falls.
E. L. Bonner, Missoula.
Jno. R. Toole, Anaconda.
W. A. Clark, Butte.
J. H. Curtis, Butte.
Thos. G. Merrill, Helena.
E. O. Dugan, Butte.

NEVADA.

Hon. F. G. Newlands, Reno.
Wm. McMillan, Virginia City.
I. C. C. Whitmore, Eureka.
E. R. Dodge, Reno.
P. M. Bowler, Jr., Hawthorne.
W. D. Jones, Austin.
Chas. Calvin, Carson.

NEVADA — *Continued.*

Hon. T. J. Bell, Belmont.
Lem Allen, Stilwater.
Alex. Wise, Winnemucca.

NEBRASKA.

Hon. Chas. H. Sloan, Geneva.
L. H. Bradley, Omaha.
R. W. Richardson, Omaha.
E. D. Stacy, Omaha.
D. A. McAllister, Omaha.
David Zimmerman, Arapahoe.
John A. McShane, Omaha.
I. A. Fort, North Platte.
Oscar Callahan, Benkelman.
Wm. Reece, Falls City.
W. H. Bucholz, Norfolk.
Geo. Hornell, McCook.
F. I. Foss, Crete.
Geo. E. Akers, Gehring.
Geo. W. Frank, Kearney.
Dan C. Heffernan, Dakota City.
Geo. Krug, Omaha.
H. A. Arnold, Omaha.
S. M. Benedict, Lincoln.
J. G. Hamilton, Norfolk.
W. F. Schwind, Lincoln.
Prof. G. A. Gregory, Neligh.
Hon. W. J. Bryan, Lincoln.

NEW MEXICO.

T. J. Helm, Santa Fe.
Thos. Guiterras, Albuquerque.
Cab Conway, Eddy.
Mrs. Grant Rivenburg, Santa Fe.
Mrs. T. P. Gable, Santa Fe.
Mrs. Jacob Weltmer, Santa Fe.
Mrs. C. L. Bishop, Santa Fe.
Mrs. E. L. Hall, Santa Fe.
Miss Stabb, Santa Fe.
L. Bradford Prince, Santa Fe.
D. P. Carr, Silver City.
Harry Whigham, Raton.
M. M. Salazar, Springer.
F. A. Manzanares, Las Vegas.
H. P. McGrorty, Deming.
Geo. P. Lane, Eddy.
Edward L. Bartlett, Santa Fe.
Grant Rivenberg, Santa Fe.
T. R. Gabel, Santa Fe.
A. H. Harris, Santa Fe.

NORTH DAKOTA.

N. G. Larimore, Larimore.

OKLAHOMA.

J. D. Maguire, Norman.
O. A. Mitscher, Oklahoma.
A. J. Sprengle, Guthrie.
T. M. Richardson, Jr., Perry.
L. H. Jackman, Newkirk.
Samuel Clay, Tecumseh.
Geo. Kerfoot, El Reno.
Edw. Hochardy, Enid.
Chas. Watson, Pond Creek.
Peter Brough, Kingfisher.
C. G. Jones, Oklahoma.
Sidney Clarke, Oklahoma.
Geo. F. Herriott, Guthrie.

OREGON.

H. B. Compson, Portland.
M. G. Butterfield, Portland.
Geo. E. Chamberlain, Portland.
Napoleon Davis, Portland.
W. F. Butcher, Baker City.
Hon. Geo. T. Meyers, Portland.

SOUTH DAKOTA.

Wm. Selbie, Deadwood.
Hon. John R. Brennan, Rapid City.
Gen. S. H. Jumper, Aberdeen.
Hon. Stephen E. Wilson, Hot Springs.

TEXAS.

Hon. Wm. E. Estes, Texarkana.
Gen. L. M. Oppenheimer, Austin.
Lewis Hancock, Austin.
O. M. Carter, Houston.
N. L. Mills, Houston.
W. B. Slosson, Houston.
C. W. Hahl, Houston.
H. A. Lloyd, Houston.
Henry Ford, Brownwood.
B. B. Paddock, Ft. Worth.
W. B. Harrison, Ft. Worth.
J. B. Collins, Ft. Worth.
Geo. Diehl, Waco.
J. L. LaPrelle, Waco.
Ed. A. Marshall, Waco.
W. D. Lacey, Waco.

UTAH.

Hon. W. S. McCormick, Salt Lake.
Hadley D. Johnson, Salt Lake.

UTAH — *Continued.*

A. Milton Musser, Salt Lake.
C. E. Stevenson, Salt Lake.
Wm. H. Rowe, Salt Lake.
Fred. Simon, Salt Lake.
Geo. Q. Cannon, Salt Lake.
C. C. Goodwin, Salt Lake.
C. F. Karns, Salt Lake.
Col. D. C. Adams, Salt Lake.
Hon. Frank Armstrong, Salt Lake.
Col. T. G. Webber, Salt Lake.
Col. N. W. Clayton, Salt Lake.
Isaac A. Clayton, Salt Lake.
Hon. John Henry Smith, Salt Lake.
Major Erb, Salt Lake.
C. R. Savage, Salt Lake.
W. H. Culmer, Salt Lake.
Miss Martie Jones, Salt Lake.
Judge L. W. Shurtleff, Ogden.
C. M. Brough, Ogden.
Hon. Frank J. Cannon, Ogden.
H. C. Bigelow, Ogden.
Hon. A. C. Warner, Ogden.
Mayor L. Holbrook, Provo.
M. M. Kellogg, Provo.
W. N. Dusenbury, Provo.
Rudger Clawson, Brigham City.
J. M. Jensen, Brigham City,
Geo. L. Farrell, Smithfield.
Wm. Paxman, Nephi.
C. Andrews, Nephi.
Hon. Abraham Hatch, Heber.
Judge T. S. Watson, Heber.
H. S. Alexander, Heber.
Hon. Henry Hughes, Mendon.
Swens O. Nielsen, Fairview.
Hon. Henry Beal, Ephraim.
Wm. K. Reid, Manti.
John Hopkins, Echo.
T. R. Cutler, Lehi.
W. W. Cluff, Coalville.
Will G. Sharp, Scofield.
W. H. Weed, Scofield.

WASHINGTON.

Col. J. S. Coolican, Port Angeles.
John Cain, Port Angeles.
Alfred L. Black, New Whatcom.
G. H. Westcott, Blaine.
L. W. Wellman, Linden.
Phil. A. Lawrence, Sumos.

WASHINGTON — *Continued.*

L. L. Adams, Spokane.
Maj. Eli Wilkin, Fairhaven.
H. W. Kinney, Fairhaven.
O. H. Culver, Fairhaven.
F. H. Adams, New Whatcom.
E. W. Purdy, New Whatcom.
Alex. Van Wyck, New Whatcom.
N. M. Neeld, Everett.
Paul Whow, Anacortes.
Hon. Henry Landes, Port Townsend.
J. S. Johnson, Blaine.
G. H. Westerell, Blaine.
D. E. Durie, Seattle.
Eugene Semple, Seattle.
J. F. Hale, Seattle.
E. L. Collier, New Whatcom.
J. Austin, San Juan.

WASHINGTON — *Continued.*

W. Finley Hall, New Whatcom.
Dr. A. S. Oliver, Olympia.

WYOMING.

Robert Foote, Sr., Buffalo.
James Terrell, Sheridan.
John F. Mall, Rock Springs.
T. J. Wyche, Van Dyke.
Wm. Brown, Big Horn.
Wm. Hinton, Evanston.
Arthur Sparhawk, Lander.
Chas F. Tew, Cheyenne.
W. C. Hall, Sundance.
J. R. Rollman, Saratoga.
Chas. E. Carpenter, Laramie.
Edward Gillette, Sheridan.

COMMERCIAL ORGANIZATIONS APPOINTING DELEGATES TO THE ST. LOUIS MEETING.

ARKANSAS.

Ft. Smith, Chamber of Commerce.
Gurdon, Ark., Lumber Mfrs. Association.
Hot Springs, Chamber of Commerce.

CALIFORNIA.

Los Angeles, Board of Trade.
Eureka, Humboldt Chamber of Commerce.
San Francisco, Produce Exchange.
San Francisco, Chamber of Commerce.
San Francisco, Miners Association.
San Francisco, Builders Exchange.
San Diego, Chamber of Commerce.
Oakland, Board of Trade.
Los Angeles, Chamber of Commerce.
Los Angeles, Cal. Improvement Company.

COLORADO.

Denver, Chamber of Commerce and Board of Trade.

INDIAN TERRITORY.

South McAlester, Chamber of Commerce.
Afton, Cherokee Indian Citizenship Asso.
Purcell, Commercial Club.

IOWA.

Davenport, Business Men's Association.
Council Bluffs, Merchants & Mfrs. Association.
Keokuk, So. Iowa Wholesale Grocers Association.
Keokuk Business Men's Association.
Dubuque, Board of Trade.

KANSAS.

Wellington, Commercial Club.
Atchison, Commercial Club.

LOUISIANA.

New Orleans, Chamber of Commerce and Industry.
New Orleans, Board of Trade.
New Orleans, Cotton Exchange.

MINNESOTA.

Duluth, Chamber of Commerce.
St. Paul, Commercial Club.
Minnesota, Commercial Club.

MISSOURI.

Kansas City Commercial Club.
Marshall, Board of Trade.
St. Louis, Merchant's Exchange.
St. Louis, Mercantile Club.
Joplin, Joplin Club.
St. Louis, Builders Exchange.
Cape Girardeau, Board of Trade.
St. Louis, Lumbermen's Exchange.
Carthage, Commercial Club.
St. Louis, Furniture Board of Trade.
St. Louis, Commercial Club.

NEW MEXICO.

Santa Fe, Woman's Board of Trade.
Santa Fe, Board of Trade.

OKLAHOMA.

Guthrie, Chamber of Commerce.

TEXAS.

Ft. Worth, Chamber of Commerce.
Waco, Commercial Club.

WASHINGTON.

Port Angeles, Board of Trade.
Fairhaven, Commercial Club.
New Whatcom, Board of Trade.
Blaine, Board of Trade.
Seattle, Chamber of Commerce.

PROCEEDINGS

OF THE

SEVENTH CONVENTION

OF THE

Trans-Mississippi Commercial Congress,

HELD AT

St. Louis, November 26th. to 30th., 1894.

MONDAY, NOVEMBER 26th, 1894.

The meeting was called to order at 11 a. m., in the Entertainment Hall of the Exposition Building, by President Henry R. Whitmore.

PRESIDENT WHITMORE: In accordance with the custom heretofore prevailing, as your presiding officer at the last session, it becomes my duty to call this Congress to order, and I will ask the Rev. Dr. Niccolls to open the meeting with prayer.

REV. DR. S. J. NICCOLLS: Almighty God, our heavenly Father, creator and Lord of all, Thou buildest and guidest all things in infinite wisdom and power. We should acknowledge Thee in all our ways. Thou madest man in Thine own image, and Thy inspiration of man giveth to him understanding. Thou hast formed the earth for his abode and richly endowed it for his inheritance, and Thou hast given him dominion over all creatures. Thou hast made all nations to dwell upon the face of the earth. Thou hast opened to each one its lot and its destiny. We are thankful for the light of our inheritance and for the blessings with which Thou hast crowned us. Thou hast placed us among the nations and crowned us with privileges. Thou hast given to us a goodly land, a land of forests and fields and of living streams, a land whose fields are fertile and whose hills and mountains are a treasure-house of silver and gold, whose valleys bear all manner of fruits and whose pastures feed our flocks and herds. We bless Thee for Thy goodness and we appeal to Thee that we may not forfeit our heritage or be false to our high calling.

And now, we beseech Thee, look with favor upon these, Thy servants, who are assembled to-day in counsel to deliberate concerning the material good of our inheritance, and fill them with the spirit of wisdom, that justice and charity and harmony may prevail in all of their deliberations. May all selfish interests be sacrificed to the general good. So lead them, in their deliberations, that the result may secure increased prosperity and large rewards to industry and to honest toil, and that each section of the land, country, town and city, may be bound together in bonds of mutual interest, and that each inhabitant of the land may have his due share in the prosperity and the welfare of all.

Grant Thy protecting care to these, Thy servants, and as Thou hast brought them here in peace and safety, so keep them and return them to their homes.

We invoke Thy blessing upon our country. Grant to Thy servants, the people of these United States, and of the Commonwealth and to all who make and execute the laws, the spirit of wisdom and of counsel. Plentifully endow them with Thy holy spirit and so direct them in all affairs that the prosperity of the land may be assured and that we may dwell in righteousness and in peace.

All this we ask in the name of Him who said, Our Father who art in Heaven, hallowed be Thy name; Thy kingdom come; Thy will be done in earth as it is in heaven. Give us this day our daily bread and forgive us our trespasses as we forgive those who trespass against us. Lead us not into temptation but deliver us from evil, for Thine is the kingdom, the power and the glory, for ever and ever. Amen.

PRESIDENT WHITMORE: As the delegates are aware, we are assembled in St. Louis at the invitation of the Merchant's Exchange. Its members desire to express to you their greeting, through their President, Mr. Wm. G. Boyd, whom I now have the honor of introducing.

MR. BOYD: *Mr. President and Gentlemen of the Convention* — With the welcomes extended to you by the Governor of Missouri and the Mayor of our city, it would seem that you need no words from me to convince you of our pleasure at your coming. There is an eminent fitness, however, in a Commercial Congress, of a character as representative as this, being received by the largest commercial organization in the Trans-Mississippi Section or in the Mississippi Valley. On behalf of the St. Louis Merchants Exchange, therefore, by whose invitation you have assembled here, I desire to add a cordial greeting from our commercial interests, to those which will be tendered by the commonwealth and the municipality.

The founders of our government recognized the community of interests existing between all sections of this country by incorporating in our constitution an inhibition against any interference with the freedom of commerce between the States. While this Congress, therefore, is

Trans-Mississippi in name, and representation, I am sure it will be broad enough and wise enough to see that one section of this country, great as it is, cannot prosper without benefiting all others, nor can one be injured without affecting every other (applause).

I can say nothing in this presence that would give you any more comprehensive idea of the importance of the commercial interests of this country. You are well aware that if they do not flourish the country cannot prosper. The great political parties of to-day are divided on economic issues, rather than on principles of government, and it begins to look as if economic questions are about to divide in twain the parties themselves. It is difficult, in fact impossible, in this age to fix the line of demarcation between economic principles and political tenets. It is evident that neither indecision on the one, nor fear of trespassing on the domain of the other, will deter this assemblage from giving free expression to its views. I shall not attempt, however, to forecast your action nor presume to circumscribe it. This is a free country, where freedom of speech is permitted and the freedom of the press respected (applause).

The high grade of the personnel of this Congress is a sure guaranty that its delegates represent the prevailing sentiment of the States and communities whence they come. That fact, together with the unexpected and almost revolutionary character of the late elections which are still fresh in the public mind, lend augmented and unusual interest to your deliberations.

That your proceedings may be harmonious, your conclusions wise, their influence great and their effect beneficial, is the sincere wish of your hosts, in whose name I again extend to you a hearty western welcome. May you carry to your homes pleasant recollections of our city and her people, and may this Congress serve to bind still closer together the Trans-Mississippi region and its commercial metropolis.

PRESIDENT WHITMORE: The Merchants' Exchange, with its three thousand members, comprises less than one-half of one per cent of the population of St. Louis. The other ninety-nine and a half per cent desire to welcome you through their Mayor (applause), and I have the honor of introducing the Hon. Cyrus P. Walbridge, Mayor of St. Louis.

MAYOR WALBRIDGE: *Mr. President, Ladies and Gentlemen* — When the American people meet in convention for the purpose of honestly advising with each other and reaching conclusions concerning the whole people, those conclusions are always right. They may temporarily seem wrong in given localities, but when viewed in the light of that great truth, that the good of each depends upon the prosperity of the whole, they are always right (applause). There is no more suitable place for this Congress to meet than in this Trans-Mississippi metropolis, this center of social American life, this focus of American political lines, this most American of all American cities. Therefore, in the name of St. Louis, I bid you a most cordial welcome, in the hope and belief that your deliberations will be so honestly patriotic and so truly American as to command the attention and the approval of the American people (applause).

PRESIDENT WHITMORE: The great State of Missouri, the oldest, with one exception, in the sisterhood of the Trans-Mississippi States, the State which has sent so many of her. stalwart sons and her fair daughters to help develop those States and territories, from which so many of you come, always has a welcome for all those who come within her borders (applause). For none is this feeling more cordial than for those who are united to them by such ties of kinship and of mutual interest. In their behalf, I desire to introduce to you Gov. Stone of Missouri.

Gov. WM. J. STONE: *Mr. President* — The duty assigned to me this morning, while a very pleasant one, is a very simple one. It is that indicated by you of extending to the delegates the welcome and the hospitality of the State of Missouri. Missouri is simply a typical Western State — in everything I believe it can be said to be typical and representative. In its great agricultural interests it stands identi-fied with the States about us. It is also one of the great mining States of the Union. It is also one of the great manufacturing States of the Union, and excepting the city of San Francisco, away on the Pacific coast, it is the only one of the Trans-Mississippi States that has a great metropolitan city, and, therefore, there is scarcely an interest repre-sented here by delegates from other States that is not also in some measure represented by the delegates from this commonwealth. For this reason the place selected for your convention is appropriate. The people inhabiting Missouri are likewise representative and typical, I believe, not only of Western manhood and civilization and Western Americanism, but likewise of the manhood, civilization and American-ism of all the people of this great Union. I do not believe that the people of Missouri are any better or more progressive, or more cour-ageous, or more patriotic, or more hospitable than those of the other States having delegates upon this floor. But they are like you, gentle-men, and all of you — they recognize in you men of their own type and kind, and being Americans, and Western Americans, I need not assure you that the entire State extends to you a most cordial, hearty and generous welcome to our hospitality (applause).

You come to discuss questions of great public concern affecting the general welfare, and any convention of that character ought to and will receive a warm welcome to this city and State.

This is a convention of Western States, Trans-Mississippi States. In one sense it appears to be sectional, in that only certain States are entitled to representation in your body. My fellow-citizens, I know I vouch your sentiments when I say that I am, and you are all of you, entirely opposed to the spirit, to the idea of sectionalism, if thereby it is meant that anything is to be done unfriendly or hostile to any other section of the Union or to any other State in the Union. You represent an empire in area. You come to discuss from your stand-point great questions that affect not only your constituencies, but affect the entire Union. It seems to me that it is altogether appropriate that in the broad spirit of patriotism questions like those affecting the currency and irrigation — anything of that kind in which you are concerned, should be made the subject of your meditations and of your considera-tion and as far as possible, of your co-operation, not with a view of securing an advantage over any other section, or over anybody else, but simply with the one high and patriotic purpose of securing absolute equality (applause). I would not have this great State in which I live, to enjoy a single advantage over any other State in the Union which is not an advantage conferred by the God who rules us or which has not been won by the enterprise and courage of our own people. I would not have any advantage conferred upon the Trans-Mississippi States over our sister States east of the river or south of us that we are not entitled to in some way. What I mean is I would have no advantage conferred upon this city or this State or this section of the Union which you represent, by legislative enactment or administrative policy (applause). I believe, in that spirit, you have come to discuss ques-tions affecting the public welfare, and believing so, I most heartily approve of the purpose of your convocation.

I sincerely trust that your stay here may be a pleasant one, as I have no doubt it will be. If you shall go away from this great State of ours, the metropolis of our State, and of the States you represent, without feeling that you have been welcome here to the hearts and the homes and the confidence of our people, then I am sure it will be the only convention of delegates that ever departed in that way.

My fellow-citizens of the Trans-Mississippi Valley States, we extend to you our hearty welcome, we open the doors, not only of the city, but of the Commonwealth; take what you will, it is at your disposal (applause).

PRESIDENT WHITMORE: It is eminently fitting that the response to these words of welcome should come from some one in behalf of the Congress who is neither a member of the Merchants' Exchange nor a citizen of St. Louis nor of Missouri. It was this feeling which prompted an invitation to Gov. McConnell of Idaho to respond to these addresses of welcome. I have just received a telegram from him which I will read:

"H. R. Whitmore, President Trans-Mississippi Congress, St. Louis, Mo.: My official duties here make it impossible for me to attend the meeting. Express my regrets to the Congress and assure its members of my earnest co-operation in carrying out any resolutions which they may adopt."

In the absence of Gov. McConnell I take the liberty of calling on the Hon. Eugene Semple, ex-Gov. of Washington Territory, to respond in behalf of the Congress.

HON. EUGENE SEMPLE: *Mr. Chairman, Fellow Citizens of the West* — I have been chosen by the Executive Committee at a late hour — as late as 9 o'clock this morning — to take the place of my friend Gov. McConnell of Idaho, and because I know him so well and have known him so long, and because I know what a splendid fellow he is and how splendidly he can voice the sentiments of the far West, I realize what a disappointment for you and for me is his absence at this time. Gov. McConnell and myself were boys together. We are true citizens of the far West and in sympathy with the great West, and probably I will say to you, Mr. Chairman, and the assembled delegates here, nearly what my friend McConnell would have said, but not being able to say it nearly so well.

Mr. Chairman, in the name of the clans that have come out of the West, picked men, as you can see, I return you their thanks for the kind words of welcome that have been uttered from this stand. We have here assembled to attend to the business of our government, and while we are not here for the purpose of demanding that anything startling or radical shall be adopted, we are here for the purpose of demanding in the strongest and most emphatic terms, that this government shall be conducted in the interest of the people, and that it shall be conducted in accordance with the motto of this great State, that the good of the people is the supreme law (applause). And who shall be the judge of what is good for the people, better than the people themselves?

We are glad, Mr. Chairman, that this convention has assembled in the city of St. Louis — as has been said, a great metropolis west of the Mississippi river. The last session of this congress was in the city of San Francisco, a great city of the far West, and I am glad that this congress has chosen — and I hope it will continue to choose for its sessions leading places, cities where it will be under healthy Western influences. Our public servants at Washington are surrounded by evil influences. Especially are they surrounded there by magnificence and by the evil influences of aristrocratic institutions. We desire that this convention shall be held in cities where they are surrounded by the healthy influences of the West.

You have kindly told us that your latch-strings are hanging out, and have given us permission to take hold of them. We understand that permission in its fullest sense, and in behalf of delegates assembled, I will state that we will pull on those latch-strings in the same spirit in which the invitation has been extended (applause).

PRESIDENT WHITMORE: *Fellow-Delegates to the Congress* — We have met here to-day to consult together in regard to matters of vast importance to the territory which we have the honor to represent, with a view of endeavoring to form correct conclusions as to what will best promote its commercial interests. As to the end in view we are all agreed. As to the methods by which it is to be accomplished we shall doubtless differ and differ widely, but we will differ honestly (applause). No two minds run in the same groove or think the same thoughts. Men are constituted differently mentally just as they are physically; with this distinction, however, that mental differences seem more capable of adjustment. Truth is many-sided. No two men see exactly the same side and no one man sees all sides. The man who thinks he sees it all oftentimes sees the least, and the fellow who always says he knows all about it, simply displays the density of his own ignorance (applause). Coming from different sections, engaged in different pursuits, surrounded by different environments, it is not only necessary but natural that we should arrive at our conclusions from different stand-points. Each one catches a different glimpse of the same truth, but in these very differences lies the greatest possibility of sound judgment and wise action. If we will but compare our honest convictions and learn from each other's knowledge and experience, we shall have a wider view, clearer conceptions and broader comprehensions.

It is a matter of congratulation that we have with us so many of our national legislators, that they may hear the views of business men as to what the business interests of the country require. Under all forms of government it is well that those who make the laws should keep in close touch and sympathy with the people, that they may know their thoughts, their wishes and their wants, and thus be enabled to legislate for their welfare. But especially is this more necessary for both parties under a Democratic form of government, where the rulers are the servants of the people rather than their masters; where every man is king by divine right, and where the people are not only entitled to the expression of their opinions, but to demand of their representatives the promotion and protection of their interests (applause).

There is no class in the community whose opinion should have greater weight, or who are entitled to more consideration, than those who represent the commercial interests of the country, for upon commerce more than upon any other one agency the country is dependent for its development, its growth and its prosperity. Commerce is the very life blood of the nation, coursing through every vein and artery of the body politic, shaping its policy and determining, to a great extent, its character and its destiny.

Commerce is, and always has been, the forerunner of civilization; the merchant has always been the pioneer in progress; like John the Baptist, he has been " the voice of one crying in the wilderness; make straight the way of the Lord " — of civilization. Commerce has built up our cities, our towns and our villages; its demands have called into existence, as if by magic, the greatest inventions of the age — our machinery, our telegraph, our telephone; step by step through various stages it has evolved the steamship from the rough canoe of the savage, and the railroad from the narrow foot-paths of the beast of burden. At its command our mines yield their wealth, our fields bring forth their fruit, the wheels of industry are kept in motion, and the waste places of the desert are made to blossom as the rose.

It overcomes all obstacles, defying wind and wave, and penetrating every clime. It has tunneled mountains, bridged rivers, felled forests, traversed deserts, and girdled the earth with bands of steel which bind in indissoluble bonds of brotherhood the people of a continent. It has transformed the ocean, that impassable gulf which had served only as a barrier between nation and nation, into a great highway of intercommunication, upon which it sends forth its white-winged messengers laden with the fruits of the earth and the products of industry with which to bless and enrich the world (applause).

Commerce extends its influence beyond the domain of business, and leaves its impress upon the character and lives of the people. It is the great leveler — the powerful ally of true Democracy.

It knows no distinction of race, or caste, or creed. It breaks down the barriers which separate men and brings its subjects together on the common ground of a common manhood, seeking and supplying the wants of each other. The merchant never stops to inquire into the nationality, the social position, the religion or the politics of his fellow merchant — he may be American, English, French, Russian, German, Greek or Hottentot; he never seeks to trace his ancestry — he may have the bluest of blue blood flowing in his veins, or he may have sprung from the lowest ranks of plebeian life — it matters not; he does not concern himself about his politics — he may be Whig or Tory, Democrat or Republican, Socialist or Populist, Single-Taxer of Free Silverite; he never questions him as to his religious belief — whether he is Catholic or Protestant, Jew or Gentile, Mohammedan or Buddhist, whether he believes in sprinkling or immersion, in free will or fore-ordination, in universal salvation or infant damnation (applause). He may know all these things, but he brushes them aside and forgets them, and, for the time being, at least, he realizes that the differences which separate men are superficial, while the agreements which should unite them are fundamental — that he has only to scratch through the veneering of race and caste and creed to find the solid timber of character, which, after all, makes the man (applause), and recognizing this, he naturally becomes broader in his sympathies, more liberal in his views and more charitable in his judgment (applause). Commerce is also the great conservator of peace — the golden cord, the strongest link in the chain, which binds nation to nation, and section to section, in the bonds of common interest and mutual good-will. The interdependence of each upon the other is the surest guarantee of mutual forbearance. Thus, whatever tends to extend our commercial relations among ourselves or with foreign countries, strengthens the ties which unite, diminishes the possibilities of rupture, and promotes prosperity, civilization and good fellowship among the people; he who contributes to this is the benefactor of his country and his race.

To assist in doing this, as I understand it, is the mission of this Congress, and the earnest desire to accomplish it should be the sole motive of all our discussions.

They should be conducted not as between competitors whose interests are antagonistic, but as between citizens of the same country, whose interests and destiny are in common; not with any feeling of sectionalism, not with the acrimony and partiality which too often characterize political discussions, but as business men discuss business questions, in a business-like way, with that unbiased judgment, and dispassionate spirit of inquiry which seeks a knowledge of facts for the purpose of so applying that knowledge as to reach wise conclusions, and give such expression to them as shall command alike the confidence of our constituents and the respect and careful consideration of those whom we have elected to enact our laws (applause). It is to be hoped that our discussions may be conducted in this manner; and, if we would gain and retain the influence, the support and the hearty co-operation of our various business organizations, we must be on our guard lest we trench upon the domain of party politics. If the impression goes out that this congress can be used for any political purpose whatever, its influence as a commercial organization will be at an end and its days will be numbered (applause). If, upon the other hand, we confine ourselves to a business-like discussion of the business interest of the section of the country which we represent, we may make this congress a potential factor in moulding public sentiment and in securing such legislation as the general welfare of our people demands.

I know that I utter the sentiment of all of you when I express the hope that this congress may thus be conducted and may thus prove to be the most successful session thus far in its history (applause).

And now, Fellow Delegates, the congress is ready for business, and the Chair awaits your pleasure, after reading a recommendation from the Executive Committee (reading):—

"In order to facilitate the business of the congress, the Executive Committee respectfully offer the following recommendations:—

That, as soon as practicable after the addresses of welcome, the congress adjourn to half-past two o'clock and that, immediately after such adjournment, the delegates from each State and Territory meet and elect a chairman and a member of the following committees: Credentials, Rules and Order of Business, and Permanent Organization, whose names shall be handed to the Secretary during the recess. Also, that, inasmuch as the Secretary has a complete list of all delegates appointed, he be authorized to issue to each of such delegates a badge on application, and that this list be recognized as the official list of delegates until such time as the Committee on Credentials shall report."

On motion duly seconded and carried, the foregoing recommendations were adopted.

Gov. WAITE (of Colorado): Mr. Chairman, this resolution will interfere somewhat with the delegates that have been appointed by the Governor of Colorado. Ten delegates were appointed. Their names were forwarded to the Secretary, but quite a number of those gentlemen have been unable to attend, and, in accordance with what the Governor supposed was his authority, he has appointed substitutes. If that list can be recognized, it will be handed immediately to the Secretary.

THE CHAIRMAN: Unless there is some objection, the Governor of Colorado will have the privilege, which we have recognized heretofore, of substituting other delegates for those who are not able to be present.

A. E. CASTLE (of California): Mr. Chairman, I understand that applies to all delegations.

THE CHAIRMAN: That applies to all other delegations, unless the convention orders otherwise.

The Executive Committee also informs the congress that it has appointed the Hon. W. A. Kifer, of Iowa, and Charles E. Edwards, of St. Louis, as Reading Clerks.

The object of this action was to prevent the interruption of the Secretary, and also from the fact that those gentlemen have voices which can be heard anywhere in the room, as we may know from past experience. It was thought best to appoint reading clerks to facilitate the business and make it more convenient to the Secretaries and more agreeable to the congress. If there is no objection, that action of the Committee will stand. The Chair hears no objection and those gentlemen will serve in that capacity.

Now, gentlemen, the meeting is open for any other business you see fit to bring before it. If there is no business to be brought forward, we will, acting under these suggestions, adjourn.

While speaking the following was handed to the chair (reading):—

"The Merchants' Exchange of St. Louis tenders to the delegates to the Trans-Mississippi Congress a cordial invitation to visit the Exchange hall, either collectively or individually, at any time during their session. Delegates will be admitted on their badges."

Also: "The Mercantile Club extends a cordial invitation to the members of the congress to make themselves at home there. The badges will confer admittance."

HON. WM. JOHNSTON (of California): Mr. Chairman, I move you, sir, that the invitations so kindly tendered this body be accepted, and that the thanks of this body be returned to the Merchants' Exchange and the Mercantile Club, and that we attend in a body or at such time as we can.

This motion was seconded and carried.

HON. E. A. MARSHALL (of Texas): Mr. Chairman, I desire to know how many names shall be placed upon our committees from each State.

THE CHAIRMAN: The Chair will state that under these recommendations each State delegation is requested to meet immediately after adjournment to elect a chairman, one member of the Committee on Credentials, one member of the Committee on Rules and Order of Business, and one member of the Committee on Permanent Organization. These names, together with the name of the Chairman and the name of the State, are to be handed to the Secretary during recess.

Any delegate who has not received his badge will, upon applying to the Secretary, receive a badge in exchange for his credentials; or the Chairmen of the various delegations may collect these Credentials and hand them to the Secretary, in order that they may be turned over to the Committee on Credentials when it is appointed.

The delegates from Indian Territory will organize the same as any other Territory, appoint their Chairman and a member of each committee.

LON BRYSON (of Iowa): Mr. Chairman, have you named the Committee on Resolutions?

THE CHAIRMAN: The Chair will state that the Executive Committee thought it advisable to defer the election of a Committee on Resolutions until more delegates were present, and it is supposed that this afternoon or, at any rate, early to-morrow morning, we will be able to fix the number of members of the Committee on Resolutions, which will be in ample time, as they cannot get to work until resolutions are offered.

A. L. BLACK (of Washington): Mr. Chairman, I move that we now adjourn, according to the recommendations of the Executive Committee.

SENATOR JOHNSTON: Would it not be in order for the Chairmen of the

different delegations to announce where the delegations are to meet?
The California delegation will please remain in their seats.

A DELEGATE (from Missouri): I desire to ask one question — suppose the member has his credentials, but the Secretary has not his name — the member has his badge — should the member proceed further to identify himself?

THE CHAIRMAN: The Chair will state that, on the presentation of credentials, if his name is not already on the list, the Secretary will put it there and take his credentials and issue a badge, subject to revision by the Committee on Credentials.

An office has been provided for the Secretary in the lobby as you pass out, where you can obtain badges.

The motion to adjourn was then seconded and carried, and the convention adjourned until half-past two.

MONDAY AFTERNOON.

The meeting was called to order by the chairman at 2:45 o'clock.

THE CHAIRMAN: The chair will announce the programme for this evening, which has been changed somewhat in the order of speakers. The subject is " Irrigation." The first speaker will be Mr. F. H. Newell, of the U. S. Geological Survey, on " The Water Supply of the Rocky Mountain Region."

The second speaker will be Hon. Elwood Mead, State Engineer of Wyoming and president of the National Irrigation Congress. His subject will be " Reclaiming the Arid Lands."

The third speaker will be Hon. Wm. E. Smythe, editor of the *Irrigation Age.* His subject will be "Irrigation a National Issue."

The next speaker will be Judge J. S. Emery, of Kansas, who is the National lecturer for the Irrigation Congress. His subject will be " Homes for Millions More."

The chair has also to announce a change in the programme for tomorrow evening on the Remonetization of Silver. Gov. Patterson had been requested to take part in that discussion and had promised to be here. Last evening a note was received from him stating that his daughter was seriously ill, and not expected to recover, and his physician told him that he must not leave. Upon receipt of his letter a telegram was sent to the Hon. Wm. J. Bryan of Nebraska, asking him to take part in that programme in the place of Mr. Patterson, which he has consented to do.

This programme will be an address by ex-Gov. L. Bradford Prince of New Mexico, at 4 o'clock in the afternoon. At half-past seven o'clock an address by Hon. Geo. E. Leighton, of St. Louis, which will be followed by Representative Bryan of Nebraska, and the discussion will be closed by ex-Gov. Anthony of Kansas.

Congress is now open for business.

MR. BLACK: Mr. President, it seems to me that there is some misunderstanding as to the various committees. The various committees, as I understand it, now are simply chosen by the various delegations. They have not been announced by the Chair, and there is some hesitation on the part of the committeemen to take any step until that announcement is made. The first thing to do will be to get the Committee on Credentials to pass upon the credentials of the various committees here. That work should be commenced at once, and I suggest that the Chair at once announce those committees, so that they can at once proceed with the duties that have been assigned to them.

THE CHAIRMAN: The Chair will state that the Secretary is now preparing a list of the committees as formed by the different delegations. As soon as that report is ready it will be submitted to the congress, the place of meeting will be announced and they will be called together.

The Chair has just been furnished by the Secretary with the names of the committees as reported and in the absence of our Reading Clerk the Chair will read them.

The Chair then read the names of the committees:—

Credentials.	Rules and Order of Business.	Permanent Organization.
Arizona .....T. B. Comstock,	S. Watts,	W. J. Cheyney,
Arkansas ...H. E. Kelley,	B. D. Williams,	J. A. C. Blackburn,
California...Wm. Johnston,	Geo. H. Pippy,	A. P. Roach,
Colorado....C. E. Smith,	A. C. Fisk,	R. E. Goodell,
Idaho.......Wm. Budge,	John Donaldson,	F. S. Bramwell,
Iowa ......A. P. Gibbs,	H. Volmer,	E. B. Tucker,
Indian Ter..G. B. Dennison,	D. M. M. Hailey,	W. H. Walker,
Kansas......S. H. Fullerton,	W. R. Savage,	A. J. Harwi,
Minnesota ..Thos. Sharp,	Thos. Sharp,	Thos. Sharp,
Missouri....S. B. Cook,	H. H. Harding,	Joseph Rusk,
Nebraska ...J. G. Hamilton,	J. W. Shabata,	S. M. Benedict,
New Mexico.T. R. Gabel,	A. W. Harris,	T. J. Helm,
Oklahoma...J. D. Maguire,	C. G. Jones,	O. A. Michter,
Oregon .....E. P. Dosch,	M. G. Butterfield,	E. P. Dosch,
S. Dakota...J. R. Brennan,	J. R. Brennan,	J. R. Brennan.
Texas.......Ed. A. Marshall,	W. D. Lacy,	Geo. Delhi,
Utah........W. H. Culmer,	Judge Dusenberry,	T. G. Webber,
Washington.A. L. Black,	L. L. Adams,	N. M. Neeld,
Wyoming ...Robt. Foote, Sr.,		
Alaska......J. C. Green,	J. C. Green,	J. C. Green.

THE CHAIRMAN: Those committees will find rooms at their disposal, and if they desire stationery it will be furnished from the platform.

The congress is open for further business.

It is suggested that the Committee on Credentials meet immediately in the first room on the right after passing through the doorway.

The Committee on Rules and Order of Business is requested to meet in the room assigned them.

The Chair dislikes very much to make any suggestions to the congress, but will feel extremely obliged if the Committee on Permanent Organization will make their report as speedily as possible. Under an unwritten law of the congress, the presiding officer of the last session continues in office until his successor is duly elected. I think, however, the congress will recognize with me the impropriety of your present presiding officer presiding at a congress held in his own city, whose guests you are, and therefore he will take advantage of the privilege, accorded to all officers in such a position, to call other gentlemen to the chair from time to time during your session. The Chair will call upon ex-Gov. Prince of New Mexico to preside at this afternoon's session of this congress. If Gov. Prince is here, he will please come on the platform.

The Chairman: Ladies and gentlemen, I have the pleasure of introducing ex-Gov. Prince of New Mexico, who will preside at your afternoon session (applause).

Ex-Gov. Prince taking the chair.

The Chairman: The President informs me that there is no regular order of business at this time. Any business, consequently, is in order. The Chair would suggest that it possibly will save time in the future if resolutions which have been prepared and are ready to be presented should be presented at this time, to be referred to the Committee on Resolutions when appointed.

Frank Trimble (of Iowa): Mr. Chairman, my understanding is that there has been no Committee on Resolutions appointed.

The Chairman: That is correct.

Mr. Trimble: Then I shall object to any resolutions being presented here until a Committee on Resolutions has been appointed.

The Chairman: That is a matter for the disposition of the house. The ordinary custom is that resolutions can be presented at any time, to be referred to the Committee on Resolutions without debate. If the house prefers to wait for the appointment of its Committee on Resolutions, there is no objection to that course.

Mr. Trimble: I move that no resolution be submitted until the Committee on Resolutions is appointed, and that all resolutions be submitted to the Committee on Resolutions.

R. W. Richardson (of Nebraska): Mr. Chairman, I cannot see any necessity for this motion at this time, and I therefore move that it be not considered.

THE CHAIRMAN: It is moved that this motion be laid on the table. This motion was duly seconded and carried.

THE CHAIRMAN: The motion is laid on the table. What is the next pleasure of the house. The introduction of resolutions is in order.

DEL C. HUNTOON (of Iowa): Mr. Chairman, I move that an invitation be sent from this congress to the Government Commission in St. Louis having in charge the Government improvements of the Mississippi River to appear before this congress at some convenient time and State to this congress the improvements to this river and the result obtained. We want the Commission of the Government to state to this congress what they have done and what they intend to do. We know that in the medical profession, when the physicians have difficulty in diagnosing a case they call it appendicitis and go to carving. A great many think that is the way with this Government Commission.

THE CHAIRMAN: As the Chair understands it, the resolution from the gentleman from Iowa is that an invitation be extended to the members of the Commission which he has just named to attend the session of this congress, at some time which may meet their convenience, in order to enlighten us by a statement of the progress of that work — is that the idea?

MR. HUNTOON: Yes, sir.

This motion was seconded and carried.

THE CHAIRMAN: The resolution is adopted and the invitation will be extended by the Secretary.

A DELEGATE from St. Louis: Mr. Chairman, I see that we have with us ex-Gov. Stanard of our State and city, and as I contemplate introducing a resolution upon the reciprocity treaties, I move that he be invited to a seat upon the platform and explain to us the subject of the reciprocity treaties and their effect during the term of their continuance and operation.

This motion was seconded and carried.

(HON. E. O. STANARD (of St. Louis): Of course I am not unmindful of the honor that my friends from St. Louis have conferred upon me by requesting me to speak upon this subject, but this invitation is exceeding unexpected to me and certainly without consultation. I have a resolution prepared upon the subject of reciprocity between the United States and the West Indies, which I thought I would take occasion to introduce this afternoon, with other resolutions, but I have no thought of making a speech upon this subject now and perhaps not at all. It would seem to me that the gentleman who offered the motion asking that resolutions be now presented to this convention, was exceedingly wise in that suggestion, and I think that the resolution should be read, because I am quite confident that there are more persons than myself who have resolutions in their pockets, and I think they should be brought out, so that we may see the drift that is in the minds of the members of this convention, and be able to deliberate on the subjects that will be brought to our attention.   Hence, I am not disposed to speak upon the subject at this time, but I take pleasure in introducing a short preamble and resolution upon the subject of reciprocity.   I hope they will be read.   I am not disposed to make a speech upon this subject.

The resolution was then read as follows : —

WHEREAS: It having been represented to this Convention that, since the Reciprocity Treaties between the United States and the West Indies went into effect in 1890, a very large and remunerative trade was established between these countries, amounting as is represented to about 3,250,000 barrels of flour per annum (equal to about 15,000,000 bushels of wheat) more than 2,000,000 bushels of corn, large quantities of other farm products consisting of oats, baled hay, mill feed, etc., also large quantities of hog products together with agricultural implements and other articles of manufacture, amounting in value to about \$22,000,000.00 in exports annually from this country; and

WHEREAS: Since these treaties were abrogated by the passage of the Senate Bill some of the last days of August, our commercial relations have been almost entirely discontinued thereby and steamship lines connecting with the Latin American ports from Galveston, Texas, Pensacola, Florida, and the mouth of the Mississippi River have been obliged to practically cease operations; therefore

RESOLVED, That, under the circumstances narrated, this Convention urgently requests the Government of the United States to take early steps for the re-establishment of the old commercial treaties between the United States and the West Indies, or make new commercial treaties to the end that such business may again* be made possible as existed under the Reciprocity Treaties, or to enact new laws if found necessary, so that business may be promoted and extended between the United States and the countries in question.

THE CHAIRMAN: This resolution will be referred to the Committee on Resolutions when appointed.   It has been the custom in previous congresses to pass a resolution to the effect that all resolutions of this character, that is, not appertaining to the order of business, be read when presented and then referred to the Committee on Resolutions without debate.   Some action with regard to this matter should be taken, in order that there may be a regular rule.

MR. STANARD: Mr. Chairman, I move that all resolutions not pertaining to the order of business, when presented be read and referred to the Committee on Resolutions without debate.

JEROME HILL (of St. Louis): Mr. Chairman, I offer an amendment to the resolution offered by the gentleman from St. Louis, to the effect that the resolution extend beyond the States and be made applicable to the other countries of Spanish America with which we had treaties of a favorable character, which were unfortunately abrogated through the Wilson bill.

MR. STANARD: I should be glad to accept the amendment of the gentleman, or refer it to the Committee for such amendment as they see fit.

The question was then put and carried on the motion in regard to the conduct of business concerning the receipt of resolutions.

THE CHAIRMAN: If the gentleman from Missouri will be kind enough to reduce his amendment to writing, and present it, it will go to the Committee on Resolutions, to be considered with the resolution introduced by his colleague from Missouri.

MR. CASTLE: In behalf of the California delegation, I desire to present a memorial to Congress on the subject of the Nicaragua Canal, and ask that it be read.

The memorial was read.

THE CHAIRMAN: It will be referred to the Committee on Resolutions when appointed.

DAVID LUBIN (of California): Mr. Chairman, I offer the following resolutions in reference to the protection of staple agriculture: —

WHEREAS, American principles demand equality before the law, in life, liberty and taxation; and,

WHEREAS, The prices of American manufactures are increased by the protective tariff in our country; and,

WHEREAS, The foundation industry, namely, staple agriculture, cannot be benefited by a protective tariff alone, owing to the fact that these products are exports and therefore are sold in free competition in the open markets at the world's ruling prices, less the cost of transportation from place of production to Liverpool, whether consumed at home or exported; thus compelling American producers of these staples to buy in the dearest and sell in the cheapest markets of the world, thereby discriminating against the producers of staple agriculture; and

WHEREAS, The introduction of labor-saving agricultural machinery in the hands of the cheapest labor of the world and on lands much cheaper and as fertile as ours has so lowered the cost of production as to reduce the world's price of these staples to about half their former rates, and which promise to remain so permanently; and,

WHEREAS, Such a condition must tend to the elimination of the independent land owning farmer and his replacement by a dependent peasant tenantry system, which, unless prevented, will not only prove detrimental to agriculture and the kindred industries but also to the perpetuity of American institutions; therefore

Resolved: (1) That just so long as manufactures are enhanced in value by protection, equity, justice and expediency demand an equal measure of protection for staple agriculture by enhancement of their prices in our country;

Resolved: (2) That, inasmuch as these products are exports and not imports, their prices cannot be enhanced by a protective tariff alone, no matter how high, but an increase of their prices in our country can only be secured by the use of a limited portion of the tariff collected for protection to pay a premium on exported agricultural staples.

S. F. Smith (of Iowa): I desire to offer a resolution in behalf of the delegation from Iowa, as to the Illinois and Mississippi Canal: —

Resolved, That the Illinois and Mississippi Canal (known as the Hennepin Canal) one section of which is completed, making now available about twenty miles of canal navigation, should be vigorously pushed to completion, thus connecting the Mississippi river and the lakes, making a through water route from said river to the eastern seaboard.

And we recommend an annual continuous appropriation by Congress sufficient to complete the same as speedily as possible.

George Sengel (of Arkansas): I offer this resolution in reference to the creation of a tariff commission to regulate the tariff of the United States: —

Whereas, The disturbed condition of the country has greatly disarranged the commercial affairs of all sections without regard to political affiliations, so that one section of the United States is prospering at the expense of the other, and believing that it is the duty of the government of the United States to regulate the affairs of the country, so that no section will suffer or prosper at the loss of the other, and whereas the disturbed condition of the commercial and agricultural affairs of all sections is due to the frequent elections throughout the land, changing the political parties too often, and whereas all the political parties have incorporated the tariff in their platforms, and whereas the tariff directly affects each and every citizen of the United States in one way or other, without regard to his political belief; therefore

Resolved, That the Congress of the United States be asked to frame a law that will create a commission to act for the whole people, in all sections of the United States, and that said commission have full power to regulate the tariff so that it will not be a burden to any one section of the country, and that all industries and people be protected alike; be it further

Resolved, That the congress of the trans-Mississippi States petition the political parties of the United States to eliminate the tariff question from their political platforms, and unite with the trans-Mississippi congress in influencing the Congress of the United States to place the tariff question in the hands of a commission — whose duties will be regulated by congress when the commission is created, and that a law be passed whereby a change in the tariff will not take place with the change in the political management of the government.

The Chairman: The Chair begs to request gentlemen offering resolutions to indorse on the resolutions their names, in order that no mistakes may occur with regard to the ownership of the resolutions.

C. O. Frye (of Missouri): Mr. Chairman, I have a resolution which I ask that I be allowed to read for myself, for the reason that my voice is peculiarly strong upon this subject.

Mr. Frye then took the platform and read his preamble and resolution, occupying upwards of twenty minutes in the reading, and during the reading he was interrupted by Hon. C. C. Goodwin, of Utah, who said: —

JUDGE GOODWIN: Mr. Chairman, if that is not out of order, I think it will be a kindness to the Committee on Resolutions if the Chair will announce that they will only have four days and nights to consider the matter (laughter).

Resolutions were then offered as follows:—

By MR. PARSONS of Cal. favoring the establishment of Deepwater Harbor in Southern California.

By MR. BOWEN of Utah in favor of Restoration of Silver.

By MR. COLLINS of Ark. relating to the Coinage of Silver.

By MR. STODDARD of Col. relating to the use of Coin Certificates.

By MR. GALE of St. Louis amending the Reciprocity Resolution offered by Mr. Stanard.

MR. CASTLE: Following the lines laid down at our last session, and in order to bring this matter before the congress for consideration at this time, I move the appointment of a Committee on Resolutions to be composed of four delegates from each State and Territory represented, the appointments to be made by the delegates from said States and Territories, and to be announced at the opening session to-morrow morning.

MR. COLLINS: Mr. Chairman, how many States are represented?

THE CHAIRMAN: The Chair is unable to say — perhaps the Secretary will be kind enough to state.

MR. CASTLE: In regard to that matter I desire to state, at San Francisco there were 88 members of that committee, but at no time were more than 20 members of the committee present, and therefore we believe it is necessary to make the committee large, in order that the business of the congress may be properly attended to.

GOV. WAITE: Mr. Chairman, it seems to me, to take 88 members out of this convention, it will not leave us much of a convention. If this discussion is going on that has been commenced, it possibly would not do any particular harm if the convention did not hear most of it, but it seems to me that this committee in order to amount to anything will have to be small. I do not believe 88 gentlemen can agree any quicker than this convention can in a body, and if we appoint 88 members and only a quarter of them attend, I think we had better cut it down to a quarter on the start. I am opposed to the number. I move an amendment that we have two members instead of four.

This motion was seconded.

It was moved as an amendment to the amendment that the number be fixed at three.

A motion was then made that the body constitute itself a committee of the whole on resolutions (laughter).

THE CHAIRMAN: There are two amendments pending to the original motion at the present time. The question is on the amendment to the amendment; that is, that the committee consist of three members from each State and Territory.

The question was then put and lost.

THE CHAIRMAN: The question now occurs on the amendment to the original motion made by Gov. Waite of Colorado.

MR. CASTLE: The amendment is accepted by the original mover.

THE CHAIRMAN: The question is as to the adoption of the original motion as amended and accepted — that is, that a Committee on Resolutions be appointed consisting of two members from each State and Territory.

It was then moved by a delegate from Missouri that the Committee consist of one member from each State and Territory.

MR. WHITMORE: Mr. Chairman, it was not my intention to occupy any time of this congress beyond the necessities of my official position, but as Chairman of the Executive Committee and a delegate to several of these congresses, I desire to state, simply for the information of the congress, that we have always found it necessary to have a large Committee on Resolutions, in order that it might be subdivided into smaller committees and different subjects assigned to them. At San Francisco we found it necessary to have four. At New Orleans three. You will find it utterly impossible to divide this work up among a committee of one from each State and Territory and have that work done effectively. I simply express that as the experience of the past, and I am sure it will be repeated at this congress. We want a committee large enough to handle these subjects intelligently and not have resolutions rushed through because the committee have not time to consider them. I see no objection to a large committee, so that you may have four or five sub-committees meeting at the same time, to whom the most important subjects can be assigned, and another committee on miscellaneous subjects.

The amendment to appoint a committee of one from each State and Territory was then withdrawn and the motion as amended to consist of two members from each State and Territory was accepted by the mover of the last amendment.

The motion was then seconded and carried.

THE CHAIRMAN: This resolution also carries with it the proposition that the members of this committee shall be announced to-morrow morning at the opening session.

MR. STANARD: Mr. Chairman, I have one more resolution to offer — only one. I offer it, if I may be permitted to say it, as a sort of a counter-irritant to some of the resolutions which have been read and referred, especially to the resolution and stump speech of my friend from Joplin, Mo.

The resolution was then read relating to the use of silver in the coinage of this country to the fullest extent consistent with the maintenance of our present standard, and referred to the Committee on Resolutions.

Resolutions were offered by Hon. Frank J. Cannon of Utah, in relation to the appointment of the Uncompahgre and Uintah Indian Commissions.

By Mr. Lubin of California, in relation to the appointment of a committee of five to attend the National Grange.

By J. C. Green of Alaska, relating to the government and development of Alaska.

By Thos. J. Sharp of Minnesota, favoring an appropriation for the Deepening of Duluth Harbor.

THE CHAIRMAN: What is the further pleasure of the congress?

MR. WHITMORE: I am in receipt of a communication from the Kearney State Irrigation Convention Committee, which the Clerk will read.

The Clerk then read a letter from the foregoing convention sending greetings to the Trans-Mississippi Congress, and requesting the appointment of delegates to attend said irrigation convention, to be held at Kearney, Neb., December 18th and 19th, 1894.

On motion duly seconded and carried the communication was ordered placed on file.

A resolution was then offered by Senator Johnston of California relating to the improvement of harbors and navigable streams.

Mr. Rich of Idaho offered a resolution relating to the coinage of silver.

It was then moved, seconded and carried that immediately after the adjournment of the convention the delegates from each State and territory meet in this hall and select their two representatives of the Committee on Resolutions.

THE CHAIRMAN: The Chair would suggest that the names be handed to the Secretary before the evening session.

The Chair desires to state that resolutions will be in order at any time prior to the report of the Committee on Resolutions. It must not be understood that when we adjourn this evening no more resolutions can be offered.

COL. A. C. FISK (of Colorado): Mr. Chairman, if it is in order now, I would like to move that Mr. S. T. Hamilton of Nebraska, who represents the Norfolk Beet Sugar Company of Nebraska, address the convention this afternoon. It is one of the subjects that will come up.

THE CHAIRMAN: If there is no objection, it is in order.

REMARKS OF S. T. HAMILTON, OF NORFOLK, NEB., ON BEET SUGAR INDUSTRY.

Mr. Chairman, Ladies and Gentlemen: I will not detain you but a few minutes, but I think I can interest you in a thought that we ought to consider in this congress. We are here to exchange views and thoughts and to pass resolutions asking national legislation on these resolutions that shall benefit our Western country, our Southwestern country, our entire land, and all of the wage-earners and farmers who are to-day suffering from depreciation. There are over three million idle men in this country now, representing possibly ten to twelve million souls. These men are idle because of many reasons. Factories have been closed up. We in the West are more interested at this particular time in several matters that are going to be brought up here than most people imagine.

There is to-day an immense depreciation in agriculture. The price of cereals is very cheap — very low. The farmer is complaining, and I see no special reason for a change unless wise legislation is brought to bear on the subject. We can legislate in many ways, but those that are really interested in the welfare of the laboring man and of the farmer, I think, will find, in what I say, something to think about.

Thirty years ago there appeared a star in the firmament of agricultural pursuits, which twinkled and went out. To-day that star has come back with brilliancy that assures its permanence. I refer now to the manufacture of the sugar that we consume in the United States, from the sugar beet. It is especially shining — this star — on the West and the Southwest, and with irrigation there is no reason why many of our Western States cannot attract hundreds of thousands of people, and then from a small tract of ten acres of well-cultivated beets a man can support his entire family. At Norfolk, Neb., where we have one of our plants, the farmers this year will absolutely receive little or nothing from their crops other than the sugar beet crop. They have had a drouth there that has been very severe, but the beet crop, growing under the ground and receiving its nourishment from the little tap root which goes down twenty feet into the subsoil to get its drink of water, has turned out a wonderful tonnage. In some places where there was no rain from the 19th day of May, until the 17th day of July, we have received a result of twenty tons of beet per acre, for which we have paid five dollars a ton, or one hundred dollars an acre. The importance of manufacturing our own sugar must be to all of you very clear. To-day we are paying out about one hundred and thirty millions to one hundred and fifty millions of dollars to foreign nations for the sugar that our people consume, and there is no reason why we cannot produce every pound of it right here in our own Western country. The result of doing so would not only keep at home this vast sum of money, but it would divide up our large farms into smaller tracts. It gives labor to little children in cultivating the beets.
enables a poor man, who cannot buy a farm or even rent a farm, to rent ten acres and to produce from that ten acres a sum sufficient to support his family. It has so many advantages and its benefits diverge into so many channels of trade that in this Western country, where we have no river navigation, and no forests of lumber, it seems specially adapted to this section. I feel that States like Oregon, Washington, Utah, Iowa, Nebraska, Arkansas and other Western States — California as well — for California has a very large factory there — are especially interested in it, for it is hand in hand with irrigation.

At Utah, where they have a factory, their beets the first year were poor, because they did not know how to irrigate. To-day that factory is working to great advantage and their beets are very rich, because they do know how to irrigate. We at Norfolk consume three carloads of limestone every twenty-four hours. In the State of Nebraska we use four and one-half carloads of coal, one-half a carload of coke and turn out three carloads of sugar, and this year we have brought into Norfolk from surrounding farms six hundred carloads of sugar beets, outside of those which have been grown and produced by farmers who have brought the beets in by wagon loads. The factory will probably run until the 15th day of next January, consuming about 140 tons of beets per diem, and paying out to wage-earners for everything that we use, about $1,600.00 per day. This money is felt in that town, so that land that was worth $8.00 to $10.00 an acre when we located there, is now renting for from $5.00 to $7.00 a year for the cultivation of beets, and cannot be bought for less than $100.00 to $150.00 per acre.

At Chino, Cal., where we have another plant, and which is now closed, having finished its campaign about two weeks ago, we consume a thousand tons of beets a day, and the land there at the Chino Valley ranch could have been bought when we located that factory four years ago for about $10.00 to $12.00 an acre, if bought in a large body. During this last year, in June, they had an auction sale, and that land sold for $175.00 to $212.00 an acre, showing what was the result of an industry giving the farmer a crop that was not affected by speculative influences.

When a man grows corn and wheat (and the ordinary farmer is a man, as we know, of not very much education) he places himself immediately in the hands of the speculator in Chicago, but when he grows a crop that is contracted for before it is put in the ground, he only runs the risk of what result he will get from his cultivated beet.

As I have said, it will withstand frost, drought or heavy rain better than any crop that can be produced.

It would require 1,000 factories such as, we have in Nebraska to give the people of the United States the sugar they consume every year. We are now consuming about 60 pounds per capita, and only producing about 9 per cent, mostly in Louisiana. But Louisiana is a cane district, and the cane can only be grown to advantage in certain localities, while the beet can be produced in all our western States, in a number of our southern States, and in the Southwest generally. The consumption of sugar doubles about every ten years, so that as fast as we could build these factories, we would be gaining on the consumption, so that it may be estimated to be a matter of twenty-five years, before we could build sufficient factories to catch up with the consumption.

Now, we were induced to go into this industry by a contract which we supposed and still believe to be a contract made by the U. S. government, wherein they specify a reasonable time of fifteen years that they made sugar free. This was a very wise act, for sugar is used by every man, woman and child in our land. To induce the development of this industry they put on, unsolicited, a bounty of two cents per pound for fifteen years, and then it should cease. They took off, to do this, a duty of 3 3-4 cents a pound, and during the last legislation in Washington they have repudiated that contract and put on a duty of 40 per cent *ad valorem*, which was a Sugar Trust duty.

I want to say here that we are not directly or indirectly connected or associated with the Sugar Trust, or they with us. We are in fact direct competitors of the Sugar Trust.

Now, an *ad valorem* duty means 40 per cent on the value of the article where it is purchased. Much of our raw sugar comes from the West Indies, where there is no market. For instance, at Port au Prince they have no market, but they send up large quantities of sugar to the New York market in its raw state, which the sugar refinery makes white, while we take the sugar out of the ground and turn it into the finest grade of granulated sugar, and it is commanding the full market price that the sugars of the trust are commanding.

This *ad valorem* system, we seriously object to, because it opens up room for all kinds of fraud. The Sugar Trust can say, "This sugar is worth so much, or so much," and get it in on 40 per cent of its supposed value, and make the difference, when they know that it is really worth more than it is valued at. But they insist upon it; they spend their money and they get their bill through.

Now, gentlemen, I would like to have you consider in this congress whether it is advisable for this country to make its own sugar. If it is not wise, then we should not consider or think anything about it.

What is the result to our people and our wage-earners? A factory such as we have in Norfolk, Neb., gives subsistence to about 6,500 souls, taking into consideration the farmer that grows the beets, the man that works in the coal mine, in the limestone quarry, in the machine shop and in the factory; and at Norfolk it has had such an effect there that if you would offer them a million dollars to close that factory up for a year or two the people would not consider it. It has relieved the depression that existed in that particular point. It even reaches out and we are getting beets from 100 miles distant. The farmers cannot grow corn to advantage at present prices. The product of lime cake is the best of fertilizers. The product of the beet, which is pulp, is the finest cattle feed. We have now some 2,000 head of cattle which we are feeding at the rate of 80 to 90 pounds per diem, and the fattening of them is something wonderful. We sell that pulp for 50 cents a ton, while in Europe it is worth $8.00 to $10.00 a ton. We give away the lime cake.

All these things we have had to contend with and they will necessitate the closing up of those factories unless we have some fair and adequate protection against the cheap labor of Europe and against the grasping monopoly of the Sugar Trust. Those people see that this industry is bound to spread, that it is bound to extend, that it is an industry that makes the farmer its partner. There is at least $50,000,000 in New York to-day ready to embark in it.

We have never yet received a dividend, or made one, or received the value of a postage stamp from the work in Nebraska. But we have in California, for the reason that the farmers in California have been a better class of farmers. Men have gone there in the delightful climate of that State, and have wanted to do something themselves, and therefore they have grown beets. In Nebraska we have had to contend against a more ignorant class, and it has taken a long time to gain their confidence (applause and laughter). I do not wish you to understand that I am extolling California against Nebraska. I simply say that the climate of California is superb. I say that the soil there is splendid. But we have just as fine a soil and equally as good a climate for this particular industry in Nebraska as we have in California, and I am interested financially in both places. I have dear friends in both States.

I want simply to ask this Congress whether this industry is worthy of development, whether it is worth while for us to save $150,000,000 of the money of our own people and make our own sugar and build up these factories all over this Western and Southwestern country, or whether it is wise to drop it; whether it is wise to have free sugar and give the advantage of that price of sugar to the poor man, or whether it is better to have a duty of $40,000,000 or $50,000,-000 imposed on sugar every year and at the same time to destroy the industry, because an *ad valorem* duty would give protection when it is not needed, and when it is needed we do not get it. When sugar is high, 40 per cent is not needed; when sugar is low, 40 per cent cannot protect it.

I said to a Congressman in Washington last year, "Why do you put in this *ad valorem* duty — what is the reason of it?" His answer was, "Oh, that is the fair way." But it was done solely for the Sugar Trust. They did not want a specific duty. They knew that a specific duty meant protection for this home industry that is to-day growing at a great rate, while it would destroy this great monopoly, and therefore they wanted the advantage of this *ad valorem* duty, which we are going to see to it, if I can induce you gentlemen to help me, is changed to a specific duty.

I ask you therefore to think, you gentlemen who are interested in the West, whether this industry is worthy of the consideration of this convention. I would be glad to state that at my hotel I have a bag of beet sugar made last year in Nebraska, which I would be glad to give a sample of. to anybody who wants to see it. I would like to show them the product of our factory and show them what an institution we have there.

In 1890 when this McKinley law was put on, I was in the banking business in New York. We did not ask for this bounty, but it was put on to commence at a certain time and end at a certain time. Owing to that promise, which we ought to be able to rely upon, made by one of the greatest governments on the globe, we were induced to come in and invest over $2,000,000. We intended to go on and build other factories, and we still intend to it that promise is kept good.

It is a question I would like to have thought of here, whether any resolution can be passed in this congress which should sanction the repudiation of a promise accepted in good faith by people who have nothing to sell, but who want to buy their goods of the farmer and give labor to the laborer. By building a thousand of these factories in the United States we would give labor to over 7,000,000 people. It would diversify our crops; it would add to the value of our land, and in a thousand ways it would benefit our people and promote nearly every channel of trade from one end of this country to the other.

THE CHAIRMAN: The gentleman desires it stated that his room is at the Southern Hotel, No. 315.

HON. GEO. Q. CANNON (of Utah): There is only one little objection we have to the gentleman's speech. I indorse everything which he said heartily, but would not like the impression to go out, which his remarks would create, that we in Utah do not know how to irrigate beets. If there is anything in the world we understand thoroughly, it is irrigation, for we have practiced it there 47 years, and the failure, or the partial failure, of our first crop of sugar beets, was not due to our ignorance of irrigation.

GOV. WAITE: Mr. Chairman, I understood you to say that unless resolutions were introduced this afternoon, there would be no chance.

THE CHAIRMAN: On the contrary the Chair stated distinctly that resolutions would be in order at any time until the Committee on Resolutions reported.

A DELEGATE (from Nebraska): I do not think my colleague, Mr. Hamilton, intended to reflect upon the intelligence of the farmers of

Nebraska in his remarks in comparison with the State of California. I would like to say that California may take the palm in raising beets, but in everything else we stand head and shoulders her equal, if not above her.

MR. HAMILTON: I would like to say to the gentleman from Utah that I did not intend to convey the idea that you do not know how to irrigate. My good friend, Mr. Thos. Cutler, the President of your sugar factory, told me two years ago that the reason that their beets were a little low in purity was owing to having been irrigated too late in the season — not that they did not know how to irrigate, but they did not have the experience in irrigating beets. Beets need no rain after a certain time in the late summer, and that is the reason that this Western country is especially adapted to beet culture. We want a dry, cold fall. It brings the sugar into the beet, which is brought by the effects of the rays of the sun and the atmosphere on the leaf, and the sugar is stored in the leaf. The beet is like a honey-comb, filled with little cells, in which is the sweet matter, and therefore if you put too much water on it it will not show the richness and purity, because it will grow too much. I do not, sir, intend to convey the impression that they do not know how to irrigate. I specially said, I think, that irrigation goes hand in hand with this industry, and we only did not know the first year how soon to stop irrigating the beet. This year, I understand, they are making a grand success in beet irrigation.

So far as my colleague from Nebraska is concerned, I do not want it understood for one moment that I am speaking disparagingly about the farmers of Nebraska. They are my friends, and I am glad to say that, after four years of labor, I have the confidence of nearly every one of them who live close to our factory and who have been there. I only wanted to convey the idea that in Nebraska, owing to the different class of farmers, we had had a struggle to go through there, that we had not met in California. In California they have no weeds to contend with, owing to their having no rain there after a certain time of the year, while in Nebraska we have showers all the summer, thus encouraging the growth of weeds, and the weeds made beet culture more difficult for those who did not know just how to go to work. They do know now, and are raising the finest kind of beets. A sugar beet that is said to be a 15 per cent beet or a 20 per cent beet, does not mean 15 or 20 per cent of sugar: it means 15 per cent of saccharine matter, some of it being sugar, some of it being molasses, and that molasses is not good to refine, like cane molasses. It is only used to make alcohol. This will develop into putting up distilleries alongside of the sugar factories.

SENATOR JOHNSTON: I take it for granted, sir, the gentleman in referring to Nebraska farmers had no allusion to those present (laughter).

Mr. Black: Mr. Chairman, it seems to me that one of the main purposes of this Congress is to devise some plan for carrying its resolutions into effect. As I understand, the Executive Committee have that matter in charge. In order that the matter may be brought up and fairly discussed before the house, I move that that committee be requested to present whatever plan for permanent organization they may have at a time not later than Wednesday morning.

(Mr. Whitmore resuming the chair.)

The Chairman: The chair will state that the motion refers to the action taken by the San Francisco congress, under which the Executive Committee were instructed to submit to this Congress some plan of organization of the Congress itself on a business-like basis. The motion now made by the gentleman from Washington is that that committee be requested to report not later than Wednesday morning.

This motion was duly seconded and carried.

The Secretary then read an invitation from the Liggett & Myers Tobacco Co., to visit their works.

The Chairman: The Chairman of the Committee on Entertainment has requested some announcements to be made. It was the special request of the Executive Committee of the Congress that nothing should be done in the way of entertainment to interfere with its business, but that such entertainment should be postponed if possible until after the business was transacted. The Committee on Entertainment, however, have felt that some courtesies should be extended in the way of entertainment of the guests during the session of the congress. They have therefore arranged so that any delegate may have a ticket to our theaters any evening during the session by applying at the Secretary's office in the front of the building. Those tickets, however, will not secure reserved seats, from the fact that no arrangements could be made for reserved seats unless a definite number were secured. Therefore gentlemen taking those tickets will have to get their seats at the box office of the theater.

A general programme of entertainment is outlined as follows: —

Thursday being Thanksgiving Day, it has been taken for granted that there will be no session during the day. It is proposed to start from the Planters' House, take a drive through the city and out to the Fair Grounds, where a lunch or collation will be served, drive to Forest Park and then return in time for dinner at five o'clock.

On Thursday evening there will be a grand symphony concert in the Grand Music Hall of this building, to which each delegate will be entitled to tickets, which will be ready for distribution on Wednesday.

I need not express the urgent desire of the Executive Committee that as many delegates as possible will attend our evening sessions.

SENATOR JOHNSTON: Mr. Chairman, the Committee on Credentials will be able to report in a few moments.

THE CHAIRMAN: Another resolution has been offered to the Chair without any name attached, and not from the floor, and it will be sent back to the mover if he will claim it.

MR. TRIMBLE: Mr. Chairman, a resolution was carried that as soon as the gentleman got through with the speech we would hear the report of the Committee on Credentials. I would like to hear that report if it is ready.

THE CHAIRMAN: The Chairman of the Committee on Credentials has just stated that that report is not ready, but it will be ready in a few moments if the congress desires to wait for it.

The Committee on Order of Business is ready to report; the report is in order, or it may be deferred until morning.

It was moved by a delegate from Nebraska to adjourn until to-morrow morning's session.

THE CHAIRMAN: Before that motion is put, the Chair desires to state that this evening we are to have a session, at which "Irrigation" has been made the special order, therefore the motion should not be put in that particular form.

THE DELEGATE: I mean until the next regular session.

THE CHAIRMAN: If that motion prevails, the first thing in order at our morning's session will be the reports of those committees which are ready to make them.

MR. TRIMBLE: If you please, there was a resolution presented here and passed that the Committee on Credentials was to report before this convention adjourned, and that the names of the delegates selected by the different States and territories would be handed into the Chairman of this convention this evening.

THE CHAIRMAN: The Chair rules that the motion to adjourn, made by the gentleman from Nebraska, is in order. The motion is that we now adjourn until the time fixed for the next session, as the Chair understands it.

SENATOR JOHNSTON: Mr. President, I will ask the gentleman from Nebraska to withdraw his motion for just a moment. We are about ready to report from the Committee on Credentials, and some members are anxious to find whether we have any members or not. I would ask the gentleman to withdraw his motion to adjourn until we hear that report.

Motion withdrawn.

SENATOR JOHNSTON: The Committee on Credentials is ready to report.

THE CHAIRMAN: The Chair will state that the Committee on Rules and Order of Business has already handed in its report, and, therefore, in the absence of any motion to the contrary, it takes precedence.

The report of the Committee on Rules and Order of Business was then read, as follows:—

"Your Committee respectfully reports that it organized as follows: Chairman, Sylvester Watts of Arizona; Secretary, Henry Volmer of Iowa, and agreed upon the following order of business:

(Signed) Sylvester Watts, Secretary.

1st. Reading, correcting and approving the minutes.

2d. Introduction, reading and referring of resolutions.

3d. Reports of committees.

4th. The congress will meet at 10 a. m., 2:30 p. m. and 7:30 p. m.

5th. Cushing's Manual to be used as a guide on all parliamentary questions.

6th. Tuesday morning shall be devoted to miscellaneous business.

7th. Tuesday afternoon and evening shall be devoted to the consideration of the financial question.

8th. Wednesday morning to miscellaneous business.

9th Wednesday afternoon, transportation, railroads, public and arid lands.

10. Wednesday evening, Nicaragua Canal.

11th. Miscellaneous business may be called up at any time after the regular order is exhausted.

12. On roll-call each delegation is entitled to vote 10 votes, as representative of its State or Territory. If more than 10 delegates are present from any State or Territory, it is entitled to as many votes as it has delegates present, provided it shall not exceed 30 votes for each State or Territory.

13th. Introducers of a subject may speak 10 minutes and close the debate with a 5 minutes' address, the other speakers to be restricted to 7 minutes.

14th. All resolutions shall be referred to the Committee on Resolutions without debate."

The adoption of the report was moved.

Mr. F. J. Cannon moved to amend by striking out the words " provided that no State or Territory shall cast more than 30 votes."

The point of order was then made by a delegate from Iowa that this being a delegate convention, no one has a right to vote in this convenvention except upon proper credentials passed upon by this convention, and as long as the Committee on Credentials has not submitted its report, no business can be conducted.

THE CHAIRMAN: The point of order is well taken and sustained. The Committee on Credentials should have made its report first, and the Chair will state that when the Committee was·ready to report it was his intention to have asked a delay in acting upon this until the report of the Committee on Credentials had been made. If no objection is offered, the Chairman of the Committee on Credentials will make his report, and immediately after that report is made, the action on this report which has just been read will be in order.

SENATOR JOHNSTON: I will ask the Secretary to read the report.

The Secretary then read the report of the Committee on Credentials, recommending that the list of names presented by the Secretary be adopted as the list of accredited delegates to the convention.

THE CHAIRMAN: The Chair understands then that the names in that book are the names which the Committee decided to be entitled to the position of delegates on the floor.

SENATOR JOHNSTON: Yes, sir. I will state for the benefit of the members present, that there has been a great deal of care taken in the filing of all the credentials, and a great deal of credit is due the Executive Committee for the very excellent manner in which they have taken care of this business by filing carefully every credential that has been presented to them. The Committee on Credentials has taken those and the credentials that have been presented to it and from those credentials we make our report and the names are inserted in that report.

THE CHAIRMAN: As Chairman of the Executive Committee, I desire to state just the position of this report before the house. The Executive Committee has kept a complete record of every delegate appointed, with the appointing power and the post-office address of the delegate. This list was handed to the Committee on Credentials, to which, as the Chair understands, they have added some names of persons who have brought their credentials with them, and their report is that the official list of the Secretary as submitted by him be made their report of those who are entitled to seats on this floor. As he has already said, all the official documents connected with these appointments are in the hands of the Secretary, and this is a transcript of the names. The Chair supposes you do not wish to have them all read. As he understands it, the report of the Committee on Credentials amounts to this — that the Secretary's list of delegates be made the official list of this congress.

SENATOR JOHNSTON: Yes, sir; that is correct.

MR. F. J. CANNON: I rise to a point of inquiry. Does the Secretary's list provideany names other than those of persons who presented credentials?

THE CHAIRMAN: The Chair will state that the Secretary's list consists of appointments made by the appointing powers. For instance the governor of a State notified the Executive Committee that he had appointed 10 delegates, and gave their addresses. Those names were entered as delegates appointed by the governor. And the same in regard to delegates appointed by others.

MR. CANNON: Permit me to continue the inquiry — regardless of whether the individuals themselves appointed have appeared at this congress or not?

THE CHAIRMAN: The Chair understands that to be the report of the Committee — that this be made the official list entitled to seats.

SENATOR JOHNSTON: In addition to the persons who have presented credentials, we have made a recommendation at the end of our report, which will be read. The Committee have no other authority, no other means of coming to a conclusion than to take the names presented to them. We could not tell whether those gentlemen are present in St. Louis or not. We could not go out in St. Louis to find a man. We simply took the papers and acted upon them, and all the papers that have come to us duly accredited, we accredited as members of this convention.

It was moved and seconded that the report be adopted.

Gov. WAITE: It seems to me it will be very proper to read this list.

THE CHAIRMAN: The Chair will state that it will take an hour at least to read those names.

SENATOR JOHNSTON: I will say again that every person coming here duly accredited from the appointing power, has been placed upon that list.

Gov. WAITE: That is satisfactory to me.

MR. CANNON: Mr. Chairman, if I properly understand the character of this report, I object to it, for the reason that it may admit to membership upon the floor of this Congress men who are not here. In other words, it may entitle a delegation to vote the strength of men who are not present, and men who are here who come properly accredited, will not be entitled to vote on the floor of this convention. This report of the Committee on Credentials proposes that all the States which were entitled to appoint a certain number of delegates shall have the names of those delegates accredited here as members of this convention. The report of the Committee on Rules proposes that no State, no matter what its representation, and no matter how many men appear, shall have more than 30 votes, a double injustice. I object to this report, because it may give names of men who have never appeared here, and whose credentials have never yet been presented. No man should be entitled to have his name on the list of delegates who has not appeared at St. Louis and offered his credentials to this assemblage.

A DELEGATE (from Nebraska): I left my credentials in the bank.

SENATOR JOHNSTON: If your name has been sent to the Secretary and properly credited, your name is on the list. No State will vote an absentee. If they have more than 30 members here, according to the report of the Committee, they shall have but 30 votes. If there is only one man here — if the Governor has appointed two men and only one of them is here, he will be entitled to 10 votes. If there are more than 10 persons present, they will be entitled to vote for each individual present until they reach 30.

THE CHAIRMAN: The Chair desires to state that this discussion is not in order. We are not discussing the report of the Committee on Order of Business. That Committee determines how you shall vote.

This simply determines who shall be recorded as on the list of delegates. The objections urged will be in order when the report of the Committee on Order of Business comes up.

JUDGE GOODWIN: Mr. Chairman, it seems to me the fairer way would be to accept this report, refer it back to the Committee, with instructions to the Chairman of each delegation from each State and Territory, to submit this evening the names of the members entitled from their respective States and Territories, and report to-morrow morning.

The question was then put on the motion to adopt the report and it was carried.

SENATOR JOHNSTON: There is one recommendation —

The Clerk (reading): "We further recommend that the following names be added to the list:—

Hon. Geo. T. Anthony of Kansas,

Mrs. H. C. Roach of California,

Mrs. Wm. Johnston of California,

J. C. Green of Alaska."

SENATOR JOHNSTON: We ask that they be added as being members of the Congress.

On motion duly seconded and carried this recommendation was adopted.

THE CHAIRMAN: The business before the house now is the consideration of the report of the Committee on Rules and Order of Business.

E. R. RIDGELEY (of Kansas): Mr. Chairman, I rise to ask that we finish up this credential work, so that we may not in our carelessness forget delegates who may be honestly on their way to the city at this hour. I therefore move that any delegate who may arrive, not included in this report, coming with his proper credentials, upon presentation and filing of the same with the Secretary, may be added to the list as entitled to vote and allotted to his seat.

THE CHAIRMAN: This will be done, if there is no objection.

It was then moved to adjourn until 7:30 p. m.

GOV. PRINCE: Mr. President, before that is done will some time be specified when the report of the other committee is to be taken up? Some of us may not be here to-night. This matter of the basis of representation is fundamental. The change that is proposed will change the entire character of this organization in its voting power. It is something that deserves the fullest consideration and fullest discussion, and it certainly should not be brought up, for instance, late to-night, when there is a small attendance. If the gentleman who moved to take a recess until half-past seven will kindly withdraw that for a moment for the purpose, I would like to move that the report of the other committee be made the special order at the opening session to-morrow morning, in order that then these matters may be fully discussed.

Motion to adjourn withdrawn.

It was then moved by Gov. Prince and duly seconded that the consideration of the report of the Committee on Rules and Order of Business be made the special order for Tuesday morning at 10 o'clock, or as soon thereafter as it can be reached in the ordinary course of business.

Col. Leighton of St. Louis then requested that delegates assemble to select members of the Committee on Resolutions, these names to be handed to the Secretary, under the resolution adopted by the congress, to-morrow morning before the session opens.

Adjourned until 7:30 p. m. Monday evening.

Monday Evening.

The meeting was called to order by President Whitmore.

THE CHAIRMAN: The Chair no doubt expresses the feeling of the members in voicing his regret at the small attendance this evening. This is probably partly due to the entertainments arranged by the Entertainment Committee and partly to the delay in the hotels owing to their crowded condition. The time is now so far spent that in order to complete the programme it is necessary to get down to work. The Chair would suggest to the gentlemen in the rear that they come forward. It will be better for the congress if the audience is as much in a body as possible.

Carrying out the view expressed this morning in regard to presiding over the congress in my own city, I shall call to the chair to-night the pioneer of irrigation in America, especially among those who are here present, and I will request the Hon. George Q. Cannon of Utah to preside at the evening session (applause).

I have the honor of introducing Hon. George Q. Cannon of Utah.

MR. CANNON: This question of irrigation is one that we have been compelled to study practically, and that which we have done has been done through the experience of long years. It is most interesting to us who have lived in Utah, and who have lived by irrigation, who have proved its efficacy, and the many advantages of the system of irrigation, to see the almost universal interest which is now being taken in this important question. It is very gladdening to us, because the day has been when we were looked upon as occupying a very inferior position in our country, and liable to disadvantages which the rainwater sections of the country did not possess. But we have proved now for 47 years that men and women can live, and live comfortably and happily and contentedly in a region that is irrigated. Generations have grown up in our land possessing all the advantages and all the culture and all the means of enjoyment that are possessed by any section of our country from the Atlantic to the Pacific. I say, therefore, again, that we are very heartily glad to have this subject considered.

I have recently come from Kansas, where I attended a convention at the city of Hutchinson, and the condition of Western Kansas is something deplorable. But I think measures are now being taken that will result in great good to that people and to that land — the system which is being looked upon with favor, of farmers cultivating small holdings and devoting their attention to intense cultivation of the soil — this system is receiving general favor, and no doubt if it is followed up it will be attended with the best of results for that people.

It is my pleasure to introduce to the Trans-Mississippi Congress this evening Professor F. H. Newell of the United States Geological Survey, who will deliver an address on " The Water Supply of the Rocky Mountain Region." (Applause.)

PROFESSOR NEWELL'S ADDRESS.

Mr. Chairman, Ladies and Gentlemen of the Convention: — The water resources of this country, especially of the Rocky Mountain regions and the great plains, are little understood or appreciated by our people, and even by you gentlemen who have spent a life-time in the West. It is still far from being appreciated in its true value. It had been my intention to-night to try to give some facts bearing upon the resources especially of this somewhat unknown and little utilized area, but a hoarseness, contracted whilst speaking at Hutchinson with our friend Mr. Cannon, makes speaking somewhat painful, and I must content myself with a few generalizations, as to the development of these resources, and proceed in an unsystematic way to follow the immediate needs of the pioneers.

Water for irrigation has been used in many places rashly and wastefully, with no regard for economy or future needs. Our ideas as to how much water can be acquired, and consequently how much can be done with this water, are often crude and unreliable. In this, we have not estimated the possibilities of development, or cast them aside as too insignificant for our attention. On the other hand, interested persons have overestimated the volume of some of our streams and have projected works which were worthless, or have sold water rights which were in effect valueless, these being purchased by innocent farmers, who have endeavored in vain to make a living. In short, this has cast disrepute in many cases upon laudable projects which should now be under way. The public at large is far from that accurate conception of possibilities leading to confidence in the future. Not only is this true in the Rocky Mountain regions, but also on the great plains. There are sources of water, often small in themselves, but in the aggregate of a good deal of importance in the development of that vast area. Among these may be mentioned waters which run underground in the pervious gravel, and which to a large extent may be pumped by mills of wind or steam, rendering possible the supplying of the production of a sufficient amount of food for the farmer's family and having perhaps something to sell to the market.

It has been my business for a number of years to investigate the condition of the water resources of the United States, and the results have been shown in a general way in the volumes which lie before me. It will be better for me to refer in a general way to these details than for me to take your time in passing upon them. These volumes, which are part of the Series Report upon Irrigation and Water Supply of the Geological Survey, I propose to present to the Trans-Mississippi Congress through your President, in order that those who are interested may have an opportunity of referring to them. I also would call to your attention a volume published by the Census Office, giving the statistics of irrigation of the Western part of the United States, and giving the water supply of the mountain region by States and counties.

Instead of presenting the diagrams which I had designed, I will merely call attention to a number of maps on the wall. The farthest map from me represents in a general way the distribution of the rainfall in the United States, the heavy blue showing the largest amount of rainfall during the year, some 60 or 70 inches, and the lighter blue showing less and less rainfall, showing least in the portion of the country immediately West of the Rocky Mountain region. That map is doubtless familiar to you all. You are all familiar with the enormous amount of rain along the Western coast and along the Gulf, and the shading off of the supply on the plains.

I have presented another map which shows in a similar manner the amount of water which flows over the ground into the streams. The first map shows the amount which flows into, and the second which flows over. You will see on the Atlantic Coast, the Appalachian region, the enormous amount of water that flows off the ground, twenty inches or more; but as we go West the amount which flows off is less and less until in the great region from central Texas to central Washington there is a vast region where the amount of water aggregates from nothing up to two inches in depth, flowing off the ground during the whole year. The darker patches bordering that area, indicate the larger amount of water which flows away from the mountains. That shows in a very general way the result which we have arrived at, by a study of individual rivers scattered throughout the country. It would be possible to show the diagrams giving the fluctuations of these rivers from month to month and bringing out the possibility of holding this water in storage in suitable reservoirs.

As connected with the subject of water supply, I will call your attention to the third map, which shows the vacant public land belonging to the national government. The red, the most brilliant, is the land which has been disposed of by the national government, either given away, or sold, or homesteaded. The lighter color shows the amount of land still in the hands of the national government, and as a rule open for entry and settlement under the homestead act. This in the aggregate amounts to one-third of the United States, exclusive of Alaska. The bands of light red running across the map are the transcontinental railroad grants; within these belts every alternate section being given to railroad corporations. The green patches on the map indicate the forest reservation, aggregating some 18,000,000 acres, lands being held by the government for forestry purposes. The greenish or yellowish tint shows the Indian reservations.

Now, as you will see from that map, a close examination of vacant public lands shows that there is some in the States of Florida, Alabama, Mississippi and even up into Wisconsin and Minnesota, but they are to a large extent located West of Western Kansas, or the middle of Nebraska. In other words, they coincide most nearly with the portion of the United States where the run-off and the rainfall is exceedingly small, or where the mountains are so high and rough as to render agriculture almost impracticable. The fate of these vacant public lands now rests with the people, and I present this map in order that you may have at a glance some conception of the magnitude of the public domain still remaining in the hands of Uncle Sam. Regretting that I cannot go into the subject more satisfactorily, I will merely say in conclusion that the work which has been carried on by the Geological Survey in this line is for the benefit of the people and should be brought more directly to the people's attention, that they may judge of its value, as to whether it is well done, and they may be able to aid its continuation in order that it may lead to a more definite knowledge of the resources of the country and to the utilization of those resources, especially of water for irrigation or for power, such as to bring about prosperity, to bring employment to the West and to lead to happy homes and contented population (applause).

The Chairman: We shall next hear from Hon. Elwood Mead, State Engineer of the State of Wyoming, and President of the National Irrigation Congress, whom it is my pleasure to introduce.

ADDRESS OF HON. ELWOOD MEAD — RECLAIMING THE ARID LANDS.

In almost two-fifths of this country the conditions of nature must be transformed before it can become the self-supporting habitation of man. An inadequate rainfall must be supplemented by a water supply secured through the work of man before the soil can be made to produce its harvest.

In this region the United States is the greatest land-owner. Over six hundred million of acres of this domain is under the ownership and control of the Federal authorities. Thus far, this authority has done little or nothing to secure a rational or satisfactory solution of the problem of reclaiming these lands. The attitude of the General Government in regard to the development of the arid States has been that of an alien landlord who made no improvements and paid no taxes. The time has come when this condition of affairs should cease, when the arid region should have laws suited to its conditions, when the requirements of its climate and the necessities of its conditions should be met by suitable legislative enactment and industrial conditions.

The arid West is the hope of the future homeseeker. Its reclamation is the greatest industrial problem now before the people of this country. On the success of this rests the growth and prosperity of the seventeen arid States and Territories. Its accomplishment offers the greatest and most profitable avenue for the investment of capital and for the employment of idle and homeless labor which this century has yet witnessed. It is a problem, therefore, which does not concern the arid States alone. The magnitude of the obstacles to be overcome and the importance of the results to be secured makes it a great national question and one well worthy the consideration of this body. I know of no more appropriate place to discuss this question than this city. From the days of the Oregon Trail to the present, it has been the great gateway through which has passed the discoverers of the arid region, the settlers in that region and the wealth and enterprise which have done so much to develop its resources. Not only has this city been the great gateway of discovery, settlement and enterprise, but this State has contributed in a larger degree to people the remote sections of the West than perhaps any other State in the Union. There is scarcely a settlement too small or region too remote to contain one or more sons of this State, and I have no doubt that a large percentage of the attendance upon this congress have been drawn here as much by a prospect of a renewal of home ties as by a hope of furthering the business interests of the homes of their adoption.

It is my purpose to outline what, in my judgment, is the best means of accomplishing this work; to lay before you the requirements to be fulfilled; in order that there may be a satisfactory return to canal builders and prosperity and content for users of water. Many plans have been proposed. Some favor the building of canals with appropriations from the national treasury; others favor State appropriations. I am here to explain how it may be accomplished by private enterprise.

There are many objections to making this work depend upon national appropriations. The construction of a Federal building costs twice as much as the construction of an equally commodious and handsome structure by private means. It also takes more time. Uncertain and inadequate appropriations nearly doubles the cost, and time of completion, of river and harbor improvements. In many of these, the outlay required to maintain unfinished work is almost as great as the cost of the work itself. To place the diversion of the rivers of half a continent under such management would be to make the growth of that section depend upon political influences. It would be a move in the direction of increased, instead of lessened, cost of irrigation works, a vital objection whether the whole country or the users of water ultimately pay for it. So far as State works are concerned some will ultimately be built, but, at present, lack of means and lack of available resources in the arid States will prevent. In my own State it is, at present, out of the question. The constitutional limit of bonded indebtedness has been reached. In addition the causes, which have retarded individual and corporate effort, have been equally effective in preventing the inauguration or possible success of State works.

A State government extending over 63,000,000 acres of land, with a

total population of only 60,000 people, with less than five per cent of
the lands in the hands of its citizens, and subject to taxation, is not in
a condition to undertake the most stupendous transformation of nature
yet witnessed on the globe.   Such a State is only great in the extent of
its   unused   opportunities.   How   great   those   opportunities   are
we   have   as   yet   a   very   inadequate   conception.   The   four
great rivers which have their origin in Wyoming will water an
acreage as extensive as that fertilized by the Nile.   The land which
can be reclaimed in a single arid State is as great in area as that which
in Egypt requires for its cultivation the labor of 2,000,000 of people,
supports the court with its multitude of idle and profligate attendants;
the illimitable number of religious and fanatical sects; the army; the
crowds of native and foreign dignitaries which throng its cities, in all
over seven million people; a national debt of five hundred million; all
these draw their support from the bounty of one river and less than
six million acres of irrigated land.

All that has been accomplished thus far has been the result of individual and corporate effort.   The experience gained has shown con-
clusively one thing, that existing Federal land laws are wholly unsuited
to the conditions and needs of an arid region.   The public lands
instead of being first settled are the lands which await reclamation.
Financial success and rapid growth have been most marked in those
sections where the land was removed from the operation of the Federal
land laws.   State lands, Mexican grants and railroad land grants have
proved most remunerative to canal builders and most attractive to
settlers.   This is exactly the reverse of what should be.   If the public
lands are the heritage of the people they ought to be made available
for the occupancy and use of the people.   It is a reproach to a self-
governing people that it should be said, as it must be said, that the
reclamation of *public land* has in the past involved heavy losses to canal
builders and has witnessed the greatest absorption of the irrigable land
by holders who have not utilized it but held it for speculative purposes.

Because of the fact that Federal land laws permit the valuable lands
below a ditch to be occupied on exactly the same terms as the worthless
lands above it, ditch building has been made a hazardous enterprise.
Because of the fact that the homestead law permits the lands below a
ditch to be secured without reclamation or cultivation, we find that
more than half of the lands under ditches are unused and that over
ninety per cent of the canals built to water *public* land have been
financial failures.   Because the public land laws disregard the fact that
the actual home-seeker in the arid region needs less land instead of
more land, we find that large areas of the land most easily reclaimed
have been absorbed by non-residents under the Desert Land Law.
These results are altogether unnecessary.   They could have been

avoided in the past by proper investigation of the requirements of irrigated countries and the framing of laws to meet those requirements.

It has been proposed as a primitive reform, to change the homestead law and make title depend on the reclamation of the land and the presentation of evidence of title to water as is done in the desert land law. No homestead in the arid region can be a home in fact without it is provided with a water supply. To require that settlers should provide this before securing title to the lands would, therefore, work no hardship to the actual homeseeker while it would cut off the abuses which now attend its operation. We would have another result. It would reduce the size of half the homesteads secured, from 160 to 40 or 80 acres. So long as it costs no more to secure title to 160 acres than it does to a smaller area, filings will be made for the full amount, but if it is necessary to provide a water supply, and use it, the greed for land will speedily diminish. That 160 acres of irrigable land is in excess of the actual requirements of the majority of settlers, was shown in an investigation made by me this season. Letters of inquiry were sent to each user of water on four of the adjudicated streams of Wyoming, asking for a statement of the actual acreage under cultivation this year. The replies from three of the streams have been compiled. Under the first stream the average size of the cultivated farm was 88 acres; on stream number two, 62 acres; and on the third stream 45 acres. An 80 acre farm would have more than supplied the average requirements of the irrigators on these streams.

Such a reform would, however, fail to meet the most important requirements in the settlement of the arid domain. Irrigation laws must recognize the fact that the social and industrial relations of the farmers of an arid region are much more intimate and complex than is true of the agriculture of humid lands; that communal interests are much more important and that such interests must be recognized and protected by adequate legislation. The settlers on humid lands are independent of each other so far as their business interests are concerned. The prosperity of the settlers under a ditch is not assured by fertile soil and favoring climatic influences. All these may go for naught if the management of the water way which fertilizes their land is not honest and efficient.

The settlers under a ditch will all be stockholders in a transportation company. The successful management of this property and their protection from abuses and extortion require that it be governed by well-settled principles of law, and, that there should be an agreement and a definite understanding between the settlers before their occupancy of the lands, has been abundantly demonstrated by experience. The community interests of the settlers is not limited by their canal alone. Agricultural success, the value of water rights, and the comfort and content of water users depends upon the efficent supervision and division of the water of a stream. If the diversion of a stream is left wholly to individual inclination and interest its water will be wasted by useless and improperly located ditches; the users of water at the head of the stream will rob the users of water below. To prevent this, to make irrigated agriculture a success in the most limited sense, it is absolutely indispensable that there be an exercise of governmental authority to protect the rights of those dependent upon the common supply. To secure the best results, this supervision should begin before ditches are begun, not after their completion. To make this supervision effective it must extend over both land and water. It is useless for the State to refuse appropriations of water from a stream so long as the Federal government permits of the unrestricted construction of ditches, through the land, to divert the water from the stream. It is useless for the State to seek to protect the rights of users of water so long as it can exercise no control over the location or number of works to divert the common supply. It is useless to seek to protect investments in canals so long as the public land laws permit the lands under canals to be absorbed on terms which invite their confiscation. Heretofore, adequate supervision, adequate protection, has been impossible. The United States owned the land, the State controlled the water, and there has been no concert of action between the two authorities.

The opportunity has, however, presented itself to put an end to this divided authority. At the last session of Congress there was tacked to an appropriation bill one of the most important laws enacted within twenty years. It has been designated as the cession of one million acres of land to each of the arid States. Strictly speaking it is not cession. The title to the land does not necessarily pass to the State. It is held by the Federal government until reclaimed, and until a settler has a rightful claim to the title. If the title passes to the State it will be simply an intermediate transfer between the government and the settler. What this law is, is an attempt at concert of action between the Federal and State authorities, between the owner of the land and the owner of the water. It is believed, however, that it will accomplish the end desired by those who have advocated absolute cession; it will enable the State authorities to fix the conditions of reclamation. If this trust is accepted in the proper spirit and administered wisely it will mark a new era in the development of the West. The responsibility resting upon the legislatures of the several arid States will be greater this winter than ever before.

The State Engineer's Report, of Wyoming, for 1894, will contain the maps of canals which have been surveyed, but which present conditions have prevented being built, which will cover and reclaim in the aggregate over one million acres of land. To insure the building of these canals and the proper protection of both the investor in their construction, and the settler who is to use them, the State should do two things: Plans for canals should be subject to State approval, and no canal should be undertaken except under a specific contract with the State which will fix both its character and the maximum price at which it is to be disposed of to settlers. No canal should be undertaken except under conditions which provide for the actual transfer of the property to the settlers, because experience has shown that canals owned by settlers are operated at less expense, with less friction, and more satisfactory results than canals which furnish water for hire. This much is required for the protection of settlers.

On the other hand no rival project should be permitted to water the land it is intended to reclaim. No one should be permitted to acquire title to land who will not, or cannot, provide a water-right therefor. This is for the protection of the canal builder, the State and the settler. A multiplicity of canals means a waste of water and a waste of money in their construction. It means either increased cost to the users of water or a loss to the owners of the surplus canals. To require that no one shall be permitted to hold the land under the ditch except actual cultivators of the soil, and users of water, is a provision indispensable for the protection of interest in canals, in the interest of users of water, because the less the hazard in the construction of canals, the cheaper the price at which they can be sold.

The law transfers to each State the control of one million acres. The selection of the land is unrestricted. The control of the land by the State for ten years, absolute. It can only dispose of the land to actual settlers after it has been reclaimed and in tracts not to exceed 160 acres. The restrictive provisions are only those which each State should insert if the cession had been absolute. The interest of all parties, ditch builders, water users, the public at large, is in having the land occupied and ditches used. The question most often asked is: " Does this law offer sufficient opportunity to protect and secure the money invested in canals?" It is urged that the land can not be made a basis of credit; that the people who provide the money must do so in advance of settlement, that not being able to control or use the land or to sell it, they will be helpless in case settlers fail to occupy the land and use the water. Canal companies under such conditions will be simply construction companies, building a water-way for a fixed price and taking their chances on finding a purchaser. In one sense this is true. There will be no opportunity to speculate in the rise in land values, nor to charge extortionate prices for water, but the disadvantage is not real. In my personal experience more bankrupts have been made through ownership of large tracts of irrigated land than fortunes secured. The only advantage to the builder of a ditch in owning the land under it, is in being able to dispose of it to users of water and preventing its speculative absorption. The law I have outlined does this, it saves the outlay required for the purchase of the land, it saves the taxes on the land before its reclamation and disposal and leaves only the question: Will settlers come to occupy land practically free and purchase canals at a price fixed by the State and based upon cost?

So long as the people who occupy the land to be reclaimed must be users of water, there will be no trouble in disposing of the canal. There is scarcely a place in the arid region where the construction of a canal does not change the value of the land which it will reclaim, from being worthless, to being worth three or four times the cost of a water right. There is no place in the arid region where canals should be built, where the annual return from irrigated land will not be greater than the cost of a perpetual water-right. So long as this is the case there will be no difficulty in securing settlers to occupy the land nor hardship to those settlers in paying a satisfactory price for a perpetual water-right. Canal building under such conditions would be one of the most secure, if not lucrative, avenues for investment. It would relieve settlers from the danger of extortionate changes for water because they would know exactly the conditions before they entered upon their new employment. It would open up one of the most inviting avenues for the employment of idle capital, in the creation of homes for those who need them and who will use them. It would enable homeseekers to secure a share of the public domain under conditions involving less hardship and expense than in the past, and with far greater promises of security and prosperity than is possible under conditions now prevailing.

I have thus far considered the building of ditches by one agency, the cultivation of the land and the use of the ditch by others; and have assumed that the party who built the ditch would dispose of the same to the settler on the land. Under this assumption canal builders are simply construction companies, having no ownership in the land or in the water to be diverted. Both canal and water-rights to go with the land to be served.

I have not considered the construction of canals to furnish water for hire. Such canals will undoubtedly be built in some sections, but are not likely to be in the section in which I have the most direct interest. One objection to such canals has already been stated. The other is the creation of carrier rights as distinct from user rights in appropriation of water.

I have endeavored to discuss the phase of this question which presents the most difficulties. In reality I believe a large number of canals will be built and a large percentage of the land reclaimed through colony enterprises and community efforts, in which the ownership of the canal and land will exist in the same individual at the outset. The ability to secure preliminary control of the land under projected canals, to reserve it for the use of the builders of the canal until such time as they can profitably occupy it, creates an opportunity for homeseekers in the East to unite their means in securing it. This is impossible now. The present land laws are based upon the assumption that each 160 acres is to be reclaimed independently of its surrounding quarter sections. The historic Greeley colony was harassed from its inception by this weakness in our land laws. The land under the canal was only reserved for the people in the East, working to supply the money to build it, and the enterprise saved from collapse and disaster, by the managers on the ground, having the sense and courage to become land-grabbers and violators of the law by making filings on the land under fictitious names and thus preventing it being absorbed by those desiring to reap the benefits of the improvements without contributing thereto.

The time has come for the sage brush and cactus to give way to something more ornamental or useful, for the nomadic range industries to give way to settler's homes and diversified industries. The mountains in all lands have been the home of the poet and patriot. Our own ought to be peopled. The farmer of the arid domain has his toilsome life brightened and enriched by the beauty of his surroundings. The silver of the snow-clad mountain joins to the gold of the rising sun and the purple splendor of his going down. It was no accident that civilization had its birth in rainless countries nor that it is destined to find there its latest development and most perfect expression (applause).

THE CHAIRMAN: The next subject to be discussed this evening is "Irrigation, a National Living Issue," by Hon. Wm. E. Smythe, editor of the *Irrigation Age*, whom I now have the pleasure of introducing to you.

MR. SMYTHE'S ADDRESS.

The average ill-informed American — and about 90 per cent of all Americans are ill-informed concerning the resources of their own country (applause) — thinks irrigation is a local issue. So our Southern friends thought about slavery. So General Hancock thought about the tariff. So Eastern bankers think about silver (applause). The fact is that the American people can live longer in shrouded ignorance about their own conditions, and then awaken faster to the truth of the situation than any other people known to history (applause). If it be true that this is a nation, and not a bundle of provinces; if it be true that we have a national life and a national destiny, then nothing which affects any vast area of the Republic can properly be regarded as a local issue (applause). Put a bullet into the brain or into the heart, and the hands and feet cannot claim that that bullet is a local issue (applause).

This nation, with its vast and complex industrial and economic system, must rise to the height of a broad and enlightened statesmanship if it would endure, not to say prosper (applause). There are no better patriots than the men who inhabit the old States of our Eastern seaboard, but they do not travel, and hence, they do not know (applause). They are wrapt in the ample mantle of inherited provincialism (applause). They live too much on the memory of their ancestors (laughter). Columbus discovered, 400 years ago, nearly all of that portion of the United States which is interesting to our Eastern fellow-citizens in the evening twilight of the nineteenth century. There is but one imperial American. He is the American who finds his outlook on the highest peaks of the Rocky Mountains and who fills his lungs with the free air of the great West (applause). In his veins mingle the various strains of blood of New England, of the old South, of the middle West, of Central Europe. All parts of his country are known to him by contact. All impulses of his time find easy entry into his tolerant brain. His dream is of a greater America. He leaves the old home to face the wilderness and he is borne up by the spirit of conquest rather than of sordid adventure. He opens mines, turns mighty rivers, reclaims deserts, builds railroads, and then, with a pride like that which Columbus felt on returning to the court of Isabella, he lays new States at the feet of the mother nation (great applause).

To these imperial Americans of the West there are no local issues, save horse-thieves. And of all issues that to his mind seem national in dimension irrigation is the first. Long after the tariff shall have been settled and embalmed in history with slavery; long after a stricken commercial world shall have grasped the helping hand of silver as a means of averting disaster (applause) irrigation will be seen to be the overshadowing issue, involving not only the safety of our own institutions, but measuring also our capacity to sustain the surplus energies of overgrown foreign peoples. Then it will be plain to all that irrigation is a vital part of the broad foundation, while tariff and silver are but the doorways and cornices in the structure of our national existence.

What is the history of the past two years? We need not review it. It is burned into the memory alike of beggar and of millionaire. No matter what the cause, the results were idleness and unrest, hunger and danger. And this condition is practically unchanged to-day. The truth is that national progress has given place to national stagnation. I, for one, believe these conditions are principally due to a great fundamental cause which has attracted but little attention. Tariff uncertainty and the subtle appreciation of gold had their part in it, but the real cause lies deeper, and even if you adjust the tariff and currency to the reasonable satisfaction of all classes of our citizenship, you must still apply another remedy to restore the nation to the old paths of peace, prosperity and progress.

The inhabitants of this continent, first as English subjects and then as American sovereigns, have enjoyed something more than two centuries of high average prosperity. Give such credit as you may to the public policies which have come and gone in endless procession during that long period and you have not yet mentioned the chief cause of our stupendous material progress. The truth is that our people were dealing with the vast resources of a virgin continent. In the process of felling the forest, of turning the prairie sod, of building railroads, of creating mighty States, of making great cities, and of developing the manifold employments of a complex civilization, we have employed vast energies and tremendous amounts of capital. And this process yielded a vast prosperity distributed through all avenues of industry and all ranks of society. This was the explanation of our unfaltering onward march, generation after generation, alike in war and in peace, in sunshine and in shadow. Now, why this period of appalling stagnation? I will tell you.

Look at a map of the United States. Draw a line down through the middle from the Canadian to the Mexican boundary, cleaving Kansas and Nebraska in twain, and you will have marked off the limitation of what we know as the humid region, and indicated the beginning of the semi-arid region. To the east of that line there are living to-night some 64,000,000 people. To the west of that line live only about 4,000,000. In other words, the work of conquering this continent is only half done (applause). The greater and better half is still open to the conquest of human genius and human industry. The western half comprises four-fifths of the national area. And surely no Western man will dispute with me when I assert that this greater West, because of its diverse and rich resources, offers at least four avenues for gainful employment and for the creation of wealth where one is offered by natural conditions in the eastern part of the continent. Now, what is the remedy for the stagnation which has fallen upon all parts of the country, all channels of trade, all classes of society? The men of the East say, if General Schofield voices their sentiment, as I think he does, "Increase the army." The men of the West reply, "Increase the homes" (great applause). We say we can make homes for 70,000,000 people. But when we say this there arises in Washington a brilliant member of the Cabinet, of dazzling and scintillating intellectual capacity, and bids us pause for the reason that this land of hungry men is already overproducing the necessities of life. And then he proceeds to employ an eminent statistician of Boston to prepare a pamphlet designed to show the overfed American people how they can live on soup bones and other refuse for a few cents a day. But with due respect for Secretary Morton and Mr. Atkinson, the men of the West are of the opinion that great civilizations cannot be evolved from soup bones (applause). They do not fear overproduction, because they are planning an industrial system on new lines, designed to meet the needs of a new century with high ideals and enormous population.

There are two kinds of farming. One is born of the instinct of speculation, the other springs from the instinct of industrialism. One is based on the single crop of wheat, of corn, of cotton, and it is just the same principle if you substitute for these staples oranges, prunes or raisins. We have passed through an era of one crop or extensive farming, which is based upon a false economy, and leads always and everywhere to disaster in the end. The man who raises wheat, corn, cotton or any other staple for export, deliberately dooms himself and his children to hopeless competition with the servile labor of lands whose very aristocracy scarcely rise to the American standard of living (applause). The American farmer who does this is the author of his own degradation. The character of his home and the hopes of his children descend with the price of his product. All this is plain in every man who thinks.

Now come with me from the plantations of the South, and the wheat farms of the Mississippi basin into the valleys of Utah. Perhaps the time has not yet come when it is popular to acknowledge the greatness of the founder of the Mormon industrial system. But the time will come when this proud nation will learn lessons of a people whom they once pursued, however justly, with a vigor untempered with kindness (applause). The census tells you that the average size farm in Utah is 27 acres. It tells you that 90 per cent of the Mormon people are proprietors of the soil. It tells you that scarcely any of these farms are mortgaged. Did you hear of any Mormon recruits in the Coxey armies (laughter)? No, for the reason that Brigham Young and the able men with whom he was surrounded, some of whom I see before me, taught the Mormon people that it was the first duty of every farmer to produce from the soil what his children needed to eat and wear. No Mormon thinks of a surplus crop for export until he has first provided for those things which his family consumes.

The Mormon plan of farming, briefly stated, is this: To have a small farm unit, devoted to diversified production, intensely cultivated and faithfully fertilized. To group the people in agricultural villages, that the women and children may be near to the church, the store, the post-office, and thus to blend the advantages of town life with the charm of rural existence.   Another link in their industrial policy is manufacturers to consume the products and thus enhance the independence of the State.   At my request the historians of the church have gathered statistics to show the financial and material results of this policy over a period of 40 years.   Allowing $20,000,000 for personal property brought into the Territory, we found that they have taken from their 20-acre irrigated farms and expended it in the cost of living, constructing irrigation works, improving farms, building factories, churches and temples and sending missionaries to the uttermost parts of the earth, the magnificent total of $542,900,000 (applause).   Every dollar of it was coined from arid soil, irrigated with the sweat of industrious men (applause).   Looking at it from the stand point of individuals, we find that the average annual income realized by each proprietor of their 10,000 little farms was $1,357.25, or $482.25 to pass to the credit of a competence after defraying the cost of a living.

With such an industrial system, improved as it will be by our later and better intelligence, our larger enlightenment, we can sustain at least 70,000,000 of the freest men who ever walked the earth (applause). They will be land owners, ready to shed their blood in defense of the soil which belongs to them and those they love.   And this, my countrymen, is our solution of the difficulties and dangers which confront the Republic to-day (applause).   Are these local issues?   Yes, as much as the battle of Lexington was local to Massachusetts (applause), as much as the shot upon Sumpter was local to South Carolina.   Those events are part of the fabric of our common history.   The train of events which followed after them molded our common destiny, and the reclamation and settlement of the western half of this continent, under just laws and in a spirit of lofty patriotism, is to be the next stupendous national achievement of a nation which will die only when it ceases to march forward (loud applause).

Our new civilization will not be one-sided.   We begin with agriculture because all civilization begins there.   There can be no enduring civilization which does not rest on this broad basis.   But with the prosperity of agriculture every other element of a complex industrial and social life will be brought into being.   Towns and railroads, banks, stores and factories — all these will come when we have conquered the soil.   And I must not forget to mention electricity.   It will be the handmaid of irrigation and its twin factor in working out the destiny of arid America.

Now, what are the practical steps by which we shall make this progress?   What can this representative body of Western and Southern men do to help us?   We come to you from the National Irrigation

Congress and ask you to lend your influence in favor of certain measures. We do not ask much. We purpose to be as self-reliant as possible. We do not assume the attitude of Oliver Twist, and hold out our plate always for more soup. We favor a policy of co-operation between the nation and the States, acting with private enterprise under proper restrictions.

We ask, first, for the repeal of the desert land law. If this law ever had a reason for being, it has fulfilled its purpose. In the majority of instances it is not available for settlers, nor can it be made useful by private corporations, except by a tortuous process of perjury and fraud. Corporations have not hesitated to use it in this way. We ask you to favor its repeal before all the valuable lands are stolen from the people by means of this instrument of injustice. We have the Carey law, which opens a million acres in each State to reclamation and settlement and bridges over the period which must elapse between the repeal of the desert land law and the adoption of a really enlightened and enduring national policy.

We ask, in the second place, that you go on record in favor of the creation of a National Irrigation Commission. Our forests are being destroyed, our irrigable lands are being largely misappropriated, our pasturage lands serve as the theater of bitter warfare between cattlemen and sheep men, our interstate streams are becoming entangled in rival appropriations, and it is high time that the American people paid some attention to this greatest of all their national assets — the public domain. We ask the appointment of a National Irrigation Commission which shall take up these complex problems and seek to evolve a comprehensive national policy. This commission should be independent of existing departments. It should be modeled something on the lines of the Interstate Commerce Commission, with power to draw upon the departments of the Interior, of Agriculture and of War for such information and facilities as it may need. Above all, this commission should be composed of Western men, who know the difference between an irrigation canal and a watering trough (laughter).

We also ask for the appointment of a temporary commission to adjust serious differences already arising over international streams between the United States and Mexico, and other differences certain to arise between the United States and Canada. If we permit these grave matters to go unsettled until they finally bring us to the verge of war, what will the world think of American statesmanship? It is now comparatively easy and simple to settle them on a basis of justice and equity.

The forestry problem is most urgent. The forest reservations secured under the administration of President Harrison command the approbation of all thoughtful students of this question, East and West alike. Urge President Cleveland to go forward with this policy without delay. But this is not enough. The bill now pending in Congress at the instance of the distinguished gentleman from Arkansas (Mr. Mc-Rae) is a measure of urgent and pressing necessity. It will serve a wise temporary purpose, and we ask you to favor its enactment. Beyond this, the National Irrigation Congress favors the plan proposed by Prof. Sargent of Harvard University, providing for the education of skilled foresters at West Point and the control of the forest reservations by the army, by means of a local forest guard. This plan would create a forestry policy on a scientific basis.

We ask for it, not on the sentimental grounds which some have urged in behalf of noble scenery, but because these mountain forests are nature's storage reservoirs, and because if you permit them to be destroyed you rob posterity of the means by which vast populations must be supported in the valleys and on the plains. We beg you to give your hearty indorsement to these measures, none of which are radical, all of which are but tentative, looking to the final adoption of a symmetrical and enlightened public policy on which a mighty civilization must rest so long as time endures.

I regret to see it stated in certain quarters that the recent Irrigation Congress was controlled by the representatives of corporations and monopolies. Such a statement arises either from misinformation or prejudice. The Congress was composed principally of delegates named by Governors of States and other elected servants of the people. It certainly represented a fair average of Western intelligence and patriotism.

Gentlemen, I hope I have said nothing to foster sectional prejudice or animosity. We must arouse the country, even if we have to startle it, to open its eyes to the great national issues involved in our cause. I speak not as a Western man but as an American of that imperial school which knows the West only as a part of the Republic (applause). A child of New England, I love the West because its budding commonwealths rest under the same flag as my native Massachusetts (applause). If danger ever arises for the Union it will come not from the West. From that source will come the great leaders of the future doctrine of nationality. Their views and their policies will be on a scale with their mountains and plains. There is no room in the Western heart for anything so small and petty as local pride.

We ask the nation to take some interest in the West, not for the sake of the West, but for the sake of the nation, of which the West is a momentous part. We ask for the fostering hands of national interest in the development of national assets. Nationality, not separatism, is the great tenet of our creed. We believe with Webster that this is "an indissoluble Union of indestructible States." We ask not to be separated from our countrymen of the East, but to be bound the closer by great policies of legislation and administration and by new ties of blood, represented by armies of settlers from the East and South. And as we go forward in the pathway of national destiny, we shall march to the music of that other note of Webster's: " Union and liberty, now and forever, one and inseparable " (prolonged applause).

Mr. Whitmore then resumed the chair.

The Chairman: The Chair regrets to announce that the other speaker for the evening has not arrived, and this will end our evening session. To-morrow afternoon at 4 o'clock the discussion on the Remonetization of Silver will be opened by ex-Gov. Prince of New Mexico, who will be followed at half-past seven o'clock by Hon. Geo. E. Leighton of St. Louis. He will be followed by Representative Bryan of Nebraska, who takes Col. Patterson's place on the programme, and the discussion will be closed by ex-Gov. Anthony of Kansas. With this explanation in regard to the programme to-morrow, the congress stands adjourned until 10 o'clock to-morrow morning.

TUESDAY MORNING.

November 27, 1894.

The meeting was called to order by President Whitmore.

The Chairman: The first business in order is the reporting of the names of the Committee on Resolutions.

The following list of members of the Committee on Resolutions was then read :—

Alaska — J. C. Green.

Arizona — W. J. Chamberlain and W. J. Cheney.

Arkansas — George Sengel and C. S. Collins.

California — D. Lubin and George W. Parsons.

Colorado — John F. Shafroth and I. L. Johnson.

Idaho — William Budge and Ben E. Rich.

Indian Territory — G. B. Dennison and Fielding Lewis.

Iowa — Bart E. Linehan and S. F. Smith.

Kansas — W. H. Toothbacker and Stephen Crane.

Minnesota — Thomas Sharp.

Missouri — E. O. Stanard and Chas. E. Yader.

Montana — T. O. Morrill and W. H. Wood.

Nebraska — W. J. Bryan and R. W. Richardson.

New Mexico — T. H. Gabel and L. B. Prince.

Oklahoma Territory— Sidney Clarke and J. A. Maguire.

Oregon — E. P. Dosch.

South Dakota — S. E. Wilson and J. R. Brennan.

Texas — Louis Hancock and Ed. A. Marshall.

Utah — Frank J. Cannon and C. C. Goodwin.

Washington — D. E. Durie and A. L. Black.

Wyoming — Elwood Mead.

The Chairman then announced that a room had been provided for the Committee on Resolutions in the front of the hall, where they could meet at such time as they desired.

The Secretary then read a letter of regret from Gov. Rickards of Montana.

It was then seconded and carried that the Committee on Resolutions meet at 2 o'clock.

It was moved as an amendment that the Committee on Resolutions meet at 12 o'clock.

The amendment was lost and the original motion was adopted.

MR. RIDGELEY: Mr. President, will it be in order to submit a resolution?

THE CHAIRMAN: No, sir; the regular order of business must be taken up. It has already been delayed too long. The special order of business this morning is the consideration of the report of the Committee on Rules and Order of Business. The Secretary will again read this report as a whole, and unless the congress orders otherwise, the vote will be taken on this report *seriatim*, and if no objection is made, it will be considered as the sense of the congress that each section as read shall be adopted.

The Secretary then read the report of the Committee on Rules and Order of Business as follows: —

1st. Reading, correcting and approving the minutes.

2d. Introduction, reading and referring of resolutions.

3d. Reports of committees.

4th. The congress will meet at 10 a. m., 2:30 p. m. and 7:30 p. m.

5th. Cushing's Manual to be used as a guide on all parliamentary questions.

6th. Tuesday morning shall be devoted to miscellaneous business.

7th. Tuesday afternoon and evening shall be devoted to the consideration of the financial question.

8th. Wednesday morning to miscellaneous business.

9th. Wednesday afternoon, transportation, railroads, public and arid lands.

10th. Wednesday evening, Nicaragua Canal.

11th. Miscellaneous business may be called up at any time after the regular order is exhausted.

12th. On roll-call each delegation is entitled to 10 votes as representative of its State or Territory. If more than 10 delegates are present from any State or Territory, it is entitled to as many votes as it has delegates present, provided it shall not exceed 30 votes for each State or Territory.

13th. Introducers of a subject may speak 10 minutes and close the debate with a 5 minutes' address, the other speakers to be restricted to 7 minutes.

14th. All resolutions shall be referred to the Committee on Resolutions without debate."

"The Admission of Territories to Statehood" was added to the Wednesday afternoon programme.

Referring to the 10th section, the Chairman said:—

THE CHAIRMAN: The special order of business for Wednesday evening has already been arranged, for the Nicaragua Canal, the Hawaiian question, and such other questions as may be incidentally brought up. It is understood that this report will not interfere with the order of business arranged by the Committee.

MR. F. J. CANNON: Mr. Chairman, I move to strike out the words, "Provided it shall not exceed thirty votes for any State or Territory," in section XII. (Motion seconded).

MR. CANNON: Mr. Chairman, the method of calling this congress together was no doubt very well considered, the basis of apportionment for this congress was perhaps very well considered, but it appears to me to cast a stigma upon the character of the congress to send out an invitation officially to the several States and Territories to send their chosen men here and to answer to those men when they shall appear with their credentials, that they are not wanted. It is a little too arbitrary — for "many are called but few are chosen" after we get to St. Louis. I do not speak for Utah alone, although we are here in strong numbers. The few men here in excess of thirty could no doubt devote their time to the programme of the Entertainment Committee, but it is not in accordance with the dignity of an assemblage which bases a large share of its membership upon population, and against the recognized rights of every State, to have its representation cut down on this floor. So far as the representation on population and enterprise are concerned, we ought to adhere to the rule which obtains in the lower House of Congress. It would be rather absurd for Missouri to appear in the House of Representatives of the United States with her full delegation and to have that delegation cut in two because she happened to have a larger population and more enterprise than some other State had. In other words, if we should adopt this rule the State that has answered this call in the feeblest way, the one that is the least interested, will have every man who appears here in behalf of that State, a larger proportion of representation than the State or Territory which has sent a full delegation. The State that has but sufficient interest to send one man here is going to give that man 10 votes. A State or territory which answering this call has sent a full delegation here is going to give its delegates but half or three-quarters of a vote each. It appears to me that if we want to send the proceedings of this congress out to the country west of the Mississippi river with a stigma which the territory east of the Mississippi would like to place upon it, the best way is to adopt the rule offered. The only way to treat the men fairly who have come here is to adopt the amendment which I propose.

Ex-Gov. Prince: Mr. President, when I asked yesterday afternoon that this might be made a special order of business for this morning, it was because the subject is one of such serious importance that it deserves the fullest consideration. And glad as I always am·to hear my friend from Utah, and ready as I have been on almost every occasion to concur in his views, I almost fear that, without some such consideration, the manner in which he would put the argument might perhaps carry this convention away from that which it seems to me is the straight path in this matter. Now, this is not a new question — it has come up in congress from the beginning. It is easy to see that there is a fair argument on each side, that is, to a certain extent. When the congress met in the city of Denver we found there what was perfectly natural, that the State of Colorado had more members present than all the other States of the Trans-Mississippi country. This congress represents an enormous district of territory, extending from the Mississippi to the Pacific. It is impossible that very large delegations should come from the remote parts of this vast district. It is always to be expected that the State in which the congress is held and the States which are immediately contiguous will have by far the largest delegations. Now, this is a representative body. It is not intended as a town meeting, or as simply a representation of the city in which it meets, or of the particular sections of this trans-Mississippi country in which it happens to hold its session. When the session was held in New Orleans, Louisiana and Texas had the great preponderance of the delegates. When it was held in San Francisco the Pacific Coast naturally had the preponderance. If there is not some basis of representation making a limitation, the particular locality will control the entire complexion of the congress which is held there. If it had not been understood that there was such a limitation here, the State of Missouri could have sent about 400 delegates, and could have shaped this congress' entire proceedings. It is the same wherever it meets. If we are to preserve a representative character, there must be some kind of limitation, or else the congress will simply become the mouthpiece of the special locality at which it is held at one or another time, and it will speak with an entirely different voice from year to year, in accordance with the place where it happens to be.

Now, in Denver, and afterwards at San Francisco, the representation was made absolutely equal between the different States. Each one had 30 votes, without any reference to the number of delegates present. I concede that there are certain objections to that and that there is a good deal of force and reason in what has been said by my friend from Utah as to putting a premium — so to speak — on actual attendance. The report of the committee made to this body yesterday, it seems to me, strikes a happy medium. It gives to each State 10 votes absolutely, if it has any representation. It limits the total number to 30 votes, thereby giving this whole range betwean the 10 and 30 as a premium on actual representation. To extend this limitation beyond 30, it seems to me, would be simply to invite the danger which I suggested, of having local influences in every case control the convention, and I submit that in order to preserve our representative character, in order that this may be a representative assemblage of the whole Trans-Mississippi country, in order that every section may have something like its proportionate weight in the deliberations and conclusions that are arrived at, a limitation of that kind is not only fair but necessary.

MR. BLACK: Mr. President, I desire to amend the resolution as read by striking out of that part of the resolution the words, " as representative of its State or Territory," and adding thereto a recommendation, "shall have as many votes as there are delegates present, provided they do not exceed 30." It seems to me that a resolution reading in that manner, viz.: that each State shall have 10 votes of right, and have in addition thereto as many votes as there are delegates present, is a happy medium between the proposition as made by the gentleman from Utah and that as made in the original resolution, and supported by the gentleman from New Mexico. Each State which is interested in this congress sufficiently to send its representative from a distance is entitled to extra consideration. For instance, take the State from which I have the honor to be a delegate. We have come here 2,500 miles — there are several members present. It seems to me that we should be entitled to more recognition than a State nearer by, who sent but one man. It seems to me that each man here, unless he be of a delegation so large that it would control this whole congress, should be entitled to a representation for himself. It is true, that if there is but one delegate here, he should have more than that power, and therefore I think the provision that each State have 10 votes is a just provision, and it should be adopted. I think the amendment I make is just, fair and equitable.

THE CHAIRMAN: The gentleman will send the resolution to the platform.

MR. RIDGELEY: Mr. President, I desire to state that I am in favor of the report of the committee, from the fact that it gives to each State and Territory just the representation that it was intended to have by the power that made the appointment of delegates, and secondly, because it gives every State or Territory a representation, whether all the delegates are here or not. No matter whether a State or Territory only has one delegate or two present, its interests are just the same as if it had 20, and it may be that even one delegate or two can reflect the sentiment of that State or Territory as ably as it can when there are 30. For this reason I am in favor of the report of the committee. As far as Arkansas is concerned, she is in the middle of the road. She will not suffer very materially from anything that has been presented. I hope the report of the committee will prevail.

H. H. HARDING (of Missouri): Mr. Chairman, as a member of that Committee I wish to state, the Committee wrestled with that problem for more than an hour, and with the experience of members who had attended former congresses, in which the same question had come up. Now, as a representative from Missouri, I have not been actuated at all by any selfish consideration. Had I taken the same view as was taken by the gentleman from Utah, Missouri would have had a large vote in this convention, but as the matter was presented in committee to me, it did not seem just, that because we were here in Missouri so near the convention, we should be entitled to so large a voice in that convention; it ought to be limited. I acknowledge there was great force from an abstract stand-point in the argument of the gentleman from Utah, and I acknowledge they are entitled to great consideration coming from a distance and at great expense, and I would almost be willing, sir, as Utah has had plural ideas, that they be made an exception and given a vote for every man they have got here. But still I think the number directed by the committee is the correct one — there should be a limitation.

THE CHAIRMAN: The Chair will read the amendment offered by Mr. Black, in order that delegates may understand to what point they are talking (reading): " On roll-call each delegation is entitled to vote ten votes, as representative of its State or territory, and in addition thereto as many votes as there are delegates present, provided they do not exceed thirty."

B. D. WILLIAMS (of Arkansas): Mr. Chairman, I had the honor of being a member of the committee which made that report. The committee was over an hour in session, and most of the time was engaged in the discussion in reference to that portion of the report. The gentlemen from the different States were present and the committee was all present, and after discussion and argument they unanimously agreed to make this report. Utah was reported upon that committee, and she with the rest of us, unanimously agreed to make the report. We believe it was just and right and proper that each State should have ten votes, and that the balance of the State should be represented by their delegates, not to exceed thirty in all. That being the case, we made that report, believing that there would be no friction and no difficulty in passing it, and that it would give all

parties an equal chance in this convention. Arkansas has twenty delegates on this floor. She could have had many more if necessary, but
here we ask to vote no more than ten votes at large and the balance up
to thirty. We feel that it is right and proper each State should have
ten votes, and for Utah, if these gentlemen have more than thirty, I
think it nothing but right that they submit to the proposition and
accept that. I believe that Missouri here joins in the magnanimous
feeling of the gentleman on my right, who has said that they ask no
more than thirty. We perhaps could muster and bring into this convention two or three hundred, but we stand with the other States —
we stand asking no more rights, no more privileges in this convention,
than the State that is represented by only one man. Therefore, gentlemen, I feel that the report of the committee should be adopted and I
move to lay the other amendment on the table.

THE CHAIRMAN: The Chair will state the two propositions. Both
allow each delegation ten votes as representing the State or Territory;
the report provides that, if it has more than ten delegates, its vote
shall be limited to the number of delegates; the amendment gives a
vote to each delegate in addition to these ten votes; both, however, limit
the total vote to thirty.

The motion now is to lay the amendment on the table.

The statement was then made by a delegate from Iowa that if
the motion is adopted it carries the original resolution with it, and to
get rid of that motion and act upon the resolution it is necessary to
vote down the motion to lay upon the table.

The Chair stated that this was corrrect and the motion was withdrawn.

HON. W. J. BRYAN (of Nebraska): Mr. Chairman, in deciding this
question it seems to me our object should be to make the utterances of
this Trans-Mississippi Congress as valuable to as wide a section of country as possible, and if we expect it to have weight, the voice must be the
voice of the States represented and not the voice of individuals who may
gone to the trouble to come to the congress. Now, we appreciate the
force of the argument made by the gentleman from Utah, and it is a
great compliment to the State to have so many people willing to come so
far to attend this congress, and yet the papers who report this meeting
will pay to that State this compliment in reporting that so many were
on hand, but if we allow each person to vote, the gentleman certainly
recognizes that one or two States may have a majority in this congress,
and what the congress does will go before the country as the expression of merely two or three States and it will fall flat upon the country.
In my judgment, the report of the committee which allows 30 votes to
those States which sent 30 delegates, is a very liberal allowance. It
seems to me they have gone to the limit.

Now, we are assembled here not to represent ourselves, but to represent the people of our State, and each person is supposed to be entitled to equal consideration in the making of these laws.   Take the case of Utah — Utah has one member of Congress or delegate, possibly two, and two senators.   Here are other States which have two senators and ten or fifteen members of Congress.   Now, these represent people interested in all questions which concern the Trans-Mississippi country. Is it fair that because a few States may send a large number of delegates, that therefore the people living in those States shall control the action of the congress?   It seems to me the argument made by ex-Gov. Prince is an unanswerable one, and that the argument made by my friend from Utah, while it may appeal to the pride of the State and be a deserved compliment to the enterprise of those people, I think they ought to be willing to take their apportionment as it is made here, without asking too large a place in its deliberations.

SENATOR JOHNSTON: I ask the Chairman, is a motion to lay upon the table debatable?

THE CHAIRMAN: It has been withdrawn — the discussion is on the adoption of the substitute.

A DELEGATE FROM IOWA: Gentlemen of the Congress, there is a disposition on the part of every gentleman present to be fair.   An invitation was sent throughout the Trans-Mississippi region and the basis of representation to this congress was made known to the people of that portion of the Union, that each State was entitled to a certain representation upon the floor of this house.   It seems to me, if the delegates from Utah have been legally sent, if their credentials have passed the scrutiny of the committee, and if Utah has sent no more delegates than she was entitled to, considering the basis of representation sent out before this congress convened — that if they are entitled to 30 or 35 or 40 members on the basis sent out to her people, and they have had enterprise enough, at an expense of eight or ten thousand dollars, to send their delegates here, and they come with proper credentials, I cannot see why there should be a disposition on the part of any gentleman from another State where the people have not had the same enterprise, to shut Utah out of the vote she is rightfully entitled to.   It seems to me it would be more fair for this body, in the wish to set the basis of representation, to look forward to the next congress, but not look back to the time when they sent the invitation to the people of Utah, setting forth the fact that they were entitled to so many towns, or so many delegates, or to so many organizations, to send one or more delegates.   They have traveled one or two thousand miles at an expense of $10,000, and when they reach here a committee is appointed by this body saying that they are not entitled to more than a certain number of votes.   I think it touches the very fountain of representation that has governed this congress for years past, that the very constitution of it be changed, if you wish to cut down your representation. Let the representation that we are looking forward to reach to the next congress, but not to the one that has assembled here to-day with her delegates, having traveled thousands of miles and spent thousands of dollars, when not one single member thereof has come with credentials that has not been accepted by this congress. Each gentleman from Utah carries with him a credential based upon the representation sent out, and if he is passed by the Committee on Credentials, he is entitled to a seat on the floor of this body.

An inquiry was then made as to the number of delegates in the Utah delegation, which was stated to be about 40.

Mr. Cannon then withdrew his motion and offered an explanation of his position.

Mr. F. J. Cannon: Gentlemen of the Congress, the explanation looks only to a vindication of the people who have come from Utah. We have had all the newspaper attention and compliments that we desire. We have not come here for the purpose of asserting individuality nor plurality. We have come here to represent the strength and vigor of the new State of Utah. We come here to vote with the gentlemen of other States upon questions which will make the country great. We do not care for more than 30 votes, but we care for justice, and we say when any congress sends its invitations it must answer to itself and to justice when people appear on that invitation. Having said so much, I desire to withdraw my motion, and Utah will accept her 30 votes, or less, along with the rest.

The question was then put on the substitute offered by Mr. Black of Washington and lost.

The original report was then adopted.

The remaining sections of the report were then read and the Chair stated the question to be upon the adoption of the report as a whole.

Capt. Thomas Sharp (of Minnesota): Mr. Chairman, in the apportionment of time on the report I see no time set apart for Rivers and Harbors.

The Chairman: The Chair is of the impression that that will come under miscellaneous business and can be introduced like any other subject.

The report was then adopted as a whole.

A resolution was then offered by Mr. Black of Washington relating to the use of American products in the American Navy.

A resolution was offered from Oklahoma relating to the admission of Oklahoma, New Mexico and Arizona as States, also relating to Territorial form of government for the Indian Territory.

Hugh Craig (of San Francisco): Mr. Chairman, the Chamber of

Commerce of San Francisco presents its compliments to the Trans-Mississippi Congress, with a resolution referring to the Hawaiian cable; the Produce Exchange of San Francisco presents its compliments with a resolution on the Farralone cable: the Board of Trade of Oakland presents its compliments with a resolution relating to the improvement of Oakland Harbor.

These resolutions were then read and referred.

THE CHAIRMAN: The Committee on Permanent Organization is now ready to report, and the Chairman will be kind enough to take the platform and make his report.

The Secretary read the following report: —

"Your Committee on Permanent Organization beg leave to report the following names: —

For President, Hon. Geo. Q. Cannon, of Utah.

For Secretaries, the present officers to serve during this session and after the location of the meeting of the next congress the Executive Committee have power to select a Permanent Secretary and Assistant Secretary.

Your committee also recommend that each State report one name as Vice-President."

THE CHAIRMAN OF THE COMMITTEE ON PERMANENT ORGANIZATION: Mr. Chairman, I merely wish to explain in regard to the Secretary it seems almost necessary that the Secretary should be located in the town where the next meeting is held. Therefore we thought it better to recommend that the old officers hold over for this meeting, and when the place was selected for the next meeting, to elect a Secretary from that city.

On motion of Mr. Black of Washington, duly seconded and carried, the report was unanimously adopted.

THE CHAIRMAN: The chair desires to congratulate the gentleman named upon the honor conferred upon him, and the congress upon the honor it has conferred upon itself. The chair will appoint Messrs. Stanard, of Missouri, Black, of Washington, and Johnston, of California, a Committee to escort the President-elect to the chair.

THE CHAIRMAN: Delegates to the Congress, I have pleasure in introducing to you your presiding officer until the next session, Hon. George Q. Cannon of Utah.

PRESIDENT CANNON: Ladies and Gentlemen of the Trans-Mississippi Congress, I can assure you that it would have been a much greater pleasure to me to have had any other gentleman, any other member of this congress, selected for this position, than to have been selected myself. At the same time, I appreciate very highly the honor that has been conferred upon me, and through me on the Territory of Utah, which I hope soon will be a State. I may say, speaking for our people who inhabit that territory, that we have taken a deep interest in the questions that are likely to come before this congress, as we do with all questions which affect the great West. We want to keep abreast of the public sentiment of the West and to take an active part in everything appertaining to its development. We believe that there is a great future before the Trans-Mississippi States and Territories, and that there is a people inhabiting that region, that will receive sooner or later a much fuller recognition from the East than they do at the present time. The question of irrigation has come to the front within the last two or three years with astonishing rapidity. It is a question, perhaps, which the people of St. Louis and those along the Mississippi river do not feel as much interest in as those farther west, but undoubtedly the time is near at hand when this important matter will receive the fullest attention. Even Illinois, I am told, feels the necessity of adopting some system of supplementing the rains which fall from heaven.

Of course, the silver question is one of deep interest to all who belong to the silver-bearing States and Territories, but there are other questions that have been mentioned in connection with the meeting of this congress which may not affect us who live in the far West so seriously as they do along the Mississippi and contiguous thereto. These undoubtedly will receive attention and should receive careful consideration.

I heartily indorse the sentiments expressed by our President, Mr. Whitmore, in his opening address. I feel that it was broad and it applied to us all — that there should be no distinction, that there should be no sectional feeling, no matter what part a delegation came from, that they should be broad and take comprehensive views of all the questions that would be submitted to this congress. I feel personally, and I think I speak for the delegation of which I am a member, that there is no question that has been mentioned in the call for the Trans-Mississippi Congress as likely to be discussed before that congress, that we do not take the deepest interest in. Not wishing to trespass upon your time, ladies and gentlemen, longer, I heartily thank you on behalf of my own Territory and myself for the honor conferred upon me.

Mr. Castle: Mr. Chairman, on behalf of the California delegation, I move that a vote of thanks be tendered to our retiring Chairman for the able manner, in which he has discharged his duties (applause).

This motion was put by President Cannon after being seconded and was duly carried.

President Cannon: President Whitmore, I take pleasure in voicing to you the feeling of, I might say love — I do not think it is too strong a word to use to our retiring President, for I can speak for myself; his conduct during our deliberations has won my admiration and love — therefore I can in behalf of this congress tender to you this hearty vote for the expression of the good feeling the members of this congress entertain for you, and their thanks for the able manner in which you have presided over this body.

MR. WHITMORE: Mr. President and Fellow-Delegates, those of you who were at the San Francisco congress will bear witness to the hesitation with which I accepted the honors and the duties which were there assigned me. I did so with reluctance, partly because I felt that the honor should have been bestowed upon some one who was better entitled to it, and partly because I doubted whether I should be able to so fill that position as to meet with your satisfaction. If I have done so, it is a source of the greatest gratification to myself, but — I say it honestly — I deserve no thanks. I have simply done that which it was my duty to do — nothing more — and I have tried to do no less. If this meeting is to succeed, if we have succeeded in calling the attention of the people in the Trans-Mississippi region to this congress and its work, that success is attributable far more to others than to myself, to those who were not under the same obligations to do that work, to the members of our Executive Committee, to the gentlemen in the different cities who have taken an interest in this congress — to them more than to me you owe any success which may attend your efforts here, and in accepting this vote of thanks I desire to include them as well as myself, and on their behalf and my own, I thank you.

MR. WHITMORE: Mr. President, before adjournment I desire to call the attention of the delegates to the fact that yesterday we received an invitation from the Merchants' Exchange to attend any one of their sessions which you might choose to. Their sessions close every day at a quarter past one, and the members will be exceedingly glad to welcome any of you who may present yourselves. The building is only about a block from the Planters House, and I think you will be interested in seeing the building in which they hold their daily sessions.

Adjourned until 2:30 p. m. to-day.

TUESDAY AFTERNOON SESSION.

The meeting was called to order at 2:30 p. m. by President Cannon.

THE CHAIRMAN: The hour having arrived to which the congress adjourned, it is now open for business. The introduction of resolutions or miscellaneous business will be in order now.

The Chair has been requested to recognize a gentleman from Colorado who is only going to be here to-day.

THE CHAIRMAN: Congressman-elect Shafroth of Colorado is going to leave in the morning and would like to make some remarks before he leaves.

ADDRESS OF CONGRESSMAN SHAFROTH ON THE SILVER QUESTION.

Mr. President, Ladies and Gentlemen of the Congress: As I understood the programme, the discussion of the silver question was to be taken up this afternoon, and knowing I had to leave in the morning, I desire to say something upon this question. If I do not say it at this time I feel I will have no opportunity to do so. I therefore thank you for the courtesy you have shown me in permitting me to say a few words upon this question. The President of this congress yesterday stated that he hoped that inasmuch as we represented the States west of the Mississippi river, that we would not look at the questions to be presented before this congress from a local stand-point, but from the stand-point of the nation at large. Those sentiments I heartily commend, and though I am from the State of Colorado, that is the greatest silver producing State in the Union, yet I may say that we do not desire the free and unlimited coinage of silver in that State because it is a product of the State of Colorado. We have no right to demand legislation in behalf of that State, if that legislation is detrimental to the interest of the nation, and it is purely from a national stand-point that we have a right to discuss this question before the people.

Ladies and Gentlemen of the Convention, the first thing that we can say is that all men will agree, no matter what their political belief is, no matter whether they are single gold standard men, or whether they are bi-metallists — they cannot help acknowledging that the unit of money must be unvarying. They all agree to that. If we do not agree to that, we are not honest in our views. Consequently I take it that all parties will concede that the unit of money must be as unchanging as the human mind can conceive and can fix. We find then, upon the threshold of this matter, that the first inquiry is, under the present standard that exists, "Is that standard an unvarying standard?" If it is, then our cause has got to retire. If it is not, then the standard must be remedied. We find upon looking at this question that previous to 1871 there were two metals that formed the base upon which was built up the credit and commerce of the world. They formed the moneys of ultimate payment, of ultimate redemption. These two metals were peculiarly fitted for money metals, on account of their quality of indestructibility, and on account of the difficulties with which they are extracted from the earth.

Although mining has existed for centuries, and although free coinage has existed for centuries, the amount of gold coin and silver coin in the world up to 1871 was practically the same. We find that by legislation one of these metals is stricken down as a money of ultimate payment. Now, what is the inevitable consequence of that? The burden which both of those metals bore was shifted on to one metal. The

shifting of the burden of twice the amount on to one metal, doubled the
burden upon that one metal. Doubling the burden upon one metal
doubles the demand upon one metal, and doubling the demand upon
one metal doubles the value thereof. It seems to me that there can be
no other logical consequence from that condition.

Now, I am not here to say that gold has doubled in value, because
this demonetization did not take place all at the same time. We know
that it was one nation after another that began demonetizing silver.
We know that if demonetization complete had taken place all over the
world at the same time, and the burden which both of two equal metals
had been carrying had been shifted on to one, the inevitable principle
of supply and demand would have made that burden double the demand
for that one metal — and doubling the demand for that metal would
double the value thereof. I am aware to-day that all the nations have
not demonetized silver, and that to-day there are some free coinage
silver nations in the world, relieving the great demand which the rest of
the world is making upon gold. Consequently, we know that although
gold has not been doubled by the demonetization of silver, yet we know
that the increase has been enormous from year to year on account of
this demonetization taking place on different years. Consequently, it
seems to me that no one can deny in the face of that proposition that
the gold has increased in value.

Now let us see what the situation of the nations was at the time
demonetization began. Before I go into that, I want to call your attention to the effect which ultimate demonetization of all silver in the
world, if it doubled the value of gold, would have; what enormous and
pernicious results must happen from that act. What effect has it upon the
world? We find that the man who has his wealth invested in securities,
after a given time realizes that his wealth has been doubled in value.
After complete demonetization takes place, the man who has his wealth
invested in anything else wakes up to the realization that his wealth has
been divided half in two. What is the consequence of legislation?
One man's wealth has been doubled by legislation, another man's
wealth has been cut in two. That is by complete demonetization of
silver when it takes place. We find that even that would not be so
great a hardship, although it is pernicious indeed. But we find there
is another class of people, who have had the bravery and the enterprise
to borrow for the purpose of developing the resources of their country,
and we find that as to those people, the effects of demonetization — the
effect of increasing the value of the gold dollar, has been as to his wealth,
to absolutely wipe it out of existence. It means that all the capital
that he put into it, is swept out by the mortgage which he placed upon
the property. It means to the man who has been a borrower, total
annihilation of his wealth. That would be the result of demonetization,

if it took place all over the world.   When we see now that demonetization has taken place in two-thirds of the nations of the world, we can easily understand why this demand for gold is becoming more constant, why this demand for gold is being eagerly made by all the nations.   It is because some one-half the quantity of money is trying to do the business of all the commerce and credit of the world.

But, Gentlemen of the Congress, we find that this would not be of such a nature as to crush us if we are to get a new start.   But when we find that there is a gold standard that has been adopted and that the nations of the world are adhering to it and we examine into the annual product of gold, we find that it looks dark and gloomy in the future.   We know that the total amount of gold coined in the world is $3,600,000,000.   We know that the annual product of gold for 1892, which is the last that I have, was $130,816,628.   It has been estimated by Mr. Giffen, a gold mono-metallist, the statistician of the London Board of Trade, that of the annual gold product, not one dollar of it goes into coin.   He does not mean to say that there are not new coins made, but that the arts melt as much coin each year as there is new gold coined.   We find that Sir Lyon Playfair has estimated that 15 per cent of the annual gold product goes into the arts.   We know that Professor C. L. Faucet, another gold mono-metallist, estimates that of the annual product of 1892, $110,000,000 of that gold went into the arts.   This is the testimony of the men who are against us upon the theory of the free coinage of silver.

Taking the most liberal of these estimates, we find that only one-fourth of the annual gold product goes into coin, and one-fourth of $130,000,000 is simply $32,500,000, that each year goes into the coins to keep up this great bulk of credit, this great bulk of commerce.   In other words, we find $32,000,000, less than one per cent of the total amount of gold coined in the world, and consequently we are having the money of ultimate payment increased by the ratio of less than one per cent per annum, and it is bearing up and supporting a mountain of commerce that has for the past 20 years been increasing at the rate of more than six per cent per annum.   We find as a consequence that when the base is increasing at less than one per cent per annum and the upper structure is increasing at the rate of some six per cent per annum, the demands upon gold are getting so constant and so strong that the inevitable result must be for gold to grow dearer and dearer.

Why, Gentlemen of the Convention, I find, upon examining as to when the demonetization of silver began among the nations in the world, that there were but two nations in the world that were using gold exclusively as a money of ultimate redemption. There were three nations in the world at that time that were simply upon a gold standard. Great Britain was one with a population of 32,000,000, Portugal was one with a population of 2,000,000 of people, Turkey had a gold standard, but at that time made no demand upon gold, on account of the fact that it had an irredeemable paper currency, consequently when the demonetization of silver began there were but two nations representing a population of 36,000,000 of people that were making a demand upon gold. We find that at that time there were seven bi-metallic nations; they were France, Italy, Belgium, Switzerland, Greece, Spain, and the United States, and only two of these seven nations were using coin, gold and silver, the rest of them having an unconvertible paper currency. Those two nations were Belgium and Switzerland. Adding the population of those to the population of the gold-standard nations, we find that not to exceed 44,000,000 of people were all that were making a demand upon gold in this world. At that time Germany had a silver standard; Austria had a silver standard; Russia had a silver standard; Sweden and Norway, Denmark and Holland; and of these nations, silver nations, two of them were upon an irredeemable paper currency.

We find then in 1871, when the demonetization of silver began, that there were but 44,000,000 of people in the world that were making a demand upon gold as the money of ultimate payment. Now what do we find the conditions to-day as to the demand upon gold? We find that Great Britain with a population of 38,000,000 is using gold, we find that Germany with its 50,000,000 is making the demand upon gold, we find that Austria has just resumed the specific payment and is using gold. Our reserve must be kept up, or we will go again to an irredeemable currency. We find that Russia is striving in every manner that she can to draw to that country gold for war purposes, or for what purposes we do not know, but we know that they are continually making that demand upon the world. We find that Turkey now with a population of 35,000,000 of people is making a demand for gold. Norway, Sweden and Denmark with 9,000,000 of people are making the same demand for gold. Egypt with 7,000,000 and the United States with its gigantic population of 67,000,000 are entering the race and the contest for gold. What is the result? When the demonetization of silver began there were but 44,000,000 of people demanding gold: to-day we have 440,000,000 of people using all the efforts that it is possible for them to make in order to get gold to keep their reserves good. The minute this reserve in the United States falls below a certain amount, this government insists that it is the proper thing for this nation to issue more bonds, in order to get gold in its treasury. The fight is constant among all the nations, and is it any wonder that gold has been increasing in value? If part of this burden were shifted upon silver, the relief would come. But when

we find that here is ten times the population now making the demand
for gold that was made in 1871 when demonetization began, we find
then that there is such an incessant and such a strong demand for gold
that no one, it seems to me, can deny that it has appreciated largely in
value.   That system indeed is pernicious that has a unit of measurement that continually. increases.   If it affected only gold and silver it
would be insignificant, but when we know that this unit of measurement measures not only gold and silver, but measures everything else
in the world, measures every other kind of property, and every unit
increases with every decrease that it will buy, we can see the importance, the enormity of this question.

A DELEGATE (from Nebraska) (interrupting): Will the gentleman
please yield the floor a moment.   I have a resolution I would like to
offer, for the reason that the Committee on Resolutions is in session.
I want to say that while it is opposed to the gentleman's position, I
have no desire to interrupt him for that purpose.

Gov. WAITE: Mr. Chairman, I move that the reading of the resolution be suspended until we get through with this address.

The resolution was read.

COL. SHAFROTH: From the resolution which has been introduced I
would imagine that it was the mover's intention that the government
should continue the issuing of silver dollars, or the bullion contained in
these silver dollars by the government itself.   That position, gentlemen
of the congress, I do not believe will relieve the situation in any way
whatever.   And why?   As long as it is the policy of this government
that it should go to a gold standard, it evidently means that its gold
will redeem all other obligations which it has, and if we once recognize,
and I understand it has been recognized by this administration, that
the free coinage of bullion by the government itself simply creates that
many more obligations to be redeemed in gold, and consequently it
makes the demand upon gold that much greater.

Money has more than one function.   All money acts as a circulating
medium, a medium of exchange, but when we get to gold, and all other
moneys are redeemable in gold, it acts principally as a money of redemption.   It means that every obligation, no matter of what nature
it may be, ultimately, if the holder of it desires, he has got a right to
demand that that be paid in gold.   You take a promissory note—go to
the debtor and say, "I want it?"   He says he will give you a check.
You can get that check paid in national bank notes, and you have a
right to demand that those notes be paid.   They might pay in United
States treasury notes, or greenbacks, but you have a right to go to the
government and say you want your gold — consequently the government gives it to you.   Consequently every obligation, no matter of what
nature it is, ultimately is payable in a gold standard country in gold,

and when we know the amount of debt that exists in the world, and know that there is a continual demand for every dollar of those obligations, a demand to be paid not all the time in gold, but sometimes at least in gold — it creates a demand of such a nature that has been growing by reason of the nations' demonetizing silver, until at last there is no end to where the value of gold may go.

Now we find, as I have attempted to show, that first by reason of the complete demonetization of silver throughout the world, that the burden upon gold would be doubled, and the demand consequently doubled and the value doubled. We have in addition to that the fact that when silver began to be demonetized and this shifting of the burden upon the gold metal was begun, there were but 44,000,000 of people demanding gold as the money of ultimate redemption. But we find now there are 440,000,000 of people that are in this struggle for gold.

Now, it seems to me, according to the principle of supply and demand — I care not how radical any man may differ from me, he cannot but admit it, that these demands upon gold must increase its value. Now let us see whether it has increased its value. When we look around, we find that every product has sunk in value, not a little, but double. We find that wheat has sunk from $1.31 a bushel to 51 cents a bushel; cotton has sunk from 18 cents to 6 cents a pound, and thus you can go over the entire staple products and find that this reduction has followed. Gold being the unit of measurement its increase cannot be estimated in dollars and cents. Its increase of value can only be found from its increased purchasing power, and its increased purchasing power can only be found in the decline of everything that gold will purchase. When we find that the supply of gold in the world simply adds, to the base upon which all the credit and commerce of the world rests, only one per cent per annum, and that commerce is going on at an increase of more than 6 per cent per annum, we know that each year the demand upon gold is getting greater and greater. The extent to which it will appreciate is something beyond the apprehension of man.

Now, I want to say, are we going to stand a system that continually depreciates, a unit of measurement that is continually increasing? We cannot stand it. Its effects become serious. It makes it operate upon falling markets, and falling markets to our enterprise mean in the long run ruin and disaster. The inevitable result is that the only manner in which matters can be resuscitated, the only way in which we can have prosperity, will be by free coinage at the same ratio that existed in this government since 1834 (applause).

Gold and silver are automatic regulators of each other. When they are both moneys of ultimate payment, moneys that can be coined freely, the inevitable result is that when one goes up the fraction of a cent, the demand begins upon the other, and that incessant demand upon the other brings back immediately, or soon, the same ratio that existed. It is said that the decrease in the price of silver according to the gold standard, is on account of its overproduction, but when we examine into that it is fallacious — there is nothing to it. Let us see what is the amount of production. There are $66,000,000 of silver produced in a year more than gold. They say therefore that the production is so great that the silver must decline. They treat it as if silver were consumed in the using of it. They treat it as if it were wheat — as if one year's supply had got to be consumed. That is not the fair way to determine what is the production of a metal that is everlasting. The only way to do is to add the annual product to the total amount of silver in the world, and then you will find that the relative increase over gold is the slightest fraction. I have made a calculation as to what that was and when you compare them, and find the ratio of that annual product of each to the total amount of gold and silver respectively in the world, we find that the ratio is, simply $\frac{38}{100}$ of 1 per cent, the increase of the entire amount of silver over the entire amount of gold in the world — that is according to the very highest amount of silver that is produced in any one year. It is unfair to treat it as a common commodity that must be consumed. You take a period of forty years and there has been more than a billion more of gold produced in the last forty years in the world than there has of silver. It is unfair to take each year's production, for silver will amount to more some years and gold more other years, and consequently it is only by a comparison of a long series of years that you can get at the question of overproduction of one metal as compared with the other, and we find that even according to these figures our claim is startling all the gold-standard men. We find when we make a proper comparison, that silver to-day is increasing. If that ratio would increase only one-fifth or one-third of one per cent per annum, this theory that the minting silver would give the relief is all wrong and self-exploded.

Now, Gentlemen of the Convention, it is said that we will become the dumping ground of Europe if we open our mints to the coinage of silver. But where is this silver coming from? It has been estimated by Senator Jones that there is not to-day more than $25,000,000 of silver bullion in the world ready for coinage. Where is it coming from? Will the people of Europe who have their gold and silver money in their pockets bring it to America and coin it? No. Why? Because it is worth more to them in that very nation than it would be if they were to bring it to America and coin it. Suppose we find that silver will purchase $1.33 worth of products in Europe? Is it possible that any man who has a piece of metal, or a piece of money that has that purchasing power in Europe, will coin it in America? There is a large amount of silver destroyed that is not in coin, but what is it? It is in the arts. Are they going to melt down the treasures of the arts for the purpose of coining? No, they cannot do that, it would be too costly an experiment. The manufacturing of these articles into the arts cost more than any person would gain by it, and consequently we see that all this talk about the dumping of silver from Europe on to our country is something that has no relation to us, so far as Europe is concerned, and very little relation to the other nations of the world. When we find that in 1890 with a free coinage bill passing the Senate of the United States, and while it was still pending in the House of Representatives, that silver not only in the United States but throughout all the world rose from 82 cents to $1.21 an ounce, what would have been the effect if the House had passed the bill and the President had signed it? Whenever we find that the American Congress has passed an act making the ratio of 16 to 1 — when this great nation with its consuming power of products of more than any 300,000,000 of people of any other part of the world — we know that it possesses a power that will unquestionably bring that product to the amount of $1.29 per ounce. If the mere passage through one house of the National Congress would raise the price of silver, not only in the United States and in our own markets, but in the London market, in the markets of the world, to $1.21 an ounce, can we seriously doubt that this great and incessant demand which this nation would make upon silver would raise it to $1.29 an ounce?

Gentlemen of the Convention, I have wearied you too long. I thank you for your attention and will say good-bye.

Senator Johnston: Mr. Chairman, I wish to make a motion that a special order be made — in order that the congress may understand what I mean, I desire to premise my motion with a few remarks.

There has been a grand work laid out for this congress. The irrigationists have had a special order, and the time has been well spent. The silver question has had a special order, and we have been highly entertained. The Nicaragua Canal question is a special order, and the Hawaiian question a special order, and I think that this question will entertain us well. But there are a few million people engaged in an enterprise in this great country of ours that do not seem to have had a special order, and in looking over this audience I find a few delegates here that I have met in other States. My object in getting the floor is to ask for a special order to-morrow morning, immediately after the preliminary business, for the discussion of Staple Agriculture.

This motion was seconded.

The Chairman: Any limit to the time?

SENATOR JOHNSTON: Two hours.

MR. RIDGELEY: Mr. Chairman, I desire to state in support of the resolution of Senator Johnston from California, that the Committee on Resolutions has subdivided, and a subdivision of the Committee has been instructed to take charge of all matters pertaining to agriculture, in the form of resolutions that may come before this congress, and I apprehend that unless there is a special order before us at this time, it might as well come up now and discuss it and refer it to the Committee.

THE CHAIRMAN: The motion is that two hours, after the preliminary business is disposed of, to-morrow morning shall be devoted to the discussion of Staple Agriculture. Carried.

MR. RIDGELEY: I take advantage of a momentary delay to call attention to the regular order of business this afternoon. I think these resolutions might be passed through to the Committee without reading and we could take up the regular order of business.

THE CHAIRMAN: It was the intention of the Chair to stop all further proceedings when that hour arrived.

MR. BENJAMIN (of California): Mr. Chairman, I have a resolution from the Miners' Association of California relative to the Rehabilitation of Hydraulic Mining.

The resolution was read.

Several resolutions were introduced and read.

Some discussion then followed as to the time when the Committee on Resolutions should report, with a view to having all the delegates present when the report was received.

It was then moved and seconded that the Committee on Rules and Order of Business be instructed to fix a time when the Committee on Resolutions will report to the congress.

An amendment was offered that the Committee give notice to the convention at least one session prior to the time when it shall be taken up.

The amendment was accepted.

THE CHAIRMAN: The motion is to the effect that the congress will be properly notified and progress will be reported, and nothing will be brought forward for action before the congress without a notice of one session in advance.

Senator Johnston suggested that a certain hour be fixed for the Committee to report.

COL. LEIGHTON: Mr. Chairman, I will offer as an amendment to the motion, that the Committee on Resolutions be requested to report such matters as they have perfected to-morrow at 2:30 o'clock.

JUDGE GOODWIN: Mr. Chairman, I move to lay the whole business on the table. The Committee on Resolutions cannot tell when they will get through. I heard of an Irishman once who ordered a coffin of a certain size. The undertaker asked him if the man was dead. He says, "No, but he will die before morning, because the doctor says so, and he says he knows what he is giving him." (Laughter.) Now, no one knows what is coming up in the Committee on Resolutions. It is supposed that the Committee on Resolutions understands thoroughly that the convention is anxious to get through with its work, and the Committee will make reports as fast as it prepares them. I move again that this whole matter be laid on the table.

MR. BRYAN: Mr. Chairman, that Committee has already adopted a rule that as fast as they reach a conclusion upon any subject-matter it shall be reported to the convention.

THE CHAIRMAN: Members have heard these explanations — the point seems to be by Col. Leighton of Missouri, that there shall be no surprise sprung on the congress without formal notice.

MR. CRAIG: I rise to a point of order — there can be no discussion on a motion to lay on the table.

The point of order was sustained and the motion seconded and carried.

THE CHAIRMAN: The Secretary has two or three communications to read, and we will then proceed to the regular order of business.

Invitations were then read to visit the Public Library and Miss Rorers' Cooking School Lectures, also the Anheuser-Busch Brewing Association.

MR. WHITMORE: Mr. Chairman, as Chairman of the Executive Committee, I desire to give notice that a meeting of that Committee will be held in parlor "F" of the Planters' House immediately after the adjournment of this session. Inasmuch as we have instructions to make some sort of a report to-morrow morning in regard to the matter referred to it at the San Francisco convention, every member of the Executive Committee of the congress is requested to be present.

W. H. CULMER (of Utah): Mr. Chairman, there has been a number of inquiries made of me for proceedings of the last congress at San Francisco. It was expected that copies would be on the table here. If announcement would be made that copies of the Ogden and San Francisco congresses could be had, there are a number of members who would be glad to get them.

MR. WHITMORE: In regard to the proceedings of the San Francisco congress, I desire to say that only about 40 or 50 copies were sent to St. Louis, and those were nearly all distributed at the Merchants' Exchange for whom they were sent; there are probably not over ten or a dozen copies left.

PRESIDENT CANNON: The hour having arrived for the regular order of business, the Chair takes pleasure in introducing to the congress ex-Gov. Prince of New Mexico, who will address the congress on Bi-metallism.

ADDRESS OF HON. L. B. PRINCE.

BIMETALLISM VS. THE SINGLE STANDARD.

The subject of a single or double standard for money value —
of monometallism or bimetallism — is attracting more attention the
world over, to-day, than any other.

It affects every human being living in "civilized countries," because
it necessarily controls all values; of land, of products of industry and
of labor on the one hand; of money, and hence of capital, interest
and fixed incomes on the other.

In the language of the great European authority on coinage: "It is
THE question of the age."

The chief difficulty in its discussion in the United States has been that
it has taken a sectional turn, and that the people of the two sections
so misunderstand each other on the subject, that any fair discussion
is about impossible. That the West, which is the producer of the
great staples, with its wealth in the form of commodities, and owing
large debts, payable in dollars, should desire the money basis to
retain the double standard existing through all history; and that
English and German bankers, the great creditors of the world, receiving their interest in money, should desire a contracted financial basis,
is perfectly natural. It was to be expected that those of our people in
the East who are under foreign control and others of the creditor class
selfishly interested in the increase of the value of money would unite
with the foreign bankers in their single-standard method of contraction; but the misfortune is that the great body of Americans east of
the Mississippi, really patriotic at heart and anxious for national prosperity, should have given so little attention to the subject as to imagine
their interests also to be different from those of their western brethren.
Hence has arisen the misunderstanding to which I have referred.

No better place for a fair discussion of the question could be found
than St. Louis, the central city of the country, midway between the
East and the West; and I have felt that I might not inappropriately
attempt something toward a reconciliation of sectional views, or at least
a partial clearing away of prejudices, on account of an almost equal
connection with each section.

Having served seven years in either branch of the legislature of the
Empire State, twice honored by votes of thanks of the N. Y. Chamber
of Commerce, and still holding an honorary membership in the N. Y.
Board of Trade, I am not unfamiliar with eastern sentiments; while a
still larger service as Chief Justice and Governor of a western territory,
and connections with various other bodies, commercial, scientific and
literary, including the past presidency of the important representative

body which I now address, has given some experience of feeling in the West, so that I can, at any rate, speak without favor or prejudice.

In the first place, then, let us clean away some of the rubbish of vituperation.

There is no doubt that many western people look upon those of the East as their enemies; that such terms as " gold bug," " plutocrat " and " Shylock " are not only used but believed to be deserved, and that the sole idea of eastern capitalists is thought to be a wicked desire to ruin their poorer brethren of the West. On the other hand, it is not unusual to hear eastern men speak of those of the West as inflationists, as " cheap money men," as absolutely dishonest and as " wanting to get a dollar for 50 cents." A fair-minded man, traveling from one section to another, has constantly to defend his fellow-citizens from these reciprocal slanders.

As matter of fact, the western man is as jealous of his good name and as proud of his business integrity as any one living. As a rule, he is a bimetallist, because he hears the subject constantly discussed, has given it careful study, understands the necessary results of demonetizing half the money metal of the world, and sees these results in actual existence, in the constant shrinkage of values, the prevalence of "hard times " and the destitution of the people.

On the other hand, the eastern monometalist, as a rule, is not the depraved creature he is thought to be, filled with a satanic desire to ruin his fellow-citizens; he has simply been so situated that he has given no attention to the financial questions involved in demonetization, he has seen nothing but gold views in the journals he reads, and takes it for granted that they are correct.

In the hurry of business life comparatively few Americans find time to read anything but the newspapers, and if in some locality these all concur in one opinion, it is apt to be adopted without inquiry. In short, the great majority of eastern people are not wicked in their opposition to bimetallism, but simply uninformed.

This word is not used in any offensive sense, but merely to state the exact fact, and to repel the idea of conscious wrong-doing. There are dozens of subjects with which the people of the East are far better acquainted than those of the West, but it happens that, for various reasons, on this particular topic the reverse is the case. In fact the ignorance of it by the generally intelligent eastern community is phenomenal; as an illustration of which I may mention that among hundreds of the best citizens of New York whom I have met during the last two years, I have found but one who had ever read the report of the Brussels Conference, though that is published gratuitously by Congress and is the most convenient and satisfactory of impartial statements.

If the matter were studied and discussed in the East as it is in the West, except among Anglo-maniacs who have no love for their own country in their hearts, and money lenders who know no principle but selfishness, there would not be a monometallist in the East any more than in the West.

What we should lay special stress upon, then, is the educational idea. We can never expect justice to the producer and a restoration of national prosperity until we have the aid of our Eastern brethren in undoing the pernicious legislation of 1873 and giving us again the bimetallism which is the only safeguard of stability in property values and protector of the rights of labor; and we cannot have that co-operation until they have become informed as to the questions at issue so as to act intelligently.

The great plea of the West to the East, then, should be, to educate itself on this subject, to read, to learn, to think, to *know*, of its principles and its effects. From the President down it has been too much the habit to accept the conclusion of some newspaper, without thought, though the subject directly affects the happiness of more human beings in America than all others combined. In the language of Senator Dumas, of the French Legislative Chamber, "Those who approach these questions for the first time, decide them at once. Those who study them with care, hesitate. Those obliged to decide them are overwhelmed with the weight of enormous responsibility."

In the first place, let us remind our eastern friends that bimetallists are not asking for anything new or unusual or untried. On the contrary the joint use of gold and silver as measures of value and mediums of exchange — in other words, as money — has been the universal custom of the world since the birth of civilization. Iron may have been used in Sparta and wampum among American Indians, platina was for a time coined in Russia, but all these were exceptional and never entered into commercial transactions. Gold and silver by unanimous consent have constituted the money of the world ever since money was used.

Coming down to our own times, the free and unlimited coinage of these two metals was the heritage of the American people in colonial days, as it was enacted in England in 1666 in the reign of Charles II and again under George III in 1768, and continued until long after the Revolution.

When the constitution was framed, it especially recognized gold and silver equally as the only proper measure of value, prohibiting the States from making anything but them a tender in payment of debts.

One of the first acts of Congress, under the presidency of Washington, provided for the free coinage of both metals at the national mints.

Any one possessed of either gold or silver could present it and receive its weight in coin of the same metal. This condition of things continued uninterruptedly until the act which demonetized silver in 1873; the right of the people to free and unlimited coinage never having been intefered with in any way till then. So the history of the world and the laws and traditions of the American people were all on the side of bimetallism till that date.

When demonetization took place it was by stealth, absolutely without the knowledge of the American people, and, as appears, without the knowledge of any members of Congress with the possible exception of three. No newspaper uttered a word on the subject. The title of the act gave no suggestion of any such object. It was understood by all that the bill which passed was simply a revision of the mint laws, and very little attention was given to it. When it was discovered some time afterward that by the omission of the standard silver dollar from the act, silver had been demonetized, the country was amazed. Senators and representatives all over the land rose to disavow any knowledge of the change. It is not necessary to quote many of them, but a few statements may be desirable to show the facts.

Senator Beck said (Jan. 10, 1878): "It never was understood by either house of Congress. I say this with full knowledge of the facts."

Mr. Kelly of Pennsylvania, long the "Father of the House" said (March 9, 1878):—

"Though Chairman of the Committee on Coinage I was ignorant of the fact that it would demonetize the silver dollar."

And again (May 10, 1879): —

"In all the legislation of this country there is no mystery equal to the demonetization of the standard silver dollar."

Senator Thurman said (Feb. 15, 1878): —

"When the bill was pending in the Senate, we thought it was simply a bill to reform the mint, etc., and there is not a single man in the Senate, I think, unless a member of the Committee from which the bill came, who had the slightest idea that it was even a squint toward demonetization."

Mr. Holman of Indiana, said (Aug. 5, 1876): —

"The original bill was simply to organize a bureau of mines and coinage. The bill which finally passed was certainly not read in this House."

Similar statements of eminent congressmen including Gen. Garfield, Senator Allison and others could be multiplied indefinitely. In the colloquy between Senator Blaine and Senator Voorhies, Feb. 15, 1878, each in turn emphatically denied any knowledge of the demonetization.

Senator Hereford (Feb. 13, 1878) said: —

"Beyond the possibility of a doubt, that bill, as it passed, never was read, never was discussed."

Mr. Cannon of Illinois said (July 13, 1876): —

"It was not discussed, as shown by the "Record," and neither members of Congress nor the people understood the scope of the legislation."

And even Senator Sherman, in his Marietta speech in 1876, said: —

"Both Houses were in favor of issuing the old dollar, the dollar in legal existence since 1792, containing 412 $\frac{8}{10}$ grains, and only demonetized in 1873, when it was worth 2 per cent more than the gold dollar."

No one has ever dared acknowledge the paternity of this secret and injurious act. Not a single member of either house of Congress has ever confessed that he knowingly voted for it. Perhaps there is no other example in history of any act so unjustifiable that no one would admit any connection with it.

Yet all that bimetallists contend for is that this act, thus secretly and fraudulently passed, without knowledge by legislators or people, and which no one will even yet defend, should be repealed. It never represented the will of the people, and hence should not be on the statute book. In the words of Mr. Holman (July. 13, 1876): "The measure never had the sanction of the House and it does not possess the moral force of law."

There was no excuse for its passage. At that very moment our silver coin was actually worth three per cent more than our gold coin, and brought at least one and one-half per cent more for exportation. There was no trouble arising from an oversupply. The act could not have received a score of votes if Congress and the people had understood what it was. It was the child of stealth and fraud.

While Mr. Kelly said in 1879, " I have never found a man who could tell just how it came about," yet every one knows that it was the work of the British money lenders, aided by their agents in our great cities.

Their interest in it was enormous. England is a creditor nation to the extent of about ten billion dollars. She holds the securities of other lands to that extent, and draws from them each year $500,000,000 in interest.

The best computations show that we alone are paying her $200,000,000 a year in interest; more than half a million a day! Every increase in the value of a dollar, therefore, enormously enlarged her income. By demonetizing one of the two money metals, the remaining money in the world, — reduced one-half in volume, — would rapidly increase in purchasing power. This was perfectly easy to foresee. Her money lenders wished contraction in order to increase the value of their investments, principal and interest. The demonetization of one of the two precious metals was the easiest way to accomplish this. They did not care which metal it was; the result would be the same. For some years they favored the plan to demonetize gold, and Chevalier and others earnestly advocated that course. But that did not succeed and then they attacked silver. Here they achieved success by the secret passage of the Act of 1873.

Bimetallists simply ask that this act be repealed and the law of free coinage be restored as it had always been before. Monometallists resist this. That is the whole issue. Yet the press of the East has caused thousands to believe that bimetallists are asking some new privileges for silver. I submit that it is the monometallists, who are insisting on a change from the universal custom, and asking it through a perpetuation of an acknowledged fraud, who should be on the defensive, and that the burden of proof of good results is on them.

Prominent among the misrepresentations so constantly reiterated that it has quite permeated the eastern mind, is that the bimetallists of the West are " a lot of silver miners who want to get a dollar for fifty cents worth of silver."

This is not an exaggerated statement of much current Eastern opinion. And yet we all know that nothing could be more absurd. · Of course the silver mining interest is much affected, and most silver miners are bimetallists, but their number is so small compared with the vast body of the people affected by the lists of contraction, and the silver product so insignificant, compared with the immense volume of commodities reduced to little more than half their proper value, that they need scarcely be considered as a factor.

It may clear the air of misconceptions, if it is distinctly understood that if there were not a single silver miner in the United States, nor an ounce of that metal produced within our borders, the question of bimetallism would be unchanged, and the injury to our people and destruction of the property consequent on the demonetization of 1873, would be exactly as it is to-day. The countries which have given the most careful attention to the subject, like France and Belgium, do not produce a single ounce of silver.

The total annual product of silver has never reached 60 million ounces; in 1892 it was 58,000,000; last year it was considerably less; while the product of wheat averages about 500,000,000 bushels. The average price of wheat in 1873 was $1.29; while to-day it is selling at your Exchange at 50 cents, after paying freight to St. Louis. The loss to the producer of silver, through demonetization, was never in any year over $32,000,000, while the loss, for the same cause, to the producer of wheat, was over $250,000,000.

In the same way every producer has suffered.

Taking some of the great staples of our country, we find, for example, that the cotton crop for last year was 6,600,000 bales, of about 470 pounds each. In 1873 it was worth 16 cents a pound. The crop of last year will not bring the planter 6 cents, showing a net loss through demonetization, of ten cents a pound, or over $310,000,000.

Looking at it by acreage, the fall in cotton in the 20 years has been from $28.01 to $10.65 per acre, being a loss of 62 per cent.

On wheat the fall has been from $13.16 to $6.00 per acre, or over 54 per cent.   Or, if we take the average of the five great staples, wheat, corn, oats, hay and cotton, the average acre value in 1873 was $15.65, in 1893 $8.15, showing a fall of nearly 48 per cent.

When these facts are presented to the monometallist he immediately answers that the loss in value is the result of overproduction or of improved machinery.   But the improved machinery with scarcely an exception was in operation before 1873, and the constant fall in prices continues just the same from year to year as at the beginning of the 20 years period.   Wheat and cotton have never within the century been as low as they are to-day.   And if we examine as to the production, we will find that the facts are against the theory.   The cotton crop was 9,000,000 bales in 1891, 6,717,000 in 1892 and but 6,600,000 in 1893, showing a large reduction, at the same time that the price decreased.

The wheat crop for a number of years has been about 500 million bushels, in 1892 it was 516,000,000, in 1893 it fell to less than 400 millions (396,000,000).

If the production of wheat in the whole world is taken, in 1891 it was 2,432 millions, in 1892 it fell to 2,403 millions, and in 1893 to 1,904 millions.

So the overproduction theory only betrays ignorance.

Altogether it is calculated that if the aggregate of agricultural products raised in 1893 could be sold for the bimetallic price of 1873, the gain to the farming community would be nearly or quite 1,500,000,000 of dollars.

In other words they have lost that vast amount on the crops of a single year through the demonetization of silver and consequent rise in the value of the remaining money.

This simple statement is sufficiently startling, surely, to arrest the attention of the nation; but the point I wish to suggest now is, that compared with this enormous loss on agricultural products, the loss of $32,000,000 by the silver producers is too small to call for special consideration, although it entailed on the mining community a grievous amount of suffering and destitution.

The fall in prices when measured by money is not at all confined to the products of the soil, which have been referred to principally because we have more accurate statistics regarding these great staples than other commodities.   Every kind of tangible property has suffered the same comparative diminution in value.   The selling prices of real estate, except in growing cities and localities where there is a natural increase, have fallen to a similar extent, as is abundantly shown by country property in the eastern States. While often ascribed to various local causes, the actual reason is simply the increase in the value of the money for which the sale is to be made.

And so it is of every kind of property possessed by man.

Thus it will be seen that the interest of the silver producer in the restoration of bimetallism is very insignificant in comparison with the vast interests of the farmer, the planter and indeed of the owner of commodities of any kind.

President Andrews of Brown University, at the Brussels Conference stated that the silver constituted but $\frac{4}{100}$ of one per cent, or $\frac{4}{10000}$ of the whole, of the total national product of the United States, in 1890.

The importance of silver comes from its being a money metal, a measure of value. The idea current at the East that silver miners only are interested in the remonetization of the white metal is about as sensible as it would be, in case Congress should pass an act lengthening the yard to fifty inches or enlarging a bushel to fifty quarts, to insist that the only persons opposing the change were the manufacturers of yard-sticks and bushel baskets, because of the increased amount of material required for their construction. In such a case those who would bear the real loss, of course would be the persons who had to supply their products by the new and enlarged measures, not those who simply furnish the measures themselves.

It is worthy of remark that although its principal use from time immemorial has been destroyed by legislation, yet silver has not decreased in money value more than other products of industry. It has, of course, felt the general effect of the rise in the value of gold money, but has kept on a par with other staple articles. An ounce of silver will buy as much wheat or corn, or hay or oats, or wool or cotton as it would before the Act of 1873. The tables showing this are too well known to be repeated here. Every commodity has been reduced in its money value since the single gold standard was established and money began to increase in value. To-day, according to best authorities, money has risen to about 147, calling it par in 1873. Of course, this correspondingly reduces the price of everything else when compared with it.

It is true that one sometimes meets people who think that some certain commodity, as silver or wheat, has gone down in value instead of money having gone up. They are like the ignorant man who supposes that the sun revolves around the earth each day, because it appears to do so; or like a child in a railroad car, who thinks that the people on the platform are moving backward when the train begins to move forward. But when the man sees that all the heavenly bodies are apparently revolving as well as the sun, he will gradually realize that it is the earth which turns and not the myriads of bodies that surround it; and when the child sees that the houses and the trees and all other objects are apparently moving backward, as well as the by-standers, he learns that the train in which he sits is that which is really in motion, and not all surrounding things. So if a single commodity alone had decreased in price it might be thought that for some special reason it had lost value, but when it is found that the whole range of tangible things, including every product of home industry, is worth less than it was ten years ago, it becomes evident that it is the money which has increased in purchasing power and not the commodities that have decreased in worth.

Speaking of those who thus reverse the facts, Sir Guilford R. Molesworth said at the Brussels Conference: " It is gold who is the sick man, not silver. They have mistaken the bloated condition of gold for a symptom of health, whereas it is the symptom of a dangerous disease that now threatens a fearful crisis."

Mr. Allard, honorary director of the Belgian mint, also sta ed the facts forcibly and tersely at the Brussels Conference: " The evil is not to be found in the fall of silver, but consists solely in the appreciation of gold. It is not silver which has fallen but gold which has risen." And again, " Silver has nothing to do with the result. It is gold which you have made scarce and which has, therefore, risen in value."

These matters have been more scientifically considered in Europe than in this country, but even here they did not escape prompt observation by experts. As early as 1877, four years after demonetization, the condition had become sufficiently plain for the U. S. Monetary Commission to declare " Gold has risen in all countries, while silver has fallen in none."

In 1879 Disraeli said in a public speech: " Gold is every day appreciating in value, and as it appreciates in value the lower become prices." The article on " Silver " in the Encyclopædia Britannica (and I quote that because it is English and certainly not biased in favor of bimetallism) says: " The closure of the mint to silver has enhanced the purchasing power of gold, compared with either silver or other commodities, about one-fourth." This was written about 1882, — say nine years after demonetization.

Some time later Mr. Balfour stated the increase in the value of money in Great Britain in 15 or 16 years, as no less than 30 to 35 per cent.

Sir Wm. Houldsworth, one of the British Commissioners at Brussels, said: " A general fall of gold money prices has taken place. This can only be called an appreciation of gold."

The three leading authorities of the world on the relative values of money and commodities have been the tables of the London Economist in England, and of Mr. Sauerbeck and Prof. Soetbeer in Germany.

The London Economist tables are based on the average value of 22 leading articles in the London market; Mr. Sauerbeck's were founded more broadly on the prices of 45 principal commodities in Germany, and Prof. Soetbeer took 100 different articles in the Hamburg market and added 14 others imported from England, so as to cover the whole range of commercial products. Averages such as these — including such a variety of articles — avoid the influences of temporary fluctuations in individual items by reason of short crops or overproduction or exceptional demand, and give as correct a view of the purchasing power of money, compared with commodities in general, as it is possible to obtain.

While these tables have been prepared entirely independently by their learned authors, year by year, it is interesting to see how nearly they agree in their general results. The London Economist shows a decline in average prices from 134 of its "index numbers" in 1873 to 95 in 1894, being $\frac{39}{134}$, or over 29 per cent. The Soetbeer tables make the decline a little less, and the Sauerbeck tables somewhat more (32 per cent). Taking an average of these, would make the present value of single standard money in Europe about 145 compared with what it was in 1873, when the demonetization of silver started the upward tendency of money, and the apparent depreciation of commodities. But in this country the change has been even greater, as is obvious to all from a comparison of the prices of the great staples which are most familiar, such as wheat and cotton, on which the average reduction has exceeded 50 per cent. That there is no present diminution in this reduction of values appears from the recent reports of the London Economist. Its midsummer report in 1892, to July 1, of that year, showed that the average apparent fall in values of 26 leading articles of consumption had been $7\frac{8}{10}$ in 2 years, or about 4 per cent per year; and the fall in the last preceding 6 months had been $2\frac{4}{10}$ per cent, or, at the rate of $4\frac{8}{10}$ per cent per year; and the second 6 months of 1892 showed no improvement.

The only apparent exception to this reduction in price is in wages, and they have been kept up through the efforts of organizations of great power, acting through strikes and other methods. Meanwhile, however, the number of the unemployed has greatly increased, so that the average wages paid to the whole working population, including those who are idle and not earning anything at all, are very considerably below the same average in 1873.

The wretched results of a continual lowering of prices,— of a constantly falling market,— are too obvious to require illustration. This is appreciated even in England. Mr. Grenfell, an ex-Governor of the Bank of England, says: "The fight against falling prices is an impossible one.   Men are holding on in hopes for better times, but no better times, taking trade and commerce as a whole, can come in gold countries, while gold appreciates.   The pitiable army of the unemployed must increase through no fault of their own."   And he speaks of "the misery, suffering and despair which have been so prevalent during the last twenty years, owing to the fatal policy of contracting the currency of the world."

Mr. Balfour, in his Manchester speech, said: "Of all conceivable systems of currency, that is assuredly the worst which gives you a standard steadily, continuously, indefinitely appreciating, and which by that very fact throws a burden upon every man of enterprise, and benefits no human being but the owner of fixed debts in gold."

President Andrews aptly refers to it as "that baneful, blighting, deadly fall of prices which has affected with miasma the economic life-blood of the whole world."

But the monometallist will suggest that it makes no real difference to a country whether the standard of values be high or low; if it is high and the seller receives less for his goods, that is equaled by the fact that he pays correspondingly less for what he buys.

There would be some force in this if commodities were all affected equally and simultaneously, and if there were no payments to be made in money itself.   But there are vast numbers of contracts and obligations which require the payment of *money*, many of them running over long series of years.   All of these are directly affected by the change in the value of money.   When a dollar is worth 147, and is increasing over 2 per cent every year, it is easy to see that great injustice is done by requiring compliance with such contracts.   In a somewhat similar case in Crete, the Turkish government, which we are not accustomed to consider the most humane, finally decreed, as the only available solution, that payments should be made at the value of money at the time of making the contract.   But in a vast country like ours, with all the varieties of obligation belonging to a complex civilization, this would be well-nigh impossible.   The only practicable means of securing justice to all is to restore the money basis to its normal standard by the remonetization of silver.

Meanwhile the increased value of money falls with terrible weight and injustice upon the debtor classes.   The debts being stated in dollars, and the dollars having increased in value and in cost, the debts are correspondingly enlarged.   The man who borrowed a thousand dollars in 1873, when money was at par, now finds that he owes one thousand dollars, each of which is worth $1\frac{47}{100}$ of the dollars which he borrowed.   As the nominal amount is the same, it is simpler to state the case in other terms.   It requires half as much more of average commodities to purchase the one thousand dollars in money now, than it did in 1873. Of some commodities it requires almost or quite double. If a farmer borrowed a hundred and nineteen dollars in 1873, he could repay it with one hundred bushels of wheat. To repay it now requires considerably over two hundred bushels. The measure of value—the dollar—has greatly increased in value, and yet he is compelled by law to repay just as many of them as he received before they began to rise. It is exactly the same as if he had contracted to deliver one hundred bushels of wheat and Congress had afterwards enacted that a bushel should contain 64 quarts instead of 32, and that all old contracts should be paid in the new enlarged bushel.

Archbishop Walsh, of Dublin, sums up the matter in few words, when he says: "Every one under an obligation to make yearly payments of a fixed amount of money, is under a burden which is growing heavier from year to year." Nor does this injustice fall alone upon those who are individually in debt. Every one is compelled to pay some part of the general debts of the community in which he lives, or of the corporations to which he is subject. The amount of State, county, town, city, village, school-district and other public debts is prodigious. It is all payable in dollars, principal and interest. With each dollar now worth $1.47, the tax-payer has to meet the increased burden required to procure these unjustly enlarged dollars. No amount of personal care or providence or avoidance of debt can save the American citizen from this added incumbrance. A large proportion of our taxation is not the result of current expense, but of these "fixed charges" required for paying the interest on public debts, and whatever may be the decreased price of all commodities in money, the number of dollars required to meet these fixed charges is not lessened. So, again, our railroads owe enormous amounts in bonds, and interest thereon is often the largest item in calculating their expenses. It is payable in money, and money at its greatly increased value must be had in order to liquidate it. The rates of fare and freight must be made such as to meet these charges. So every one who travels or receives commodities by rail is forced, without his consent, and without any fault or neglect on his part, to pay part of the extra 47 per cent added to every dollar of railroad interest.

Calling the amount of interest paid by this country to England each year $200,000,000, the added cost to our people is $94,000,000 in our commodities, for which we have to toil; just that much added each year to the burden on American labor, without any return, as the price on that one account for the theoretical benefit of a single gold standard.

HONEST MONEY.

We hear a good deal about "honest money" and an "honest dollar," and some of our Eastern friends use those phrases with a kind of self-righteous complacency, as if *they* were the sole advocates of business integrity. And they do it, really believing it is so.

Let us see about this.

Here is a dollar which has increased since 1873 and is still regularly increasing in value, about $2\frac{4}{10}$ per cent each year. If it would buy 10 pounds of any commodity 10 years ago, it will buy $12\frac{4}{10}$ pounds to-day. If a man borrowed $100 ten years ago, he has to pay back 24 per cent more in value to-day than on the day of the loan, besides all interest. I am not speaking now of the manifest impossibility of doing any legitimate business at a profit, when there is an annual loss in the value of whatever goods are concerned in it, of $2\frac{4}{10}$ as compared with money. I am only speaking of the honesty or dishonesty of this dollar which is rising in value every year. The most important quality in a measure of value, is stability. The measure should be absolutely unchangeable. If a person borrows a sum in 1874, he should repay the sum, with the same purchasing power, in 1894. There is a manifest injustice — a manifest *dishonesty* — in requiring the man who borrowed $100 in 1872, when it was equivalent to 84 bushels of wheat or 550 pounds of cotton, to pay back one hundred dollars which has appreciated to $147 in 1894, and equal 200 bushels of wheat or 1,700 pounds of cotton.

The United States constitution provides that Congress shall pass no law impairing the obligation of a contract. Yet Congress by its legislation has changed every contract in which a cash payment is at some time to be made, by increasing the value of the money which has to be used. Suppose that Congress should decree that each year one inch should be added to a yard measure, every one would cry out against the dishonesty involved in requiring a man who had contracted to furnish 1000 yards of cloth, supposing the yard to be thirty-six inches, to fulfill his contract when the length was increased to thirty-seven or forty inches, without any change in compensation. Yet the annual increase of two and four-tenths per cent is almost exactly an inch on a yard. Had the yard measure increased exactly as money has since 1873 (that is to 147) it would now reach fifty-three inches.

So, if Congress should enact that a bushel should increase in the same ratio, it would now hold forty-seven quarts, and every one having a contract to deliver potatoes or wheat or apples, by the bushel, would be compelled to deliver that increased quantity.

If the legislative interference extended to weight, the pound would now weigh 23 ounces.

A law regarding a single commodity only affects that one article, but one which changes the worth of the measure of all values, affects everything which is bought or sold by that standard.

Money is the embodiment, in one measure, of the measures of length, of capacity and of weight — of the yardstick, the bushel and the pound.

Congress by the demonetization act of 1873 has accomplished exactly what separate acts providing for the annual enlargement of each kind of measure would have done; the only difference is that the effect was so concealed that the indignation of the people was not immediately aroused.

And yet the increased measure of all values, which has enlarged every debt and obligation and contract, without the consent of the debtor and without any compensation, is called " an honest dollar," and every attempt to preserve its value without change is pronounced an endeavor to inflate the currency and " deluge the country with cheap money." Naturally the creditor classes, who hold the bonds and mortgages and securities, and derive a fixed number of dollars annually from them, desire the dearest possible money; the higher it ascends in its purchasing power, the more flagrantly it becomes a " dishonest dollar," the more profitable it is to them; and controlling, as they do, the banks and financial institutions and the press of the great cities, they do not find it difficult to cause the unthinking to believe that their selfish scheme of contraction is a patriotic effort to preserve the public credit.

There is another fallacy that it may be well to explode by a few facts.

Quite frequently we hear the statement from some one who thinks that his words contain the wisdom of the ages, that the value of every commodity is what it costs to produce, and that, consequently, the real value of silver is what it costs to extract.

Disregarding for a moment the absurdity of this proposition in regard to a money metal, which is a measure of value, let us see what it would mean if it were in any sense true, if, for instance, silver were simply a commodity.

The brilliant author of the statement usually follows it up by saying " And in such a mine " — naming some one of the most famous producers of the time then in the height of its phenomenal success — " it only costs so many cents — 20 or 30 or 40 perhaps, — to mine an ounce of silver." Therefore, he argues, silver in general is worth 20 or 30 or 40 cents an ounce. Such an extraordinary logician is only fit to be the victim of the next mine speculator who travels his way, or to be an early victim of the fool-killer.

On the same principle, if a man found a nugget of gold weighing 5 pounds, and carried it home, occupying a day in the operation, counting his time as worth $2.50, that gold would be worth half a dollar pound.

If the principle had *any* truth in it, it would be the *average* cost of production which would be the criterion, not the extreme either of cheapness or expense.

As matter of fact, both gold and silver — taking the whole production and expense — cost more to produce than they are worth. An official inquiry as to the cost of producing silver a few years since, showed the average expense to be nearer $2 than $1 per ounce; and it is not probable that nearly all the outlay was ascertained, as men are not generally anxious to publish their failures.

Within 20 miles of my own home is a mining camp, in which a few years ago, more than 1,400 "locations" were made. On over 500 claims considerable work was done, ranging from a few hundred dollars to many thousands — how many hundreds of thousands in the aggregate, no one can say. Unfortunately not a single mine ever paid expenses, and it is certainly not an overestimate to say that every ounce of silver obtained there cost $100. The same is the case with scores of deserted camps all through the Rocky Mountain region. Yet would any one be idiotic enough to say that silver was worth $100 an ounce because that was the cost of production?

A friend of mine recently counted up his expenditure in silver mining in various localities and found it to exceed $6,500. He had succeeded in extracting something less than 3 ounces of metal. But that is no reason to say that silver is worth $2200 an ounce.

Within a month a well-known man of wealth in New York informed me that he had made 26 investments in mining and had never received a cent of return. If I should name him you would agree that the 26 investments probably aggregated over, rather than under, $100,000. Suppose he had enjoyed somewhat better success and had succeeded in obtaining an ounce of gold or silver, would that be reason to say that either metal was worth $100,000 an ounce, because that particular ounce cost that much? Even taking the bonanza mine referred to by our brilliant friend, in which silver is being produced say at 30 cents an ounce; if we go through its history, see the time and money spent in prospecting, in development work, in all the numberless difficulties to be overcome before success was achieved, and then watch its future when the rich ore is exhausted or the vein is lost, or the mine is flooded, or the mineral becomes refractory, when new machinery and processes have to be introduced, and expensive dead work is continued in the hope of regaining the old richness, we will find that, even then, the average cost from beginning to end is vastly greater than in the heyday of phenomenal success.

Then it must be remembered that the facts in regard to gold are exactly the same as with silver; only emphasized, because a few pounds of gold accidentally found run into the thousands much faster than the white metal. In the early days of newly found placers in California and Australia, when the accumulation of ages was washed out in a year, two or three ounces a day was nothing unusual and sometimes a fortune was made between dawn and night. But no one thought that the value of the product, whether great or small, was to be measured by the value of the day's wages. A friend of mine last summer did a little placer mining on both sides of a stream, and found that on one side it cost about sixty cents to extract a pennyweight of gold and on the other, about $2.00. Yet it would be absurd to say that the gold obtained varied to that extent in value.

The fact is, that, except in the case of newly discovered regions, the production of the precious metals depends on their value, not their value on the production. And it is also true, as before stated, that with the same exception, both gold and silver, taking the whole product of each, cost more to produce than they are worth; and we may conclude that thus it will be as long as the speculative trait in human nature remains unchanged. If gold is worth $20 an ounce, every known place where it can be produced for that sum will be worked, and in addition a multitude of people will expend money in attempts which prove failures, thus largely enhancing the average cost of the metal obtained. And it is exactly the same as to silver.

But I have spent too much time on this illogical idea that the value of a money metal should be its cost of production, and vary as that varies. What is needed in a standard of value is stability. The man who incurs a debt to-day, measured in dollars, should pay it, both in justice to himself and his creditor, in dollars of the same value. Hence the value of money, and the number of ounces of a money metal to be counted as a given value are matters of legislation, not of trade.

As a rule the matter of large or small supply has nothing to do with that fixed value. It is worth remarking that so far from a large supply of one or the other metal being made to reduce its value, in a number of cases, where dominant nations looked to their own interests, exactly the reverse was the case.

Look in your Encyclopædia Britannica and you will see that the Romans, when the supply of gold from Dacia and Spain fell off, raised the legal value of silver from one-thirteenth to one-tenth that of gold; raising, you observe, the more plentiful metal, so as to have a larger supply of money. The following extracts cover more modern changes: "In Spain the ratio was $10\frac{3}{4}$. When America was plundered the first fruits were gold, not silver, whereupon Spain in 1546 raised the legal value of gold to $13\frac{1}{4}$, and the rest of the world was obliged to acquiesce. During the following century Portugal obtained such immense quantities of gold from the East Indies, Japan and Brazil, that her imports exceeded £3,000,000 a year. Portugal now governed the ratio and in 1688 raised the value of gold to sixteen times that of silver. A century later Spain again controlled, and as her colonial product was now mostly silver, raised its value in 1775 from $\frac{1}{16}$ to $\frac{1}{15\frac{1}{2}}$ for the Peninsula.

In every one of these cases the dominant power raised the value of the metal of which it had the most abundant supply, exactly opposite to the theory of the anti-silver men that a large production requires a diminution in value; and it will also be observed that the value was always fixed by edict and not by natural law.

The patriotism shown by the governments of Spain and Portugal, in obtaining all the advantages possible for their own people and products, compares very favorably with the action of our own, which struck down silver when we were its largest producers, and, when compelled by law to purchase a certain amount each month, labored incessantly to force down the price, when each cent of reduction, per ounce, meant the loss of millions of dollars to our agricultural and business community.

No better illustration of the fact that the value of the two money metals is matter of legislation and not of supply, can be found than in the result of the uniform ratio of 1 to 15½ preserved in France from 1803 to 1873, a period of 70 years. During this time the fluctuations of production of the precious metals were very great. From 1803 to 1820 the average annual yield of gold in the whole world was $9,710,-500, of silver $36,847,500; or about 4 of silver to one of gold. From 1821 to 1840 it was $11,466,000 of gold and $21,964,000 of silver; or about 2 of silver to 1 of gold. From 1841 to 1860 it was $85,150,-000 of gold and $34,826,500 of silver; about 2½ of gold to 1 of silver; and from 1861 to 1873, the annual gold product was $117,991,850, silver $68,043,900; nearly 2 of gold to 1 of silver. If we take shorter periods, the divergences are even greater. The coinage of France presents still more extraordinary contrasts. From 1821 to 1847 the value of silver coined was more than 9 times that of gold; from 1853 to 1866 that of gold exceeded the silver no less than 34 times.

Yet all these changes in production and coinage did not affect values one iota. The French ratio of 15½ to 1 fixed the value of the two money metals for all of Europe and by the existence of the bimetallic system all the dangers that would otherwise have been incurred from rapid changes in prices were averted, and the French people became the richest and with least pauperism of any in the world.

And yet the idea has been industriously inculcated by all the gold standard press of the East, that silver had depreciated because it had become so abundant by overproduction that it was against natural law to keep up its price, and that the bimetallic agitation was simply because the West desired "cheap money," a depreciated currency, with which to pay its debts. This kind of talk has a certain plausibility and is apt to affect the uninformed who confuse commodities with measures of value and do not know that the latter are necessarily creations of law in order to insure stability. But when you meet it by the single fact that at the moment when Congress demonetized silver in 1873, silver itself was worth more than par at the ratio of 16 to 1, that a silver dollar was worth at least $1.02½, and a like weight of silver was worth that sum anywhere, because it could be coined into dollars at will, you destroy in a moment all that fallacy.   Ernest Seyd said in his letter to Sam'l Hooper, in 1872, "The cause of the disappearance of the American dollar from circulation, is due to the original error of there being too much silver in the piece."   It is then plain that the large production of silver had not the slightest effect on its value so long as the ancient law of free coinage existed.   The depreciation of the metal was solely the result of legislation, not of supply.   And a notable illustration of the same fact was presented only a year ago, when the demonetization in India caused an immediate fall in the value of silver.   At that very time there was a diminution in the product, but the price was not affected by that, but solely by the legislation.

Perhaps for some it may be well to add the force of an official English opinion on the subject, the more notable as England is the leader in gold standard ideas.   The report of the British Royal Commission on Gold and Silver, made in 1886, says, speaking of the stability of the double standard during all the fluctuations of production during the century, " so long as the bimetallic system was in force, we think that, notwithstanding the changes in the production and use of the precious metals, it kept the market price of silver approximately steady at a ratio fixed by law."

Another point is worthy of notice.   That so far as Europe is concerned, it was the steadfast bimetallism of one single country, France, which preserved the stability of the ratio through seventy years of fluctuation including the violent change in relative production brought about by the gold discoveries in California and Australia.   If France could do this, single-handed, why not the United States?

So far from having been depressed by overproduction the surprising point is, that silver has not fallen in gold value more than it has, from other causes.   For not only is it affected by the rise in the value of gold money, in which its value is counted, just as other property is, but its value is naturally greatly reduced by having its principal use suddenly prohibited by Act of Congress.

Let us take a very simple illustration, which every one can understand as to this latter point.

The two great cereal articles of food are corn and wheat.   The principal use of each is to be ground into bread stuffs, yet each has a small percentage of use for other purposes.   A certain fraction of the corn, for example, is used for distillation.   Now let us suppose that a gigantic syndicate bought up all the wheat in the country and that having done this, in order to enhance its value, they should influence Congress to pass a law forbidding any grinding of corn into meal or its use in any way as food. What would be the result? It is obvious that with the whole food demand, previously divided between the two great products, thrown exclusively upon wheat, its price would be immediately enhanced and would continue to increase as it became more and more scarce. On the other hand, the great use for corn having been extinguished, the only use remaining would not require 20 per cent of the crop, and the price would descend with a rush as each owner of corn tried to secure a sale, by lower and lower offers, of his own stock, as part of the 20 per cent needed for distillation.

One would certainly think that the speculators and the Congress, which had created this great monopoly and made their selfish wishes law, would be held in detestation by the whole people and their names made subjects of execration forever.

But suppose on the contrary, that when the owners of corn complained that what was before worth 50 cents a bushel would now only bring 20 cents and asked that the legislation which thus deprived it of value should be repealed and the immemorial and natural use of corn as a food material be restored so that it would recover its former price, they were to be met by the cry that this was a most monstrous and unjust proposition because every one could see that corn was only worth 20 cents as it was actually selling for that price in the market, and the real trouble was that the production was too much for the demand; and for its raisers to ask congressional action was a piece of supreme assurance.

And suppose that when the great body of the people who were compelled to pay double value for wheat, because it was the only cereal product allowed to be eaten, arose and demanded that their ancient right to use corn should be restored, they should be told by national leaders and by the press that wheat was the only honest food, that the use of corn had always been a mistake and that its deleterious effects were now so well known that no one except those selfishly engaged in its culture, or who dishonestly wished to cheapen food, would think of asking for its restoration.

This appears to be as near a parallel to the congressional action on the silver question as can be suggested except that the latter is much more disastrous and far-reaching in its consequences because it has enhanced the value, not of a simple commodity like wheat, but of gold standard money, which is the only legal measure of value of everything else.

Gold and silver were the two money metals from the beginning of civilization. The great use of each was for the purpose of coinage. Silver had a comparatively small use in the manufactures and arts just as corn had for distillation. Now, suppose a certain syndicate, having obtained control of most of the gold of the world, actual and prospective, by means of holding interest-bearing indebtedness, should be able to influence Congress to demonetize silver. The two results are obvious. Gold, which is the only money metal left, increases in value, as the burden of pecuniary business of the world, previously divided between the two metals equally, falls upon the one alone; and silver, with its great use destroyed, and only the smaller one for manufacturing remaining, of course rapidly falls.

Then, when the owners of silver ask that the legislation which caused this condition shall be repealed and the immemorial and natural use of silver as a money metal be restored so that it will recover its proper value, they are met with the same cry that this is a most monstrous and unjust proposition because every one can see that silver is worth only 60 cents an ounce, as it is actually selling for that in the market, and the trouble is that the production is too great for the demand; and for its producers to ask congressional action is a piece of supreme assurance.

And when the great body of the people, who are compelled to pay double value for money, because it is now confined to gold, arise and demand that their ancient right to coin and use silver be restored, they are told by national leaders and by the press that gold is the only honest money, that the use of a double standard had always been a mistake, and that its deleterious effects are now so well known that no one except selfish silver miners or those who dishonestly want "cheap money" would think of asking for its restoration.

And our people at the East, reasonable and intelligent about other things, seem to overlook the fact that it is only restoration to the normal and immemorial condition of things that is asked, — not anything new; that the "supreme assurance" is on the part of those who ask Congress to reverse the action of all the ages and demonetize silver and thus deprive it of its legitimate use, not of those who simply ask that that most unjust as well as disastrous piece of legislation be repealed.

No doubt when the wheat syndicate destroys by legislation the use of corn for food, it will have power enough to control the press of a whole section and to obtain a constant repetition of the statement that corn was never a fit article for human nutrition, that it had been the fruitful source of all diseases so long as permitted to be eaten and that it was a benevolent act on the part of the wheat Shylocks to save the people from a continuance of such dangers to life and health; and the good people of that section will consequently believe that their oppressors are a set of unselfish angels, nobly devoting themselves to the saving of the nation from the dishonest endeavors of the wicked owners of unwholesome corn.

AMERICAN PRODUCT.

One other point I wish to speak of, because there is a plausibility about it, which at first sight has gained the acceptance of many excellent citizens. Yet the proposition is really so illogical that its supporters cannot have given it much consideration or else have not grasped the fundamental principles involved in this matter. I refer to the proposition to have " free coinage of the American product " of silver, only.

What does Free Coinage mean? It means the system which was established at the foundation of our Government and continued until 1873, which provided that every one having gold or silver could take it to the mint and have it melted and stamped into coin, or receive its equivalent weight in money already coined. Thus, as it stood for many years prior to 1873, any one having gold received one dollar for each $23\frac{22}{100}$ grains; or, if having silver, received one dollar for each $371\frac{1}{4}$ grains. That was free and unlimited coinage at the ratio of 16 to 1. The consequence was that every ounce of gold in the world was worth $20.68 and every ounce of silver was worth $1.29, less the expense of transmitting it to the mill; because it could at any time be converted into coin at those rates. The amount actually coined was comparatively small, for the value by weight was thus absolutely fixed and determined by law.

So it must always be when there is free and unlimited coinage. So it is still as to gold, in this country, and will be as to silver as soon as the old law is restored. But the moment there is the slightest limitation, so that owners may feel uncertainty as to the coinage of their own metal, there is a rush to the mint in order to secure the stamp of the government.

To illustrate, let us suppose that the amount of available uncoined gold in each year is $30,000,000. So long as the law provides, as at present, for its unlimited coinage, the metal has its perfect value by weight wherever it is. But let the law provide that $29,000,000 and no more shall be coined every year, and the fear that any particular lot of gold may be among the surplus million will depress the price and every owner will hasten to carry his metal to the mint. The result would be instability of value and a far larger actual coinage than under an unlimited law by which the gold is sure to be accepted whenever presented. The facts are exactly the same as to silver. So long as we had free coinage there was no rush of metal to the mint for it was sure of acceptance at any time and was therefore worth as much in the bar as in the coin.

If we had a law for the free coinage of the American product only, at the old valuation of $1.29 to the ounce, no one could determine, by looking at a bar or other form of the metal, whether it was American and consequently entitled to coinage, or not. There would always be a doubt and a fear of rejection and hence the metal would not command its full coin value. There would be a rush of silver to the mint in order to secure the coveted stamp which alone could remove all doubt.

With a law for unlimited coinage all the silver in the world would instantly be worth its weight in U. S. coin less the cost of transportation, and having that value in its uncoined condition there would be no inducement to undertake the cost and risk of sending it to our mint. But if there were a limitation either of amount or as to place of origin, we should have two classes of silver, entirely different in value, one coined and the other uncoined. There would be a continual struggle to secure coinage, lawfully or unlawfully, for the uncoined metal, and a multitude of difficulties and contentions would ensue.

The whole principle underlying the stable and unvarying values of the precious metals as measures of commercial exchange, requires an absolutely free and unlimited right of coinage at a fixed ratio. Any limitation whatever destroys uniformity, decreases value and excites distrust.

An objection often urged to the restoration of the free coinage of silver as it existed before 1873 at the ratio of 16 to 1, without concurrent action by England and other nations, is that this country will be immediately inundated with silver from Europe; that it will become the "Dumping Ground" for the surplus silver of that continent. At first sight, this idea is somewhat plausible, but a very little investigation shows that it has no foundation. There are two reasons for this conclusion, either of which would be sufficient.

First. There is no surplus silver in any country of Europe. Their silver is in the shape of coin and in no part of it is the amount greater than that required by the people themselves.

Secondly. So long as our ratio is 16 to 1, silver can only be exported from Europe to the United States at a loss. Their ratio is $15\frac{1}{2}$ to 1. In other words $15\frac{1}{2}$ ounces of silver coin in Europe are worth one ounce of gold coin, but if brought to the United States another half ounce must be added to purchase the same amount of gold. This means a loss of $\frac{1}{32}$ or a little over 3 per cent on every transaction, besides the expense of transporting the silver across the ocean. This matter has been very thoroughly discussed and the "Dumping Ground" theory effectually set at rest by various authors, but this brief statement shows how unfounded it was.

While the United States at this moment is feeling the effect of demonetization most severely, many parts of Europe are suffering almost as greatly. In England the small land-owners were practically swept out of existence in less than 20 years after the demonetization of 1816. Archbishop Walsh has graphically portrayed the condition of Ireland arising from the single gold standard. And Prof. Suess, of the Austrian Parliament, perhaps the greatest continental authority on this subject, ends his recent great work with these significant words:—

"The question is no longer whether silver will again become a full value coinage metal over the whole earth, but what are to be the trials through which Europe is to pass to gain that goal."

Such are some of the facts in this case, plainly stated. In their presentation I have indulged in no rhetoric and have used no expressions to arouse sympathy for the sufferings of the masses of the people or indignation at the selfishness of their oppressors.

The need of the hour is such an awakening of interest in this question in the East as will cause inquiry and investigation and independence of thought.

We are one nation, our interests are identical; that which affects one section, affects all; and in this matter the conditions are practically the same, East and West, North and South. The idea studiously inculcated in the East that this is a western matter and one in which the silver producing States are principally interested, is utterly deceptive, as I have endeavored to show. The farmer of New York or Ohio is interested precisely as is his brother in Iowa or Kansas. The man who owes a mortgage in Massachusetts feels the increasing pressure of the obligation as strongly as his fellow-debtor of Missouri or Dakota. The increasing number of foreclosures, the lengthened list of sales for unpaid taxes, the armies of the underpaid and unemployed, tell the same story everywhere.

On theory it was easy to say what the results of demonetization must be; actual experience is showing what they are. A steady decrease in all property values and a steady increase in the burden of all fixed charges, can bring but one result. The cry of the suffering goes up to heaven. The most despairing and the most touching of their prayers are never heard on earth, for they come from those who suffer in silence. The aggregate of human misery caused by this grinding of the upper and nether millstones is a thing to make angels weep.

We live in the most favored of all lands. God has given us a goodly heritage. The natural resources of our country should make it one of universal prosperity and happiness. There is no reason for suffering and want. Its causes are purely artificial. By the selfishness of man the good gifts of Providence turn to ashes in our hands; the food is taken from the mouths of the weak and the defenseless.

No judgment from on high has been visited upon this people; neither war, nor famine, nor pestilence has been suffered to afflict us.

Yet in the midst of physical health the nation is sick. In the midst of wealth there is poverty, and in a land of plenty there is suffering and starvation.

God grant us all the will and the wisdom to seek the causes of these things, and having found them to apply the remedy (great applause).

Adjourned to 7: 30 p. m. Tuesday evening.

TUESDAY EVENING SESSION.

The meeting was called to order at 7:45 p. m. by Senator Wm. Johnston, of California.

SENATOR JOHNSTON: In the absence of our worthy President he has asked me to preside. Our discussion this evening will be upon the silver question, and the meeting will now come to order. I am informed that this is an early hour for St. Louis people to gather. We western people, when we say 7: 30, mean 7: 30 and not 8 o'clock, but I find it means 8 o'clock in St. Louis. We do not blame you for being a little late on this occasion, for it is the custom.

I have the honor and the pleasure of introducing to you Col. Geo. E. Leighton, of St. Louis, who will address you upon the all important money question of the day.

ADDRESS OF COL. LEIGHTON — WHY WE OPPOSE FREE COINAGE.

Mr. President and Gentlemen: I wish to express my extreme gratification for this very generous reception. The fact that such an audience should assemble to listen to a discussion of this somewhat dry and technical character, confirms my belief in its importance to the country, and in the earnest interest which you have as citizens, in its wise and proper solution. I think there are times when the thought comes to all of us, that we wish not especially to be confirmed in our present views or to have them changed, but that we wish to have more light—to know the whole truth, whether in accord with our present views or not, and that at the present time there are few public questions upon which this desire is more positive and pronounced than upon the question which is now under discussion by the Congress.

I wish at the outset to express my obligation to Gov. Prince of New Mexico for the very clear, able and dignified presentation to the Congress of the cause of silver to which we have listened. I can not say that it was convincing, for I shall have occasion to-night to differ with him in his premises, his logic, and his conclusions. I cannot agree with him that the only light on this subject pervades the West, or that the East, as he has told us, is enshrouded in the densest ignorance from the President all the way down, for I believe that his view of the question and the view of the silver States is perhaps just a little narrow, and possibly just a little locally selfish. By the East, I presume he means those who live east of a meridian which is continually getting further west, and which now includes the entire range of States from Minnesota to the Gulf on the west side of the Mississippi and who are rapidly getting a foot-hold in the second range including Dakota, Nebraska and Kansas. I believe this view of the East, as he calls it, more fairly takes into consideration the relation of free coinage to the whole country and to its great agricultural, commercial and manufacturing interests, with which they are more in daily and immediate contact than are our friends in the Rocky Mountain States.

But we both agree upon one point — that the great need of some parts of the country is enlightenment. The opponents of free coinage ask nothing more than free, fair and open discussion before thinking men. He and I would differ very widely as to which is the antidote and which is the poison, but I am sure I should be glad if the " case for silver " as he has so eloquently presented it to the Congress and the " case against silver " as I shall endeavor to present it to-night, or a better or clearer one, could go together into benighted regions, East or West, to be talked over, and thought over and discussed, and picked to pieces, in every country store, in the gatherings at the country post-office, and by every intelligent farmer's fireside. The American people both East and West are very apt at this sort of thing, and are sure to get pretty near the truth on any question if you give them time.

DANGEROUS CONDITIONS.

It has been wisely said by an English statesman, that there is no period involving greater danger to the good government of a nation, than one in which industrial depression is general, and the masses of the people, restless and dissatisfied, join in the general cry that *something must be done, and at once.* Such a period is not only the opportunity of the political demagogue, masking his personal ambition under zeal for the interests of the people, but scores of honest and patriotic men everywhere sincerely hope by the application of some favorite legislative nostrum, suggested by their own limited environment and range of observation, to alleviate the real or apparent evil. The history of civilization is dotted with these periods, and there is scarcely one in which a proposition to issue fiat money, or for the creation of a bountiful currency in some form, has not borne a conspicuous part. At such times money, however abundant, is inactive. Inactivity is readily confounded with scarcity. With the conclusion reached that hard times are due to the scarcity of money, the demand for the issue of more money readily finds support. What is really a result, is confounded with the cause of the evil.

Just now faith in debasement of the monetary standard, in various ways, as a remedy, is shared by several other faiths in the popular mind.

Mr. George offers us the "Single Tax" upon land as the pre-eminent remedy for all the ills of organized society. In his view, currency and tariffs are of small moment. State ownership of the railroads seems to another class to be the means of securing universal prosperity; and if there is any way of getting them without paying anything for them, and having the State operate them free of cost to the public, it presents, on the surface, pretty strong claims, as a relief to some of our ills. The socialists have their remedy, the production and distribution of everything by the State. Mr. Bellamy and the nationalists have theirs. The populists would have the nation issue and lend to the people all the money required. The great national parties find an adequate cause for all, the one in the policy of protection; the other in that of taxation solely for revenue.

But there is a class and it is a large and aggressive one, especially in the West, who think they see in the free coinage of silver at the old ratio, a remedy for all our industrial ills. In their minds all our trouble has been occasioned by the action of the United States and of Germany and other European States, more than twenty years ago in unifying the coinage of the German States, under the Empire, and in adopting the gold standard. A large number of people are discontented, naturally so, with prevailing industrial conditions, who are unwilling or unable to study the underlying causes which have brought about present conditions, are anxious to try anything that is suggested, with the hope of improving those conditions. In a word — *something has got to be done*, and the whole troop of suggested remedies, any or all, are readily welcomed by some portion of our people, as a possible, if not a probable, means of improvement.

THE REAL CAUSES.

I do not think there is any proposition more easily capable of absolute proof, than that our present condition is not due in any considerable degree, to a refusal to adopt Mr. George's remedy, or Mr. Bellamy's, or to the fact of corporate ownership of railroads, or our method of securing necessary revenue through the tariff under either system, or to the appreciation of gold, or to what is called the demonetization of silver. There are many causes. But stated broadly, it is due in a great degree to a too rapid development throughout the world of agricultural and industrial interests. It has been a development too rapid and too irregular for the proper and natural adjustments to distribution and consumption. A part of this development is due perhaps to our enormous immigration and to too stimulating legislation favoring corporate organization, but a great deal more in this country to the enterprise, inventive genius, and push of American character, which, while increasing production to extreme limits, has failed to measure the capacity of the market for consumption within the limit of practical distribution, and is brought up very suddenly by the stubborn fact that there are not purchasers enough for the steadily increasing output. Our difficulty is not in providing for a healthy normal and growing production — but a production increasing beyond the increase of population, or its capacity to consume.*

We cannot go over this matter now, though I believe this explanation is the true one, and as capable of absolute proof as any proposition in industrial history. The same thing has occurred before, and the same thing will occur again, as long as the American spirit of progress gives character to all our industrial work. Reaction is the inevitable sequence of too rapid development. A " boom ", to use our western phrase, is always followed by a collapse. We shall get it through our heads some time that mere growth in numbers or in aggregate material wealth, is not necessarily growth in the sum of happiness and contentment of a people.

WHAT UNLIMITED COINAGE MEANS.

I propose, however, to-night, to speak upon but one of these proposals, the demand for free coinage of silver on a basis of 16 to 1, as a national need, or a remedy for our national ills. It is a living, practical question, not to be avoided, or explained away, or safely compromised. The people of St. Louis, who I am here to represent, have never occupied a doubtful position upon this proposition. By the repeated expression of their commercial organizations, by their representatives in Congress, representing both the great parties and by their press they have, always with great unanimity, regarded the free coinage of silver at a ratio of 16 to 1, not as a remedy, but as a certain aggravation of all our troubles.

Fortunately, it is not as yet a distinct party question. It is to be regretted that it is a question, inspiring or creating factional differences within the parties. It is unfortunate that it is a question of apparently great local importance to a large section of the country. It does not

---

* NOTE.— This rapid development within twenty years is not confined to agricultural products. In manufacturing: —

	1870.	1890.
Capital employed	$2,790,000,000	$6,525,000,000
Value of products	5,370,000,000	9,370,000,000
In mineral industries — tons of iron produced	1,692,378	9,269,382

help us to solve a question of this character wisely for the whole country, that there is a local industry claiming to be fostered, which we would like to foster, a local interest to be protected, which we would like to protect, for which it is assumed something of principle ought to be surrendered or waived.   But its true solution and the only safe and enduring solution, must be predicated, not upon the advantage to Leadville, or Denver, or Helena, but upon the need of the whole country. I think it may be demonstrated that, considered even as a local interest, there is no enduring advantage to be derived by the silver producers or their States, from free coinage.   Adjustments of real values are sure in the end, and all artificial supports lose their force in the long run. Our experience with the Bland-Allison Act of 1878 and the Sherman Act of 1890 as legislative props ought to be conclusive upon this point.

Speaking, however, not from the stand-point of local interest, but from a broad national stand-point, the real question to be determined is: What is to be gained and what is to be lost to the country by free coinage?

It is a measure of tremendous import, how tremendous I think very few fully appreciate.   The currency of a country is the life blood of its commercial existence.   It flows to the remotest limit, and its quality affects every interest.   The unwise appropriation of a few millions, means only a few millions lost.   But to change the standard of the nation's currency, under the conditions of difference in value existing to-day, inevitably affects every interest, modifies every commercial transaction, forces liquidation and re-adjustment of great undertakings at terrible cost, paralyses new enterprises, and will come home to the remotest hamlet in the land.   All parts of the country will suffer, but none more surely than the great West, which you represent here to-day.

Have you ever considered what the current commercial transactions of this country of ours represent in one year — the transactions into which dollars and the character and quality — in a single word, the *value* of the legal tender dollar enters?

The clearings of the banks with each other are not far from seventy thousand millions annually.   The transactions between individuals, and between individuals and banks, and the retail business of the country, not represented in clearings, represent probably half as much more.   Here we have one hundred thousand millions, as the annual business of this country,— two thousand millions a week, in all of which the real *value* of the standard dollar is the controlling element. Not a bale of cotton, a bushel of wheat, a pound of sugar, not a day's labor, not a paper of pins or a spool of thread, into which this value does not enter.   Surely this may well cause us to pause in any legislation disturbing that value.

To disturb that value in such a vast commerce, in any way, even in a slight degree, we know from experience in all countries, means the hoarding of the best money, the suspension of new ventures, until conditions are again settled, and the unrest and doubt, which paralyses all progress. Commercial prosperity can only exist under permanent and settled conditions. If slight disturbance can produce this result, how much more disastrous, when a change so radical as that proposed in the free coinage of silver at the rate of 16 to 1, with unlimited legal tender quality. The real ratio in value to-day as between silver and gold is about as 30 to 1.

I do not believe that anything is to be gained to the prosperity of the country by free coinage, even upon a real ratio, but coinage at a real ratio even though entirely unnecessary, has or once had a logical basis and if it were a *settled* ratio, would in a degree avoid the tremendous shock occasioned by a coinage upon a false and artificial ratio, enforced by the fiat of the government. If there is anything in bi-metallism — it is a system which seeks to have but *one standard of value* — *one monetary unit*, of value, but to have that value represented in two different metals adjusted in quantity to a real ratio — the real value of each being the same. There cannot be two standards — or two monetary units; two DIFFERING dollars in value at the same time.

THE RATIO OF 16 TO 1.

The ratio of 16 to 1 has been set up as a fetich to be worshiped. Because it was a real ratio, or substantially so once, it is assumed that it must always be so. Let us get rid of the idea that there is anything sacred in the ratio of 16 to 1. Time was, perhaps, when silver was worth as much as, or more than gold, weight for weight.[*] In the time of the Roman Empire, it had reached a ratio of 9 or 10 to 1. The great production of silver in the centuries following the discovery of America, increased the difference in value, and for many years 13 to 1, 14 to 1 and 15 to 1, were accepted as ratios. Sometimes this ratio of value continued apparently fixed through long periods, but, however slow the change, it has never escaped the everlasting law of final adjustment.

It is to be remembered that in earliest ages, and down even to the last half century, the age of steam, international intercourse was very

---

[*] In the earliest Egyptian period, the old empire, silver was valued higher than gold; under the new empire at Thebes (Thothmes III.), either through new discoveries or a brisker trade with Phenecia and Syria, there was a considerable fall in the value. History does not tell of the probable racket among the politicians of the day occasioned by the demonetization. *Erman. Life in Ancient Egypt.*

limited, hampered by a thousand obstacles, and with the money metals, as with the great staples, the movement of a surplus from one nation to another was slow and uncertain.

The age of steam has made the whole world one. There can be now no surplus of money or commodities anywhere in the world that it is not hurried to fill the shortage elsewhere, if one exists.

It is this ability to move rapidly from nation to nation, throughout the world, that now equalizes values rapidly. We know at the breakfast table what was going on yesterday in India, Egypt, China and Japan, Australia and the Argentine, not only the events of political or historical importance, but the condition of the crops, the number of bales of cotton, or bushels of wheat, afloat for the very markets in which our cotton and wheat are sold.

As values of cotton or wheat or corn change as it is wanted elsewhere or not, by the same law the value of silver changes as it is wanted or not. Legislation is impotent to help or hinder these changes to any material extent.

It is the part of common wisdom to recognize these new conditions. There is no sense or reason in blind devotion to an old ratio, simply because it was acceptable once. It is not founded on an ordinance of Providence as some of our friends seem to believe.

We do not gain anything by shutting our eyes to real change of value or condition in anything, in agriculture, in mining, in manufacturing, in commerce, in political or social development. We must, if we wish to reach a sound and sure conclusion, recognize every ascertained fact, however unwelcome. There is no gallantry or patriotism in resisting a fact. It is simply folly, and the penalty is sure.

It is an abuse of language to talk about friends of silver or enemies of silver. It obscures, rather than clears our view of the question. The whole question is one of commercial utility. It is one of the greatest obstacles we contend with in presenting this question to the average inhabitant or average statesman of the sparsely settled States, West or South, that he has no conception of the nature and monetary requirements of our larger commerce. Coin money seems to him to answer all the purposes of buying a horse, or selling his load of cotton or corn or wheat. The moment the matter is considered by the merchant, even in the silver States, the conditions, which make silver monometallism impossible to a great commercial nation, become apparent. We need money, just as we need railroads, telegraphs, post-offices, steamships. They are all and alike our servants. As that is the best railroad, the best post-office, or the best steamship, which serves the purposes of commerce best, without reference to our friendship or enmity, so that is the best money which serves the purposes of commence best. And it is just as important that our money should be safe, and sound, and efficient for our use, as that the steamship should be seaworthy and efficient in its duty.

There is no more reason for adhering to old and obsolete ratios in the money metals, than for adhering to the use of the barge, the flat boat, or the sailing vessel for transportation, all valuable in their day, and in many places and under many conditions just as valuable still. There is a great deal of talk about demonetization of silver. Silver is used as money as much in volume as it ever was. It will always have, and must, have a large place in the money of the world — a place which it fills perfectly. It will no more go out of use than the sailing vessel will go out of use. Under wise legislation, it will have a steadily increasing use, increasing within the lines of safety. Its use will be, in a measure, different from what it has been, but it will be made just as valuable and as necessary to the world, as it has ever been.

DIFFERENT CLASSES OF ADVOCATES.

Free coinage of silver is advocated in this country to-day by two classes of persons reasoning from totally different and inconsistent stand-points. They cannot both be correct in their claims of what it is to do for silver, or for the commercial prosperity of the country.

Let us examine these claims as fairly as we can.

By one class it is claimed that what is called demonetization *has produced* the decline in relative bullion value from 16 to 1 in 1873, to 28 or 30 to 1 in 1894, that free coinage by the United States will restore the value of silver throughout the world to the old ratio, with gold — that a parity will be re-established, and we shall all be happy in a true bimetallic millennium.

Governor Prince has just presented to us this view; — I think it fairly represents the genuine claim of the silver producers. It is an honest position and its defenses are to be met, not with denunciation, but by honest argument.

By another class the permanent change in relative value is frankly admitted, but it is claimed that the monetary unit as now established in gold is too high, that by substituting silver and thereby reducing the value of the monetary unit one-half, gold will be demonetized and it will give the country more and cheaper money *under the old names*, a sort of getting two dollars for one, and paying one dollar for two, scheme.

The first class believe that parity in value and freedom of interchange at the old ratio will be maintained. The second class do not desire or expect to maintain the parity in value, but desire and expect to bring the country to a silver basis, the monetary unit to be the silver dollar of 412 1-2 grains, now worth about fifty cents. This is the view of the long list of political floaters — who believe in fiat money and are willing to range themselves under the flag of free coinage, populism or unlimited issue of paper, either or all, as the time is most opportune for their own political preferment.   Free coinage just now happens to be their banner — but they will all desert it for paper, if opportunity occurs.   I believe that position is fundamentally dishonest in its purpose.

THE FIRST CLASS — WHO CLAIM THAT A PARITY WILL BE RE-ESTABLISHED.

Let us look at these claims separately.   What is called demonetization in this country is scarcely worthy of consideration in a discussion to an intelligent audience, and although so much is made of it, may be briefly disposed of.   As there had been only 4,000,000 silver dollars coined in the United States since 1804, a period of seventy years, it is absurd to say that the elimination of the dollar of silver in the Coinage Act of 1873, destroyed any market which had formerly existed for silver.   At that time, as you will remember, 412 1-2 grains of silver were worth more than a dollar, and it was not supposed by any body, not even our Rocky Mountain friends, that another 412 1-2 grains would ever be presented for coinage, or that a silver dollar would ever be required in our currency.

The adoption of the gold standard by Germany in 1873, and the Latin Union in 1878, had an undoubted influence upon the future value of silver, as it was a limitation of future consumption, but the influence has been immensely overrated.   The action of Germany in 1873 and of the Latin Union in 1878 was but the defense of their monetary systems against influences destined to overwhelm and destroy it, if not counteracted.

INCREASED PRODUCTION OF SILVER.

The depreciation of silver is accounted for fully by the common facts of production and consumption.   To claim that the depreciation from $1.29 per ounce in 1873 to 68 cents per ounce in 1894, the depreciation of silver contained in the dollar from $1.00 in 1873 to 50 cents in 1894 is due to that cause, ignores the most palpable and certain influences at work.

The production of silver in steadily increasing volume under new discoveries and improved methods of working, and the artificial stimulus given by the act of 1878 and that of 1890, explain the cause fully and completely.   Had it not been for this enormous increase, an increase without parallel in the history of the money metals, a material depreciation would not have occurred.   The production of 1893 exceeded the total production for the first fifty years following the discovery of America.

We produced $150,000 in silver in 1860, $16,000,000 in 1870, and

$75,000,000 in 1893. Mexico produced $23,000,000 in 1870 and $59,000,000 in 1893. South America about $10,000,000 in 1870, and over $25,000,000 in 1893.

The world's product of silver in 1870 was only about $51,000,000 as against $107,000,000 gold; in 1893, largely under what I cannot but call the artificial legislative stimulus given to production, it was $196,-500,000 in silver to $138,000,000 in gold, a complete reversal of the relative product. The annual gold product had increased about 30 per cent — the silver about 300 per cent.

Demonetization is not the word to apply to the action of Germany or the United States. The gold standard was in each adopted in the unification of the coinage. In Germany $100,000,000 of silver in use as coin was recoined into imperial silver coins and it is still coining about $1,250,000 annually.

The action of Germany was not a war on silver, as it has been so often styled. The consolidation of the empire after the war, found the constituent States with seven different coinage systems, with seventeen kinds of gold coin — 66 different silver pieces — 46 kinds of notes issued by 35 different banks, besides a considerable amount and variety of State paper.

The unification of such a system was inevitable, and the adoption of the gold standard, was simply the adoption of a system best fitted to promote, as it has promoted, her commercial growth. At that time silver had not depreciated, the old ratio was still substantially a true one, and the sole consideration was the adaptation of the currency to the best use of a great civilized nation.

The net average annual silver coinage of Germany for a long series of years prior to 1871 only amounted to about $10,300,000, while the statistics show that in the sixteen years following, so great was the impetus given to the use of silver in the industrial arts that the imports of silver exceeded the exports by over 77,000,000 marks, about $19,-000,000.

The average annual coinage by France for sixteen years prior to 1876 was only $7,400,000. Belgium for ten years prior to 1876 coined annually only about $6,700,000 and Italy $5,900,000.

The coinage of Germany, France, Belgium and Italy together, amounted to less than $30,000,000 annually.* If this full amount of average annual coinage had been continued it would only have consumed in 1893 about 20 per cent of the increased output of nearly 300 per cent.

The real ground of complaint against Germany and France is not that they ceased to take their annual average of silver for the purpose of

* *Soetbeer — Production of Precious Metals.*

coinage, but that they ceased to take it in continual increasing proportion as the product increased so abnormally throughout the world.

The nations, which, to protect their monetary systems, ceased to continue upon the dangerous path of unlimited coinage — shared with all other nations in a largely increased consumption of silver in industrial work.

If this suspension of demand for silver for coinage by European States was the sole or even the principal occasion for the depreciation, the coinage of about $30,000,000 annually by the United States from 1878 to 1890 would have more than supplied a market for all the demand suspended by the action of the States. If it did not restore the value, it would have checked the decline. For Germany and France, Belgium and Italy to have continued the coinage of silver on the old ratio under the increased output from 1870 to the present time, would have been to invite a demoralization of values throughout the world, which no nation in its senses would assist in producing.

The extent to which silver has been increasingly used in the industrial arts is often overlooked.

From 1861 to 1870 the average annual import of silver into Great Britain was about £9,000,000. In the ten years from 1871 to 1881 it averaged £12,750,000, an annual increase of £3,750,000 or in round numbers $17,000,000. Much of this of course went finally to the East, but allowing the normal consumption by the eastern nations to be maintained with a natural increase, the statistics show an annual increase of £1,000,000 in industrial consumption of silver. France, after it ceased to coin, imported over $5,000,000 above exports; Italy over $3,000,000, and Belgium and Austria in like proportion.* History does not present a case in which monetary and industrial interests have so struggled in every possible way to adjust themselves to this overwhelming avalanche of silver, to take and use it in some way. In this effort the United States, to please the silver States, has gone to the farthest point of safety, if not beyond it. It has done more, far more than could be reasonably asked. But with every effort, annually increasing production has crowded upon the effort to use, and the inevitable decline in value could not be stayed. Probably upon this extreme production the fall in value has been too great. If this be so, time will correct it. Price is not always made in the unconsumable commodities like silver, by the amount of production in any one year. The tendency towards continuous increase or decrease is even more potent. This dread of an annual avalanche of silver from the United

---

* The Director of the Mint estimates the consumption of silver for industrial purposes last year at about 9,000,000. See also *Soetbeer, Consumption of Metals.*

States, has had an undoubted influence upon all the markets of the world.

The scheme by which the United States tried to stay the decline by purchasing and storing in the treasury over two thousand tons annually of uncoined American silver hastened the fall it was intended to prevent. This accumulated mass hangs over the market of the world to-day, just as unconsumed iron or cotton or wheat or any other product. Be it early or late, some time it must be disposed of. It is an unused and in its present form an unusable product.*

Upon the adoption of free coinage by the United States, say its advocates, the old ratio will be re-established. Silver will be doubled at once in real value, throughout the world.

Let us see what that means in its application to the world.

The purchasing power of silver to-day is about as 30 to 1. Free coinage by the United States thereby re-establishing the old value of 16 to 1, is to at once nearly double the purchasing power of silver held elsewhere — not our own, for by our fiat we have upheld the power of purchase at home.

Where is the silver of the world, and who is to benefit by this doubling in its value and in its purchasing power?

India has about $1,000,000,000 whose value is at once to be doubled. China has about $725,000,000, whose purchasing power is to be doubled.

Spain, Mexico, the Straits, and the South American States have about $400,000,000 whose purchasing power is to be doubled.

The Director of the Mint, substantially in accord with other careful estimates, fixes the silver in the world at about $3,500,000,000. We are, then, it is claimed, by a simple act, providing for free coinage in the United States, to enrich all these countries at once by doubling the present value and purchasing power of all this mass of silver, everywhere throughout the world. Think what this really means — an appreciation of the value of the whole currency of the silver countries of 100 per cent in a single day, through a legislative act of the United States. Such an *appreciation* inevitably means the doubling of the burthen of all current or fixed indebtedness, and measured in the new currency values, a *depreciation* of all commodities and fixed property. This means universal bankruptcy.

There are men in the world who claim to believe this, for this is

---

* Under the Bland Act of 1878, the United States purchased 291,272,000 fine ounces at a cost of $308,279,260 in gold. It is now worth $186,414,091, or a loss to the people $121,865,170.

Under the act of 1890, it purchased 168,674,682 fine ounces at a cost of $155,931,000.

This 7,000 tons is now worth $108,951,796, a loss of $46,979,204.

what restoration of value necessarily means. Governor Prince takes this position squarely and it is the only consistent position for those who expect *bimetallism* on a ratio of 16 to 1. Surely if real value can be so easily created, Alladin's lamp has been found again, and the Congress of the United States holds it. Let us see if we can change the seasons by renaming the months, or the time of sunrise and sunset by a re-arrangement of the dial of the clock.

Do not be deceived. There is no possibility of bimetallism of any kind under free unlimited coinage upon the old ratio. I have a great respect for an act of Congress, especially if it is a moderately wise act, but it cannot perform miracles. If what is called bimetallism is ever to obtain, it can only be by the combined action of the great commercial nations building it upon a new ratio ˙approximating actual value.*

-----

* NOTE.—The use of this term, *Bimetallism*, by the advocates of the free and unlimited coinage of silver at 16 to 1 is one of the most deceptive and, if they were conscious of it, dishonest forms of argument to the people. The names of Suess, Laveleye, Courtney, Balfour, Foxwell and others in Europe, and of Prest. Andrews and Gen. F. A. Walker in this country, are quoted as "Bimetallists," *hence* advocates of free coinage. The persons named are supporters of *International Bimetallism*, a totally different thing. *Not one* of the recognized defenders of international bimetallism has ever declared in favor of free coinage by the United States alone. Gen. F. A. Walker, its most eminent exponent in this country, has declared distinctly his opinion that free coinage by this country alone would delay, if it did not prevent adoption of an international agreement establishing a par of exchange between the gold and silver using countries.

As to our former legislation he says: "Our coinage of two millions a month under the Bland-Allison act of 1878 was directly *against* the interests of bimetallism, while our purchase of four millions five hundred ounces of silver bullion a month under the Sherman act of 1890, was an even worse strategic blunder." *Tract for the Times.*

Mr. *Balfour* says: "If it be possible by *international* arrangement to establish a joint standard throughout the world, it would not be open to the objection which a single standard is open to." *Mansion House speech, August, 1893·*

Sir David Barbour says: "No final or satisfactory settlement of the currency question is possible except by an *international* agreement." *Manchester speech, Feb. 6, 1894.*

Sir. Wm. Houldsworth says: "It is an *international* question." "It is the duty of her majesty's government to negotiate without delay with *other* nations." *Prof. Foxwell* says: "Bi-metallism is new and involves *international* agreement, the question of *valuation* as well as the *question of ratio*." "These matters can not be settled by *isolated action*." "We shall never settle the monetary difficulty without *international* action."

·From the *Official Statement of the Bimetallic League:* "The aim of the Bi-Metallic League is to secure by *international* agreement the opening of the mints of the leading commercial nations to the unrestricted coinage of gold and silver at such a fixed *ratio as may be mutually agreed upon* amongst those nations.

No secure system can be established on the idea of favor in either metal, and it must be so extended that either metal may freely flow from nation to nation without loss, as a surplus accumulates in one or the other. The moment the idea obtains to any considerable degree anywhere that one metal is the best to get rid of and the other is the best to keep, that moment bimetallism is gone in fact, and no legislation, unless it can change human nature itself, can save it. As a matter of historical fact there never has been any actual period of bimetallism, in a strict sense, in this country. It has been a system of alternating standards. We have a gold standard to-day because under the ratio of 1834 and 1837, silver was worth the most, and the business of the country adjusted itself to the lower standard of gold, as it always does — a law as old as human history.

There can be but one result of a free coinage act, by which it is attempted to give, by legislation, a fiat value or any other than a bullion value to silver. If we are willing under any wild delusion, to stamp and label it, and compel its circulation among our own people for more than it is worth, the world will provide us its hoard as long as the delusion lasts. Silver will come from the four quarters of the earth, as long as we are willing to take it at more than it is worth elsewhere. Gold will go out to pay for it, and a mono-metallism of silver will be established.

At best, say some of our friends who want to be " friendly " but have been intelligent enough to see this inevitable result, let us only coin *American* silver. This is an admission of the whole case against silver. Considered as coin, with all the qualities that must be inherent in coin — there is no difference in value between American gold or silver, and the gold or silver of any country, and the whole problem remains, and will always remain, as long as we try to coin American, or any other silver, upon a false basis.

Good wine needs no bush. A good coin, whether of gold or silver, needs no favor. It can dispense even with legal tender acts, it can take care of itself without impairment in any crisis, in every part of the world.

The government can create a coin but it cannot create *value* in coin. Its only office is to give assurance of purity and weight by so shaping a given quantity of metal — that it will pre-

---

"No settlement is, however, in our opinion possible without *international action*. The remedy we suggest is essentially *international* in its character and its details must be settled *in concert with the other powers*." Sec. 34.

"The particular *ratio* to be adopted is not in our opinion a necessary preliminary to the opening of negotiations and can be left for *further* discussion and settlement." Sec. 35.

serve that quantity and its value unimpaired. The notion that a coin can be made safe upon any other basis than that of intrinsic value, obtains nowhere else than in the United States. Cernuschi, the ablest and most consistent bimetallist of the generation, says, '' That is the only true coin which will stand the test of fire — that is worth as much melted, as it was before.''

Here in the United States, the idea that an act of Congress can give a *value* to a coin, not inherent in the substance, is of recent growth.

Up to the act of 1878, all coinage of the United States was made upon ascertained actual value, whether of silver or gold. The mint merely gave the stamp of uniform weight and fineness. So indifferent was this country as to whose stamp it was, so that it was an honest one, that by the acts of Congress of 1793, 1816, 1819, 1823, 1834 and 1843, the *gold coin of England, France, Spain, Portugal*, and the silver coins of *France, Spain, Mexico, Peru, Chili and Central America*, were not only made receivable by the United States, but were made *legal tender* throughout the *United States*, at rates established according to their actual weight and fineness as compared with the standard of the United States. I may remark in this connection, that the gold eagle ($10), of the United States, is legal tender throughout the dominion of Canada, to-day.

How false our whole position is in coining silver on a ratio of 16 to 1 is made apparent by this simple test. The result is irresistible in its exposure of our weakness. Let us apply it.

An act of Congress to make legal tender the *gold* coin of any country, or every country on the face of the earth, at rates established according to their actual weight and fineness as compared with the 25.8 grain standard dollar of the United States, would not produce a ripple of disturbance in the commercial world. Not a sovereign, or franc, or mark, or florin, or peso, would come or go, except in the normal flow created in the settlement of international balances. There would be no movement, simply because the coin would have no more value in one place than another.

To pass an act to receive the *silver* coin of the world as legal tender, at rates established according to weight and fineness, according to our false 412 1-2 grain dollar, would bankrupt the country, as it would mean taking the world's silver at double its present value. Does not this prove that this position is inconsistent and untenable?

By an act of Congress, it is made the duty of the Director of the Mint to estimate quarterly the value of foreign coins, and that the same shall be proclaimed by the Secretary of the Treasury. The silver coins of other countries are rated at commercial value and in the valuation of October, 1894, the Mexican dollar is valued at 51 cents. If our American silver dollar were coined in any other country it would now be rated at about 50 cents. But we compel our own people to take it for 100 cents. Is this sensible, fair or honest?

If there is a fact absolutely determined, and without exception in the history of the world's money, it is that two currencies of different standard value cannot circulate together. If either one is worth more elsewhere than it is at home, it will go away just as surely as corn or wheat or cotton, or any other commodity, will go where it is worth the most. In France and in the United States, silver at the old ratio is maintained at a parity with gold, but in both cases it circulates, not upon its own value as coin, but because the respective governments have not only pledged themselves to sustain this parity as to existing coinage, but have so administered their financial policy as to make them to the extent of the present coinage practically inconvertible. Free and unlimited coinage by France or the United States would make this impossible, and gold and silver would part company at once. Both countries have all they can do to maintain what they have already coined.

In the popular discussions of the silver question, on the stump, even in Congress and often by the press, the word " bimetallism " is often used carelessly to describe very different things. If by the word is meant *a common and general use of both gold and silver* under a system of absolutely free and unlimited coinage, it does not exist, has never existed anywhere and cannot exist. If it is intended to mean a common and general use of both metals under conditions which will promote the largest use of both, it cannot be attained by *unlimited* coinage of silver. No gold would be coined, for it would be worth more as bullion. The only hope *for a large use of silver with gold is under the shield and protection of gold as a standard*. This, although technically not bimetallism, is the condition in France, Belgium, Holland and the United States, to-day. Silver may be maintained in very large though always limited volume under a gold standard, but in no country on the face of the earth at any time in its history, has a dollar of gold ever been maintained in common use under a silver standard. I challenge our silver friends here to-night to cite a single example of such a case. If we are to have monometallism of silver, free coinage cannot make it any worse. But if we desire to use both metals as freely as it is possible to use them both, which, though not the scientific, is the popular meaning of the word " bimetallism," it can only be accomplished by *limiting the coinage of silver* under the gold standard. We are doing that and maintaining a volume of silver almost too large for safety. This is what France is doing by limiting the coinage of silver. There is and can be no other possible bimetallism, a common and general use of both metals in one country. I believe that this is what most of those in the West have in mind, when they claim to be *bimetallists*, and that they can be made to see that that end is not attainable by the free and unlimited coinage of silver at a false ratio. That means silver alone, as it does in Mexico and the South American States where free coinage obtains.

THE SILVER MONOMETALLISTS.

Let us now consider the claim of the other class who are advocating unlimited coinage, the reasons upon which it is based, and the results to the country. There is not the slightest doubt that the claim of this class is right, to the extent that free coinage by the United States means not bimetallism, under any definition of the word, but a sole silver standard. Silver will come into the country in abundance but our gold will leave.

Does any interest of this country, agricultural, manufacturing or commercial, wish to bring about this result?

We have a standard now in accord with that of the civilized world. We are one of the most advanced nations in every respect of civilization, in intercommunication, in production, in intelligence and political progress.

Humboldt made the observation more than half a century ago, that while advancing civilization had for centuries moved toward the West, the steady trend of the use of silver, reversing that order, had been toward the East.

It is not only a fact, but it is a fact grounded in the very differences between the Eastern and Western nations. Advanced civilization means a large varied and extended domestic and foreign commerce, the production and interchange of a great variety of commodities, in large volume, the most efficient and perfect facilities for aggregation, and distribution, and a perfect monetary system adapted to the larger as well as the smaller transactions. In the Eastern nations, labor is poorly rewarded, transactions are small, and are usually discharged in coin. In nations like China, Japan and India, where the smaller coins in every-day use affecting all business are, as in the case of China, worth about one-tenth of our cent (1000 to a dollar), or in Corea about 4000 to a dollar, it is easy to understand how it is that silver may be king — that a dollar which is the largest practical limit in size of a coin, may look large. But the commercial transactions of great and powerful civilized countries are not small. Daily transactions occur in all our cities, and even larger towns, where commodities are aggregated for distribution, whose purchase or sale it would require tons of silver to discharge. Gold simply by its own fitness, has became necessary in settlement of the larger balances of commerce, and it would be only a question of degree of inconvenience, between using silver *alone* in the larger commerce of the world, and using the iron of the ancient Greeks, or the bronze and copper of the Chinese.

Each has, or has had, its true place where it has obtained, but to force it into a place for which it is not suited, simply imposes upon commerce an unnecessary burden, which in the end, must be borne by the whole people.

All money has not the same adaptability to commercial use. Even if relative value could be perfectly adjusted, we could do efficiently with silver, what we cannot do with copper, or nickel, or bronze, yet the nickel, or copper, or bronze, are as surely money within the range of their use as gold or silver. The world has determined by experience beyond all law, that gold, by possessing large value in small bulk, is the most efficient standard money for use by the great commercial nations, in their intercourse; that silver has, and ought to have, an extensive use, where gold would not answer as well, and that nickel, and copper, have their limited uses, but that any sound monetary system must bind them together by a real, not an artificial ratio, or, as in the case of our subsidiary coinage, by some system of redemption or interchange by which the one may always command its equivalent in the other, if needed.

There is no prejudice against silver, any more than there is a prejudice against the sailing craft, when we take the steamship, or against the horse, when we use the electric road. Gold answers the purpose better, as for certain purposes the steamship or the electric motor does. Silver will always continue to be used extensively, and more and more under wise legislation, for a large part of our volume of money. In England, France, Germany and the United States, probably the largest number of every-day transactions are discharged in silver,— not the larger amount.

That money metal is the best, and ought to be used just when and where it best fulfills the need to be supplied.

Silver can no more be forced beyond this point, by law, even if coined upon actual and settled value, without disturbance of commerce, any more than nickel   copper can. We once coined gold dollars, half cents, and twenty-cent pieces. The coinage was discontinued because they supplied no monetary need. We found the same thing true of the silver dollars c⁰ ⁻⁻78. Of the $419,332,000 coined, there were on July 1, 1893, less than $50,000,000 in circulation, and all of the efforts of secretaries of the treasury of both the great political parties to get more into circulation, have failed. We got up the device of the certificate, by which five or ten or twenty dollars could be represented in one note, concealing the objections to weight and bulk. If a certificate for 10,000 copper cents were by law made a legal tender for 100 dollars, we might blind ourselves just as easily as we blind ourselves with the silver certificate, but it would not be more objectionable in substance.

EFFICIENCY AND SUPPLY OF GOLD.

We have to-day in this country a volume of gold of about $660,000,-000, sustaining our whole currency, a volume larger than any country in the world except France; our *visible* supply (in the Treasury and banks) is even larger than that of France.

We are large and increasing producers of gold. We have a national credit which can call gold from all quarters of the earth to any extent needed. We are a creditor nation, and the natural flow of gold is toward us. Under wise legislation, by which a sound, safe and elastic banking system adapted to the wants of the whole country — the West and South, as well as the North and East — no country in the world is better fitted to maintain a gold standard, and provide a general currency absolutely safe and adapted to the wants of the whole people.*

The world does not need gold for a *circulating* currency. Its larger commerce, by which I mean every conceivable form of interchange, from the producer in any part of the world to the consumer in any other part, can be far more efficiently handled through safe and appropriate banking systems. It needs gold enough, and only enough to settle international balances, to guarantee the safety of such systems under the severest stress, and furnish the assurance that every dollar, however represented or expressed in silver or paper, can be converted into gold of a definite weight and purity. The objections so often made in the West to a banking system, next to the post-office, the most economic and efficient instrument of commerce, is one of the most unaccountable phases of opinion in an intelligent and progressive people. It is a survival of an old prejudice formed when the primitive frontier bank was as unlike the perfected bank of to-day, as the Mississippi steamboat boiler of that period was unlike the boiler of to-day. This world has progressed in the knowledge of what constitutes safety, security and public service in banks, as it has in what constitutes safety, security and public service in steamboat boilers.

If there were no other consideration but that of convenience, it would be an unpardonable folly for a great commercial nation to abandon the gold standard for the silver standard, except under the direst stress, still more when it has all the gold that it requires, and can with ease command more if needed.

DANGER IN ABRUPT CHANGE OF STANDARD.

But I think those who advocate free coinage have failed to measure the tremendous shock to the country in the abrupt shifting of standards so widely differing as they do to-day under the ratio in use.

---

* The gold coinage of the United States for the year ending June 30, 1894, amounted to $99,474,000, the largest in the history of the mint.

When the established ratio is based upon real values comparatively fixed as they once were, change of standard from gold to silver may only mean the abandonment of an efficient system for one inefficient and cumbersome. But where the ratio in use is false, as in the United States, change of standard means necessarily a radical change in the value of the monetary unit — a dollar is at once to have a value of 50 or 52 cents instead of one hundred cents.

It is a comparatively easy matter to come down the stairs of a ten story building, even if one is sharply pushed all the way, but to be pitched off the roof, involves considerations of danger from which the most courageous may well shrink. Yet that is just what it amounts to, by a simple act of legislation, to change the monetary unit to such an extent. Such an act of supreme folly has never yet been committed by any civilized or uncivilized nation. In every case where standards have been changed it has been, in fact, accomplished under the working of natural law, without abrupt change in values. Legislation has simply confirmed what has already practically existed. Difference in value was relatively slight and barely measurable, and, while often disturbing to a degree, such change has not been destructive, as it would be under present ratios.

England has become a gold country by a slight difference in the legal ratio by which silver was undervalued, and it left the country.

We became a gold country in precisely the same way. Under the ratio established in the act of April 2, 1792, the bullion value of silver in 1804 was greater than its full value as coined, and its coinage practically ceased. Up to 1834 we had theoretically a double standard, but in fact a gold standard. By the re-adjustment of this ratio not a dollar of legal tender silver was coined between 1804–1834; under the acts of June 28, 1834, and January 18, 1837, silver remained still, in a slight degree, more valuable as bullion than as coin, and left us theoretically still with a double standard, but in fact a gold standard. The difference was slight — reaching only two or three per cent, and that gradually, and without disturbance.

ABUNDANCE OF MONEY.

Do we need more money? The real supply of money is all the money in circulation wherever it may be. If this is accumulated in money centers, and any man cannot get it, it is because that which he has to offer in exchange for it is not wanted, or the world can get it somewhere else for less money. It may not be his fault, but there is no sentiment about it. No increase of a surplus already great, will enable those to get it who have not that to offer which the purchaser wants. If under conditions of ample supply, it is hoarded, or held from active use, or there is an unwillingness to buy or to invest, it is time to look for some other cause than that of scarcity. The world is full of schemes, unwise in purpose, projected upon an unsound basis, or defective in their assurance of security and revenue, which do not command the attention of the investor, the man who has money, whether a dollar or a thousand. Projectors instead of revising their schemes, are quite ready to cry scarcity of *money*, when the real scarcity is one of *credit.*

The final test of abundance of money is the *rate of interest.* Not for any particular month or year where exceptional causes may operate, but its general tendency towards increase or decrease. Taking this city as a center, let me cite the fact that within a generation a rate of ten per cent prevailed for years, then eight, then six. Now, on unquestioned security, five per cent is usual. Our State and city, within a generation, were compelled to pay seven per cent. Now a rate of four and even three and one-half per cent will command all the capital required.

Can money be scarce when such rates obtain on long time, and money can be had in abundance? Remember that while we all want money, no one wishes to keep it, if he can safely put it to use. The depositor of five or ten dollars in the savings bank is governed by precisely the same motive as the large capitalist, the desire for some return, and when large sums are accumulated as they are to-day in all the great cities of this country, and the lending rate in New York is only about two per cent per annum, and in Boston, Chicago, St. Louis, Baltimore, New Orleans, relatively as low, it is time to inquire whether unsettled confidence and credit is not the cause, and not the scarcity of money, and to take steps to re-establish rather than disturb it.

THE PER CAPITA TEST.

Taking all our currency together, we have now a per capita of about $25.50, the greatest in our history, and the greatest in the world except France. It is 30 per cent more than Great Britain; it is nearly 50 per cent more than Germany, nearly three times the per capita of Italy or Austria, more than four times that of Mexico, and two and a half times that of Canada, a prosperous country in commerce, manufactures and agriculture, not differing materially in its methods from our own. Taking our whole country together, we have more complete and rapid communication, more perfect personal and business relations, and the facilities for transfer of money to points where needed, surpassed by no nation on the face of the earth.

In the prosperous years 1867 to 1873, when prices of everything ruled high — cotton, wheat, corn, iron — our per capita of currency was $18.25. In the prosperous years 1879 to 1884, it was only $22.60.

Is it reasonable or sensible then to claim that with a currency per

capita of over $25.00, the largest in our history, our present ills are in
any degree due to a scarcity? May it not be worth while to remember
that this great increase in per capita since 1884 has been all in depreciated silver, which has threatened the integrity of the whole body of
our currency? Has not the quality of currency more to do in the matter
than the amount? Does not a reasonable fear of the quality account
for the inactivity which is mistaken for scarcity?

" But though there is an abundance of money in the East and the great
cities, we cannot get it in the West and South." Such a statement is too
general. There are many portions of the West and South, which can
command on public and private credit all the money they require, even
at the present time. But they are the portions where a high sense of
public and private credit prevails — where there is not a shadow of
doubt to the investor about the security and protection of his property
under the law. High sense of credit, by which I mean not great wealth,
but a general popular recognition of private right and public duty as
applied to property, will command money for all safe and legitimate
uses, everywhere, as well now as at any time.

Thousands of tons of silver in our currency at any ratio will not
change the conditions upon which money or capital will flow to or avoid
any section or State.

But, say our friends, gold has appreciated in value.* The monetary

---

* NOTE.— The world's product of gold for 1893 was $155,522,000 — larger
than the great product of 1853, when Australia and California were producing their largest yield. It will probably reach $175,000,000 this year. *See
Report of Director of the Mint.*

During the seven years since 1887, the annual gold product has increased
about 75 per cent, a rate far beyond that of population — or commercial
requirements. If prices have declined in the face of such an increased production of gold, the cause must be looked for elsewhere than in appreciation
of the value of that metal.

NOTE.— The *per capita* wealth of the country — the aggregate real and
personal property, is given by the census as follows:—

1850	1860	1870	1880	1890
$308	$514	$780	$870	$1039

These figures completely refute the charge that there has been any such
general shrinking in value, as would be caused by an appreciation of gold.
The increase has been the largest in the *Western States.* The classification as
given in the census shows the increase of wealth *per capita* in the decade
1880-90 was:—

For the whole country.................................. .... 19 per cent.
For the North Atlantic States.............................. .... 19 per cent.
For the South Atlantic States ....:........... 17 per cent.
For the North Central States...................................... 19 per cent.
For the South Central States.. 30 per cent.
For the Western States. ....74 per cent.
See Abstracts of Eleventh Census.

unit, the standard dollar of $25\frac{8}{10}$ grains, is worth more than formerly, and is steadily increasing in value.

I think I have shown that there is abundant reason to account for the depreciation of silver in the abnormal production. Prices of our chief commodities have fallen, it is said. But there can be no greater fallacy' in reasoning, than to select any one or two or three commodities, though important ones, and jump to the conclusion that if prices have fallen, the money in which prices are measured has become more valuable. Cannot we account for the fall in prices upon other adequate and sufficient grounds?*

It would take too long, in an address of this character, to go over all the tests and comparisons, and there are many, but there is adequate explanation of decline in the price of cotton and wheat, our great commodities, in the tremendous impetus given to their production over increased areas not only in this country, but in India, Russia, Egypt, Australia and the Argentine, all of which countries compete with us in the markets of Europe, operating together with the immense decline in the cost of transportation in our own and other countries, brought about by the unexampled construction of railways,† and the great increase of cheap steam transportation upon the ocean.

The gold supply of the world was estimated in 1885 at about 21,-207,000,000 marks,‡ over 5,000,000,000 dollars, held almost entirely in civilized countries of Europe and America, thus giving it great mobility. The supply is being increased about $150,000,000 annually. No country experiences a scarcity, and supplemented for commercial uses, as this supply is in all civilized countries, by sound and efficient banking systems, it is ample for the world's needs.

VALUE OF MONEY.

As the test of *abundance* is rate of interest, the one supreme test of *value* of money is the reward of labor, and that test applied, a day's labor is worth more in gold than at any previous period in the world's history.§ If gold had appreciated wages would have declined. A day's labor in this country can, to-day, not only command more gold, but can secure more for the gold. That cannot be said of any country in which the silver standard is established.

---

* NOTE.— A careful analysis of the situation, which space does not permit elaboration, leads to the conclusion that even agriculture, though affected most seriously in the great commodities of *cotton* and *wheat*, in which development has been most marked, has not in other respects materially suffered. *Corn, cattle, hogs, hay, oats, barley, rye, butter, cheese, potatoes,* have fairly maintained the average of prices of ten or fifteen years ago.

† Railway Mileage of the United States, 1880—87,801. 1890—163,562.

‡ Soetbeer, *Supply of Precious Metals, 1885.*

§ *See Senate Report, No. 986.*

To the laborer in every department of industry, the maintenance of our present monetary standard is of supreme importance. Even conceding that his wages would eventually be nominally higher if paid in a depreciated money, the processes of adjustment through which he must pass in the five or ten years of doubt, and distrust, would be destructive of every comfort, and involve the most serious interference with steady employment. Disordered finances in all countries and in all periods produce only idleness, poverty and suffering of the masses. The strong survive, and the weak go to the wall.

It is the unerring record of the history of depreciation in coin money, from whatever cause, that the poorer classes are those who suffer most. They are less able to understand the processes of decline, to anticipate and follow them to their logical results, in the complex re-adjustments of value which are inevitable. In all these adjustment processes, the capitalist indeed suffers, and by the capitalist I mean the owner of fifty or a hundred dollars in the savings bank or the shop or on the farm, as much as the owner of a thousand or many thousands, employed in the larger industrial works. But the capitalist will suffer less, his difficulties be less a hundredfold, than those of the laborer in any avocation. Fixed property can adjust itself far more quickly to cheap money than production. Commodities from the soil are always for immediate sale, and in the ordinary course must be sold. Fixed capital can wait more easily until values are established in new measures. The manufacturer may stop his machinery, the mine owner may leave his coal in the pit — his iron or lead or zinc in the earth, the fire may go out at the forges and furnaces, the ship remain anchored in the stream. Even through the dark and forbidding path of national bankruptcy, the processes of liquidation are slow and time is acquired. But the products of the soil and labor must inevitably accept from day to day all the fluctuations and uncertain rates that obtain. They are helpless and cannot wait.

THE IMMEDIATE NEED.

At no time in the history of the nation, in my judgment, has public duty pointed the patriot citizen more clearly and unmistakably in one direction, than it does to-day to the effort to secure a comprehensive reform of our whole currency system, and its establishment upon a sound, safe and enduring basis. We need, not a patching up, we have had enough of that, but a full, adequate and complete reformation. No part of our country needs it more than the West and South.

Will it advance the prices of wheat, and corn, and cotton, and iron, and lead, and cattle, and lumber?

Will it increase the wages of labor, the earnings of industry in all its forms?

Immediately and directly — No. Eventually — Yes, as surely as the summer rains assure an abundant harvest.

No legislation will at once enable us to get as much per pound for 10,000,000 bales of cotton as we got for 7,000,000, as much per ton for 6,000,000 tons of iron as we got for 4,000,000, or so much per ounce for two thousand tons of silver as we got for one thousand tons.

But there cannot be, there never will be, a restoration of public credit and confidence, promoting that increased consumption, upon which price depends, until a sound and settled currency system gives that stability, which lies at the very foundation of all prosperity. Give it to the nation and hope will return.

The silent wheels will surely move again, the mine deliver its wealth of coal and iron, more precious far than its gold or silver. The capital of the world, now abundant everywhere, but idle and waiting its opportunity, will gain new courage for new adventure here in the great West. New enterprises will spring into being, to call for the work of thousands of busy hands, whose earned reward of honest labor will promote increased consumption in a hundred varied ways.

We shall have such a currency system in the end, some day or other — in some way or other. The problem confronting us now, is simply whether it is to be reached by a wise, courageous, conscientious and thorough study of question, availing ourselves of the costly experience of our own and other nations, or through a general financial convulsion, leading to national bankruptcy, from which, poorer in wealth, but richer in experience, our children may build anew. Upon the courage, patience and wisdom of this people, which never yet have failed it, the answer depends.

There can be no greater national folly than to disturb an *established* standard, to willfully launch out upon an unknown sea of disturbed values, whose farther shore no human vision can penetrate.

I believe that we shall not do so. Our people can be made to see the truth, to know the danger, as it is written over and over again in the world's history. That history contains no page so undisputed as that upon which is told the trial and trouble, the loss, distress and suffering, brought about by conditions wherein uncertainty of value has pervaded the currency of the nation. The great truth can be brought home to our people, and to know the danger, is to avoid it.

In the closing years of the Seventeenth Century, England experienced all the derangements of trade brought about by a disturbance in the value of its silver. The decline had not been occasioned by decreased market value per ounce, as in the present case, but by the steady wear and constant clipping of the silver coins in use. The result, however, was the same. Real *value* of the coin was disturbed. Twenty-one shillings in silver coin was not worth a guinea in gold as the law declared. Twenty-five or thirty of these debased shillings were required to buy a guinea sterling.

Macaulay in one of his most graphic chapters (chapter 21) depicts the situation.   I cannot forbear quoting a few paragraphs.

"Whether Whigs or Tories, Protestants or Jesuits were uppermost, the grazier drove his beast to market; the cream overflowed the pails of Cheshire: the apple juice foamed in the presses of Herefordshire: the piles of crockery glowed in the furnaces of the Trent: and the barrows of coal rolled fast along the timber railways of the Tyne. But when the great instrument of Exchange became thoroughly deranged, all trade, all industry, were smitten as with a palsy. * * * The evil was felt daily and hourly in almost every place, and by almost every class: in the dairy and on the threshing floor, by the anvil and by the loom, on the billows of the ocean and in the depths of the mine. Nothing could be purchased without a dispute. Over every counter there was wrangling from morning to night. The workman and his employers had a quarrel as regularly as the Saturday came round. On a fair day or a market day, the clamors, the reproaches, the taunts, the curses, were incessant; and it was well if no booth was overturned, and no heads broken. No merchant would contract to deliver goods without making some stipulation about the quality of the coin in which he was to be paid. Even men of business were often bewildered by the confusion into which all pecuniary transactions were thrown. The simple and the careless were pillaged without mercy by the extortioners whose demands grew even more rapidly than the money shrank. The price of the necessaries of life, of shoes, of ale, of oatmeal, rose fast. The laborer found that the bit of metal, which, when he received it, was called a shilling, would hardly, when he wanted to purchase a pot of beer, or a loaf of rye bread, go as far as a sixpence. The ignorant and helpless were cruelly ground between one class which would give money only by tale, and another would take it only by weight."

It is a warning, — may it not be a prophecy.

In the physical world we seek to discover natural law, and by making our human actions conform, we compel the great forces of nature to be our servants.   Steam, fire, electricity, the winds, the rivers, the ocean, co-operate in promoting our purpose.   If we neglect to conform, they break forth in wide-spread destruction.   It is just as true in the economic world.   There is a natural law founded in our human nature.   It has been worked out, and defined by ages of costly experience.   We may recognize it in our legislation and make it our constant friend and helper.   Antagonized or ignored, it will break the flimsy web of human legislation as surely as flood, and fire, the lightning or the cyclone, break the puny barriers which human hands have reared.   Disaster will follow in the wake of the broken laws of commerce, just as surely as prosperity and smiling peace will bless their observance.

No sentiment, however elevated, not impulse, however generous, not local interest, however commendable, not eloquence, however impressive, but truth alone

" *is still the light,*
To guide the nations groping on their way."

(Applause).

PRESIDENT WHITMORE: As Chairman of the Executive Committee, I desire to state that the programme this evening includes an address by Congressman Bryan, of Nebraska, and Ex-Governor Anthony, of Kansas. Those gentlemen have both come here at the express invitation of the committee, for this express purpose, and while the programme will have to be somewhat curtailed, owing to the lateness of the hour, the committee trusts that the audience will remain until the programme is completed (calls for " Bryan, Bryan ").

THE CHAIRMAN: Ladies and gentlemen, members of the Congress, it is my pleasure, and my duty as well as my pleasure, to present to you the Hon. Wm. J. Bryan, who will now address you upon the money question of the day.

MR. BRYAN'S ADDRESS.

Mr. Chairman, Ladies and Gentlemen, Fellow-Citizens: In half an hour, and in half an hour only, I am expected to say what is to be said for the silver cause to-night. I am glad that this meeting of the Trans-Mississippi Congress is held in the city of St. Louis. My attention has been called to the fact that in this city, and not very far from the place where we now meet, the transfer was made which gave to this nation what was known as the " Louisiana Purchase," wherein most of the States of the Trans-Mississippi country are located. In this city, where that purchase was finally consummated, in this city which sits at the gateway of the west, we have met to-day in convention, to discuss the interests of this great section of the Union.

The gentleman who has preceded me has done the silver cause a favor which I only wish all our opponents would do us. (Laughter.) He has boldly advocated what few of them will dare to declare to be their purpose. Our great difficulty has been that we have had to face foes in the dark and have had to tear the masks from hypocrites before we could recognize our enemies. We have been compelled to face men who have pretended love for the cause of bi-metallism, while they stabbed it to the death. But I rejoice that to-night we have heard from an opponent who holds before you the glittering hope of an universal gold standard! He holds out no promise of international bi-metallism, no hope for silver, but says that natural laws are driving out the white metal and bringing an intelligent world to the use of gold as the only real money — unless, possibly, silver can be used as pennies and nickels are now. That is the issue, my friends. That is the issue which gives us this great Trans-Mississippi Congress; it is the issue which comes before the people of the United States; it is the issue which comes before the whole civilized world, and men are taking one side or the other of this great question, the question of a single or a double standard for the human race.

I call your attention — I must speak briefly and very hurriedly — to the fact that there is a difference between the interests of men on this subject. We sometimes listen to men who talk as if most of us were sordid and base and selfish, but that God had raised up a few unselfish financiers to spread light before the ignorant. Who are these unselfish men who would teach us what a sound currency is? My friends, there are differences between the interests of people in this world, in this country, and even in this city. Let me call attention to what great men have said, because it might be presumptuous to give my opinion only against the opinion of a financier. Let me tell you what men have said, whose names you know and whose opinions you respect. Let me read you what Mr. Blaine said about the destruction of silver, my friends, because it is the destruction of silver we are to meet now — it is not international bi-metallism. It is not the restoration of silver, delayed for a little while, but it is the complete destruction of silver that we have to face (reading). "The destruction of silver as money must have a ruinous effect upon all forms of property, except those investments which yield a fixed return in money. These would be enormously enhanced in value and would gain a disproportionate and unfair advantage over every other species of property."

My friends, a moneyed man is as good as anybody else, but I challenge any man to prove before an intelligent audience that a moneyed man is not as selfish as any other man. Mr. Blaine says that the destruction of silver as money would give to those who have fixed investments an enormous advantage, that it would enormously enhance the value of their property, and that they would gain a disproportionate and unfair advantage over other kinds of property and over people owning other kinds of property. Do you believe, therefore, that every man who tells you he wants silver destroyed is an unselfish patriot, and wants it destroyed in the interest of all the people? Or, can you not believe, from what you know of men, that they may be selfish and that their desire to destroy silver may be due to the fact that they know that when they do it, they will gain an unfair advantage over other people?

Let me read you what another statesman has said (reading): —

"The contraction of the currency is a far more distressing operation than Senators suppose. To every person, except a capitalist out of debt, or a salaried officer, it is a policy fraught with bankruptcy and disaster." That is the language of Senator Sherman. To every one except a capitalist out of debt, that is the excepted class. If it is the capitalist out of debt who will be exempt from the dangers of bankruptcy and, by the rise of the value of the dollar will gain an advantage — we may ask, is he entirely unselfish in advising the destruction of silver? Mr. Sherman tells you that the capitalist is interested in the destruction of silver, because he gains by it. Let me read from another authority: Mr. Carlisle said in 1878, "According to my view of the subject, the conspiracy which seems to have been formed here and in Europe" — how mildly my friend (Mr. Leighton) spoke of the changes in Germany and other countries — Mr. Carlisle says, "The conspiracy which seems to have been formed here and in Europe to destroy by legislation and otherwise, from three-fourths to one-half of the silver money of the world" — is what? National law? No! He said, it was "the most gigantic crime of this or any other age."

My friends, have you ever tried to select the most gigantic crime recorded in the pages of history? Try it, and then think that this conspiracy formed in this country and in Europe, is the most gigantic crime of all. But Mr. Carlisle did not stop there. He says, "The consummation of this scheme would ultimately entail more misery upon the human race than all the wars, pentilences and famines that ever occurred in the history of the world." (Applause.)

Yet, my friends, we are told that "cheap money" gives to the "demagogue" a chance. We are told that to advocate the restoration of the gold and silver coinage of the constitution, is to put one's self upon the plane of the ignoramus, the man who does not know anything about economic truth or financial principles, or if he does, does not tell you what he thinks!

Why have we met here to-night? Why has this convention been called? I believe one of the great reasons for it, is that the people of this Trans-Mississippi country believe what Mr. Carlisle said and that they are trying to prevent a misery which would be greater than war, pestilence and famine. Be not deceived. As I said, we are to be congratulated that the issue has been clearly outlined, for now we are on ground where we can fight, with the authority of the great statesmen who have spoken upon this subject. We are told that it is natural now to eliminate silver. The advocates of silver are simply seeking the application of natural laws to our financial system — that is all. I have noticed in my short life, that He who made and planned all things has planned more wisely than we can, and that by following natural laws we will come nearer to the truth than by following laws of man's making (applause).

The Creator, as infinite in love as in power, has supplied legitimate means for the gratification of every human need. When He implanted in man's body the desire for food He scattered over the face of the earth an abundance with which to satisfy his hunger; when He gave him thirst He filled the ground with veins of water and planted living springs along the hillsides; when He permitted weariness to creep over the limbs of the toiler He sent sleep, "Tired nature's sweet restorer," to renew his strength; when He gave to man a mind capable of development and filled it with a yearning for knowledge He placed within his reach the means of instruction and surrounded him with opportunities for study ; and when He made man a social being, fitted him for companionship with his fellows, and fashioned the channels of trade, He stored away in the mountains the gold and silver needed for the world's currency.

I may be in error, but in my humble judgment he who would rob man of his necessary food, or pollute the springs at which he quenches his thirst, or steal away from him his accustomed rest, or condemn his mind to the gloomy night of ignorance, is no more an enemy of his race than the man who, deaf to the entreaties of the poor, and blind to the suffering he would cause, seeks to destroy one of the money metals given by the Almighty to supply the needs of commerce. (Prolonged apylause.)

And yet, my friends, we who ask that God's laws shall be observed and his bounties used, are told that we are suggesting an innovation. On the contrary, he who advocates a gold standard, turns back the history of six thousand years. He who would tell you to-day that the world has outgrown gold and silver, must tell you that for thousands of years mankind has labored in the dark and only saw the light when the conspiracy was formed " here and in Europe to destroy by legislation and otherwise one-half of the world's metallic money."

My friend said that if we had a sound and elastic currency, a bank currency, that we would be all right — that the banks are safer than they used to be. I wish the gentleman would go to Lincoln, Nebraska, and tell the depositors in the Capitol National Bank that banking is safer now than it used to be. You can scarcely pick up a newspaper but you find that some trusted employe has robbed the bank ; and yet, in the Baltimore plan, we are told if we want a good, sound currency, we must let the bank issue money to one-half of their capital stock and let the government guarantee it. I believe you once had a man in this State, who undertook at times, the collecting of the fares on the railroads — came along sometimes and stopped the train and collected the fares. (Laughter.) I suppose he thought he could do it better than the conductor could. And, my friends, I want to impress upon you the fact, that the underlying purpose that actuated Jesse James, is the same purpose that actuates the demand for a bank of issue. (Cheers and applause.) Now, when I say that, I do not mean to compare a banker to Jesse James. (Laughter.) What purpose actuated Jesse James? It was the desire for money. What is the purpose of the bank that desires to issue paper money? It is the desire for the profit; that is all. It is the love of money. The love of money, we are told, is the root of all evil, and it is the duty of government to lessen the evil as much as it can.

Jesse James sought money in violation of law, the bank of issue seeks money through the aid of friendly legislation.

I was passing through Iowa, not long ago, and I saw some hogs rooting in a field, and it took me back to the time when I lived on a farm and when we used to put rings in the noses of the hogs — not to keep them from getting fat, but to keep them from destroying more property than they were worth, while they were fattening. Now, my friends, an idea is the greatest thing a man can get into his head, and we gather our ideas from everywhere; from an urchin upon the street we may gather an idea that will turn the course of a life. From those hogs, rooting in the the field, I got an idea that will never leave me as long as I live, and that is, that one of the duties of the government is to put rings in the noses of the hogs. (Laughter.) And, my friends, when I say this, I mean no reflection upon anybody, because we are all hoggish. (Laughter.) I want to admit for the silver miner — I am not one, I never was one and never expect to be one — I want to admit that he is selfish and likes to see silver go up, just as well as the farmer likes to see hogs grow fat. The farmer keeps his hogs in a pen, goes out and looks at them and sees them growing fat. He is selfish, but we do not condemn him, it is natural. Some men keep their money in a pen, they go and look at it and see it getting fat. I do not believe that a financier who watches his dollars grow fatter every day is any worse than the farmer who watches his hogs growing fat, but he is as apt to enjoy the sight. But they object to any man who owns a mine saying a word about silver; they say he is selfish, and only wants silver used because it brings him a profit. May not the financiers have a selfish interest in the legislation he advocates? Our financial legislation has been controlled for twenty-five years by gold men, who have reaped where they did not sow, who have been able to gather in more than they are entitled to, who have been securing a dollar of ever increasing size.

Now, you will have to restore silver, my friends; there is not enough gold to do the world's business with. My friend talks about the supply of gold. You might as well try to clothe a man in the garment of an infant, you might as well try to feed a grown person upon the food of a child, as to attempt to supply a great nation with the money that was sufficient for a small nation. It is only four years since Mr. Sherman said, we required about fifty millions a year to keep pace even with population, and population is not the only factor to be considered. He considered it required something like fifty millions then. Where is it coming from? They repealed the Sherman law and have not added other money to the circulation. The National Bank circulation is less than it was a year ago. But some say that we have enough money now and do not need any more. They remind me of my father-in-law's assurance.   When I was married, he said, " William, while I have, we shall not both of us want."   (Laughter.)

Yes, my friends, while they have plenty, *all* will not want!   What do some of them know about lack of money?   A man who has a full pocket does not always sympathize with the one who does not know where the next meal is coming from.   What is their test of plenty? Why, interest is low, they say, therefore, money must be too abundant. It has been shown over and over again by the advocates of bi-metallism that a low rate of interest may be, because, with on appreciated dollar, all enterprise being unprofitable there is no man who can afford to borrow money.   Money stays in bank idle; the rate of interest is low; and yet they tell us that is proof positive that we have plenty money in the country.

We are gradually throughout the world approaching the gold standard.   Every step of the legislation for the last twenty years has been to increase the demand upon gold and as it increases the demand upon it — it is a natural law, the law of supply and demand — it increases the purchasing power of each dollar.   And what is the result?   Other prices fall.   My friend tells you that gold has not risen, that a dollar has not appreciated.   I need not discuss that question with him; I will point him to the Royal Commission of England, and to the monetary Commission of Germany, which admitted that gold has risen; I point him to any man who is not interested himself in the appreciation of money, and he will tell him that the value of the dollar has risen.   We think we have had hard times — we have only commenced.   Just a few nations have demanded gold and the result is that gold has been made more precious and misery is on the increase.   What will be the result when we drive India to the gold standard and her 250,000,000 of people reach out after their share of the world's gold? what will be the result when we drive China to the gold standard and her almost countless millions reach out after their share of the gold?   We simply put the world's gold on an auction block and the people stand round and bid. (Applause.)

My friend says that the laboring men will suffer from the free coinage of silver.   What do they themselves say?   We give the ballot to the individual because we know that nobody can look after his interests as well as he can himself.   What do the laboring men say when speaking for themselves?   Why, they have recently sent a petition to Congress, signed by the leaders of all the labor organizations of the United States, demanding the free coinage of silver at 16 to 1, and I appeal to the laboring men themselves, to learn what they want, rather than to those who assume to speak for them.

But, my time is up, I think; I only have two or three minutes (cries of " Go on, Go on "").   No, my friends, Governor Anthony has to follow me and it would not be fair for me to encroach upon his time.

I will take about two minutes more. Now, there are two or three phases of the question, and I wish I had an hour on each. (Cries of "Take an hour.") Not now, we will have some time to discuss this question when it comes up on the resolutions and I may have a chance to speak them. There are three suggestions which I have to make: as to ratio, quantity and independent action. There is no prominent advocate of free coinage who is advocating any ratio but 16 to 1. If you have it at all, you will have to take it at 16 to 1. Will you have unlimited coinage, or a limited coinage? My friends, true bi-metallism means that the value of a dollar shall be regulated not by artificial laws, but by natural laws of supply and demand, and that every ounce of gold and silver that comes from the mines shall be permitted to go into the currency. I am in favor, not only of the free coinage of silver, but of the unlimited coinage of silver at the ratio of 16 to 1. Our opponents are great obstructive statesmen, but they are not constructive statesmen. They find fault but do not propose to restore silver at any ratio or in any way. They simply object to what others propose. And now the last question. Shall we act alone, or wait for some foreign nation to help us?—that, my friends, is, perhaps, the most immediate question we have to face. Most of our enemies to-day call themselves international bi-metallists. Mr. Hendricks of Brooklyn, in a recent speech in Congress, said that if we would repeal the Sherman law, in three months England would be asking us for an international agreement. The Sherman law was repealed. You remember the prosperity that followed? (Laughter.) We waited three months and England did not come; we waited three months longer, and three months longer, and now we have waited a year and England has not come, and we are still patiently waiting. These are the people who do not want bi-metallism at all. They tell you the gold standard is the natural standard, and that it must come.

I appeal to your patriotism. If we have some in this country who know more about the sunny skies of Italy than about the invigorating breezes of the Western prairies and who receive their inspiration from other lands, let it be known that there are people between the Alleghanies and the Golden Gate who are willing to trust their all to this Republic and rise or fall with it. And these people, whom we represent, though delayed over and over again, are contending for the restoration of the gold and silver coinage of the Constitution, and are ready to declare now in favor of the immediate restoration of the free and unlimited coinage of gold and silver at the present ratio of 16 to 1 without waiting for the aid or consent of any other nation on earth (applause and loud cheers).

THE CHAIRMAN: Before introducing the next speaker, I desire to ·make an announcement. The Conference on Free Coinage will have a meeting to-morrow morning at nine o'clock, at the Southern Hotel. All friends of free coinage are invited to meet them there.

I now have the pleasure of introducing to you, Governor Anthony, of Kansas, who will also speak on the Silver Question.

ADDRESS OF GOV. ANTHONY.

Mr. President, and Gentlemen of the Congress: I arise before you to-night under a heavy burden, a darker cloud of embarrassment than ever rested upon me before at the entrance upon a like undertaking. You·have been listening for hours to able, wise men; and I may say, with no intended disrespect, to plausible, ingenious men, on the pending subject of discussion,—the free and unlimited coinage of silver at the mints of the United States. You have just been held to this late hour of the night by the matchless eloquence of the orator and statesman of Nebraska, Congressman Bryan, who has woven a web of sympathy about you until some of this great audience have clamored for him to continue, and occupy the time allotted to me. To follow him, and his almost irresistible attractions of the finished orator, is indeed an embarrassing task. But, gentlemen, there are mitigating circumstances that greatly reduce my fears, and put me quite at ease. You will all remember that Mr. Bryan was the late candidate of two political parties in his State for United States Senator, on a distinctively free silver platform. They designated him in separate conventions to go out as their trusted representative. In this capacity he went from schoolhouse to schoolhouse, from rostrum to rostrum, all over his State, with an appeal, a portion of which you have heard from him here to-night, for free and unlimited coinage of silver, as the cure for all their financial ills.

Responding to an invitation from citizens of Nebraska, it came to be my lot to follow the rhetoric and captivating eloquence of Mr. Bryan, as I am called upon to do to-night, with my plain, prosy statement of great fundamental truths. Since then the people of Mr. Bryan's State have passed upon the merits of his contention for free silver, and decided, by some 15,000 majority, that they do not want him as an advocate of financial heresies to misrepresent them in the counsels of the nation. It is not alone my own judgment, but a sublime faith in the ultimate fruits of wisdom in the common people, that gives me courage to speak to you as I shall speak to-night.

It were not strange that you should be nettled and weary from what you seem to have borne with such close attention since early this afternoon, and until this late hour. You have been fairly stuffed with statistics and crammed with figures, foreign and domestic. You have had comparison of weights and measures, of weights and measures of substance and value, and all woven together with strings of silver and strands of gold, in a fabric as wide as the world and as long as time. Indeed, at the close of that wonderful address of my friend, Governor Prince, I was so full of figures that I could feel them struggling to get out through the skin all over me. I am not sure that each of you was not near the fate of the poor man who trifled with a new invention. Your time is too valuable to waste upon amusing stories, but this one seems so pertinent and illustrative that it must be told.

It was down on that portion of the Massachusetts coast where the herring-fish is the chief food of the people, and you who have tried to gather sustenance for the body from the bones of this fearfully and wonderfully made fish will understand how they had to work for a living. An inventive genius came to their relief by the construction of a machine to eat herring with. They put the fish in a hopper, and on turning a crank the bones went out one way, and the meat into one's mouth the other way. The inventor was fairly canonized as a public benefactor, no one dreaming that so innocent and valuable a device could work harm to any one. But there came up to it one day a hungry, left-handed man, put his mouth to it and seizing the crank with his left hand, turned it the wrong way, and it filled him so full of bones that his clothes could not be taken off, and they had to bury him robed as he fell (laughter). Governor Prince, and the young gentleman from Colorado who preceded him, seem to have taken the statistical crank with their left hands, and turned it the wrong way, giving their hungry listeners bones instead of meat, leaving us in a condition hardly better than the victim of the herring machine (applause).

Be assured that your miseries shall not be further magnified in this direction. You shall not be asked to follow me in meaningless mathematical combinations to confuse, nor in the mazy wilderness of theory and speculation to bewilder and mislead you. It is my ambition to bring the business proposition of the free and unlimited coinage of silver by our mints, at the ratio of 16 of silver to 1 of gold, to the test of common sense, the common solvent to which this and all kindred questions must in the end be submitted for solution and settlement. Neither appeals to interest and passion, resort to sophistry and eloquence, nor the quoting of what some impassioned theorist has said about it in Great Britain, or anywhere else, can aid you in passing a correct judgment, or protect our country from the results of unwise action on so great a problem.

First and fundamentally, then, let us find what the duties and powers of the government are in this relation. It will be admitted that the power of a government cannot be greater than that of the source from which it is derived, and that the sources of governmental power are, and ever must be, limited to three. First. The power of might, of superior physical force. This is a form of despotism based on the theory that might makes right, and that the strong may rule the weak because they can do so. Second. The divine right of rule, a theocratic government, based upon the assumption that man is incapable of maintaining or governing himself, and is dependent upon his Creator, God, for both care and control, under a crowned ruler, divinely ordained and set above human impeachment or dictation. Our government is based upon the third, and only remaining theory: Self-government, absolute sovereignty in the enfranchised citizen, as the unit of governmental power, and a majority of these units of original power the ruling monarch, charged with every duty and responsibility involved in the framing and administration of human enactment in the form of law. It is based upon the claim that the human race is endowed with the attributes of wisdom, justice and mercy, equal to their own government and regulation as communities, and provided with ability and industrial impulse equal to self-care and maintenance as individuals. In brief, we have anchored a government in a belief that every human being, in normal development, is a self-governing, self-supporting entity; requiring no outside power to control, no intervening paternalism to support; that all the government required or justified relates to community interests and their regulation and control; and that "all just powers of government are derived from the consent of the governed themselves," as expressed in the Immortal Declaration of the fathers and founders of it.

As a matter of immovable fact, then, this government had no original existence, no inherent power resting on the law of superior might, or of divine right. It was called into existence as the agent of the people to meet an admitted necessity of community life. Its every power is a delegated, representative power; an inherent power of the individual, surrendered voluntarily to the government for community use. The government of the United States has no power, no prerogative or privilege, in peace or in war, that is not inherent and absolute in the individual citizen for his use in the maintenance of himself, in his right to "life, liberty and the pursuit of happiness." The government is but the aggregation of the surrendered powers of the individual citizens included in the governmental compact, and when it attempts to go beyond this it is usurpation — revolution. The citizen is not the waif to be cared for under the obligation of paternalism by the government, but the government is the thing created, a helpless child of the people, to be fed, cared for and protected by them.

Bear with me in an illustration or two, showing that our government in its sphere of duty is but the peer of the citizen in his, and must be governed by the rules and limitations fixed by the natural rights of the individual. If on to-morrow the government comes to this city to trade in, or purchase, property, does it come with any prestige or privilege relating to such transactions not common to every one in this city and country? It wants cloth, and finds it on sale. The merchant asks a dollar a yard for it; the government offers fifty cents, which is refused; whereupon the accredited officer of the government says to him: " By authority and direction of the Govern-. ment of the United States I command you, sir, to deliver this cloth at the price it has offered you." Does the merchant obey this command? No, he simply tells the Government to " get out " and give room for other customers. But cloth is finally found and price mutually determined, the invoice calling for a thousand dollars. The officer writes on a slip of paper: " Due the bearer hereof one thousand dollars " and signs it by authority of the Government. The merchant refuses to accept it, saying: " My goods are cash, pay me money, or if you want them on time, that period must be fixed and expressed, together with a rate of interest until it matures and is paid." The government then assumes the power claimed for it by our free-silver-fiat friends, and hands out another bit of paper, silver or alluminium, on which is engraved or printed the legend: " This is one thousand dollars, its value created by act of Congress, without regard to the value of the material from which it is made; without promise or obligation to pay, and a full legal-tender for all debts and obligations, public and private." Signed: " Carlyle, Secretary of the Treasury."

How long would it take the merchant to again tell the Government to " get out, " and if met by insolence to put him out? Not a minute! He would fall back upon the fundamental fact that the Government can no more make something out of nothing, and make that nothing a legal-tender, than can he, or any other citizen, do the same thing. True it is, that in assuming this attitude the merchant incurs the risk of being classed by Mr. Bryan with " gold bugs," but it will be found that this government will not be one-half strong enough to " put a ring in his nose " as the distinguished statesman suggested should be done (applause and laughter).

But you may have been startled at the declaration, that the war power of the government is a delegated power, original in the citizen, with the right to use it at all times for the protection of himself, and under precisely the same conditions prescribed for its use by the government for the people, as a political body. Let us see, Mr. President: If I invade your premises unbidden by you, I am a trespasser; if I take from those premises property without your consent, I am a thief; if I break its fastenings and enter your house by force in your absence, I am a burglar; and over against each of these lawless acts is set a heavy penalty for my punishment. But, sir, if my life is put in danger by the assault of man or beast, I can then seek your premises for protection, and am not a trespasser; I may take any article or thing found of yours on those premises, for my defense, and am not a thief; and if need be I can break down your doors and make your house a castle for my defense, and I am not a burglar. And why? Because the paramount duty of man is to protect that which is paramount in man — his own life; and before that duty, the right and all considerations of property ownership and use must give way. This is the war power of the individual, in its relation to the property rights of others; and here is the source and origin of the war power of the United States of America; a delegated power for public use. When the life of the nation is assailed by foes without or within, then it may come to your merchants for their goods; to the farmer for his grain and animals; to the toiler for his labor, and it need not higgle about prices or terms of pay, but take that which it finds and needs, to be settled and paid for as best can be done when the danger is passed and the life of the government saved from peril. Again, let me say, that every power and prerogative of a republic must respond to, and come as a trust from, the individual, environed by the same law of limitation that governs their use in the hands of their original possessor.

No one will, I think, question this analysis of popular government, nor dispute the source and limitation of its powers as I have defined them. Now let us put this proposed governmental scheme of free and unlimited coinage of gold and silver into legal-tender money, at a fixed ratio of sixteen to one, to the test of comparison with the right and power of the government to put it into execution.

On May 20th, 1890, Senator Jones, of Nevada, in addressing the Senate upon this subject, said of coin money: —

"Its value does not arise from the intrinsic qualities which the material of which it is made may possess, but depends entirely on the intrinsic qualities which law or general consent may confer."

About the same time Senator Peffer said: —

"It matters not of what money is made, or what its intrinsic value is. What gives value to the coins is law, nothing else."

Here antipodes meet in agreement as to facts, but in irreconcilable antagonism as to results desired. Senator Jones seeks refuge behind this definition of the word money, in the interest of a silver-producing constituency, and to the end that the government might take from them a half dollar's worth of silver, or less, and declare it a legal-tender dollar, when coined and returned to them, free of charge or cost for coinage. Senator Peffer was airing one of his fiat money vagaries, in the interest of a debtor constituency. The one a cool, calculating schemer for personal gain, at the ultimate cost of the people, the other an unbalanced theorist, seeking to escape honest obligations through legislative jugglery. The one a silver *monometallist*, the other a silver *destructionist*. Oh, what a consistent pair of twins for government adoption (applause).

Each of these gentlemen has doubtless grown in the grace of socialistic despotism since these utterances. But as to this, Senator Peffer has not left us in doubt, as we may learn by reference to the Congressional Record. On August 16th, 1893, Mr. Peffer introduced Senate Bill No. 486, from which I read : —

"Whereas, a nation that can make good bonds can make better money; and Whereas, a nation that can make a dollar on gold can make another dollar on alluminum, or on paper; and Whereas, a nation that won't or can't pay its debts has no right to exist on earth; and Whereas, Congress can coin money to pay its debts in six months. Therefore, be it enacted, that the Secretary of the Treasury be directed to prepare six hundred million dollars ($600,000,000) of declaratory, not promissory — full, not partial — legal-tender money of this republic, of various denominations, on sheets of alluminum or silk-threaded paper, as the people may prefer, and then forthwith call all the outstanding interest-bearing bonds of the United States for immediate redemption, and pay for them with this said surplus money."

Again on Oct. 6th, 1893, Mr. Peffer introduced Senate Bill No. 1050, from which I read the following : —

"Sec. 3. Gold and silver shall be coined at the mints of the republic, at a ratio of one in gold to sixteen in silver."
"Sec. 4. The Secretary of the Treasury shall *coin* a sufficient amount of full legal-tender *paper money* to make up the sum of six billion dollars ($6,000,000,-000) and cover the same into the treasury."

You may be curious to know for what purpose this trifling sum of paper money was to be *coined*, and how made available to the people. Here you have it, in the section following : —

"That the sum of six hundred million dollars ($600,000,000) be appropriated to each of the States and Territories, in pro rata ratio to inhabitants, for public improvements; and all persons offering their services to any State or Territory shall be given employment at four dollars ($4.00) per day of eight hours work."

As I have said, I do not know whether Senator Jones has kept pace with Senator Peffer or not, nor do I know whether the free silver advocates in this Congress are ripe as this yet, or not. But, gentlemen, it is the logic of the situation, the end to which the doctrine of free and

unlimited coinage will surely carry you.   If it is within the province
and power of this government to coin and certify a piece of metal as a
dollar, and send it out as a legal tender, that contains metal worth a
single cent less than a dollar — as uncoined metal, a commodity in the
open markets of the world — without accompanying it with a pledge of
redemption, then Senator Peffer is right when he says, that "a government that can make a dollar on gold, can make another dollar on
alluminum or paper."   Then it becomes senseless, idiotic, to mine
gold or silver, to be wasted in coinage, when the substitution of alluminum and paper for coinage will give us coin-money of equal value
with those precious metals.   Then the declaration of one of the leading journals sustaining free coinage and fiat paper money, in my State,
will become axiomatic.   It said: —

"The monumental idiocy of the age is in the fact that governments have
been foolish enough to borrow money, instead of making it."

But this definition of money as the creation of law, instead of the
embodiment or pledge of value, together with all the fatal financial
fallacies and false hopes to which it leads, can find no support in reason, nor justification in the genius of our government or the constitution of our country.   Noah Webster, who has never been suspected of
having mining interests or fiat money fallacies to prejudice him, gave
this simple and comprehensive definition of the word, "Money:"
"Wealth, affluence."
My contention is that all money, whether possessory or promissory,
that is made a legal-tender by force of law, must come up to this definition.   It must be "wealth, affluence."   It must either be coined
from a metal the purchasing power of which, by reason of its intrinsic
value as a commodity on the market, will be and remain co-equal with
its legal-tender, debt-paying power; or, it must be in the form of a
bill of credit, a promise to pay and redeem in money of possessory
value on demand.   To make such promissory notes worthy of confidence, and to justify their use as representative money, "wealth,
affluence" must be put in escrow, ample for their redemption, the
government, National or State, becoming the custodian of such security.
Lawful money, then, must consist of value within and of itself; coin
money, the material of which is worth as much as the coin itself, and
therefore requiring no intervening obligation for its redemption, or it
may be evidence of debt in the form of a promise to redeem on demand, dollar for dollar, in self-redeeming, coin money.
This government has no right, no power short of usurpation, to issue
coined money as a legal tender without its expressed value being contained
in the material of which it is made; nor to authorize the issue of credit
money without "affluence" — abundant wealth — held in trust for its

certain and prompt redemption. It may coin "tokens" for use as change-money, with less intrinsic than nominal value, such as the copper cent and nickel five-cent tokens and subsidiary coins, their legal-tender qualities being limited and their redemption provided for in the law authorizing their coinage. Beyond this it cannot go.

The wise and thoughtful men who framed our Constitution foresaw the necessity of a fixed and uniform standard of weight and measure in the interchange of property and commodities. They recognized also the equal necessity of a like measure of the value of property and commodity in such exchanges. Hence, in Sec. 8, Art. 1, of that instrument, they gave to Congress the power " to coin money, regulate the value thereof, and of foreign coins, and fix the standard of weights and measures." This means, if it means anything, that Congress was to provide a fixed unit of distance, weight, bulk and value, to be accepted and respected by all the people in their trade relations. Then why was the power to "regulate" one of these measures given, and withheld from the others, when all of them were required to be fixed measures in order to meet the demands of their creation? The answer is plain and simple. The measure of distance and substance could be "fixed" by reason of the rigidity and steadfastness of the material of which they were made. A yard stick would always measure a yard; the bushel measure would always hold a bushel, and the pound weight, weigh a pound in the balance. But value was an immaterial thing, an unknown and variable quantity, depending upon laws and conditions beyond the power of governments to enact or control. They believed, as I do, that a stick with which to measure a yard must be as long as the legal unit of measure it was made to determine; that a peck measure must contain a peck; a pound weight weigh a pound, and the measure of a dollar in value must possess a dollar of value. They never . dreamed that value could be measured without value in the measure, more than distance could be measured without length in the rod or chain it was measured by. Hence the power to "to regulate the value thereof, and of foreign coins." It was to fix a measure of value from the most stable commodity known, so regulated as to have a coincident commercial and legal value; and to regulate the value of foreign coin by determining the relative weight and fineness of them and our own, and making public proclamation of what each denomination of foreign coin was worth to its owner, as money or as bullion. In the exercise of this regulating power judgment cannot err, nor caprice prevail, without prompt exposure. If the material in a money coin is valued less than its commercial value, it will be demonetized at once and fall to the condition of merchandise. If it is over-valued it will circulate as money at its face value in the payment of debts just so far as it can be forced by mandate of law, but in purchases it will be made to conform to its bullion value, by an added amount, equal to its shortage, in the price of whatever is purchased with it. It will, however, be just as fictitious and dishonest a measure of value as would be a yard-stick, less than thirty six inches, as a measure of cloth.

But now comes the Jones-Peffer-Free-Silver-Fiat school of states-men, and declares that value in money is the creation of law; that the legend stamped upon $412\frac{1}{2}$ grains of silver, or upon $25\frac{8}{10}$ grains of gold at the mint, if stamped upon an equal surface of alluminum or paper, would give to these comparatively worthless materials the same instrinsic value as the silver and gold.   That " a Government that can make a good bond can make better money," and of course would be a very great fool to make a bond, or provide for the coinage of silver or gold at any ratio.   To meet the case, the constitution should read: " Congress shall have power to create money and determine its value, to print or stamp the legend, ' this is a dollar,' without regard to the value of the thing upon which it is printed or stamped, and it shall immediately become a dollar, in fact and in intrinsic value."

You may esteem this line of argument far from the subject in hand, but if you will trust me in patience to lay this foundation, I will under-take to place our subject upon it a little later, and in a manner to justify, in your estimation, the plan being pursued.   We must get down to the root of this contention, if it is ever to be settled in wisdom and safety.

Governor Prince, in his elaborate and ingenious address, this after-noon, in which he suspended before us an object we knew to be jet-black, and came near convincing us that it was snow-white, said some things which cannot be allowed to pass unchallenged. It seems hard to say, and much harder to believe, that the Governor would with intent be guilty of distorting or garbling the words of any one to gain undue advantage in debate.   And yet he seems to have done so.   You will remember his declaration that there were those who say, " that the cost in labor invested in the production of a thing, is the value of the thing when produced."

I do not believe that any man outside of an asylum for the insane, or a retreat for idiots, ever said any such thing.   But coincidence of lan-guage forces me to believe it has reference to declarations of mine, mis-quoted by reason of careless reading.   My words will be found in an address before this Congress, in the official report of its proceedings at the Denver meeting.   I was then, as now, endeavoring to find a solution of this silver question by the test of fundamental laws.

What I said then, in this connection, it were well to repeat here: That the cost to the producer of silver and gold was governed by the same law as in the case of coal, iron, copper, wheat, corn and cotton — the same as every product of industry, from mine, farm or factory.

Their cost, not their value, as represented by Gov. Prince, being measured by the amount of labor invested in their production. It was laid down then, and repeated now, that the cost to the producer of the product of hand, or brain, was the equivalent, always, of the value of the labor expended in its production.

But the value to the producer of the thing produced was determined by quite a different law, by conditions beyond his control, or his power to foretell with any degree of certainty. Values are determined by the necessities of the consumer, and are controlled by the relative supply and demand of each and every article or thing, in an open market.

The farmer invests his earnings in land and farm implements; plants, cultivates and harvests his wheat. When in the granary he can readily determine its cost in the measure of interest on his investment and labor from seed time to harvest. But he must depend upon the market price, where he has to sell, for an answer to the question: What is the result of my investment and labor worth to me? If wheat is scarce, and the hungry plenty, he will realize profitable return: if wheat is abundant, and consumers scarce, his returns may involve actual loss.

The mechanic builds his forge and buys iron and coal. With his brawny arm he beats out horseshoes and strings them upon a pole. He counts the cost of material, and adding the value of labor at the anvil, knows exactly what the string of shoes have cost him. But their value to him must be determined later, by the necessities of men with unshod horses. If barefooted horses are abundant, and competition light, he will realize quick sales and large profits; if these conditions are reversed, slow sales and small profits, or possible loss.

In like manner the silver miner invests his capital and labor, subject to the same law as the farmer and mechanic, in the fixing of the cost and value to him of silver bullion. If the demand for wheat and horseshoes is not such as to make the business of producing them self-sustaining what follows? Do the farmer and mechanic clamor for aid, and demand that the government take the complete product of farm and shop, at an arbitrary price double that for which they can be sold in the open markets of the world? Do they proceed to organize a political party, and kindle the flames of sectional strife, on the issue of free and unlimited use of wheat and horseshoes as measures of value, on a fixed ratio with gold, of double their intrinsic market value; and the issue of legal tender certificates therefor? Oh, no, they just quit the business of growing wheat and turning horseshoes, until changed conditions again demand them at paying prices! And this is just what the silver producer should do, and in the end must do. Let them pursue the course already entered upon. Close up non-paying silver mines and push the enterprise of mining gold. By this method, this respect for paramount natural law, will relief be found for the existing disparity in the market value of silver and gold. It cannot be accomplished by human enactments, any more than the laws of man can be put in the place of the laws of God in the moral world.

That I may not do injustice in charging free silver advocates with the unreasonable purpose of invoking the aid of government, to make good to the silver mining industry its impairment incident to the law of supply and demand, which has depressed the price of silver bullion in the open markets of the world from $1.34 an ounce in 1850, to 63 cents an ounce now, let me call as a witness in my defense a distinguished advocate of free silver, now a delegate in this Congress. The Globe-Democrat of yesterday prints the following, in quotation marks, from the Hon. Frank J. Cannon, of Utah:—

" We must have free and unlimited coinage of silver at a ratio of 16 to 1 if this country desires prosperity again. Silver is now so cheap that miners can not run their mines at a profit. There are a large number of mines containing both gold and silver, the latter predominating; and other mines contain lead and silver, but these mines cannot be worked at a profit because the silver is worth nothing. The value of silver must be increased before these mines can be worked without loss, and the best way to increase the value of the white metal is by its free and unlimited coinage."

Here you have it all in a nutshell. The Government is not only asked to provide a market for the surplus silver of the world, but must coin it into legal-tender money at a fictitious, arbitrary value, more than twice its worth in the market as a commodity to-day. And for what? That the waning enterprise of silver mining shall be made the most sure and profitable of all known vocations. He says that " silver is worth nothing " now, and in the voice of the " fiatist " demands that the Government shall make " something " out of " nothing," and create a class aristocracy .by giving that " something " to the silver miner, at the expense and wrong of all other industries.

There are numberless other industries in our country to-day that may be. fitly described by the words of Mr. Cannon, by substituting the word wheat, cotton, or something else, for silver ; and farm, or factory, for mine, and which could with equal reason and justice demand relief by the same paternal method. As a matter of fact, free and unlimited coinage of silver is only another phase of the " Sub-Treasury System," proposed for the relief of the farmer. As a matter of experience, silver coin cannot be forced into actual use as circulating money except to a limited extent, not in amount equal to one-fourth the amount already coined. The silver is resting in the vaults of the National Treasury, whilst certificates representing it are in circulation as money, at double the value of the silver they represent. By the same method corn and cotton, pig iron and lead, may be made legal-tender at double their value, by their purchase and deposit, and the issuance of legal-tender certificates thereon; and I am free to declare my conviction that there is just as much power vested in the Government to do it with one of the commodities named as another, and no more or less of justice or reason in assuming the power to do it.

What I wish to say, and to express it in very plain English, is this: The Government of the United States has no more right, either legal or moral, to respond to the necessities and demands of the silver miner, for a market for his output of silver by purchasing it at a price double that fixed for it by the law of supply and demand in the open markets of the world — no more right to take fifty cents worth of that silver and issue a legal-tender certificate in payment for it of one dollar, than it has to take a fifty-cent bushel of wheat at the fictitious price of one dollar, and pay for it in a like certificate (applause).

(Some members leaving the hall.) I hope my silver friends will not go away, as this may be the last opportunity I shall ever have to carry the truth to them.

I desire now to undertake the correction of history, that has been so sadly disfigured by my friend Governor Prince in your hearing this afternoon. You will remember with what force and pathos he depicted to us the crime of silver demonetization, and the awful results following it, in destruction of values, the withering of trade and crushing of labor, incident to the reduction of the volume of currency, by taking silver from its function as money. How values of factory and farm, mill and shop, and all the fruits of toil had been dragged down by it. Both the Governor, and the eloquent young gentleman from Colorado who preceded him upon this platform, pointed us to 1873 as the fatal date of the crime and disaster which had drawn that dark and dismal line of unthrift across our beloved country, this side of which had been a very "valley of the shadow of death" to us as a people. They told of the thrift and profit of enterprise under bi-metallism prior to that date, and of unthrift that followed under monometallism thereafter. If I have overstated, or in the least misrepresented these gentlemen, I wish to be corrected, and make apology right now.

In these so-called arguments, truth and error were so nicely blended, fact and fiction so ingeniously woven into the same frabric, as to confuse the coolest head, and mislead the most stable judgment, into an approval. For myself it may be confessed, that I got completely lost in the wilderness we were led into, and had to pinch myself to determine whether it was I or somebody else.

Having discovered myself, and recovered my senses again, it may be as well for me to spring a surprise upon you now as later, and here it is: As a matter of fact, silver was not demonetized in 1873, and Gov. Prince knows it, whether the gentleman from Colorado does, or not (laughter).   They have talked loud and long to us about the beauties and blessings of bimetallism under free and unlimited coinage laws, when Gov. Prince knows, when every man who has given thought to it knows, that gold and silver money were never maintained in circulation together under a free coinage law, for a single year, by any government in the history of the race (applause).   A free coinage law may not demonetize silver; it may not demonetize gold; but one or the other of them must yield to the inevitable, and go out of use as money, under the action of such a law.   Let me repeat this, as it is fundamental: Never in the history of human government have gold and silver been maintained on a parity, and in coincident circulation as money, a single year, under a free coinage law (applause).   In the experience of our own Government, each has been demonetized by the other, under the resistless force of a free coinage law.   Let us see when and how.

The first mint act of the United States was in 1792.   It was a free coinage act, pure and simple.   Under its provisions any citizen of the Republic, any inhabitant of the world, could bring gold or silver to our mints and receive gold or silver coin, as they might elect, in return, at a fixed ratio of 15 to 1.   That is, the depositor of one ounce of gold would receive for it just fifteen times the value in coin money that the depositor of an ounce of silver would receive.   This ratio was an arbitrary one fixed by law without respect to the natural law of relative values, it was not the ratio existing in the open markets of the world, where gold and silver were daily bought and sold.   It was at variance to the legal ratio in the countries of Europe, where commercial values had been respected and a ratio of $15\frac{1}{2}$ to 1, adopted.   Just why our government did not beat the same path of common-sense that had been marked out by the other nations I cannot say, unless by suggestion, that its infatuation with the idea that a country strong enough to whip Great Britain, and set up an independent Republic, was strong enough to defy the natural laws of God.

Let us now recall the results of this free coinage law.   The ratio of law not being the ratio of commerce, one of the metals was necessarily overestimated, the other underestimated.   Gold happening to be the underestimated one, came at once to be worth more in dust or bar than in coin.   In other words, an ounce of gold bullion would buy more of the necessaries of man than fifteen ounces of silver, whilst its legal tender value in coin was no more than the silver.   Hence gold ceased to be money of circulation, and its coinage a fruitless burden upon the government.   The great crime of demonetization and monometallism. then, was not perpetrated first in 1873 in the interest of the "yellow metal," as stated by Gov. Prince in your hearing to-day; but in 1792, and in the interest of the "white metal."   From 1792 to 1834 our country worried along with a single standard of money measure, and that silver; and seems to have done fairly well at that, and without breaking up the gold mining interests of the world either.

For a period of nearly forty years gold had not been seen by the people of this country, except in the windows of bullion brokers, when about the year 1830 there came to be an organized determination to adopt means for the restoration of gold and bimetallism. That contest, however, was fought on quite different and greatly broader lines than the present one. It was more a national sentiment than a class interest; a question of public policy, rather than private concern. The interests of the ostracised gold miner cut no figure, so far as I can read. The only question was one of feasibility, of means for its accomplishment. Those who claimed that it could be reached through a change of ratio, in the then free coinage law, were met by the objection that this was a mere temporizing policy, a guessing on the future commercial relations of the metals, that would again demonetize one or the other of them. The environments of the question at that time it were well to study now, and I venture to recall a little of that history. On this subject Hon. Campbell P. White, of the Finance Committee of Congress, said in 1831:—

" There are inherent and incurable defects in the system which regulates the standard of value in both gold and silver; its instability as a measure of contracts and its mutability as the practical currency of the nation, are serious imperfections; whilst the impossibility of maintaining both metals in concurrent, simultaneous circulation seems to be clearly ascertained."

From a report made by the same man to Congress I read the following: — (This report of the Finance Committee was made a year later, in 1832.)

"The committee cannot ascertain that both metals have ever circulated simultaneously, concurrently and indiscriminately in any country where there are banks or money dealers; and they entertain the conviction that the nearest approach to an invariable standard is its establishment in one metal, which metal shall compose exclusively the currency for large payments."

In 1834 one of the most distinguished statesmen this country has ever produced, whose name will be revealed to you a little later, in a speech in the United States Senate, gave the following exposition of the then existing free coinage law:—

" The false valuation put upon gold has rendered the mint of the United States, so far as gold coinage is concerned, a most ridiculous and absurd institution. It has coined, and that at large expense, 2,962,177 pieces of gold, worth $11,852,890, and where are the pieces now? Not one of them to be seen, — all sold, and exported; and so regular is the operation that the director of the mint, in his latest report to Congress, says that the new coined gold frequently remains in the mint, uncalled for, though ready for delivery, until the day arrives for a packet to sail for Europe. He calculates that two millions of native gold will be coined annually hereafter; the whole of which, without a reform of the gold standard, will be conducted, like exiles, from the national mint to the seashore, and transported to foreign regions."

In a final appeal for the passage of the bill intended to reform the mint law and save gold for money use in our own country, this same Senator-Statesman uttered the following words: —

"To enable the friends of GOLD to go to work at the right place to effect the recovery of that precious metal WHICH THE FATHERS ONCE POSSESSED — which the subjects of European kings now possess — which the citizens of the young republics of the south all possess — which even the free negroes of San Domingo possess — but which the yeomanry of this America have been deprived of for more than twenty years, and will be deprived of forever, unless they discover the cause of the evil, and apply the remedy to the root."

And who was this eloquent advocate of the "*gold dollar of the daddies*" in 1834? It was that great statesman, whose name is so linked with the name of St. Louis that this city will be known and remembered by coming generations, as long as the hand of time shall continue to weave years into centuries — it was Thomas H. Benton (applause). And there was no Congressman Bryan then, to denounce him as a "gold bug" — a "hog," that should have a ring put in his nose (applause).

But Congress responded to this appeal for gold, and decided that the American citizen was as good as a San Domingo negro, and of right should be permitted to handle a gold coin occasionally. They sought and found a remedy, but in doing it ignored the lessons of history and the warnings I have read to you from Congressman Campbell P. White, as well as many others who believed with him, that the trouble was not so much in the ratio, as in a free coinage law itself. They changed the ratio from 15 to 1, to 16 to 1, which overreached the European and commercial ratio just as much as the old law fell short of it. In their desire for gold they had overvalued it, and undervalued silver, with the logical and inevitable result — they remonetized gold and demonetized silver. It was in 1834, my friends, and not in 1873, as you have so many times been told to-day, that silver was demonetized in the United States of America.

Gov. WAITE (interrupting): May we ask you a question?

Gov. ANTHONY: Certainly.

Gov. WAITE: Was that change an increase of silver in the dollar?

Gov. ANTHONY: That change was a decrease in the gold in the dollar (applause). I see nothing strange in this. Honesty demanded a decrease in gold in the dollar then, just as it demands an increase in the silver in the dollar now. This is the only way to fix a ratio and keep it in harmony with the governing law of values, the open market price which the separate metals will command.

We find, then, as a historic fact, that silver was demonetized under the operation of this act of 1834, changing the ratio of metal values; not in 1873, and as a base conspiracy, as charged in your hearing so many times to-day. It was the result of error in judgment; too much confidence in the power of human enactments, and not enough in the force of a great and paramount natural law. The ratio of 16 to 1 made silver in the bar, as a commodity, worth more than in coin, as money. In the language of Senator Benton, which I have read to you, "silver coin was conducted, like exiles, from the national mint to the seashore, and transported to foreign regions," just as gold coin was exiled and transported to foreign regions before this change in coinage-ratio.

Young men cannot verify this statement from memory, but I see many gray-haired men before me who can. They will confirm what I have stated to you from my own personal knowledge. No man saw an American silver coin — "a dollar of the daddies" — in circulation as money in the transaction of business, from 1834 to 1873. Nor were minor silver coins of the United States seen in circulation until after 1854, when the minting of subsidiary coin at a ratio of $14\frac{8}{10}$ to 1, with a limited legal tender to five dollars, was provided for. No, Mr. President, you could no more find an American silver coin passing from man to man as money in all those years, than you could find business brains in the head of a flat-money-financier now (applause).

Gov. WAITE: Is it a fact that while sixty millions of dollars were coined, that ninety-five million dollars of subsidiary coin was coined?

Gov. ANTHONY: It is not a fact, for any period known to me; but for the period from 1793 to 1894 there was a little over $39,000,000 of silver coined, of which less than $1,500,000 was in standard silver dollars, and over $37,500,000 in subsidiary coin. But this subsidiary coin, having the same ratio of silver in them as the standard dollar, went from the mint to the bullion market the same as the dollar.

Gov. WAITE: While I have the floor let me ask another question. When the mints of the United States were open to the coinage of silver at 16 to 1, and as you say the ratio in England being $15\frac{1}{2}$ to 1, the bullion silver was worth more than the coined silver—is it a fact that the price of silver bullion was fixed, whenever the mints were open in the United States and in France, at the ratio of either one government or the other?

Gov. ANTHONY: Oh, no, my friend. In the first place the mints of France were never open to the free coinage of silver. France maintained a parity between gold and silver coin at its legal ratio, by a pledge of interchange and redemption, each with the other at the will of its owner, precisely as this government does now; so that whatever was short in the value of the metal, was made good by the credit of the government. It is this obligation of the government that makes our fifty cent silver dollar equal to the one hundred cent gold dollar now.

Gov. WAITE: I mean that the mints of France coined silver at the rate of $15\frac{1}{2}$ to 1?

Gov. ANTHONY: Yes, sir; the mints of France coined silver at $15\frac{1}{2}$ to 1, and we at 16 to 1. That is right, and just what I have been saying; and this difference in ratio made it profitable to send French gold here to buy our silver coin, at its face value, as fast as it dropped from the mint, to be carried there and coined under the French ratio.

Gov. WAITE: How, in the United States, could the price of silver bullion go down below 16 to 1, when the mints of the United States were coining it at this ratio?

Gov. ANTHONY: For the same reason that gold went up relatively to silver, under the coinage ratio of 15 to 1, prior to 1834. The price of bullion, gold or silver, is determined by the law of supply and demand, and no coinage ratio can affect to annul that law.

Gov. WAITE: Let me say to you —

THE CHAIRMAN: Governor, you certainly are enough of a parliamentarian to know that you must ask permission before you can ask a question. You know how to get the floor — by addressing the Chair.

Gov. ANTHONY: Mr. President, I beg your pardon, but I never want to be discourteous. We are here in search of the truth, and any one asking a question with an honest purpose to illuminate and set out the truth more plainly than I am doing it, is my friend and not an intruder.

Gov. WAITE: Governor Anthony, I intend to treat everybody perfectly fair, and do not ask any questions for the purpose of annoying anybody. If you have any idea that I do, I wish you would disabuse your mind of it. I am here for the purpose of getting information, and for the purpose of getting at the facts. The question that I put to you was: If at any time while the mints of the United States were open to the coinage of silver at the ratio of 16 to 1, did the price of silver bullion ever go below those figures?

Gov. ANTHONY: No, sir; not if you mean to apply your question to the time of the enactment of the 16 to 1 ratio law of 1834, to its repeal in 1873. During that period silver never reached so low a commercial ratio as 16 to 1, and consequently could not be kept in coin. But if you ask it with reference to the period since 1873, I answer with an emphatic, yes, sir. We have coined full legal tender silver dollars at the ratio of 16 to 1, more than four hundred million dollars of them, and with the pledge of the government to maintain them on a parity with gold dollars, and yet the bullion price of silver has gone down, down, until the silver in one of our dollars is worth less than fifty cents in the markets of the world.

Gov. WAITE: (Rising to speak.)

THE CHAIRMAN: Now, Governor Waite, you are too good a parliamentarian to undertake to get the floor without coming under parliamentary law. You must ask permission of the gentleman you are asking the questions of.

Gov. ANTHONY: That so-called demonetization of silver in 1873 requires no more attention from me, in exposing its utter absurdity, but my duty would not be performed, my obligation to country and conscience redeemed, did I fail to rebuke that awful indictment of my government — your government — of the grandest and wisest government in its inception, the most just and generous in its administration, the most comprehensive in range of possibilities for the race in the world — that was drawn and presented to us this afternoon by Governor Prince. We were told by him that at a period, less than twenty-five years past, the President, the Senate, the House of Representatives of the United States, united and joined with enemies of our country abroad, conspired and combined in a plot more damnable in purpose, more destructive to the peace and prosperity of man, than was ever before wrought by legislative crime. He told us of the shrinkage of values, of fortunes broken and wasted, of hopes blasted and homes made desolate, of miseries multiplied, by the stealthy "striking down of the white metal," in the act of February 12th, 1873.

I submit that this is not an overstatement of the Governor's awful arraignment. Indeed, imagination could not picture a conspiracy, born of hell and nursed by devils, more hideous in injustice and cruelty than this act of our Government. If what he said to us is to stand unchallenged, as historic truth, then indeed the train-wrecking robber of the plains is a man of honor, when compared with the men elected to make and administer our laws.

I stand here to protest with all the fervor of my nature against this, and all kindred inflammatory appeals to passion — these perversions of history for the purpose of cultivating the soil of popular distrust and discontent; it can do no less than destroy love for country, respect for home, and breed disloyalty to the Republic. I can perform no higher duty than to denounce it, here and now; to bring to you convincing evidence that all this talk of free silver advocates about a "secret conspiracy," with its midnight meetings and its mysterious dark-lantern pathways, by which this bill was carried through both houses of Congress and signed by the President, without the knowledge of any one outside of the conspirators, is but the policy of selfishness, or the prating of demagogism (applause). And now to the proof of this.

As early as 1870, Secretary of the Treasury Boutwell, in his annual report for that year, recommended amendment of the mint law, substantially as appears in the act of 1873. Every one knows, or should know, that at this time neither silver nor gold were legal-tender, by requirement of law; that payment in specie had been suspended for years, and its possible resumption a thing of the future, suspended between hope and doubt, in the minds of statesmen and financiers; that silver, in bullion, was worth 3 per cent more than its face value in coin; that to have passed a law of Congress, at that time, demonetizing a silver dollar of 412½ grains, would have been no more effective, nor less idiotic, than an act legalizing the natural law of gravitation.

In 1871, bills were introduced and discussed in both houses of Congress embodying the recommendations of Secretary Boutwell. The bill which, as amended, finally became a law, was introduced by Mr. Hooper of Massachusetts in the House, not by Sherman in the Senate, as most free silver men delight to believe and declare. It was first considered in the House on April 9, 1872. (See page 3, Cong. Globe, 2d session, 42d Cong.) Mr. Hooper, from the Committee on Finance, presented the bill with explanations, by sections in their order. On presentation of sections 14 and 16, which include this subject, he said: —

"Thus far it is a re-enactment of the present laws; in addition, it declares the gold dollar of twenty-five and eight-tenths grains of standard gold to be the unit of value, gold having been practically in this country for many years the standard, or measure of value, as it is legally in Great Britain and most European countries. The silver dollar, which is by law the legally declared unit of value now, does not bear a correct relative proportion to the gold dollar; being worth intrinsically about one dollar and three cents in gold, it cannot circulate concurrently with gold coins. As the value of the silver dollar depends on the market price of silver, which varies according to the demand and supply, it is now intrinsically worth, as has been before stated, about three cents more than the gold dollar."

"Section 16 re-enacts the provisions of existing laws defining silver coins and their weights respectively, *except in relation to the silver dollar, which is reduced in weight from 412½ to 324 grains; thus making it a subsidiary coin in harmony with the silver coins of less denominations. The silver dollar of 412½ grains, by reason of its bullion or intrinsic value being greater than its nominal value, long since ceased to be a coin of circulation, and is melted by manufacturers of silverware.*"

"The committee, after careful consideration, concluded that twenty-five and eight-tenths grains of gold, constituting the dollar, should be declared the money unit or metallic representative of the dollar of account."

Here we have a full and frank declaration of the purpose of this Bill, made by its author on its presentation to the Congress and people of the

United States for consideration, and a year before its enactment into law. Its purpose was to make the law conform to the higher law of supply and demand, which had demonetized silver under the amended ratio of forty years before. It was proposed to do it this time by remanding the silver dollar to the condition of a subsidiary coin, with a limited legal-tender function, and a ratio of intrinsic value with that of gold coin that would keep it in circulation as money. For the eighty years of our national existence we had been engaged in the vain struggle of maintaining a bimetallic currency, under a free coinage law, only to succeed in the demonetization of gold under the first ratio, and silver under the second one.. The statement I have given you, from Chairman Hooper, was verified on the same occasion by other members of his committee, and that without protest or unfriendly criticism from a single member of the house, on account of its hostility to silver. Mr. Stoughton of Michigan, a member of the committee, said : —

" The only change in this law is the more clearly specifying the gold dollar as the unit of value. This was publicly the intention, and perhaps the effect of the law of March 3d, 1849, but it ought not to be left to inference or implication. Silver depends, in a great measure, upon the fluctuations of the market and the supply and demand, for its value. Gold is practically the standard of value among all civilized nations, and the time has come in this country when the gold dollar should be distinctly declared to be the coin representative of the money unit."

" The silver coins provided for in this bill are the dollars of 384 grains troy, the half-dollar, quarter-dollar and dime, of the value and weight of one-half, one quarter, and one tenth of the dollar, respectively; and are made a legal tender for all sums not exceeding five dollars at any one payment. The silver dollar, as now issued, is worth for bullion $3\frac{1}{4}$ cents more than the gold dollar, and $7\frac{1}{2}$ cents more than two half dollars. Having a greater intrinsic than nominal value it is certain to be withdrawn from circulation when we return to specie payment, and to be used only for manufacture and export of bullion."

" The office of silver coin is to supply the public want for small change. They are made the token of value, and not the value itself, and are designed only for change and circulation at home up to, but never in excess of, the requirements of trade."

Mr. Potter of New York said (see page 2310 same Vol. Cong. Globe) : —

" This bill provides for the making of changes in the legal-tender coin of the country, and for substituting as legal-tender coin of only one metal, instead of two. I think myself this would be a wise provision, and legal-tender coins, except subsidiary coins, should be of gold alone."

You will remember a quotation read to us yesterday from Congressman Kelly, of Pennsylvania, then a member of Congress, declaring that this bill was smuggled through surreptitiously, and absolutely without his knowledge at the time. Charity to the memory of the dead Statesman leads me to hope that the quoted words are a forgery; but if not they must stand against his fame, as a confession of moral cowardice. For on page 2311 of the Congressional Record, from which I have been reading to you, will be found the following evidence, in his own words as officially reported, that he not only knew all about the bill, but was one of its most distinguished advocates. He said: —

"By a mistake in our law it has become impossible to retain an American silver dollar in this country except in collections of curiosities. They would, if coined in considerable numbers, be a source of enormous profit to the silver bullion dealers of New York. Let me show you. The silver refined by our laws is worth 3½ cents more than the gold dollars, and is worth 7 cents more than two half dollars. *Now, sir, is the government of the United States to be made the prey of the people of the world in order to give larger profits to a few silver bullion brokers in New York? For this is the whole question.* But I have shown you but a small part of the *profits that the bullion gamblers and dealers of New York City are making under our loose laws.* The gentlemen who oppose this bill insist upon maintaining a silver dollar worth three and a-half cents more than a gold dollar. So long as these provisions remain you cannot keep silver coin in the country. *Certain bullion dealers in New York are making from fifty thousand to one hundred thousand dollars a year out of our government.* One of them admitted to my colleague and myself, that his business averaged from one million eight hundred thousand dollars to two millions a year, and that *he put the silver into the mint, and drew out for every two dollars four half-dollars and a ten-cent piece.*"

As I have said, we had no use for coin money at the time this bill was recommended by the Secretary of the Treasury and enacted by Congress. Silver was but the means of speculating upon the Government, as the words of Mr. Kelly so clearly show. Only in California was specie in use, and that gold. It was the only State that stood up against the Government standard, "greenbacks," and made gold coin its only legal tender. And for this it was arraigned by Senator Sherman in debate on this bill, as disloyal to Government, keeping $40,000,000 of gold in its own selfish use, at a time when it was greatly needed to buy foreign material for war purposes.

SENATOR JOHNSON, of California (interrupting): I hope the Governor will not abuse my constituents, here in St. Louis (laughter).

GOV. ANTHONY: Oh, no, Senator, every man, when we get through with this, will recognize me as his friend.

Referring again to the debates upon this bill, from which I have read, it becomes apparent that it was more in the nature of protection from the greed of "silver bugs," than in the interest of "gold bugs." Nor is any evidence of cunning or concealment disclosed at any stage in either House. The Hooper bill passed the House, and went to the

Senate, but failed of passage 'that session. On re-assembling, it was revived by House Resolution No. 2394; again discussed, passed, sent to the Senate, and referred to its Finance Committee; and by Senator Sherman, its Chairman, reported back with amendments, on December 16th, 1872. Here it became the subject of extended debate, in which Senator Stewart took an active part. Singularly enough, the only opposition to the bill came from the silver bullion brokers of New York, and the gold worshipers of California.

The Senate finally returned it to the House with some twenty amendments, which were non-concurred in, and it went to a conference committee; some of the amendments were ratified and others receded from, and it became a law on the 12th of February, 1873.

During all these years no bill was more constantly before Congress and the country than this one. And I now submit that its supporters should be taken out of the entomological kingdom, where they have so long been doomed to dwell as "gold bugs," and returned again to family and friends, as members of the human family (applause).

Mr. Fisk (Interrupting): Would not that all have been cured if the ratio had been 15 to 1?

Gov. Anthony: Not under a free coinage law. But of that later. What I want to show is that this bill was passed with the full knowledge of all, and show it by the record.

Mr. Fisk (Interrupting): I have read all that record.

Gov. Anthony: That may be, but if so you have never divulged it to your hearers in any speech I have heard from you (applause).

Mr. Fisk: You did not answer my question: What is the reason that a dollar that left the country for coinage in Europe did not contain any more silver than the subsidiary coins?

Gov. Anthony: That question may be somewhat abstruse and involved for my little mind, but, as a matter of fact, no such thing ever occurred, and therefore no reason can be given for it. Our subsidiary coins were of the same ratio in richness of metal and weight as the dollar coin, until 1854, and were gathered up and exported with the same profit. After that they were minus seven cents in value of metal, and remained at home.

Mr. Fisk: Answer the question.

Gov. Anthony: I think I have, and want now to close the question in hand. Does any intelligent citizen of this country really believe this law of 1873 to have been the fruit of a conspiracy, in which the American Congress and President were allied with the gold interests of England? And that it was "smuggled through" Congress without its own members, or the country, knowing anything about it? Is there a man here in this house who believes it (cries of no, no)?

Gov. Waite: Let me say a word on that.

Gov. ANTHONY: No, sir. I am not going to give up any more of my time.

We must all know, and I want you to carry this thought home with you, that if this charge of corruption in our government, as then or at any time in its history constituted, can by any possibility be true, that it must shake the confidence and impair the faith of every citizen of this Republic in the solidity and perpetuity of his government. It must go far to confirm, as axiomatic, the statement of the man who reared an Empire over the grave of a Republic — Napoleon Bonaparte. He laid it down as a political axiom, that " a government resting upon a popular ballot contains the seeds of its own destruction, and must sooner or later flee from its own cruelty to the more tender mercies of a despotism."

I have a single illustration — an object lesson in free and unlimited coinage — which will demonstrate its fallacy, and protect me from any selfish motive in assuming a position on this subject. I have interests in Mexico which were acquired at a time when exchange between silver and gold in that country was but ten per cent, now it is about one hundred per cent. Some of those interests are still retained, although I am selling them when I can; my experience in that country for a period of years having taught me to love my own country more than ever before. Talk about poverty and its attendant miseries in this country? Why, if any of you have traveled in Mexico, you have seen more of poverty, misery, and squalid wretchedness, greeting and imploring you at Chihuahua, Zacatecus, or any like station, at every passing train, than can be found in ten States like Missouri; and they enjoy the full benefits and blessings of free and unlimited silver coinage there, too (applause).

We have been given to-day, as the crystallized judgment of the advocates of free coinage at the ratio of 16 to 1, that it would immediately bring silver up to gold in market value as bullion — that silver is now below gold in commercial value only because we do not freely coin them at that ratio. Mexico has had exactly that law and its uninterrupted practice for all these years, except that the Mexican silver dollar contains six and a fourth grains more of pure silver than does our dollar. Now what has been the effect of this law in Mexico? And why should not its results be the same here as there? In this experience is found a complete answer to the question put to me a little time ago: "Did not the ratio in this country and France fix the price of bullion silver in each country?" It could not do it in the countries named in the question more than it has done it in Mexico. And there, a ratio of a little less than 16 to 1, in use for nearly a century, has had no control over the bullion price of silver, but has seen it go above that coinage ratio, and then below it, until at this moment, when the bullion price is but half of the legal-tender value of the coin.

I sold some machinery in the city of Mexico on the 4th of last April, and here is a duplicate of the draft received for the proceeds of one of those sales. It is issued by the bank of London and Mexico, payable in gold, at the bank of British North America, in New York (showing the paper). For the machine I received $1,782.00 and for that number of Mexican silver dollars received this draft, for $900.00 gold. Rate of exchange, 98 per cent. Or $882.00 premium in silver on $900.00 in gold.

Now, who paid this premium? This is a vital question that I want made plain to you. It cost me not one cent. I could have as well paid $3,000.00, if that had been the known cost of exchange. The price of the property sold was based on gold, and what I asked was received for it. But who did bear the burden of that enormous exchange? And right here we come to the pith of this matter, and expose the demogogic claim that the common people, the poor working man, wants a "cheap" dollar. The man who bought the machine was establishing a starch manufacturing plant. In capitalizing that plant he could only protect himself by putting the machine in at the price he paid for it in his own money — $1,782.00, not $900.00 — and the price of his starch is made to meet the interest on the larger, not the smaller sum, and the poor people, who starch their garments as much as do the rich, have the chief burden to carry.

But our free-silver friends tell us that unlimited coinage would not tempt silver from other countries, to be loaded upon us. Yet if free coinage had have existed here, do you that suppose I would have bought this draft? Not much! I would have started with that silver in my "grip" for St. Louis, or New York, and converted my Mexican dollars into legal-tender American dollars, making $882.00 thereby — plus the excess of silver in the Mexican dollars. With free coinage and a guaranteed parity, the St. Louis merchant, who would order $10,000 worth of foreign goods, to be sold here at a possible profit of ten or twenty per cent, would be a business idiot, when he could order the same amount in silver and double his money on it at the mint, on delivery. The merchant who did order foreign goods would at the same time order silver sufficient to pay the duties on them, to come on the same vessel. He would only have to slip over to Philidelphia with his silver to make 100 per cent on it, and be able to pay his duties at half price, leaving the government to recoup by the sale of its bonds, or other expedient.

Under free and unlimited coinage, without the guarantee of parity maintenance, and this is what is demanded, no such opportunities would offer, for three months time would be ample to Mexicanize this country, reduce our circulating money more than $600,000,000 in the loss of gold, and $300,000,000 more in the purchasing power of silver coin and certificates, which would go at once to the plane of the commercial value of silver bullion, where Mexican silver coins are, have been, and must remain, so long as they adhere to their present system of free and unlimited coinage.

In conclusion, I am not called upon by any personal interest to protect or defend the American banker; as a class, I am under no personal obligation to them, except such as are expressed on the face of " bills payable." And yet I listened with pain and profound concern when they were compared to " train-robbers" by Mr. Bryan, from this platform to-day. A banker is no more a robber than any other business man in our country — if an honest banker. And if he is not an honest man behind the bank counter, he is no worse than a dishonest man in any other vocation. A member of Congress from my own State, when robber-ruffians from the Indian Territory murdered some of our best citizens, in an attempt to rob a bank, uttered the same sentiment. He said: " Why arrest, try and hang these men; they only sought to steal the money in the bank, and that is just what the owners of the bank had already done — why not hang them?"

Oh, shame on any cause that makes it necessary to assail the character and credit of my country, as they have been assailed from this rostrum to-day. Oh, despised be the advocate of that cause, who drops to the plane of denouncing that great class of men, who did in defense of their country what I could not do, what you, my soldier comrades, could not do. We could put our lives in the breach, and bare our breasts to the shot of the foe, to save our country with its constitution and flag to posterity; but we had no money to contribute or loan to the Government, and of what avail were soldiers without money to feed, clothe and pay them; to supply them with arms and ammunition? But for the capitalists of our country who were patriotic and trustful enough to advance money and protect the national credit; — who went to Abraham Lincoln with money, as we went to him with service; — but for that union of confidence and patriotism, which risked life in the field and fortune at home, this country would long since have ceased to exist as one of the family of great nations, where it so proudly stands to-day (applause).

My judgment condemns these demagogic appeals to the prejudice of class and section, as little better than treason; my soul revolts against them with unutterable loathing.

And now, gentlemen, it only remains for me to thank you, who have listened with such patience until this late hour of the night. If I have said anything severe, beyond the measure of necessity in an earnest, honest purpose of awakening thought and provoking reflection, I regret it. But, Mr. President, it is safe to say, in parting with you, that if I have said anything that I am sorry for, I am heartily glad of it (great applause).

Adjourned to Wednesday morning.

WEDNESDAY MORNING.

November 28, 1894.

The meeting was called to order by President Cannon at 10:30 o'clock.

Miscellaneous business or the introduction of resolutions was declared in order and resolutions were introduced and referred.

THE CHAIRMAN: The order adopted yesterday was that after miscellaneous business had been. attended to, there should be two hours devoted to debate on Staple Agriculture. If there be no other business now, that time for that debate will be granted.

SENATOR JOHNSTON: Mr. Chairman, in pursuance of the question now coming before us, I send up a majority report and also a minority report, and ask the Secretary to read them.

The reports were read by Mr. W. H. Culmer, acting as Secretary.

MAJORITY REPORT.

" The Committee on Resolutions reports the accompanying resolution with the recommendation that the resolution be not adopted."

MINORITY REPORT.

" The following members of the Committee on Resolutions respectfully recommend the favorable consideration of the following resolution."   (Signed) D. LUBIN,

W. H. WEED,

GEORGE W. PARSONS,

B. EDMONTON,

BEN. E. RICH.

WHEREAS, American principles demand equality before the law, in life, liberty and taxation; and

WHEREAS, The prices of American manufactures are increased by the protective tariff in our country; and,

WHEREAS, The foundation industry, namely, staple agriculture, cannot be benefited by a protective tariff alone, owing to the fact that these products are exports and therefore are sold in free competition in the open markets at the world's ruling prices, less the cost of transportation from place of production to Liverpool, whether consumed at home or exported; thus compelling American producers of these staples, to buy in the dearest and sell in the cheapest markets of the world, thereby discriminating against the producers of staple agriculture; and

WHEREAS, The introduction of labor-saving agricultural machinery in the hands of the cheapest labor of the world and on lands much cheaper and as fertile as ours has so lowered the cost of production so as to reduce the world's price of these staples to about half the former rates, and which promise to remain so permanently; and

WHEREAS, Such a condition must tend to the elimination of the independent land-owning farmer and his replacement by a dependent peasant tenantry system, which unless prevented will not only prove detrimental to agriculture and the kindred industries but also to the perpetuity of American institutions; therefore

Resolved, (1) That, just so long as manufactures are enhanced in value by protection, equity, justice and expediency demand an equal measure of protection for staple agriculture by enhancement of their prices in our country.

Resolved, (2) That, inasmuch as these products are exports and not imports, their prices cannot be enhanced by a protective tariff alone, no matter how high, but an increase of their prices in our country can only be secured by the use of a limited portion of the tariff collected for protection to pay a premium on exported agricultural staples.

SENATOR JOHNSTON: I move as a substitute for the majority report, the minority report of the committee. On that I desire to have Mr. Lubin take the floor and address the convention.

THE CHAIRMAN: The question of the adoption of the minority report is now before the congress.

The minority report was then reread.

MR. RICH: Before this discussion opens it would be well to know the pleasure of the congress concerning the manner in which it is to be debated. Under the rules reported by the Committee on Rules and Order of Business, 10 minutes are allowed to the gentleman introducing a resolution, who is the author of it; 5 minutes' address to close, and 7 minutes to other speakers. But yesterday the congress adopted a resolution that there should be two hours' debate upon this subject of Staple Agriculture, and it might be well before we enter upon the debate to understand how this debate shall be conducted. I would like to hear from the gentleman, Senator Johnston, who introduced the resolution yesterday, asking the congress to allow two hours for this debate.

SENATOR JOHNSTON: The Worthy Master of the State Grange of California will occupy a few moments, and I think about a minute and a half will be about as much as I want. Mr. Lubin, the author of this idea, the originator of it, would like as much time as the convention will grant him, as there will be some opposition probably in the discussion. I would like to have him make his talk and the rest of us will submit to the rule of the Congress.

THE CHAIRMAN: How long will it require?

MR. LUBIN: I have an address which will probably take about an hour.

SENATOR JOHNSTON: Mr. Chairman, last evening one gentleman occupied half an hour in discussing the money problem. The time was not equally distributed, and we would like the indulgence of the convention so that he can make this matter plain to every one. I believe he understands it thoroughly and that he can get through with the subject in an hour.

A DELEGATE (from Missouri): Mr. Chairman, when that resolution was passed yesterday to grant two hours to the discussion of agricultural products, it was not intended that the economic questions of tariff would be brought up under any such delusion. A question of the production of agricultural products of the fields and cereals of our land is one thing — the discussion of a political question, such as this resolution both in the majority and the minority reports refer to and as the resolution professes to be, is another thing. We understand this is a commercial body. Talking about agriculture is one thing and the question of economic laws is another. Now, if this is to be thrown open to a two hours' debate I would move that it be postponed until some other day. I understand this body has granted you gentlemen, representing the agricultural interests of California, to talk for an hour upon agriculture, but we do not want you to introduce the questions of tariff. The people of this country on the 6th of November proclaimed that they were tired of discussing it, and what the country wants, Mr. Chairman, is a rest upon that subject. We would be delighted to listen to the gentlemen who want to represent Agriculture; if they can give any intimation of how to produce any of the cereals in a better or speedier method, or if there is any economic method about that, as a matter of course I would raise no objection. I do not think this body wants to listen to a long harangue on a political or tariff question, and I, as one, would object to the extension of two hours on that subject.

SENATOR JOHNSTON: Mr. Chairman, the question of tariff does not occur in that proposition that we bring before you. This question, Mr. Chairman, has been decided by a certain sound, by the people of these United States within a very short time. This is not a question of tariff or of free trade. We do not bring any such question to this body to discuss. We think we know our business better. We understand what we are discussing, and it is the extension of the present voice of the people to the tillers of the soil that we are about to discuss here. It is not a question of whether we will have a tariff or free trade. That question has been decided, and we now simply ask the extension of that decision to the three millions of people who till the soil, who own a very large portion of the territory of this country, whose commercial interests would not be worth a dollar were it not for the tillers of the soil, and we claim the attention of this body for a few moments to discuss that question. Mr. Chairman, this has been said to be a commercial congress. I think the gentleman is correct, that it is a commercial congress, and we are about to introduce a subject here which will further the commercial interests of these United States just as much as any other question we have discussed. Silver? Does that come any nearer the commercial interests of this country than do cotton, corn, pork or beef? Now, Mr. Chairman, we ask fair play, and I do not want to occupy too much time here. We simply by a vote of this body have been granted this order of business, and it will require a two-thirds vote of this body to change that order of business at this time. Now, Mr. Chairman, I hope this time will be granted to brother Lubin, and if this congress gets tired, you may call him down and he will quit.

A·DELEGATE (from Missouri): Read the resolution, so that this body can understand whether it is a question of agriculture, or tariff, or economic principles that the people of this country have sat down upon.

The reports were then read again for the third time.

THE DELEGATE: Now, Mr. Chairman, if they will eliminate all features in reference to the tariff and insert, in place of that, "Agriculture," I do not think there could be any objection to it, but it would avoid that question that has been so tiresome to this country and give us all that refers to agriculture.

SENATOR JOHNSTON: Mr. Chairman, does the word "tariff" occur in the reading — so long as protection is the will of the American citizen, the humble hayseed asks his share of it.

THE CLERK (reading) "Staple agriculture cannot be benefited by a protective tariff alone."

THE CHAIRMAN: "By protection alone" — will that alteration suit?

MR. LUBIN: I object to the change. I stand here, Mr. Chairman and gentlemen of the Trans-Mississippi Congress, to present a measure of equity and right of a most important interest in the United States. If this Trans-Mississippi Congress is what I thought it was when I accepted the invitation to be a delegate to it, a representative body of men this side of the Mississippi river for the purpose of ameliorating adverse conditions and for the purpose of furthering the interests of these vast States and territories, then we are all right and then this question is properly before this congress. But if this congress — I say it with all due respect — from what I have learned this morning of my own observation is practically a mutual admiration society for silver alone, you will do the cause of silver much more harm than all its friends can do it good, and I say it now and right here (applause). I prefer to take that resolution from the table as the introducer of it and go before a fair American audience, be they a congress or no congress, and receive justice and right, rather than have it treated as it has been spoken of. I demand the resolution.

A DELEGATE (from Arkansas): Mr. Chairman, I rise to a point of order. I understand that this is the report of a committee, and if it is not in proper shape, I do not think that this house has the right to amend it in this arbitrary way. If it is not in proper shape for the reception of this body, it ought to be recommitted. They have no right to change it in that way. It has to come before this body as it is, in the form of a minority report or majority report, and if it is susceptible of change, it is only by amendment. I infer that the question of tariff is not settled. It may be settled in the minds of some gentlemen here, but in the minds of the American people it is not settled. It is like Banquo's ghost, that comes up always until it is settled, and settled right. I have no objection to any reference that is made to protection or free trade, or to any modification. My point of order is that that report, if not in proper shape, has to be referred to the committee from which it emanated, and it cannot be amended in this arbitrary manner.

THE CHAIRMAN: The point of order is well taken, but the proposition was to take out this by mutual consent.

SENATOR JOHNSTON: To the point of order I desire to say a word: the Committee, as was its right, voted against this proposition. That is, a majority reported the proposition and recommend that it do not pass. A minority of that committee, as it is their right to do, bring in a minority report, and now, sir, we move to substitute the minority report for the majority report, and I think I know just exactly what I am talking about.

A DELEGATE (from Arkansas): You are right about that.

SENATOR JOHNSTON: I rise to a point of order. The special order is the discussion of that question, and it takes a two-thirds vote of this body to change it, and I demand the special order.

MR. ROACH: Mr. Chairman, I desire to say a few words, more as an introduction than anything else. The gentleman who introduced this resolution was first known as a fruit farmer in California. He became interested in the question of the transportation of our California fruits to the East. He came before our California State Grange, which is a conservative body of men and women, non-partisan and non-sectarian, numbering up in the thousands in membership, and presented this idea. It was referred to a committee of five citizens of our State who stand well in the commercial and legal circles of our State. As soon as they saw the import of this they asked that they be given further time to report, that the matter intrusted to their hands was of such great moment that they did not feel justified in making a report in the limited time given to it. They took this matter under advisement for six days and reported at the Grange Congress at the Midwinter Fair in San Francisco, and reported to amend in favor of this proposition. Our executive committee adopted it and referred it to the various boards of grangers in our State. It was adopted and referred to the National Grange, which just closed its session at Springfield last week. That body, representing one and a half million of people, is organized in thirty-five States of our Union. As is the custom of that body, it referred it back to every subordinate State grange, and it will come up next year for final action, and I have no doubt that that action will be favorable.

Our difficulty, especially on the Pacific Coast, is such that we cannot longer maintain ourselves. We have to do something. We have tried all kinds of legislation — we have hoped that this party or that party or some other party would introduce some measure of relief, but we have no relief, and if we are to maintain our independent yeomanry in the United States, we will have to have this measure, or some other one. And when the farmer goes down, the Republic goes down with him (applause).

We present this matter from a non-partisan and non-sectarian organization. You cannot take politics or religion into a grange, thank God. It is a free institution. We present this here because we believe it is right; we believe it is entitled to consideration more than it has received, and while we do not propose to ask whether tariff is right or wrong, we ask that as long as other industries are protected, we have an equal share. That is all we ask. That, Mr. Chairman, is all that that resolution desires, and thanking you for attention, that is all I have to say. We ask it as a matter of justice and right as men.

Mr. Lubin: Mr. Chairman, Ladies and Gentlemen of the Trans-Mississippi Congress, the prosperity of the United States can only be maintained when there is a just equilibrium between manufacturers on the one hand and agriculture on the other.

When these two balance there must be prosperity. In order that a state of civilization be carried out in these United States differing essentially from the civilization of the foreign countries, a wall of protection has been erected, which enhances the price of commodities within the United States, enabling a higher wage-rate and a better state of civilization. Unfortunately, the mechanism of this protection is one-sided; it protects effectively against the cheaper labor of foreign countries, but it has no such effect upon anything going out of the United States. It can have no such effect, and, as long as this cannot be equal, the protection is not equal. It necessarily follows that the industry, which is not protected by the mechanism in operation, pays for the protection of the industry which has its prices enhanced by this wall. This is not new; it has been said thousands of times; it has been said by much abler men. What I say to you now is based upon practical experience with this question, practical experience as a merchant and importer and engaged in the business of agriculture.

It is commonly supposed that when a case of goods comes over from Europe to the United States and the duty on it be $50.00 that the enhancement is $50.00. ·This is not true; the enhancement on $50.00 is $86.25; because when the goods reach the hands of the importer he adds a profit of 15 per cent and this is very low; then it goes into the hands of the distributor, the jobber, who adds 20 per cent; it then goes into the hands of the retailer, who adds 25 per cent. Please bear in mind that this is not on goods; it is on fiat, on duty, on law, pure and simple. Now then, the man who pays the cost of the entire thing is the man, or the great industry, which is compelled to pay the advanced price and at the same time sell its product at the free trade price of the world.

How does agriculture sell at the free trade price of the world? England, to whom we sell the bulk of our products, will pay us no more than she can obtain the same products for from any other country in the world. As soon as she obtains the product at that price then the rest of the product sold for home consumption is appraised. In that great exchange which some of you visited yesterday, the Merchant's Exchange, we found the prices quoted, Liverpool on the one side, New York, Chicago and other cities on the other side, and all prices based upon the price at which we sell our export, and this price controls the price of our entire production of staple agricultural products. As we have 65,000,000 of people to feed in the United States and a much smaller ratio to send abroad, if we sell this much of it at the prices ruling at Liverpool, necessarily the entire balance is sold at the price of the small quantity exported. This is not new. This has been stated thousands of times, perfectly clearly. The result is that every single dime of protection, and it runs into billions of dollars, is paid by that industry which is compelled to sell everything it has in Liverpool and buy everything at artificially enhanced prices. There is not a laboring man in the United States who pays a copper for protection; there is not a merchant who pays a copper; not a lawyer, butcher, teacher or any person you can name until you come down to the man that raises wheat and cotton, and they foot the bill. This was the condition in the United States for this past 30 years under high pressure and would undoubtedly have been the condition for many more years* to come, because agriculture and manufacture balance, and this man here never knew that he footed the bill. A great many of them did not know it.

But something remarkable has occurred. It was not necessary for this fellow to realize this position. Why? because with the powerful aid of labor-saving agricultural machinery he could defy the whole world. But Western and Central Europe, even in this present day, use agricultural machinery. Agricultural machinery has recently been introduced, though chiefly by England; her desire for cheap food and cheap raw materials has led her to introduce agricultural machinery in vast tracks of country in the Argentine Republic, that a few years ago supported only the jack rabbit. This country a few years ago imported flour. What does it do to-day? The Master of the State Grange of California gave these figures which are corroborated because they are facts:

In 1893 according to a report of Mr. J. H. Brigham, Master of the National Grange of the United States, read about 4 or 5 days ago, there were exported from the United States to Argentine, agricultural machinery, $1,620.450, and Great Britain sent to the same country the same year harvesters, $235,430 ; Agricultural steam engines, $1,174,028 ; agricultural engines, not steam, $791,620.   Total, $3,821,528.

Now, when agricultural machinery went into the Argentine Republic and into India, Egypt, Asia Minor and Russia, then came the trouble with the peon and the coolie — the cheapest labor in the world.   We gave them these machines and the result has been the cutting in half of prices on agricultural staples.   If silver alone had been the cause, all things would have fallen.   Why has not corn fallen?   Why is not corn worth 12 cents a bushel?   Because Argentine only produced 750,000 lbs.   But she is preparing to raise it on a larger scale, and those of you who raise corn will find the time will come for corn as it came for wheat.

What is the condition of agriculture to-day?   It is this staple agriculture, which is the first thing we receive to buy our manufactures with, which is cut in half.   Then comes an economic disturbance.   What is the remedy for this?   As soon as we can restore the equilibrium we are all right.   What is the method of restoring the equilibrium?   One of two ways.   One is to have manufacture reduced to the same level as agriculture, relatively, by absolute and unrestricted free trade.   The other is the lifting up of agriculture to the same artificial place that manufacturing is placed in now.   People then say, "Oh, there is another remedy.   Let us curtail the area under cultivation — we will have a small quantity of these great staples and then they will bring better prices."   This is seemingly true, but there are a few things fatal to its being carried out.

We find that the United States bought of foreign nations in 1893 — and this is about the purchasing amount for the five years following — $800,000,000 worth of goods and over.   She owes, on a very conservative estimate, $100,000,000 — some say $200,000,000 — interest which has to be paid.   We have got to pay that as long as we buy from foreign nations, and we must pay in commodities ; no nation can pay in gold and silver.   If we had all the gold and silver in the world piled up here, and we paid only in gold and silver, it would not take more than about eight years to clean us out.   No country in the world pays in gold and silver.   The only commodities we can pay in are those from agricultural staples, and just as long as we pay in these agricultural staples we will receive not a copper more for them than Great Britain can buy them for from the cheapest labor countries of the world, and as long as we sell them at this cheap labor price, the price for everything else that is produced is precisely the same.   Let me give you an illustration.   Here is Liverpool and here is San Francisco.   Say the price of wheat is $1.00 here, less the cost of transportation. It will be worth 80c, 70c, 60c or 50c as you go further back. Here is a factory and you have it loaded with 10,000 men working there — what is the result? Why, the protected man will buy this wheat at the Liverpool price, less the cost of transportation from his place to Liverpool. The manufactures are sold with the price added for transportation; agriculture is sold with the price deducted for transportation, even when the stuff has not traveled at all.

.Now, while I am in favor of protection, the time has come when this is a question superior to section. It is a question of the perpetuity of this nation. It may be that the question of silver will supplement this. I do not say you must not talk of silver. I simply say: I have a right to present this measure and to show that unless this is rectified, it is one of the means of scuttling the ship. There never was the danger before in the United States of these economic disturbances of which we have only had a simple taste the past year and this year the thing must intensify itself. This has got to reach an equilibrium. How is it to reach that equilibrium even if silver were worth a dollar and above at this moment? Why, the Liverpool price is controlling the price in the United States, even though the price of wheat be in every port 45 cents or $1.25. It would not remove the injustice that this industry pays for the protection of every other industry in the United States.

Now, the perpetuity of a Republic depends upon the equity of its laws.

The greatest purchasers of labor in the United States are the purchasers of staple agricultural products.

Some say that if we give any protection to staple agricultural products that it will so stimulate the production of staple agriculture that the price will lower still lower than they are now. This is not correct. The adoption of this proposition is not new. It is the old English plan. It was in operation before the abolition of the corn-law. There is not a single statement I have made here this morning that is in any way new.

It is only the application of the idea in this country that may be called new. They had a scale and an export Board, and whatever product they desired to maintain up to a certain price, when it rose up to that price, there was no bounty, when it fell below that price there was a bounty. The bounty is intended merely to keep those men on the land without driving them off.

If he should have his rights it should be in the same relative protection, 40 or 50 per cent on the dollar's worth, as manufacturers receive. But this proposition is only asking for 5 or 6 or 2 or 1 per cent advance on the price. Therefore this will not conduce to overproduction.

Then again they say " Let us diversify our products." This may be all right in New Hampshire, but this is not farming as it is done in the West, where diversification on such lands as we have is not possible. What is to become of our California products this year? They say " Diversify your products — go into hops." I have seen hop fields un-picked, because it would not pay to pick the hops. I have seen vine-yards in which the hogs were let in to feed on that which should be the food of man, because there was a surplus. The only thing it is abso- · lutely necessary for us to produce is staple agricultural products be-cause with these we not alone feed our people, but we send them abroad in payment for our imports.

Again an objection is made " Why should we import?" — put a wheel around the United States and import nothing.

Very good, I would like to rest my argument on that, if that is the sense of the Convention. I hardly think it will be the sense of the American people in this nineteenth century to take any such step or remedy as pointed out.

I will close my remarks by giving this example incidental to protec-tion. Protection is against the cheap labor countries, I claim, and, with the authority of the very best legal minds of the world, that Government pure and simple has not the right to a copper of the money collected for protection, because this is a paternal function and not a government function.

There is no way to protect an export but by offering a premium on the export.

Now, in justice to the great interests of agriculture, if any industry is at all to be protected it should be agriculture, because the integrity of this nation rests upon agriculture. We demand here no privilege. We demand here a right, and the American people must ultimately listen to a right — no privilege, no favor but a right which they are denied. They have not had the right for years, and every year that they did not have the right they were robbed and it should be done for agriculture as well for manufactures.

THE CHAIRMAN: The Chair has a notice from the Committee on Resolutions, Hon. Wm. J. Bryan, informing the Chair that one of the members of the Committee, Mr. F. J. Cannon, has charge of the major-ity report, on Staple Agriculture, the report which opposes the adoption of the report as I understand it.

It was moved that Mr. Cannon be heard.

MR. CANNON: I desire to ask what preliminary attitude this question has at the present moment. We were engaged in the Committee on Resolutions, and I do not know what position the question has been placed in during our absence.

THE CHAIRMAN: The motion was made by Senator Johnston of

California, that the minority report be substituted for the majority report. Mr. Lubin and Mr. Roach have occupied the floor about three quarters of an hour in speaking favorably to the minority report, urging its adoption.

MR. CANNON: Do I understand from the gentleman who advocates the minority report that we have a division of the time?

THE CHAIRMAN: That has been mentioned, but no decision has been reached. There is time, however. Two hours was allowed by special order yesterday for the discussion of this question: three-quarters of an hour have been consumed,

MR. CANNON: All on the affirmative side of the motion?

THE CHAIRMAN: Yes, sir.

MR. CANNON: Mr. Chairman, I should like to ask if it would be agreeable to the minority to consent to an equal division of the time, not necessarily arbitrarily, but because personally, as having charge of the majority report, and not having opportunity to consult with the gentleman who would advocate the majority report, I do not know how many of them would choose to speak.

SENATOR JOHNSTON: I do not think the gentleman asks anything unfair; we are not here for technicalities. There has been some little objection to the length of time taken up with that portion of the subject and Mr. Lubin has cut himself down to less than one-half. There is no objection for all sides to be heard on this question, and I think I voice the sentiment of my colleagues. If we have asked anything that is unjust, we are willing to go before the world with our proposition. We are not afraid to have it discussed.

THE CHAIRMAN: There need be no trouble on this question.

MR. CANNON: Mr. Chairman, on behalf of the Committee I will then open our side of this case, with the privilege of closing for our side, if it shall seem desirable. Mr. Chairman and gentlemen of the Convention, this duty falls upon one who will perform it with pain to himself, because I was reared on a farm, and I know that the farmers are the men who support the world. No man knows, however strong his advocacy of this proposition, better than the representative of the majority seport of this Committee, the evils of these times; but despite that, I stand here in opposition to the resolution under the minority report, because I do not believe that it will answer the ends proposed by the gentlemen who offer it here. It seems to me that it will pile up mountain upon mountain, of burden upon the shoulders of the agricultural population of the United States. It seems to me that it is a wrong remedy, in that it is, first, impracticable; secondly, that it is special; thirdly, that it does not bring out the history of these days and the certainty of to-morrow. Owing to the fact that the Committee considered this question only a few moments ago, and that there had been little or no time, as well as expectation on my part, for the preparation of any statistics, in behalf of the Committee, and myself as its representative, I must ask the indulgence of the audience if we shall fail to make so strong a case in behalf of the majority report as might have been made if further time had been allowed.

First. We take the proposition, that the final resolution is untrue, in that it says the only way to enhance the value of agricultural products in the United States, is by the payment of an export bounty.

SENATOR JOHNSTON: Will the gentleman allow me to correct him — my impression is that the word " only " is stricken out.

MR. CANNON: Mr. Chairman, the word " only " has been stricken out then without any authority of the Committee, if that be true, because the word " only " appeared in the resolution, and in fact I have the original resolution here (reading) :—

" *Resolved*, That, inasmuch as these products are exports and not imports, their prices cannot be enhanced by a protective tariff alone, no matter how high, but an increase of their prices in our country can only be secured by the use of a limited portion of the tariff collected for protection to pay a premium on exported agricultural staples."

SENATOR JOHNSTON: Now, Mr. Chairman, the original resolutions did not read that way. In our conference, we agreed to that, that the word " only " should be stricken out; that was our understanding. It was our agreement to take out the word " only."

MR. CANNON: Mr. Chairman, I waive the point; I hold in my hand the original resolution and it contains the word " only." I will not continue the discussion of that point, if it be waived, except to emphasize to the attention of this audience that, if the majority report shall not prevail, in the interest of truth the resolution should be amended to strike out the word " only."

SENATOR JOHNSTON: I will agree to that.

MR. CANNON: I maintain, in behalf of the majority of the Committee, that this is an impracticable attempt at solving a great difficulty. The payment of an export bounty upon agricultural goods will necessarily stimulate the production of the particular classes of goods. We find now that the great difficulty arises from the fact that our staple agricultural products come into competition with staples produced elsewhere in the world, and a market once our own and remunerative to the farmer, once wealth-giving to the nation, is being lost to us to nations which have shown the superiority of degradation over civilization in the production of agricultural staples at low prices for the world's demand. I maintain further that it is not only impracticable in a general sense, but it is impracticable in the sense of its application. This is a general resolution. We call upon congress by this resolution to perform and put into effect certain acts. But we have a right, and it is our duty, to examine the character of the law by which such bounty shall be paid. The idea is, I presume, to give to the agricultural producer indirectly through the hands of the exporter a certain premium or bounty, which shall compensate him for the lack of sufficient price in the markets of the world. In other words, if it costs him 80 cents a bushel for his grain and he nets but 60 cents, he is to be paid in this way, not questioning the assertion of the devotees of the proposition, that the money would actually reach the farmers — he is to be paid in this way, that 20 cents out of a special fund held by the nation in trust for him. What then will be done for a people whom it costs 90 cents a bushel to raise their grain? If in California near to the seaboard, almost within reach of the Pacific, a 20 cents a bushel bounty is needed, what shall we say of the valleys that have to pay 28 cents a bushel railroad toll to get their grain to the ports of the Pacific? Not only must we have a sliding scale by which the staple agricultural products will go into the markets of the world under the bounty, but we must have also a liberal scale by which a man further from market shall have a higher bounty than the one nearer to the seaboard. I place it to you to show the impracticability of a proposition of that kind, and if the law would in its details be impracticable, then we have no right to recommend it.

I oppose the resolution because of what goes with it. The statement was made here that we cannot protect an export, because this is class legislation in behalf of the class that I admire as much as the gentleman who proposed it, but in whose behalf I do not want to see invoked any class legislation. We have protection on cotton goods — we export them — cotton manufactures, and, according to the theory of this proposition, we must put an export bounty on manufactured cotton goods because they are not protected by a protective tariff. We export iron goods in large quantities. I have here the statistics of our exports for 1892 and 1893, the only figures which the limited time permitted me to obtain. Then, according to this theory, to be absolutely just, we must put an export bounty upon iron manufactures. We must put an export bounty on machinery. Do you see to what point it would lead? If the day shall ever be when the United States shall pay its indebtedness to the world, we must export and encourage exports. That day is not here now. If the export bounty shall be established in this country, it must be just to all classes, otherwise it is the kind of legislation which our friends who advocate this measure oppose. I maintain that it is not necessary to discharge the debt of the United States every year, whether by the shipment of agricultural staples to the extent that we now export them. The statement was made here yesterday, or the day before, that we import into the United States every year $100,000,000 worth of sugar. We pay for it, according to the theory of the advocates of this measure, for staple agricultural products with products sold in the markets of the world in competition with the production of the cheapest forms and lowest priced labor under God's sun, and then we buy the sugar in the markets of the world and bring it back here and the farmers pay the freight both ways. Instead of doing that, let us diversify our industries, and when we have sufficiently done that, that we do not import the things that we need, then we will find the $600,000,000 of staple exports every year reduced to $300,000,000. By the development of all the industries in the United States, we shall probably find that we do not have need for any considerable quantity of export goods in order to pay for import goods. But if it shall be necessary to export some article in order that we may have money with which to discharge our obligations to the world, let us first find out how much money we actually need, and then let us encourage all classes of industries to engage in that export.

The very argument of the advocates of this measure is the strongest opposition to it. When they tell us of the increased development of the new lands of Argentine and other countries of Spanish America in the production of staple agricultural goods, they tell us of a menace to the agricultural industry of the United States, and they show to us the source from which will come the death blow to our export trade in staple agriculture. Not only Argentine, a representative of the new countries of the world, but the older countries of earth; India, for instance, and the old civilized nations rearing the crops with which to feed Western Europe, and we must come in competition with them. We cannot meet their crops to-day, and this resolution is a confession of that fact. How will we be able to meet a constantly falling market when from every point there comes into the markets of the world a constantly increasing surplus?

My friends, the remedy is otherwise than as suggested, but the remedy is so broad that it comprehends the whole social and commercial system by which men are inter-related. We talk about the law of supply and demand, but we do not understand the law of supply and demand. We poor people who are not of the school of political economists, we look about us and we see the demand and we say that that is as sacred a demand as humanity ever saw — and we see the supply of labor going back and forth idly in the streets looking for the toil it cannot find and we say that that is as sacred a supply as heaven ever gave to man There was the demand and there was the supply and yet from some mismanagement, we cannot bring them together. The remedy therefore is as broad as the ends of all humanity and it will not be supplied by any proposition for class legislation. It must be by the new evangel of all peace for earth, and I simply fear that he is not in this assemblage. I hope that when he shall come he may have the gospel by which the wants of man are to be supplied and the toil of man is to be constantly employed; -- he will deliver to us a new redemption and we will hail him as a new redeemer (applause). My friends, there are others, I trust, to speak in behalf of the Committee, and I will call upon Senator Wilson of South Dakota, a member of the majority, to occupy ten minutes in behalf of the majority.

SENATOR S. E. WILSON: Mr. Chairman and Gentlemen of the Congress, as a member of your Committee on Resolutions and as a member of the sub-committee to which was referred the resolution now before you, I desire to say a few words against the adoption of this resolution and in behalf of the majority report. I do not believe that the American farmer needs protection under the system of American protection which has been so long in successful operation in this country, not by any means, but for reasons that seem to me, upon a casual examination of this question, must be apparent to this country. The gentlemen who have advocated the adoption of this minority report, are asking a great deal from this congress, composed of gentlemen of all classes west of the Mississippi river, lawyers, doctors, merchants and agricultural men. When the gentleman who advocates the proposition says that it took the State Grange six months to deliberate upon this proposition before it was adopted, it does seem to me that in the deliberation of a few hours that we are permitted to give to this question, it is asking a great deal to ask this congress to take this advanced step in favor of this proposition, that has not, so far as I know, received any stable support by either the writers or speakers upon political economy for the last fifty years.

MR. ROACH: The State Grange of California did not have this for six months under consideration. The committee to whom it was referred had it under consideration for six months.

SENATOR WILSON: How large was that committee?

MR. ROACH: Five.

SENATOR WILSON: Then that increased the responsibility which is brought here, if a committee of even five members of the State Grange of the State of California deliberated over the proposition for six months.

MR. ROACH: The committee only meets twice a year.

SENATOR WILSON: This congress only meets once a year. How long does the committee stay in session?

MR. ROACH: Say about a day.

SENATOR WILSON: It is asking a good deal of this congress to take up this proposition to protect the American farmer — and I am in favor of protecting the American farmer as much as anybody else in this country, but no more. He is asking for a protection that nobody else has asked, except the sugar producer, and that is for a purpose in opposition to the reasons advocated here to-day. If I understand the object of protection — and I am a protectionist — the primary principle and intention of it is to secure a diversity of industry, and these resolutions will have exactly the opposite effect upon the interests of the agriculturists. Now, I asked that question in the committee, but they did not undertake to answer it satisfactorily to my mind. It will have an opposite result — and why? Because there is a multitude of agricultural products that cannot be so successfully produced as to enable the farmer to export them with any degree of prosperity.

Now, what would be the tendency of this measure? It seems to me that it would be to lessen the diversity of industries on the part of agriculturists and induce them to give their attention to that particular class of agriculture which he may profitably develop to such quantities that it may be exported, and the object of protection will be thwarted by that measure.

I do not know that I am prepared, or that any gentleman is prepared, with the consideration I have been able to give this question since it came up before the committee, to follow out in detail the effect that the adoption of this measure will have. I say, you are asking more than the manufacturers ask. I believe in a protective tariff upon commodities shipped here in competition with ours. That is all the American manufacturer asks. He does not ask for a bounty upon what he makes or for a premium upon these things if he is beginning to export them into another country, that he may thereby be induced to manufacture a greater quantity, but when the farmers of the country are asking that there shall be an export duty imposed upon the articles that they produce in competition with those produced by foreign agriculturalists, it seems to me that this is class legislation, and that the ultimate effect upon protective measures in this country is to bring them in disrepute, rather than to augment and increase the desirability of protection for the American people. I thank you, ladies and gentlemen.

MR. BRYAN: Mr. Chairman and gentlemen of the Convention, there are several reasons why, it seems to me, that this minority report ought not to be adopted by this convention. In the first place, it is a new subject which has not been considered by the people who sent us, and if we should express ourselves on it we might be misrepresenting the views of those whom we assume to serve. If we were simply speaking for ourselves, we might exercise more freedom as to the subjects we discuss, but I believe if we want to give force and effect to the resolutions we do adopt in this convention, we ought to take those subjects which are subjects of intelligent discussion among the people, so that our views will really reflect the views of those who sent us. So far as I know, this proposition made in the minority report has never been seriously considered in any large body of people. It is true it has been introduced by some of the granges, but it has never been introduced in any of the legislative bodies, and it introduces a principle which is of as great importance as the question of the tariff.

Now, the principle involved in the tariff question is whether we can by legislation give an additional advantage to persons engaged in particular industries. This resolution goes on the theory that the farmer is engaged in an industry which cannot be benefited by other means, and that therefore we must apply a different principle or policy to him to give him in that way the advantage which we give to others in a protective tariff. So that this principle is as broad as the tariff question, and as has been said by the gentleman from Utah, if we are going to apply it to the farmer and give him a bounty on his farm products; then every person who exports, will have a right to demand a bounty on his exports, and we think every person engaged in producing a thing that can be benefited by tariff will insist that he ought to be helped because somebody else is. If we start a system of bounty on exports we depart into a new field just as broad and full of embarrassments. Now, this resolution is perhaps the only one which refers to the tariff in any way. If I were at liberty to discuss the question from my own standpoint and to express my own convictions on the subject, I would say that it is not wise to allow it to the farmer. I doubt if he would get any advantage out of such a system. His safety lies not in attempting to extend a vicious system to him, but in protecting him from the vicious system already in existence. In other words, the safety of the farmer does not lie in legislation which is conceived with the idea of getting his hands into somebody else's pocket, but his safety lies in legislation that will keep other people's hands out of his own pockets.

Mr. CANNON : Mr. Chairman, not knowing the gentlemen present and not having any consultation with them — there will be five minutes for any delegate who wishes to speak in opposition to the minority report now pending.

A DELEGATE (from Iowa): Mr. Chairman, I can readily see where these gentlemen get their proposition for a bounty on wheat. The production of sugar in this country is away below the consumption; the production of wheat in this country is in excess of the consumption, and that is the reason why we cannot apply the principle of a bounty to your production of wheat. The advocates of a bounty on sugar assumed that by that bounty they could bring the production up to the necessities of the people of the United States. When it reached that point, they proposed to cease that bounty. Now, these gentlemen start out and do not put that limit on. They do not propose to abrogate that bounty when they get up to an export basis, and the conditions are entirely different. The farmers certainly consume per capita as much sugar as anybody else does, and are benefited by this bounty, but they cannot be benefited by a bounty on wheat, because you cannot make that bounty fit every portion of the country. These gentlemen are on the Pacific Coast. There they start with cheap transportation, ocean transportation, the cheapest in the world, because there is no limit to it. Why, they can get out of the harbor with water sufficient to load a vessel to 25 feet. They can get transportation that cannot be equaled in cheapness on the earth. But what will you do with the people of South Dakota, Nebraska, Kansas and Iowa? Will they get any benefit from such a bounty as this? No, sir; it will take 28 cents per 100 for them to get where those gentlemen already are. There is no justice in such a thing, and to build it upon the foundation of the bounty already in effect, or which has been repealed — yet I believe it is in effect notwithstanding it is repealed — and it is an injustice to this convention to ask them to act on it for the reason that it is based on this other bounty that is as different as day is from night.

MR. CANNON: Mr. Chairman, if there is no one else who desires to speak for the majority side of this question, we will now consider our case closed with the few words which I wish to say.

SENATOR JOHNSTON: Do you mean to occupy your time now?

MR. CANNON: I am not permitted to occupy my time now — you have the floor.

SENATOR JOHNSTON: Mr. Lubin has the floor to close. We have only occupied three-quarters of an hour.

MR. CANNON: If all your speakers except the closing one will now take the floor, it will be a gratification to us, as there are some of your arguments which no doubt I have not heard. I will close immediately preceding Mr. Lubin.

THE CHAIRMAN: The request is made that you speak now, Senator Johnston, excepting your final closing remarks, and that the majority side have the opportunity of replying to any new argument that you may advance, and you have the closing five minutes.

Mr. Bryan announced that the Committee on Resolutions would meet at 2 o'clock.

QUESTION: Will the sub-committees report to your committee by that time?

MR. BRYAN: The sub-committees have nearly all reported.

QUESTION: Will you inform them all so that they can report?

MR. BRYAN: Yes, sir; I will.

The Entertainment Committee announced that tickets were provided for all delegates to the theaters to-night and to-morrow night, and explained where to get them.

Mr. Savage of Kansas then moved to adjourn.

MR. CANNON: Mr. Chairman, by agreement with Senator Johnston of California, not more than twenty-five minutes at the outside will be occupied in concluding this matter, as we will waive part of our time. and I trust the discussion may be finished at this session.

Motion to adjourn withdrawn.

A. J. WEDDERBURN (of California): Mr. Chairman, I do not intend to occupy but a very few minutes of the time of this convention. I have listened with a great deal of pleasure to the gentleman from Utah and to the Senator from Dakota and to the distinguished gentleman from Nebraska. I am thoroughly incapable of entering into a combat with men of that caliber. I am simply talking as a plain, unvarnished farmer. I will try in my plain way to answer some of the arguments of the gentleman from Utah. He says that the scheme is impracticable, and I say it has not been found to be impracticable when applied to manufactures. The manufacturer has received a bounty all the way through. You cannot make a tariff anything else than a bounty. That is the absolute fact and it cannot be disputed. We come here in behalf of the farmer of this country and ask for equality and do not want anything else. The gentleman says he favors equality, and we ask him to do just what he says he is willing to do. He says he opposes special legislation, and I tell you that the grange, from its foundation in 1866 to 1873, when it announced the broad policy of this country, was in antagonism to special legislation, and my colleagues here who represent that motion in this delegation are decidedly opposed to any such idea. We do not want special legislation. We stand upon a broad platform here to-day and demand equality before the law, and equality in taxation. That is the only thing we want, nothing else, nothing more.

The gentleman has spoken about California and her nearness to the seaboard. If he would take the facts, he will find that on the eastern seaboard wheat is selling for 50 cents a bushel, in California 35 cents, in Oregon 31 cents, in Washington 25 cents. These are facts, and it costs more to produce that wheat than it brings in the open market. The report from the Department of Agriculture issued in 1893 brings out these facts: that to produce corn in this country in 1893 cost $3.65 per acre more than it brought; that to produce wheat in this country in the year 1893 costs $5.85 per acre more than the farmer got for it; to produce cotton cost at present price 6 cents a pound, and it is selling at 4 cents a pound. Now, these are facts, gentlemen. We are not here pleading for anything but right and justice. We are here, asking you, the representatives of the mercantile interests of this great country, as representatives of the mining interests of this great country — we are asking you not to see killed the goose that has laid the golden egg, that is helping you along, upon which you live and upon which the eastern manufacturer lives; we are asking you to protect and save the life of this goose; that is all we want.   We know we are considered geese by the majority of mercantile men.   We know we are nothing but clod-hoppers, but we have certain rights and we come in justice and in equity and ask you to give us those rights.   Take wheat, cotton, tobacco, beef and pork, and take the prices to-day — and some gentlemen here in their speeches yesterday showed how nearly they were allied to silver— most of you gentlemen are silver men and indorse the silver idea.   I see before me one of the first members of the Bi-Metallic League when it was organized in the United States.   I believe in the white metal, but I tell you it is too close a friend to these agricultural products for you not to recognize that they must have their right share and justice under this Government, as well as the white metal.   The eastern manufacturers have their bounty and we should have ours.

Now, the gentlemen from Utah and South Dakota both said that there was no bounty upon exports, which shows that they have not looked into this question.   The manufacturer of the East is allowed to bring his pig iron, his steel, any commodity that is protected, no matter how high — he is allowed to bring it into this country, manufacture it into agricultural machinery and every other kind of machinery that he chooses, and when that product is exported he is given 99 cents bounty back on every dollar that he has paid.   Are they not protected again? These are facts, and you ought to look at them fairly and squarely and do agriculture justice.   These resolutions here are not wrong.

The gentleman of the sub-committee said that he did not find any fault with the whereas nor with the first resolution, but he found fault with the last of these, calling it an impractical proposition.   Well, if it is impractical, you have got to find some way to protect the farmer, and that is all we want.

SENATOR JOHNSTON: Mr. Chairman, I will only occupy a moment or two, because the time is getting short, but there is a question we would like you to consider.   We come over from the Pacific Coast, asking you people from Utah, from Kansas, from Arkansas, from Iowa and all the other places this side of the Rocky Mountains, to come over and help us as you will be asking us to come over and help you.   I see before me gentlemen who have been accustomed to deal with questions of practical experience and with questions of political economy, and I ask you, gentlemen, have any of you ever been in a legislative body and found a single individual coming up there with a proposition entirely alone, that he was successful in carrying that proposition into a law? Such a thing hardly ever occurs.   Now, if I understand the object of this Trans-Mississippi Congress, it is for the purpose of conferring together with the people west of the Mississippi river, in order that we may assist each other in demanding our rights from the people east of the Alleghanies. I say to you, gentlemen of this Congress, that there is very little sympathy in the people east of the Alleghany Mountains with those that are west of the Mississippi river. I have been among those people, I have been with them, and trying to persuade them to assist us in projects that we have in hand. They are not interested in our agriculture. They have a good home market. They are protected and we are not. Now, this is a problem that is within the power of this Congress; it is within the power of the people west of the Mississippi river to solve this problem of political economy. The irrigationists come here to present us with a key or a panacea for all the ills that this republic is heir to. The silver men come and state that they have the key which will unlock this problem. The Nicaragua canal people come and say that they think that these are all subsidiary questions and should not be considered, but give them the Nicaragua canal and they think they would be happy.

Now, the agriculturists come here. We do not say to you that we have the only problem to present that will relieve us at this time. But I tell you, gentlemen of this congress, that the key to unlock this problem has many slots. It is not a key of a single slot that you can thrust into the lock and turn the lock. If you are going to have any strength, if you are going to do anything for this part of the country, all of these slots must be properly adjusted. This key has a slot for silver, a slot for irrigation and a slot for the Nicaragua canal, and it will have the largest slot for the agricultural interests of this country. Now, then, gentlemen of this convention, you take this key that belongs west of the Mississippi river, this key that we all adhere to — if the irrigationists are right in their proposition, grant them what they demand; if the silver men are right, grant them what they want; if the Nicaragua canal men are right, grant them what they ask. Those of us who are in favor of the agricultural proposition, we tillers of the soil, believe that these people will assist us in our position and in the welfare of the country. Now, then, with this key of many slots, let us all grasp it, thrust it into the lock of this political economy of ours and turning the bolt we will solve the problem.

Mr. CANNON: Mr. Chairman, I shall be very brief and would not speak, except my position in the Committee seems to compel it. Here is the key with five slots and no more (showing a key). So long as those slots fit the ward of the lock, we can unlock the problem, but the moment you put a false slot in that key, you destroy the entire problem.

SENATOR JOHNSTON: We are the big slot.

Mr. CANNON: If this is in the wrong place in the problem, you destroy the value of it all. In behalf of the majority of the committee, we insist it should be the sense of the congress that this is a dangerous proposition for us to advance before the country at the present time. Equity before the law is demanded and justice in behalf of the agriculturalists. A general tariff bill was passed, protecting all the industries of the United States, not a perfect bill by any means, but as nearly perfect as human intelligence, acting through the several parties which may be from time to time in power, may permit. Agricultural products are brought into this country in vast quantities, just as manufactured products are exported in large quantities. We bring potatoes from Scotland, barley from Russia. The other day 117,000 bushels of Russian barley came into the United States.

The gentleman who did not want to contend against men of such large caliber as a member of Congress and as well equipped for this fray, furnished to us the very best evidence which we want. He said that this bounty must not only be on a scale up and down, but it must also be on a lateral scale, extending from the Atlantic to the Pacific, and he furnished the evidence of that by saying that wheat brought 31 cents in Oregon, in Washington 25 cents, in California 35 cents and on the Atlantic seaboard 50 cents. Then we must have a scale for every city and every State in the United States.

Senator Johnston: This proposition is to make an equal division. If you get a bounty of 5 cents in Utah, then it will be 5 cents in San Francisco and in every other place where you have wheat; the scale does not propose to slide from one State to another.

Mr. Cannon: Mr. Chairman and Ladies and Gentlemen: That is very well for California or for the producer of staple agriculture on the Atlantic coast, but how far is 5 cents a bushel going to go with the farmer of Dakota or Nebraska, who may have to pay 28 cents a bushel to get his wheat to the same point?

Senator Johnston: He would be 5 cents better off.

Mr. Cannon: If the government has the right to make him 5 cents better off, let it make him the whole 28 cents better off at once.

Mr. Lubin: It has been stated that the matter is obscure. The gentlemen who say so have evidently not kept themselves posted. The press from one end of this land to another, and some of the most important journals in the country, and some from foreign countries, have taken this matter up. It would be different if the bounty was an enormous sum. Wheat is 45 cents now and it was $1.30, but it cannot stimulate it very much with a 5 or 6 or 7 cent bounty. Mr. Cannon and Mr. Bryan both stated that if staples received a bounty, other exports will ask a bounty. Just so — and they have it, and I have here in my hand a paper that is talking against this very bounty that the manufacturers receive, and there is probably not one in this room who knows anything about it. He receives back 99 per cent on every dollar's worth of goods.

MR. CANNON: May I ask the gentleman a question? — I hope the gentleman would not propose to convey the idea that the manufacturer receives back 99 per cent of every dollar of export of manufactured goods.

MR. LUBIN: Ninety-nine per cent of the tariff duties that have been paid.

MR. CANNON: Ninety-nine per cent of the duty paid upon the raw material imported into this country with which to maintain manufactured goods for export — isn't that a fact?

MR. LUBIN: Most decidedly — it is all right for one side of the house. People say, "We are for protection." No man is more for protection than I am, but I want justice. How eloquent and grand they can be and how attractive their speech! But what is there in it? See, here are the protected men, here are the unprotected men — and what about the unprotected men? The American Protective Tariff League said, "We applaud you for your grand protective tariff." They sent to us and asked us for a liberal subscription. I said to them in reply, "Yes, Mr. Treasurer of the American Protective Tariff League, I will give you a contribution if you are deserving of it. Here is $1,000.00 deposited in the bank of D. O. Mills & Co. Take this money if your cause is right. If your cause is wrong you shall not have it. It was placed in the hands of men well known, John T. Ely, Hon. John Wannamaker, Samuel Gompers, Senator Chandler and others. It was to be referred to the Executive Committee. They were to answer in 90 days. That time is about gone. They dare not reply, because they are wrong and they know it, and every man that has spoken to-day knows that he is wrong, because staple agriculture is not protected and cannot be protected. We must protect our products, or we must close the gates of our country. It has been commented upon by the leading journals. If it is premature for this convention, let some one offer a resolution, not to kill it now, but to submit it next year if it is so desired. If this convention decides against it, they decide against right and equity.

GOV. WAITE: Though I am not on the programme, I would like to speak about two minutes on this.

On motion Gov. Waite was granted permission to speak.

GOV. WAITE: This matter is opposed because it is to be a bounty. Does not the law provide that the importer may put his goods in the warehouse of the United States and hold them there for a year without the payment of imports — is not that a bounty? Is not the law that provides that the distiller can take his product after being manufactured into whisky and store it in Government warehouses and let it lie there for two years and save the payment of its taxes for four years or even seven years, and an arrangement made by which the whisky lost by evaporation shall be made up to him — is not that a bounty? And yet these gentlemen are astonished here because it is proposed to give a bounty. That is just what this Government has been doing for years and years. I was educated as a protectionist. We have to-day here a condition of affairs in this country in which the wheat, the corn, the cotton, every staple article of production is being produced at less than cost. The Democratic party has just lost its crop in this country in consequence of that condition (laughter), and I wish to say to the Republican party, who are about to assume the government of this country, that unless they change that condition they will also go to Hades.

There were calls for the question on the motion to substitute the minority report for the majority report and the resolution was again read.

SENATOR JOHNSTON: Mr. Chairman, I desire to have the word "only" stricken out, because that was our agreement.

THE CHAIRMAN: Is there any objection to striking out the word "only?" It can only be done by unanimous consent.

It was then moved, seconded and carried that this question be referred to the next session of the Trans-Mississippi Congress.

The Secretary then read the following letter received from the Secretary of the Mississippi River Commission.

ST. LOUIS, MO., November 27, 1894.

Mr. Geo. H. Morgan, Secretary,
　　"The Trans-Mississippi Commercial Congress,
　　　　　　St. Louis, Mo.

Sir: I have the honor to acknowledge the receipt of your communication of this date, extending an invitation to the members of the Mississippi River Commission to attend the present session of your body now convened in this city.

I will immediately transmit copies of your letter to each of the members of the Commission, only one of whom, Lieutenant-Colonel Chas. R. Suter, is in the city.

　　　　　　Very respectfully,
　　　　　　　　Your obedient servant,
　　　　　　　　　　GEO. A. ZINN,
　　　　　　　　　1st Lieut. Corps of Engineers,
　　　　　　　Secretary Mississippi River Commission.

(Letters were subsequently received from Gen. C. B. Comstock, President, and R. S. Taylor, Esq., a member of the Commission, expressing regret that they were unable to attend the Congress as requested.)

The session then adjourned.

WEDNESDAY AFTERNOON SESSION.

The meeting was called to order at 2:30 p. m. by President Cannon.

The Chairman announced that the Committee on Resolutions had passed a resolution that a special order be made if possible for the representative from Alaska to have half an hour set apart some time to-day. I learn from him, Mr. Green, that he would like to give some stereopticon views of the scenery of Alaska, which he says will be very interesting to the members of the Congress to see, and he would appreciate it if half an hour could be set apart for him. What hour will you set? The subjects before the Congress this afternoon, as arranged by the Committee on Rules and Order of Business are Transportation, Railroads, Public and Arid Lands. This evening papers on two different subjects will be read, on the Nicaragua Canal and Hawaiian question. Mr. Craig of California intends to speak on Hawaii and Prof. DeKalb will deliver an address on the Nicaragua Canal. There will be a short paper by Prof. Waterhouse on the Nicaragua Canal and a paper by Capt W. L. Merry of San Francisco on the same subject. Prof. DeKalb's paper will occupy three-quarters of an hour to an hour.

It was then arranged that the views on Alaska be presented at the opening in the evening.

MR. CASTLE: Mr. Chairman, in behalf of the California delegation I introduce a memorial on the subject of the Nicaragua Canal. That memorial was referred to the Committee on Resolutions, and I am asked to present the following resolution as adopted by that committee: —

Resolved, That the Trans-Mississippi Commercial Congress respectfully and urgently requests legislative action on behalf of the prompt construction of the Nicaragua Canal under the control and supervision of the government of the United States.

I move the adoption of this report. Carried unanimously.

THE CHAIRMAN: The subjects now before the Congress are Transportation, Railroads, Public and Arid Lands.

MR. FISK: Mr. Chairman, I do not wish to take up any of the subjects named. I would just like the indulgence of the Congress for one moment to say that the object of these Congresses in convening them was that the industrial interests might formulate some plan to be submitted to the National Congress, that they might have an equal show with the East, which has always been organized. Now, in all these Congresses, we have been represented by the mayors of cities, by county commissioners and by business organization. If the West is to be represented at this Congress, and the South, or all the trans-Mississippi countries, I submit that we ought to invite the industrial classes to join our deliberations, and I want to move now that at the next session of this Congress the Farmer's Alliance and Industrial

Unions, the Trades Assemblies and Knights of Labor be admitted to the same representation as the commercial organizations now have.

It was moved that this motion be referred to the Committee on Resolutions.

MR. FISK: I move, Mr. Chairman, that we consider it now.

THE CHAIRMAN: There is something else before us and we will probably forget that. It seems to the Chair a question of this importance should be considered with a fuller house or after more mature deliberation. It is not that the Chair has any preference in the matter, but we have now before us a large number of resolutions, which have been passed upon by the Committee on Resolutions, who are ready to report these resolutions, having sent them in for that purpose, and to inject this into the midst of the discussion would scarcely be fair to the Committee on Resolutions and to the gentlemen who have introduced the resolutions which have been acted upon. However, it is for the congress to decide.

A DELEGATE (from Arkansas): Mr. Chairman, it seems to me that this resolution ought to be referred to the Executive Committee, because the Committee on Resolutions will soon go out of existence, and this resolution has a bearing on the future work of this organization. The Executive Committee being a standing committee, should take that under advisement and govern themselves accordingly.

THE CHAIRMAN: Do you make a motion to that effect?

THE DELEGATE: I make a motion that it be referred to the Executive Committee.

The motion was seconded and carried.

A number of resolutions reported by the Committee on Resolutions were then read and adopted.

THE CHAIRMAN: Here are a number of resolutions, which it will take a long time to read. They are all on one subject, in reference to the Oakland Harbor and Sacramento and San Joaquin rivers, Islais Creek and Puget Sound.

A DELEGATE: I ask what reference there is to Puget Sound in these resolutions?

COL. LEIGHTON: Those refer only to harbors within the State of California and Washington. It seems to me that some of the members of those delegations could enlighten the congress very quickly upon the subject. It seems to me it is a very doubtful policy for the congress to pass any resolutions of a general character without knowing what they are voting for.

MR CRAIG: Mr. Chairman, I call up the motion on the Oakland Harbor resolution, as presented by the Produce Exchange of the city of Oakland.

This motion was seconded.

A DELEGATE: Mr. Chairman, as a member of the Committee on Resolutions, I desire to renew my question as to this resolution referring to Puget Sound. There is a resolution which has been adopted by the committee regarding the fortification of Puget Sound. I simply desire to know whether that is included.

MR. CRAIG: Mr. President, as far as the Oakland resolutions are concerned, they speak for themselves. I understand that my motion is now before the house and it should be adopted; it has been duly seconded.

MR. RIDGELEY (of Kansas): Mr. President, before taking action or voting favorably upon this motion, I wish to ask a question. From my limited knowledge of the improvements heretofore carried on at Oakland Harbor by the United States Government, the chief benefits have accrued to the Southern Pacific Railroad Company. I wish to inquire as to what will be the result, or who will be the chief recipient of the benefits, if we impose upon the people of the United States further improvements of this harbor. I simply ask for information.

MR. CRAIG: For the last twenty years the U. S. Government has had that work in hand, with a corps of engineers, and the work has been done a little piece at a time, and it is suffering now in consequence of not being completed. This is not a question between the city of Oakland and the railroad — that question is now in our Supreme Court, and we have every reason to believe it will be decided in favor of the city of Oakland. This is simply requesting those at Washington having this work in charge to go on with the work and finish it up. It is a burning question between the city of Oakland and the railroad people, and we have got them on the run. We expect to have a wharf at the end of every street going down to the water. We don't ask for an appropriation. The resolution is as follows:—

Resolved, That we recognize the injury that has been done to the city of Oakland and its commercial interests by the long delay in completing the improvement of its harbor, and we urge upon the Congress of the United States, not only on economic grounds, but also because of its imperative necessity, that an appropriation sufficient to finish the work be at once made, and that Oakland be also made a port of delivery.

It was then moved that the Chairman of the Committee on Resolutions be given an opportunity to appear in person.

MR. BRYAN: No — finish that up.

The question was then put and the resolution adopted.

Now, answering the question of the gentleman from Washington concerning the character of the resolution about Puget Sound, it is as follows:—

" *Resolved,* That the Congress of the United States is urgently requested to take immediate steps for the adequate defense of Puget Sound by means of war vessels regularly stationed there and by suitable fortifications on the shore."

On motion duly seconded and carried, this resolution was adopted.

THE CHAIRMAN: Now, there are remaining resolutions concerning the Sacramento and San Joaquin rivers and Islais creek.

SENATOR JOHNSTON: I will read the resolutions, and premise by saying that this is diametrically opposed to the interests of the Central Pacific Railroad, because we desire to get cheap water navigation right alongside of their railroad. There is a long preamble here and I will not occupy your time reading it (reading): —

Resolved, As the sense of this Congress, that the Government of the United States should make sufficient appropriations for, and cause to be done, such work of impounding mining debris as may permit hydraulic mining without its causing injury to the navigable waters of the State and to adjacent lands, and should provide necessary appropriations for improving and maintaining the navigation of such streams.

This resolution was then duly seconded and adopted.

MR. BRYAN: I have a report here on the coinage question, and before reading these reports I ask that an agreement be made as to the time of taking the vote. I have conferred with Gov. Stanard, who represents the minority, and he and I have agreed upon twenty-five minutes on a side to discuss. If that is agreeable to all I ask unanimous consent that the time for a vote be fixed at 20 minutes after 4.

There was no objection.

Mr. Bryan then presented the majority report of the Committee upon Resolutions, as follows: —

Resolved, First — That in direct opposition to the plan known as the Baltimore plan the sense of this convention is that all issues of paper money should be by the general government. Second — That it is the sense of this convention that the pending proposition for a reformation of our paper currency is one that, in our judgment, would create additional and perhaps insurmountable difficulties to the return to bimetallism, and that we are opposed to the same. Third — That in any currency reform acted upon, we demand that a constituent part thereof shall be the remonetization of silver or that it shall be of such a character as to be no impediment to our return to bimetallism as it existed prior to 1873.

WHEREAS, An appreciating money standard impairs all contracts, bankrupts enterprise, makes idle money profitable by increasing its purchasing power, and suspends productive forces of our people; and

WHEREAS, The spoliation consequent upon the outlawry of silver in the interest of the creditor class by constantly increasing the value of gold is underminding all industrial society;

Therefore, We demand the immediate restoration of the free and unlimited coinage of gold and silver at the present ratio of 16 to 1 without waiting for the aid or consent of any other nation on earth.

MR. BYRAN: Mr. Chairman, in order to bring the matter before the convention, I move the adoption of the resolution reported by the Committee, and yield to the minority member.

SENATOR JOHNSTON: Mr. Chairman, before we enter upon the discussion I desire to settle the question of voting. I move that each delegation that are here present vote the entire vote that the delegation is entitled to, on the final issue of this question.

THE CHAIR would suggest that the chairman of each delegation be prepared to report the number of votes unanimously cast by his delegation, or divided as they may be, so that it will save the time of the congress, and in his absence let some other member of the delegation do so. With that understanding, is the congress ready for the motion of Senator Johnston?

SENATOR JOHNSTON: The motion is that the delegates present cast the entire vote that the delegation is entitled to, whether they are all in their seats or not. By this means we can poll our delegation before roll-call, or some member of the delegation can rise and announce the vote of the delegation.

The motion was not adopted.

THE CHAIRMAN: Gov. Stanard will now read the minority report.

Gov. Stanard then read

THE MINORITY REPORT.

Resolved, That we favor the use of silver in the coinage of this country to the fullest extent consistent with the maintenance of our present standard, and that we cordially approve the efforts of the government of the United States to secure the co-operation of other nations in a more extended use of silver in international commerce upon such ratio of value with gold as may be found expedent and effective and susceptible of being definitely maintained; but we deprecate the agitation for the free coinage of silver by this country as a menace to the soundness of our currency and injurious to the public welfare.

Gov. STANARD: Without reading the names of the gentlemen of the minority report, I will state that they represent in part the States of Missouri, Iowa, Texas, Nebraska, Washington and Minnesota. Mr. Chairman and Gentlemen of the Convention: It is not possible for me to occupy more than seven or eight minutes of the twenty-five which has been allotted to us for the discussion of this question. It does not seem to me necessary that we should discuss it to any great extent at an hour so late. We believe that the resolution sufficiently explains itself for the convention to fully understand and comprehend what the minority are desirous of conveying to the convention and to the country. We believe further that this subject of free coinage, or of a sound financial basis, has been sufficiently discussed, almost even before this convention convened, and if there was any doubt upon the matter, there has been enough light thrown upon the subject from this platform at least to have the citizens of St. Louis understand it, and perhaps the regions round about. I have not been occupying a very enviable position before the Committee on Coinage. I have been one of a minority from the beginning, and now, gentlemen, I think I should have your sympathy and that I should be successful at last in the attempt which I intend to make before this convention. I did not think that my St. Louis friends had any designs on me, but I have been on the minority in about everything.

MR. CHAIRMAN.: The thought has come to my mind since I have been in this convention, from conversations which I have had, from speeches which have been delivered, and from resolutions which have been presented, that there were many people in this country who thought we were about finished up, that we should legislate for the people now here inhabiting this country, without thinking of the oncoming tide of immigration that is sure to inhabit this country in the next half century. You know of my sympathies, and much more of my association — because I have been West of the Mississippi river all of my life-time, and I know all the hardships and all the privations of the people who came to this western country, this trans-Mississippi country, and have made it blossom as the rose. I have been the observer of the things that I believe to some extent have made this country great and prosperous, this western country, this country that has more than two-thirds of the area of the United States. I know of the hard fields of labor that the western people have been in. I know of their faithfulness and their perseverance and endurance in the hardships in the days that have gone by, and my deliberate judgment is to-day that there is no country on the face of the earth, in the United States or anywhere, that has to-day a greater measure of prosperity in all that it takes to make a great and prosperous and a happy and an educated people, than in this country west of the Mississippi river. And as to the future, let me say, that our population is doubled about every 30 to 33 years since we had 8,000,000 people in the United States. The population has doubled as accurately upon the large figures as upon the small, as in 1860 we had a little over 30,000,000 people and in 1890 about 63,000,000 people. We may not double as accurately in the future every 30 years as we have in the last 30, but if we should we will have 122,000,000 people in the United States in 1920; and the extra lot of immigrants, this new population, is going to settle west of the Mississippi river, because it is the best place for them to live, because there are the best conditions. I look for a great improvement in this western country; in the southwest where the State of Texas can take good care of 15,000,000 or 20,000,000 people — and they are beginning to find that there is such a State, the State of Washington on the extreme northwest, where the possibilities can hardly be estimated; and the same with the States that are west of us.

Now, the point that I want to make is this — that the prosperity that has come to the western country has not only come through the energy and intelligence and push and progress of the West, but it has come through the intelligence of the money of the East that has gone to help develop the resources of the West. And it is the money of the East, or the money of the western centers, or the money, no matter where it shall come from, that you will need in the next quarter of a century in the development of the great enterprises of the western country, and I undertake to say that the policy is a bad one that will in any way interfere with the credit of this western country, that will in any way cast a doubt upon the kind of money that we expect to pay our debts in.

I have found in my business career that credit was an exceedingly tender thing and that an individual, as well as a country or nation, should be exceedingly careful with his credit, because it takes money as well as brains to develop a country and to bring the best results to our civilization. It needs both. My judgment is that while the recommendations of this convention may not be as powerful and as potential as some of us may think, it is bad policy to recommend to the Congress of the United States a policy that will bring about in any way a depreciated currency or any doubt as to what we were to pay our debts in.

It is estimated that Europe holds about $6,000,000,000 of the indebtedness of the United States, including railroad indebtedness, State and National, corporation and other general securities of the United States. Now, it is an advantage to us to get cheap money of all the earth. Money is worth only about one per cent to-day in the Bank of England — one per cent per annum — and it can be borrowed in New York, I am told, for two or three per cent. Now, I will tell you that it is bad policy, to say the least of it, to do anything to damage our credit and to keep us from getting the money of the world to transact our business and develop our enterprises at the cheapest possible rate. What we need is money in this western country. We think we have got brains enough, and that we have got energy and vim enough. It is what I have been wanting all my life, that same money to do business with, and get it as cheap as I could, and we don't want to do anything to hurt our credit. Any city that has a bonded issue out does not care whether the bonds are taken in their town or taken in New York, or taken in London, for that matter. We want to utilize everything in the United States, all the resources, not only of our own country, but of foreign countries.

Now, I have but one more remark to make, because I know that my time is rapidly going, and that is, in case we adopt a policy in the United States of the free coinage of silver at the ratio of 16 to 1, knowing that silver is only worth about 50 cents on the dollar in the markets of the world, the indebtedness. of the United States held in foreign countries will be sent here for our gold. They'll not wait for the chance of getting a good gold dollar after there is a probability of free coinage of silver, and, in my judgment, you gentlemen who have got money would act exactly in the same way. If you have more than $10.00 or $100.00 loaned out, you would want to get your money very quickly, and if you had your money in bank you would want to be sure to get it out. In my judgment, the adoption of the policy which is outlined by the majority of this committee would make such a panic in this country as we have never seen before, to which the panic of 1893 would be as but a gentle zephyr before a cyclone.

Mr. Chairman, my time is up, and I am sorry I have taken up so much of your time, because I want some other gentleman to speak upon this subject. I am exceedingly thankful for the very courteous attention that the Committee on Resolutions has given to me, and for the attention which the convention has shown me.

MR. BRYAN: I yield five minutes to Mr. Johnson of Colorado.

HON. J. L. JOHNSON (of Colorado): Mr. Chairman and Gentlemen of the Convention: The only reason that I have to come before you is simply to call attention to what we are fighting for. Heretofore, we have been led to believe by the other side that they were in favor of silver, either by international agreement or otherwise. But the minority resolution discloses the purpose of the other side. Permit me to read just a few words: " We are in favor of the use of silver in the coinage of this country to the fullest extent consistent with the maintenance of our present standard." Let me ask you what the present standard is — the gold standard. " We are in favor of silver, so that it does not interfere with the gold standard." That is all. Bimetallists of this convention — those who believe in silver, whether it is by the coinage of the United States alone or otherwise, will vote for the majority report. Those who believe in the gold standard will vote the other side — that is all there is to it.

Then, " but we deprecate the agitation for the free coinage of silver by this country, as a menace to the soundness of our currency, and injurious to the public welfare." That is, they are in favor of silver that does not interfere with the gold standard and any other discussion of the silver question must not occur. That is the true interpretation of this resolution. Finally we come to the point when the question is: Are we in this country to have forever the gold standard, or are we to have anything else but the gold standard?

Just one other thought that was brought out by the gentleman who has just left the floor. He states that the development of the West depends upon eastern money; — does it? Are we willing to pay usury and interest upon the development of western enterprises? The money that is produced in the West, unless it goes East to pay interest, remains there, but money that is borrowed in the East must return to the East. It is better for the West to produce its own money than to borrow it and pay interest on it. And what is true in reference to the East is true as to the whole country of the United States. When it comes to borrowing money of Great Britain, or anywhere else, money that is made and developed in the United States remains here, unless it goes abroad to pay interest, or balance of trade. Money that is produced here in this country remains here. The American people have the ability to make their own money and keep it if they will.

Mr. Bryan: I yield four minutes to Judge Goodwin.

Judge Goodwin: Ladies and Gentlemen: I heard my little son reading an account of the contest between Mr. Corbett and Mr. Sullivan, and the burden of it was that all Corbett tried to do was to evade Sullivan and jab him. Now a man who has but four minutes to talk on the silver question can do nothing but jab somebody, and I want to begin by jabbing your honored Governor (laughter). He is a lively gentleman. I do not believe he ever had a vindictive thought, but he is all off on this question and he needs some missionary work. He told you how cheap money was in New York. I guess it is (laughter). I think in New York you could borrow $15.00 on a $20.00 gold piece at probably 2 per cent a year, but nothing else (laughter). There is no property in the country that you can borrow that money on. And why? Because the money of the country is worth so much more than property that no man desires to loan money or purchase property. He wants city bonds, electric light stocks or something else. The Governor began his remarks by telling you how much sympathy he had for the West. That is all right — only the West does not ask for sympathy. The West is doing missionary work for these barbarians in the East. If the City Council of St. Louis should pass an ordinance to-night that no lady or gentleman in St. Louis should eat wheaten flour, and have the power to enforce it, and wheat should fall to-morrow four cents and corn advance five cents, I do not believe the Governor would get up and tell you that wheat had fallen in its intrinsic value, that we must all eat corn, especially if there was not more than half corn enough to give you. He tells us what a panic would come.

Now, I believe that every one, except the Governor, who has talked on the other side, has either designated silver men as irrepressible cranks or out-and-out thieves. I wish to say, that all promises that the gold men have made show they are all liars, and I can prove it (laughter). Mr. Cleveland several years ago wrote to Mr. Carlisle, that if the Bland law was not repealed, the country would go to the everlasting bow-wows. It did not go. That was not a falsehood on Cleveland's part, but he had not studied the question more than two hours and a half, under the tutelage of some gentleman who had an interest in a National bank. The trouble with him was he never studied it. He made up his mind and that was the end of it (laughter). A year ago last July, when the extra session was called, the whole New York press, with one exception, assured us that to repeal the purchasing clause of the Sherman law, all trouble would pass away and prosperity be restored. That was discounted before they got through with the repealing. Then the tariff must be fixed — that will make everything lovely. Now, you talk tariff and anti-tariff. There has not been an election of late years that has indicated any principle on earth. They have simply given expression to the unrest in the people's hearts because of their troubles. I have talked with cattle men since I have been here. They have assured me they have not made a cent in 12 years. You go out in Missouri and you will find the land has fallen 50 per cent in value. Go into any other State of the north and you will find land and all that has grown out of the land has fallen 50 per cent, because money is worth so much more than property, that property is of no account, and by no work that you can do can you get profits to the producer. If you don't change your minds, those of you who live in the East, and do the right thing by silver, we will come here again and again and have no limit on time and will talk you to death. That seems to be the only way.

Gov. STANARD: I yield three minutes of my time to Mr. Hancock of Texas.

LEWIS HANCOCK (of Texas): Mr. President, Gentlemen of the Convention: The resolution presented by the minority of your Committee on Resolutions does not call for a general discussion of all the phases of the silver question. However we may differ as to the wisdom and folly of the legislation which in 1873 in this country, and about the same time in Europe, placed restrictions about the coinage of silver, however we may differ as to the effects of those restrictions upon prices and upon prosperity, there are no living issues among the people of this country on those questions to-day. But there is a live issue between the people of this country on a decidedly different question and that is the question as to whether or not this country can alone, independently of other commercial nations, undertake the free coinage of silver at a ratio of 16 to 1. That is a totally different question. It is not a question of standards; it is not a question of metals; it is not a question of interest. It is a question of safety. The resolution presented by the majority of the Committee on Resolutions sets forth in clear, distinct words, the fact that this Government can undertake the coinage of silver with safety. The report submitted by the minority of that committee undertakes to set forth just as clearly the fact that this country cannot do it. The issue is intended to be made clear and distinct, so that the people of this country can begin to learn what they are discussing.

What is the great condition to-day? Whether we like it or not, silver is a commodity selling in the markets of the world, and all the free silver countries have not been able to help us and cannot help us. Silver sells as a commodity at about 63 cents an ounce, at which rate our bullion is worth about 50 cents. I do not believe there is a man upon this floor who will not assent at once and without discussion to the proposition that if this country adopts the policy of the free coinage of silver independently of other commercial nations, that if silver remains at 60 cents an ounce or at any figure under $1.29 an ounce, that we thereupon pass from a gold standard to a silver standard.

MR. BRYAN: I yield four minutes to Gen. Weaver.

HON. JAMES B. WEAVER (of Iowa): Mr. Chairman, Ladies and Gentlemen of the Convention: Mr. Leighton last night during his address asked the question, "Do we need any more money?" I am in favor of the majority report, because I believe the country does need in its business, a greater volume of currency than it now has. He made the assertion that during the sixties we had $18.00 per capita, that we now have about $25.00 per capita. I was astounded to hear a gentleman of the apparent information of Mr. Leighton make such a declaration as that. Now, does anybody believe that we are within the period of inflation and that the war period was, compared with this one, a period of contraction and contracted currency? If this is the case what did the Secretary mean — and I have his report here of 1865 — the first report made after the close of the war — when he said there was so much currency in the country that it was demoralizing the labor interests of the country and the remedy was in contraction of the volume of the currency. If the gentleman was correct, and we had only $18.00 per capita at that time, and that volume existed, of necessity any contraction of the currency is greater to-day than it was at the close of the war. Perhaps that is the matter with the currency.

I have the reports of Secretaries Fessenden and McCullough, and I want to call attention to a remark always overlooked by the gold-standard men in discussing the money question. It is this: that whatever volume of money we had in the United States at the close of the war, it was confined in its circulation to the people of the Northern States, and we only had 25,000,000 in the Northern States, and when the war closed a little less than that, and whatever volume of money we had was confined in its circulation to that number of people. I have also the report of the Comptroller of the Currency at that time, the brightest and ablest man that has ever filled that chair since the sixties, Mr. John Jay Knox. Mr. Knox says in a speech before the convention of the National Bankers' Association, that we had over

$1,500,000,000 of legal tender money in circulation in the Northern States at the close of the war, and we had over $1,700,000,000 of currency in circulation at that time, every dollar of it in circulation among the Northern people. When Lee and Johnston surrendered they added in a single day 10,000,000 of penniless people to Uncle Sam's money-using population, which was an addition of 40 per cent to our money-using population in a single day. Was not that equal to a contraction of 40 per cent of the money in circulation in the North when the war closed? Was not that a tremendous contraction for a single day, and did not that increase the demand for money 40 per cent? Let me give you a rule in political economy as invariable as the motion of the earth — the demand for money is equal to the sum of the demand for all other things, and when 10,000,000 of penniless people were added to our money-using population in a single day, that increased the demand for money 40 per cent in this country. But in addition to that contraction by the addition of that penniless body of people from the South, Congress adopted the recommendation of Secretary Mc-Cullough and at once entered upon the contraction of our volume of money. The bonded debt was only $1,066,000,000, at the close of the war, but June 30th, 1869, it jumped to $2,056,000,000, a contraction of $1,000,000,000 of money in three years; 70,000,000 of people are using the money to-day; that is an addition of 170 per cent to our money-using population; 25,000,000 were using the money at the close of the war and there are 70,000,000 using it now, and that is 170 per cent increase in our money-using population. Nobody claims we have over $116,000,000 in circulation now, whereas there were over $118,000,000 in the hands of the people at the close of the war.

Gov. STANARD: I yield three minutes of my time to Mr. Black of Washington.

MR. BLACK: Mr. President, Ladies and Gentlemen: I have not time to make an argument — to explain why the people of Western Washington are opposed to the free coinage of silver at 16 to 1. I can but briefly state three reasons. 1st. Because in that country we do not believe that the free and unlimited coinage of silver at 16 to 1 is honest. We believe that such a coinage is repudiation. I will illustrate; I see my friend Gov. Prince — if I could go to him and borrow $500.00 to-day and take that $500.00 and buy $500.00 worth of silver bullion, and the day after the act is passed making silver a legal tender at 16 to 1 I take that bullion bought with his money to the mint and I get 1,000 legal tender silver dollars for it. I take to brother Prince $500.00 of it to pay him back, and keep $500.00 of it myself. I say that is not honest, that is repudiation. I say that, as well as not being honest it is not fair. 2d. Is it fair, that because a man in Colorado has a silver mine, that by operation of law his silver mine should be doubled in value, when Brother Rowe living in Utah has a grain field and raises wheat? It is not fair that one citizen of Utah has his property doubled in value while the other has not. It is class legislation. I say further than that, and as a third reason why we are opposed to this proposition, that it is not a legitimate money. Take a silver dollar as it is to-day and ask any man in this audience what makes it worth a dollar, and he will tell you it is the fiat of the Government: it is the stamp of the Government. If that be true, then I say it is time this Government joins with Gov. Weaver, making a stamped dollar of paper instead of spending 50 cents on the dollar for silver for it.

Gov. STANARD: I yield three minutes to Col. Leighton of St. Louis.

COL. LEIGHTON: I feel, gentlemen of the Convention, as though I have said enough, and that you would rather listen to somebody else, but I yield to the request of Gov. Stanard to say a single word. I have given expression to my own idea, and which is the idea — excuse me for saying it — of the more intelligent people of the United States, that the coinage of silver on the basis of 16 to 1 means monometallism of all silver, and not bimetallism at all.

A DELEGATE (from Kansas): I move a vote of thanks to the gentleman.

COL. LEIGHTON: That seems to receive a response, from which I infer that it is the intelligent conviction of the majority of the silver States. It is simply a policy intended to put this country upon a silver basis, to have monometallism of silver, instead of bimetallism, which you undertake to claim before the public. If that is so, in my judgment, it is a large step toward carrying out the policy foreshadowed in the majority resolution. The minority of the committee were complimented on expressing fairly and fully what they meant in the minority report. Let me compliment the majority in expressing what they mean when they expressed their declaration of war against the banks of the country. Now, I undertake to say, gentlemen, that that policy turns back all the wheels of civilization. A bank properly organized, properly regulated, properly examined and surrounded with all the safeguards which legislation can give to it, is as great an instrument of civilization and as great an instrument in carrying on the commerce of the country as a railroad, a post-office or a telegraph.

MR. BRYAN: Gentlemen of the Convention, I have saved about seven minutes to end this discussion. I am sorry that I have not more time. Last night I did not have quite as much time as I wanted. The ratio was about 5 to 1. But when it gets to 16 to 1 we don't complain (laughter). Now these resolutions fairly express the contest and I think that, even though Solomon may not have been as intelligent as some others are who assume to be more intelligent than we are, you are all intelligent enough to know what the issue is and that you have courage enough to express yourselves when you do know. The resolution reported by the minority is a resolution in favor of the gold standard, in favor of the use of silver so far as it can be done consistently with the gold standard. That is the construction placed upon it by the gentleman who presented it to you.

Our resolution is for the double standard, and you can range yourselves up on whichever side of this proposition you believe in. Let me run over the first of these questions.

They say we are repudiating. Some people think there is only one method of repudiation; for the debtor it is wrong, but if the creditor repudiates and demands 150 cents from him when he owed only a dollar, that is honesty (applause). Now, the gentleman suggested that we needed to borrow money. Yes, my friends, and you continue the infamous policy that we have labored under, and we will be borrowers of money and hewers of wood and drawers of water for the man who makes slaves of us by financial legislation. We want legislation in the interest of justice that will let people get out of debt when they pay as much as they borrow, and not seek to gather in more than they are entitled to. If you would give us just legislation, we would not be deprived of our rights, and year to year we would not find our mortgages increasing. Give us just legislation and an honest dollar and the people of the West, with their magnificent resources, could loan money to the eastern country, that is not as rich in natural resources. Those people would not even coin the seigniorage, the money in the treasury lying idle, and yet when they need money they go and borrow money to run the Government, and tax this country. Who was it said banking was right? It is right in the proper sphere, but I denounce a banking conspiracy that drives money out of the treasury to get bonds issued because they want to run their Government and want bonds to run it with.

My friends, these men who talk about superior intelligence do not apply to the money question the most common principles of practical life. If you increase the demand, my friends, isn't it the same thing as decreasing the supply? If you increase the demand for silver by opening the mints of free coinage, does not that increase the demand and raise the price of the metal? We increase the price of gold by increasing the demand for it. Why is it that these men who so dread that you will pay for silver more than it will cost to mine it, why do not they complain of the profits that go into the pocket of the gold miner when you raise the price by legislation? They claim they don't want to discriminate. We don't. When we ask for the free coinage of silver, we only ask them to give back what law took away. You cannot give to the mine owner a single penny more than you took when you demonetized silver. I want to call your attention to two or three prophecies. They say that gold will go abroad and that bonds will come back from Europe. We have heard the same old prophecies from the same source every time we try to legislate for silver. When the Bland Act was passed the papers said our credit was destroyed, that greenbacks would go below par and gold rise to a premium. In 1878 we accumulated a supply of gold instead of letting it go abroad. Under the Bland Act and in the beginning of 1878 our bonds went abroad, and yet those people come and prophecy again, on the theory of the gambler that never having been right, they must necessarily be right now (laughter and applause).

Our coinage proposition asks for the unlimited coinage of gold and silver at 16 to 1 without any other nation of the earth. I am glad they did not base their objection on international bimetallism. I am glad they did not tell you they expected it, because they did not ex. pect it. I want to ask you whether this great nation, the greatest on God's footstool to-day, must do only what second-hand countries in Europe do. Did Italy ask our consent to take gold as a standard? Did Germany ask our consent to demonetize silver? Did the Latin Union ask our consent to suspend the coinage of silver? Did India ask our consent to suspend the coinage of silver and reduce the value of all the silver we had on hand? Do these nations ask us? Not one of them. And yet men tell you they have not confidence in their country, that the United States must go abroad and ask some other nation what we shall do when we legislate for our own people. It was more than one hundred years ago when our ancestors declared their political independence of all the other nations on earth, and I believe that to-day the people of this country are ready for the new declaration of independence. It was said that they gathered upon the streets listening for the sound of the bell that should tell them the declaration had been signed. Oh, my friends, 70,000,000 of people to-day are listening for the sound that shall tell them that this people has declared its financial independence of every other nation upon the earth. We do not have to tell you something that has no danger in it. We do not have to guarantee you against possible danger. We simply have to propose a better system than the system that has crushed us for twenty years and which they want to make perpetual now. My friends, we believe that if you open your mints to both gold and silver, that the worst possible thing that can come from it will be infinitely better than the best thing that can come to us waiting as we are.

We ask you to pass this resolution and let the Trans-Mississippi Congress be placed on record as in favor of the independence of this country in its laws by coinage at 16 to 1, the ratio that we had before it was stricken down as we believe by fraud, at least in the night (cheers).

The minority report was then read again.

THE CHAIRMAN: The question now before the house is the adoption of the substitute.

The Chairman stated that each State would vote 10 votes, whether it had more than one person present or not, but that above 10 votes it must have a man present on the floor for each vote.

A delegate from Arkansas moved that the vote on the minority proposition be accepted as the vote on the majority.

The vote was then taken on the question of the substitution of the minority report for the majority report on the coinage question, and the substitute was lost by the following vote:—

	AYE.	NO.
Arizona	...	10
Arkansas	3	12
California	...	27
Colorado	...	19
Idaho	...	10
Iowa	10	6
Indian Territory	2	8
Kansas	...	14
Louisiana	...	...
Minnesota	10	...
Missouri	21	9
Montana	...	10
Nevada	...	...
Nebraska	5½	4½
New Mexico	...	10
North Dakota	10	...
Oklahoma	...	10
Oregon	...	10
South Dakota	...	...
Texas	8	2
Utah	...	30
Washington	8	2
Wyoming	...	10
Alaska	...	10
	77½	213½

A division was called for between the coinage question and the currency question.

MR. BRYAN: I think it is a matter of right, that if they ask for a division on these propositions they are entitled to it.

MR. SMITH (of Iowa): The report of the Committee settled fully and fairly and finally the question of the division. Division of the question would be revision of the resolution, and it cannot be done.

THE CHAIRMAN: The chair rules that the rejection of the substitute does not affect the majority report. It can be divided if asked for.

A vote was called for upon the question of a division.

GOV. PRINCE: Mr. President, as a matter of parliamentary law, a division is the right of every individual to call for. It does not require a majority or a vote, but a simple call by any individual. That is as well settled as that the sun rises in the East.

The majority report was then reread.

A DELEGATE: Mr. Chairman, I call for a division on the currency question and then a vote on the others.

First clause of the majority report was then adopted by *viva voce* vote.

The roll was then called by States upon the adoption of the second clause of the majority report and it was adopted by a vote of 206½ "Aye" and 75½ "No."

The vote on the adoption of the second clause of the majority report was as follows: —

	AYE.	NO.
Arizona	10	
Arkansas	14	2
California	17	...
Colorado	19	...
Idaho	9	1
Iowa	6	10
Indian Ter	10	...
Kansas	14	...
Louisiana	...	...
Minnesota	...	10
Missouri	9	21
Montana	10	...
Nevada	...	...
Nebraska	4½	5½
New Mexico	10	...
North Dakota	...	10
Oklahoma	10	...
Oregon	10	...
South Dakota	...	...
Texas	2	8
Utah	30	...
Washington	2	8
Wyoming	10	...
Alaska	10	...
	206½	75½

A motion was made that the Executive Committee be requested to arrange for a meeting for the purpose of hearing an address from Hon. Wm. J. Bryan in answer to Col. Leighton, and the Chairman of the Executive Committee stated that it was not within the power of the Executive Committee to hold such a meeting.

Mr. Black made the point of order that this Congress had no power to call a special meeting.

The point of order was sustained.

THE CHAIRMAN: The Executive Committee is ready to make its report.

MR. WHITMORE: Mr. President and Members of the Congress: At your last session in San Francisco the Executive Committee was ordered to make a report in regard to some plan for permanent organization of the Congress. In accordance with instructions given by you to report this morning, that Committee has been ready to report for some hours past. It has a very important report, and it is therefore hoped that every delegate will remain to hear it. At the San Francisco meeting, at the suggestion of Gov. McConnell, a motion was introduced to appoint a special committee to devise some plan of permanent organization and of raising funds by which the Congress would have money to pay its own expenses, and also to see that its resolutions were properly presented in Washington. That Committee reported unfavorably. It was recommitted to the same Committee, with instructions to go over the matter again. They found so many obstacles in their way that the time was not long enough in which to remove them. The resolutions were then referred to the Executive Committee, with positive instructions to submit a report at this session of the Congress. This Committee is composed of two members from each State and Territory west of the Mississippi river. A great deal of correspondence has taken place between the Chairman of the Committee and different members, in order to ascertain their views in regard to this matter, and the report now about to be submitted is signed by every member of the Executive Committee who is here, and I think coincides with the opinion of the other members who have been heard from through correspondence. The following is the plan proposed for the permanent organization of the Congress.—

1st. The Congress shall meet at such time as shall be fixed by the Executive Committee, not less frequently than once each year, and at such place as shall be designated by the previous Congress.

2nd. The permanent officers of this Congress shall consist of a President; a Vice-President to be named by each State and Territory; a Secretary; a Treasurer who shall be elected by the Executive Committee, and such assistants to the Secretary as the Executive Committee shall deem necessary; an Executive Committee consisting of two members who shall be selected by the delegations of their respective States and Territories, one of whom shall be elected at each session for a term of two years, except at the present meeting, at which time two shall be elected, one of whom shall serve for one year and one for two years.

The President shall be *ex-officio* member of the Executive Committee.

3d. The election of officers shall take place at eleven a. m. of the second day of the session, previous to which time the Committee on Permanent Organization shall make its report.

4th. The Executive Committee shall select its own chairman, who shall be its executive officer, and who shall have charge of the interests of the Congress between its sessions, arrange all preliminaries for its meetings, and take such steps as the committee may deem proper to bring its action to the attention of the United States Congress and urge the adoption of the measures which this Congress may approve.

The funds of the Congress may be used to defray the necessary expenses thus incurred, provided, however, that in no case shall such expenses be incurred unless the funds are in hand to meet them.

5th. In order to provide for such expenses, the annual dues for membership shall be as follows: from every business organization the sum of ten dollars, which shall entitle it to one delegate, and five dollars for each additional delegate. Any delegate appointed by the Governor of any State or Territory, the Mayor of any city, or the Executive officer or officers of any county, shall pay five dollars.

Should the amount thus contributed prove to be more than is needed to defray the legitimate expenses of the Congress, the dues shall be reduced at the next Congress to such sum as may be found adequate to provide such expenses.

6th. The following shall be the basis of representation:—

The Governor of any State or Territory may appoint ten delegates; the Mayor of each city one delegate, and an additional delegate for each five thousand inhabitants; provided, however, that no city shall have more than ten delegates; each county may appoint one delegate through its Executive officer; every business organization one delegate, and an additional delegate for every fifty members, provided, however, that no such organization shall be entitled to more than ten delegates.

7th. Each delegate present shall be entitled to one vote.

8th. These rules may be amended by a two-thirds vote of any succeeding Congress.

Gov. WAITE: Mr. Chairman, some provision should be made by which the representation will be fair not only to the State in which the Congress may happen to be held, but also in all the States that send delegates.

Mr. W. H. Culmer moved the adoption of the report.

It was moved by a delegate from Arkansas that the report be referred to the Committee on Resolutions, and the Chair ruled the motion out of order, as it was the report of a committee made by instruction of a previous Congress and could not be referred to another committee.

On motion of Gov. Waite seconded by Gov. Prince the plan was amended by the addition to Sec. 7, of the following: Provided that no State or Territory shall have more than 30 votes.''

. The report was then unanimously adopted as amended.

Mr. WHITMORE: Mr. Chairman, I simply want to state to the members of the Congress that now it becomes the duty, under the rules, of every delegation to select the names of its committeemen to serve for the ensuing year, and these names should be handed in before the Congress finally adjourns.

It was then moved that on Friday morning the roll be called and that each State present the names of a Vice-President and Executive Committeemen.

It was then ordered that the question of the location of next congress be brought up on Friday morning at 11 o'clock.

Mr. F. J. CANNON: I desire to inquire of the Chair if there was not unfinished upon the table of the Clerk the report of the Committee on Resolutions. I make the point of order that we should continue with the report of the Committee on Resolutions without the intervention of other business.

A DELEGATE: I rise to a question of personal privilege: This morning, before this congress, I introduced a resolution. That resolution was read before this Congress and sent to the Clerk's desk to be referred to the Committee on Resolutions. That resolution was lost or destroyed and never went to the Committee on Resolutions. Our delegation called that up before the Committee on Resolutions and it could not be found, and therefore the Committee instructed us to re-introduce that resolution and that it be reported to this body here. I ask that that resolution which was destroyed this morning come before this body and that action be taken upon it at once.

THE CHAIRMAN: How is the Chairman to know that this has come from the Committee on Resolutions?

Mr. BUTTERFIELD (Secretary): They spoke to me about that and I have been trying to find it ever since.

Mr. SMITH (of Iowa): I was present when that was spoken of.

Mr. F. J. CANNON: I am not standing on technicalities — I am asking if there is not some unfinished business before this convention?

Motion was made to adjourn until to-night.

It was then announced that tickets for the theater and concert to-morrow evening could be had on application at the Secretary's office.

The meeting then adjourned until 7 :30 p. m.

WEDNESDAY EVENING SESSION.

The meeting was called to order by President Cannon at 7 :40 p. m.

Mr. J. C. GREEN, of Alaska, gave an exhibition of stereopticon views of Alaska, with a description of the climate and resources of that country, lasting about 20 minutes.

THE CHAIRMAN: I now have the pleasure of introducing to you Mr. Hugh Craig of San Francisco, who will address you on the subject of Hawaii.

ADDRESS OF HUGH CRAIG, ESQ.

Mr. Chairman, Ladies and Gentlemen: When the Trans-Mississippi Congress · met last in San Francisco the Hawaiian Islands were then under a provisional government. It was a very doubtful condition of affairs. It was not very well known nor very certain what the result would be. About that time it was supposed that our authorities at Washington would undertake to re-instate upon the throne there the celebrated lady whom you may remember by the name of Liliuokalani. Some of the better counsels prevailed and it is now a full-fledged Republic, which Mr. Sanford B. Dole had the honor and pleasure of declaring in a document reading something like this, " I, Sanford B. Dole, in accordance with the authority invested in me by the provision of the Executive Committee, declare this to be the Republic of Hawaii." That is very much like something we have heard of before. The American people have established another branch of our great nation, and they are very anxious to be taken into the family nest, so that they may be one of us. As you know, there are to-day some 45 States of the Union, and there are 4 Territories knocking to come in, and Hawaii does not want to be the last one. It wants to come in and make up the fifty.

Her claims for admission are that she can make, and does make, and has made a good showing, for all that has been done, and she can point that, in the period of her history since the American people have taken charge of her commerce, there has been such a development as will insure to them favorable attention when they next ask at Washington for admission.

I have been asked by your President to present you with sundry statistics, information, experience gained in the South Pacific amongst the people of those islands, and show why the Hawaiian Islands will be a valuable addition to our Republic, especially so to the States on the Pacific Coast, California in particular. As a matter of fact it is the only foreign commerce — that between Hawaii and California — which is done almost exclusively under our flag. Of their imports, amounting to $7,700,000.00, 77 per cent are obtained from California. Of their exports, over $10,000,000, 99 per cent come to the Pacific Coast States. Their foreign commerce, imports and exports, amount to $18,000,000. To give you some idea of how valuable this is becoming, the population of Hawaii through American enterprise amounts to about 90,000. Of this 90,000, 35,000 are native Hawaiians, about 6,000 half-caste, about 15,000 Chinese, 13,000 Japs and 9,000 Portuguese, about 2,000 native born Americans, about 2,500 Germans, British, Italians, French, and about 6,000 Hawaiian born children of Americans, British and Germans, altogether making 90,000. They show that such an amount of development has taken place in consequence of the American management of their commercial affairs that they will compare favorably with any part of the world.

Now, you will find if you take their commerce and exports and imports amounting to $18,000,000, and divide by 90,000, that it gives an average of $200 *per capita*. Divide the whole of the foreign commerce of Great Britain, exports and imports, by the population, and it gives about $100 *per capita*. Divide the foreign commerce of the United States by 70,000,000, and that gives you about $25 *per capita*. You see, therefore, that this small community, sprung from a few thousand Americans with their families, have within the last five years produced something abnormal in the shape of commercial development.

(Pointing to the map.) San Francisco to the Sandwich Islands is 2,000 miles; from the Sandwich Islands to Yokohoma is 3,100 miles; the Fiji Islands, 4,000 miles; New Zealand, 6,000 miles. This commerce of theirs, we on the Pacific Coast — who have helped to build it up — really own. When the people at Hawaii become wealthy and rich enough and they desire to take their families away, they come to California, or Oregon or Washington, and build themselves a house, and we are glad to have them. They have created a vast amount of wealth. Their sugar amounts to 300,000 tons a year. They are establishing coffee plantations where they are raising coffee that is equal to the Mocha and Java coffee, and they have in their hands such a property as is worth saving and protecting. And now, at this early day in the history of their Republic, they come knocking at our doors for admission; — our own countrymen, mind you — men who have gone there from us across the ocean to take up this land, not by spoliation or appropriation, but by commercial progress and commercial intercourse with a people who are anxious to have them there. They have obtained the title to this land legitimately; they have no apology to make, or explanation. When they went there, these Hawaiians had the ownership of the property and the titles to the land. President Dole is an authority on those titles and he has written an article upon it.

To give you some idea of the customs there. They are all various branches of a great family that have come across from the East, and some of the people on the other islands can trace their origin to Hawaii. In the early days, before the Europeans arrived amongst them, there was no occasion for quarrels, and when a native would hear about a row going on there he would say, "Who is the woman?" "Where is the lamb?" They had nothing else to quarrel about. Their titles were obtained in a very extraordinary way. For instance, I will relate to you something which, perhaps, will be new to some of our legal gentlemen. As you know, we have a variety of titles in the United States, by inheritance, purchase, love and affection and various considerations. The question of these titles there comes before courts called for the purpose and presided over by legal gentlemen who have become acquainted with the customs of the people and assisted by a couple of native assistants. Before them are the claimants, gesticulating and trying to prove that each man is the one who should have his name put in the grant, entitling him to the ownership of the land, all land there being held in common. Women's rights there is an immemorial custom — they have always had their rights. In fact, inheritance comes through the mother's side, as it is always doubtful, among the South Sea Islanders, who the father was; therefore, in all these courts they always trace back to the mother. They always know who the mother is, but they are not certain who their fathers were. On one of these occasions, the judge sat in court and a young man claimed that his name should be put in the grant — and you will remember the object, because the three men whose names are put in the grant will be handed the purchase money for the land and it would be their business to divide up this amongst the people interested — and it generally followed that some odd coins stuck to the fingers of the three men. This young man had a great deal to say to explain to the judge why his name should be put in the deed, because, said he, "My fathers are buried upon that land." "I was born there." When he got through, after making a very good impression, an old man entered and got up and said to the judge, throwing off every stitch of clothing that he had on him: "Listen, Chief Magistrate, this young man has spoken wind only, there is nothing in it. He asks where his fathers were buried: here (slapping his chest) I will tell you — that lad was raised on that land. When I was a young man I went with my father and my people to that land and there we attacked the men who lived on it and owned it, and we killed them and ate them all, and I had this land when this child came into my hands and was about to dash his brains out on the rocks and my wife asked me to give her the boy. I did this" — and now you see the base ingratitude of the native character — "and after raising him up and making a man of him, now he comes in and claims my property. Now, Mr. Magistrate, I will say to you that I not only have the title to the land by the might that enabled me to conquer it, but anything there was in his father went into my stomach, mixed with my blood and became part of my flesh and my bone and if there is anything that he possessed or that he owned that has not come to me, I want you to tell me." He referred to the assistants, one on each side, "How is that? What do you think about that?" "That is correct." That is the

South Sea Island method of acquiring land, and after referring the matter to his brother judges, they concluded that that was about as good a title as could be found and that the fellow who did kill and eat up the other fellow was entitled to the land. And that is recognized in the courts of New Zealand as title by digestion, and the very best title that could be brought into court (laughter and applause).

Therefore, ladies and gentlemen, these Hawaiians have reason to be very grateful to our fellow-citizens who went over to the islands and did not eat them up (laughter). They acquired property by legitimate methods and in this way they have come to us with something in thei. hands and they ask us to allow them to join with us. And we in California, who are doing so much of this business, when the proper time comes, we are going to ask you to admit the Hawaiian Islands to participation in our government.

It is said by Senator Morgan of Alabama, that when a crown falls in the Western Empire, it is pulverized, never to be re-instated, that when a scepter departs, it departs forever.

Now, our countrymen there in Hawaii for the last fifty years have tolerated this opera bouffe play at royalty, but they simply tolerated it, because they knew that the time would come when these Hawaiians would tire of it themselves, and they would be very glad to be taken into the American camp. When we go back a few years in the history of the islands, we find that it has been generally conceded that the ultimate absorption of Hawaii by the United States was expected by all statesmen. In 1843 the British Government by one of their navy captains, took possession of the island, but before the year was out he was ordered to surrender. Those representatives of their government called upon the Hawaiian minister and said, "We do not want to have trouble here. We want you to join with us in an agreement that neither Great Britain, nor the United States, nor France, shall appropriate the Sandwich Islands." "Oh, no," says Uncle Sam's representative, "We know a good thing when we see it, I am very glad you have agreed to keep your hands off, but the ripe plum will drop into our hands, and we have only got to wait."

Later in 1853, a Hawaiian Commission was sent to England and the British Minister said, "No, the inevitable destiny of the Hawaiian Islands is that an American Protectorate shall be placed over them, or they will be annexed to the United States." This is true history, so there is nothing surprising to us in the West, that our people who know the country, who have developed it, should come to our doors and knock for admission.

Now, as to the matter of investments: we have thirty millions of dollars invested in the Hawaiian Islands, belonging to the people of the United States, five millions belonging to Great Britain and two millions to Germany. You see we have the preponderance in every direction. The civilization is that of America ; the business is done in dollars and cents ; the social life is that of the United States ; they are hospitable to a fault. It is the rendezvous of the United States fleet in the Pacific. Our United States Navy people have always recognized that the time would come when Hawaii would drop into our hands, and we are very proud to know that when the time does come, we are ready to take her in. We shall do what we can to help her into the United States. She is the guardian of all our Pacific Coast, from Oonalaska down to San Diego.

It has been said that it is too far away — that we cannot govern Hawaii, excepting at a great expense. It would entail upon us there an army of men and a navy at considerable expense. Well, there is something in that, and as Uncle Sam is economizing, and the Post-master-General is cutting down his appropriations, we say, if Uncle Sam cannot see his way to take this thing in, we can arrange it over there ; we are quite prepared to attach it to California ; we will undertake to care for it ; we will send the necessary troops there to maintain order and we still have some constructors of marine shipping left there. We have the " Irving M. Scott " and others ; we can reproduce monitors in the shape of the " Monterey," the " Charleston," the " San Francisco," the " Olympia," and the " Oregon ; " we have plenty of iron, and men to man them with, men to build them and we have the gold coin. I am sure, I express the sentiment, not only of California, but of Oregon and Washington, when I say that if it cannot be done through Congress we will have to take care of it on the other side. But we never will permit any other Government to take possession of the Hawaiian Islands. (applause). I would call attention to the relative positions of San Francisco and Nicaragua and the Hawaiian Islands ; if it had been put on the map properly, it would show you that the Hawaiian Islands are the guardians also of any canal that may be opened on the Isthmus — and here again I want to compliment the artist who got this map up. We not only put through the resolutions for the canal to-day, but he has given us a canal already (laughter) only he has put it on the Isthmus of Panama instead of Nicaragua (laughter). If he could convince the French people that blue water was actually running there, that map would be worth one hundred million dollars. They spent two hundred millions doing one-fifth of the work that is necessary to put that work on the Panama canal through, so that it would cost a thousand millions of dollars, before they could successfully put through a canal there, and this Nicaragua Canal which you have heard about in the resolutions to-day, is proposed to be put through for one hundred millions.

Now it has been claimed, and claimed from Washington, that a long line of distinguished Presidents have been opposed to going beyond our boundaries, for fear of getting us into trouble with foreign nations. They say we cannot take in Hawaii, it is away beyond our coast, we would better get along with what we have, and keep between the Pacific and the Atlantic and let these outside places go. Now, the race from which we have sprung has never had any difficulty in assimilating territory. If you will just think back a little, the Anglo-Saxon race never backs out at a big thing in the shape of new property, never (applause). You never hear of the British Government rejecting something in the shape of a new colony that is offered to her — at least I do not remember it, and if we will remember back in our own history, I think we will find that the men whose memory is the greenest, the men we delight to hold up as examples to our children, and whose names are most prominent in the history of the United States, are the men who have been led forward by that acquisitiveness and that desire to extend the territory of the United States, which has always brought to us good fortune and prosperity. If you will go back to 1803, Mr. Jefferson found that some other people owned the territory on the right bank of the Mississippi, and he did not like it that 13 colonies consisting then in population of about 5,000,000 had only about 827,000 square miles of territory. Jefferson thought he had to provide for the future. He wanted some more. He did not like the idea that a foreign fleet might enter the Mississippi river and come up to St. Louis, so he called to his counsel Mr. Monroe and he sent him to France as special envoy. He said: " You must acquire that Louisiana property, no matter at what cost. We cannot afford that a foreign nation should hold that; we must have it for our children. Upon the success of your mission depends the life of the United States." Monroe was successful, and it is related as the greatest achievement of Jefferson's time, costing some $15,000,000 for 1,200,-000 square miles of territory or about $12.50 per square mile. It did not cause Jefferson any trouble, and when he was remonstrated with by people who said then, " We have more territory than we can handle; we are going away beyond the Father of Waters and we never can protect it." " Protect it," said he: " Why, this is the greatest government on the face of the earth " — and he only had 5,000,000 of people behind him. He said: " It is the only government where every man at the call of the nation will fly to its standard to protect it, without having to impress him (applause)." Then later that spirit of determination to hold what we had got and get more, if we could, was shown in 1812 and 1814, when in the time of Madison he conceived the idea that while he was having a row with England, it would be a good time to take in the whole of Canada, and he actually sent out troops for that purpose. He never gave up his determination to get Canada. When Mr. Monroe became president he did not fear any foreign

entanglements. He sent General Jackson down to stop the trouble
with the Seminoles, and Jackson took the whole of Florida. He
took possession of Pensacola, a Spanish town, and came and
reported to his chief what he had done, and he said, "Jackson, you
will have to give those Spanish fellows that Pensacola back
again, and tell them we will give them $5,000,000 for Florida."
And they took the $5,000,000. So it appears that the men
who accomplished these things are the men whose memory is
the greenest. Later, in 1844, the Americans captured Texas; and
they came with their arms full of sheaves to get into the Union. There
was a new generation that had came up then and said, "We don't want
Texas," and the bill was defeated and then there was a row. Then
came the cry, "Tippecanoe and Tyler too, the annexation of Texas
and re-occupation of Oregon, 50, 40, or fight (applause)." Twenty-
three million of people defied the whole world and said, "We will take
what we want." That was the war cry, the slogan of the election when
Polk was elected, to take in more territory. When Texas came in then
they did not have enough. There was another territory south of them
and they said they would give us that territory if we would give them
$3,000,000. And then for $18,000,000 we got part of Colorado, Nevada,
Utah, New Mexico, Arizona and the whole of California, about 2,000,-
000 square miles, costing a little more per square mile than Jefferson
had to pay for 1,200,000 square miles, but we have never regretted
it. There were only 23,000,000 people behind Mr. Polk when he undertook that. Then a little later, in about 1848, when that matter was
closed up, there came an opportunity for a Secretary of State, whose
name will be revered as long as the English language lasts, and no other
man since Cromwell has recognized the capacity of the Anglo-Saxon
race for self-government better than Abraham Lincoln, the greatest of
all the presidents (applause). When the time came that Russia was
tired of Alaska and was ready to take $7,200,000, Mr. Seward did not sit
down with a map and figure up, "Well, Oonalaska is 2,000 miles from San
Francisco, and we might get into foreign complications before we could
send a navy there." He just paid the money and took the territory, and
he acquired 600,000 square miles for $7,200,000. Is there anybody
within the sound of my voice likely to say that Mr. Seward made a
mistake, that we would take that money back and give some other nation
Alaska? Why, if Mr. Green had had the time to tell you what we
know about Alaska, it would astonish you. And now two or three
figures. You must not imagine that I am romancing; the Treadwell
mine, running 260 stamps, paid in dividends last year, $779,000. The
Alaska Packing Company which controls the Alaska canneries, might
just as well have put up 1,200,000 cases of salmon at $4.00 a case,
but they were afraid of overloading the market and only put up 600,-

000. Last year the whalers captured 300 whales, each whale worth for whalebone $5,000,—a million and a half dollars; now add the whaling interest, the canning and mining interests — and we don't know what the product of the Yukon Mine is. All along that country shown by Mr. Green to-night men mine and obtain enough in three months to come down to San Francisco, Portland, Seattle and Tacoma and have a high old time the other nine months, and they do not give it away, either (applause).

I only wish to show that the people of the United States have never made any mistake in the acquiring of territory. Therefore we on the West say to you, "We must have Hawaii, we cannot let anybody else have it. We propose to overrun the whole of that South Pacific some day; we propose to keep that as a safety point for our people with our ships and our steamers." Humboldt has said that the commerce of the Pacific will in time exceed the commerce of the Atlantic, and Wm. H. Seward said that the greatest development of the Anglo-Saxon race will be found on the shores of the Pacific. Now, this is not boasting. These are men of common sense and mature judgment, of intellect and capacity enough to take in the whole thing. And we are of the same opinion as Mr. Humboldt and Wm. H. Seward. And then we have a grand territory ourselves. It does not increase very fast, but some of the people in the East should understand that there is plenty of land there, plenty of water, good sound currency, gold and silver — no paper heritage on our side; the State is not in debt; we own everything we have got. Those of us who are in debt, we owe it to each other, and when the thing gets very tight we just say: "Well, you will have to wait — it is very unfortunate that we cannot pay the interest on our mortgage, and if you do not like it you can take the property."

One of our savings banks the other day, which has a capital of $1,000,000 and deposits of $24,000,000, said to a few of our friends in San Francisco who proposed to build a parallel railroad to the Southern Pacific in the San Joaquin, "Put us down for $50,000, because if you cannot build a road at such a price as to carry wheat from the head of the San Joaquin down to tide water for less than $4.60 a ton (which we were paying for transportation when wheat was worth $40.00 a ton, and we are still paying $4.60 a ton, and it is only worth $17.00 a ton) why, our securities do not amount to much." Thus you see we help each other. Therefore we have a sympathetic feeling for our neighbors and our countrymen 2,000 miles off from the coast, and we propose that they shall not be left out in the cold.

Now, ladies and gentlemen, my time is nearly up, and you will hear something on the Nicaragua Canal; but before I take my seat I want to say that besides Hawaii we have an overwhelming appreciation of what it is to be an American citizen, and we do not think you people East of us realize that out of the English speaking people on the face of the earth (and you can figure them up at about 117,000,000), 70,000,000 of them live in the United States, and we claim that, by one of the physical laws with which you are all familiar, the larger must in time so affect the lesser that they will all come in. We expect this in our time, and we are hopeful that the man will be raised up, perhaps from a Pacific Coast State, to point out the way by which we can do it, to accomplish not only the annexation of Hawaii but everything in sight (laughter); 3,300,000 in Australia, 700,000 in New Zealand, 4,500,000 in Canada and the 38,000,000 in dear old England, so that the dream of the philosopher may be realized, that the English-speaking race, the Anglo-Saxon race, the dominant race, that those all over the world, just the same as the Americans have done by Hawaii, will confederate and come together and become one great English-speaking nation, and we say with your poet:

> " Thou, too, sail on, O Ship of State!
> Sail on, O Union, strong and great!
> Humanity with all its fears,
> With all the hopes of future years,
> Is hanging breathless on thy fate!
> We know what Master laid thy keel,
> What workmen wrought thy ribs of steel,
> Who made each mast, and sail, and rope,
> What anvils rang, what hammers beat,
> In what a forge and what a heat
> Were shaped the anchors of thy hope!
> Fear not each sudden sound and shock;
> 'Tis of the wave and not the rock;
> 'Tis but the flapping of the sail,
> And not a rent made by the gale!
> In spite of rock and tempest's roar,
> In spite of false lights on the shore,
> Sail on, nor fear to breast the sea!
> Our hearts, our hopes, are all with thee;
> Our hearts, our hopes, our prayers, our tears,
> Our faith, triumphant o'er our fears,
> Are all with thee,—are all with thee! "

(Prolonged applause.)

Several resolutions were then introduced and referred.

THE CHAIRMAN: I now have the pleasure of introducing Prof. Courtenay De Kalb, of the Rolla School of Mines of the University of Missouri, who will address you on

THE POLITICAL RELATIONS AND COMMERCIAL ADVANTAGES OF THE NICARAGUA CANAL.

PROF. DEKALB'S ADDRESS.

It is a curious thing that where a people rest their indorsement of any project upon too broad a general principle, there is a corresponding lack of enthusiasm for its consummation. If you regard this Nicaragua Canal as being in some broad indeterminate manner a good thing, even perhaps a somewhat glorious thing, believe me, you will never avail much in the active propaganda of the undertaking. It needs not that you see all sides of this question, nor that you understand all of its manifold advantages; it is enough if you see *one* side, *one* advantage, provided only that you see it clearly, that you believe in it with all your might, and will not rest until you have done your utmost to obtain this canal for the sake of that single advantage which you have perceived.

It matters not what may be your vision, so long as it is a true one, whether being a merchant, a farmer, a miner, here in this vast West, you realize that this canal will save for you on the goods you buy and on those you sell, no less than thirty per cent in freights; whether being a railroad man you are wise enough to shift, if possible, the oppressive burden of cheap and bulky freights to a water route, so that industry may receive an impetus, and lead to vastly increased shipments of high class freights over your railroad, enabling you to receive dividends where now you receive none, or larger ones where they have been small; neither does it matter whether your interest is a purely civic one, a patriotic eagerness to blot out sectionalism by removing the barriers of discriminative rates with their attendant hardships and social discontent; or, still further, whether you seek to keep the clutch of powers beyond the sea from that point toward which the commerce of the world is destined to converge, but which will never grow familiar with vessels flying the stars and stripes unless the freedom which that banner and that alone proclaims, is guaranteed by our government for this Nicaraguan water-way.

No matter, I say, what may be the reason which to you is all sufficient, only be no longer apathetic, as our people have been in the past.

Only once has the American nation been thoroughly aroused on the subject of this canal, and that sudden interest related more directly to diplomatic troubles than to the building of the canal itself. Public feeling waxed hot in the decade of the fifties when England was scheming to undermine our conceded rights in Nicaragua. The most trivial incident would then have sufficed to precipitate a war between the two great Anglo-Saxon powers, but amidst so much excitement, with the golden sands of California drawing the eyes of all toward the far Pacific, the practical endeavor to open a shorter route by a ship canal fell crushed, a hopeless undertaking, for want of financial aid. Perhaps the hand of Providence guided us to our greater good. Had our resources then gone into that vast enterprise we would not so soon have seen our fair republic spanned from sea to sea by roads of iron; the plains and mountains of our middle west might still have been a desert; the unity of our nation still unattained; our aggregate wealth only a fraction of what it is to-day. Such speculations may be idle. We know what *is*, but cannot so surely tell what might have been. There is no doubt, however, that had our fathers built the Nicaragua Canal, we would have had the burden to-day of practically rebuilding the whole of it, for then it was thought that a depth of twenty feet would suffice for the largest ships that would demand a passage; *now*, our small freight steamers require that depth, while our ocean greyhounds would plow the bottom at 30 feet. The cost of such a reconstruction would almost equal the outlay for a new canal.

For good or ill, the canal remained a dream unrealized. We were fast losing that pre-eminence on the sea which had been the fruit of New England's trading with the Indies. We had made concessions to England in repealing the law for discriminative duties favoring American shipping, which placed British vessels on an equality with our own. Finally came the troubled years of civil war and reconstruction. By this time the ruin of our foreign commerce was complete. As we began once more to prosper, every dollar of our resources was expended in developing the natural wealth of our own domain. Never before in the history of the world had so vast and valuable a field for capital been wrought upon with such skill and daring faith. Thus is it that America stands supreme, the richest nation the world has ever seen, and the wisest nation in the comprehension and use of its God-given endowments. It is not strange that we saw with indifference the growth of England's naval power, while our ships that once had sailed so proudly lay rotting in our ports. We had no need to go abroad when there was more than we could do at home. And so our people, absorbed in their own affairs, having such feeble connections with international trade, could not be induced to take an active interest in the Nicaragua Canal. Its value is seen by many, a superficial interest in it is widespread, but the purses of our citizens have remained closed against it. For six whole years the Maritime Canal Company of Nicaragua has been incorporated and no more than $6,000,000 have been expended upon the work. Perhaps this again is fortunate. I do not mean to stand as an apostle of that peculiar faith which is a part of the religion of so many Americans; that faith which reposes in blind confidence that if you will only repress enthusiasts, and let America drift, she will infallibly drift in the right direction. America does a great deal of this unguided drifting. (We let the winds of fate drive us on in the very face of threatening storm clouds, and no one reefs a sail until the evil is upon us.) Some one, we believe, will surely devise a plan to compose the raging tempest; some one will invent a machine to blow our enemy into small pieces, and we will grow rich on the fragments. In fact we do generally rise nobly to an emergency, and, if we must, we will take possession of the Nicaragua Canal while our European cousins are adjusting their spectacles to see what we are about. This is far from being our wisest course, for we should have to pass through a crisis to be driven to it in this spasmodic manner. There is a tangled skein of treaties which may draw into a hopeless Gordian knot as we proceed, only to be undone by some Alexander's sword if we allow this matter to drift on the uncertain current of circumstances. There are two things which would compel America to own this canal. The first would be the enactment of laws favoring the growth of our merchant marine, which is not unlikely to follow the building of our navy. The existence of a great ocean commerce would render a canal under American management imperative. The second is the stagnation of our internal commerce, which is becoming more decided year by year through the high freight charges of our transcontinental railroads. The existing rates are higher than can be borne by the great volume of goods which would be offered for shipment on easier terms. And yet the railroads have reduced their charges to the lowest possible limit until some new stimulus has given to the people of the West the means to create a greatly increased traffic in high-class goods for these roads to carry. We cannot fail to recognize the solemn truth that we have nearly reached the limit of advantages which can be gained from rail communication alone through the western United States, and that they are proving inadequate for the needs of commerce. In other words, the railroads cannot afford to carry for great distances those crude products which are necessary for any great expansion of industry, save at prices which are practically prohibitory. Those reciprocal relations between every portion of our commonwealth, so vitally essential to the integrity of our institutions, are checked by such an obstacle to easy commercial intercourse. It is the obstruction of circulation in one member, disturbing the functions of the whole organism. The natural development of the entire country is impeded by charges which restrict an interchange of commodities, and a separation of interests between the Atlantic and Pacific regions of the United States will grow more marked with each passing day while these conditions remain unchanged. There are some who profess to see that this separation will lead to a severance of political union. The Civil War is a sufficient answer to this prophecy, but that severe financial distress will result can not be doubted, unless we provide relief by means of an Isthmian ship-canal.

Our fathers, fifty years age, had reached a point in national development where they saw the need of foreign capital to assist in the unfolding of our resources. They had fed upon liberal ideas. Freedom, equality, brotherly love, friendly intercourse with all the world, had been the themes of countless orations from the beginning of the republic. These circumstances created a public sentiment which hailed with approval the broad principle laid down in the Clayton-Bulwer treaty that the Nicaragua Canal should be built for the good of the world, and should exist under the protection of all the great powers of the earth. Few men in those days thought of taking a more selfish stand until the diplomatic controversies over this vexatious treaty had fired the people with indignation. The spirit then aroused was never quite extinguished. It survived the tumult of the Civil War, and re-appeared intensified in 1880 when President Hayes announced that we could but regard any Isthmian canal as practically a continuation of our coast line. Since then we have ceased not to hear of a canal by Americans for Americans. It went so far that a treaty was drawn up between Secretary Frelinghuysen and the Nicaraguan minister providing for the construction of the canal out of public funds of the United States, with special privileges accorded to our commerce. This so-called "jingo" policy, in which Mr. Blaine likewise copiously indulged, has curiously affected popular opin on regarding the canal. In the East, where our people come into close relations with foreign countries, and where the great cities are so largely composed of an alien population that even the press is too often tinctured by foreign sentiments, a broad view is taken, and there exists a general indifference as to whether the canal be built by the United States, or by European nations. In the West, where less dependence is felt upon foreign commerce, where an inland security and independence inspires a stronger sense of national self-sufficiency, a sturdy, if indeed, somewhat vainglorious Americanism asserts itself. They are, perhaps, no more truly patriotic than others, but they are patriotic everywhere and at all times, and I thank God for it. We need this healthy Americanism to correct the alienism that is growing to such alarming strength along our Atlantic seaboard. But we can not do what all these earnest patriots demand without violation of our solemn compacts; neither is it necessary. Surely America is great enough to build this canal out of her own financial strength, she is great enough to protect it, she is great enough to insure to all nations the free use of it on equal terms with herself.

The first incentive to the opening of a canal across the American Isthmus was a shorter route for the Spanish galleons to the jeweled

Indies. It was soberly thought of in Spanish councils in 1550; seriously discussed in 1620 when Diego de Mercado submitted a remarkable report on the Nicaraguan route. But we all know how Spain, as if by way of expiation for her excesses, fell prostrate beneath the blows of enemies within and without. But it was not Spain alone that foresaw the need of this canal. England, too, cast her eyes in that direction. (Marvelous England! Marvelous above all in that unswerving fidelity to a single purpose in her foreign policy, whether ruled by a puritan Cromwell, or an autocratic Hanoverian king, or directed by a Palmerston or a Gladstone under a mild Victoria, the same yesterday and to-day, grasping island, and cape, and marshy coast, wherever she can gain a footing to menace her rivals and secure control of the commercial highways of the earth.) Slowly for a century she threw her net around the isthmus, until in 1782 she flung her forces, under the famous Nelson, against the Nicaraguan colony, seeking to capture that very waterway where we now propose to build a ship canal. How one brave Spanish woman saved her country, and sent Nelson away mourning the failure of an expensive expedition, is matter of history which you may learn elsewhere. But England kept firm her grip upon the Mosquito Shore, and secured by treaty a license to cut logwood in Belize,— fatal license, which furnished a pretext for taking full possession of this valuable country, commanding both the Gulf of Mexico and the Caribbean Sea. Meanwhile the United States had risen into prominence, was expanding over the whole of North America, and England saw clearly that we would need a trans-isthmian canal for commmunication with our Pacific territories. Would that the wisdom of those British statesmen had been our wisdom, and that we had taken steps to control this waterway, without British interference, making her understand that she too must fall under the prohibition of the Monroe doctrine, even if it was enunciated by us at her suggestion when she became alarmed at the Spanish-American schemes of Napoleon Bonaparte! But Napoleon finally fallen, England defied the Monroe doctrine which had once been her benefactor, and no more than one year ago concluded an important Mexican treaty in defiance of it. So, she waited not an hour, when she saw that California must be ours, to fasten upon the Nicaraguan waterway, seizing its supposed western terminus from Honduras, and its eastern or Greytown end from Nicaragua under pretext of territorial claims of her ward, the Mosquito Coast. I am not here to give you the history of this enterprise. You know how this action of Great Britain did at last arouse our statesmen; how we wrung from England the Clayton-Bulwer treaty of 1850, and how she triumphed over us in drawing up that document, by her superior diplomatic skill; how immediately she defied the treaty, and insulted Nicaragua in demanding that she come to terms about the building of this canal by England, because, forsooth, she said, the United States had not the necessary financial strength nor spirit of enterprise requisite for such an undertaking. Again you have heard how we finally were forced by British obstruction of our commerce across Nicaragua to send Capt. Hollins, staunch old sea-dog, down to Greytown to burn American powder in their faces, and to ship these Englishmen, very much disgruntled, and "surprised" as Lord Palmerston said, over to their island of Jamaica. Then it is familiar, aye, disgraceful, history, how that we agreed to settle all these troubles by accepting treaties between Great Britain and the republics of Nicaragua and Honduras, relative to the Mosquito Coast, provided these were drawn in accordance with the American interpretation of the Clayton-Bulwer treaty. Childish simplicity! As if an ungenerous rival could contract against his own interests. So we see the old Mosquito question still hanging over our heads, fraught with germs of future mischief, unless we take hold of this canal question with a firmer grasp.

I wish that I might give you a full account of this Clayton-Bulwer treaty, and its subsequent history. Every American citizen owes it to himself and to his country to know somewhat of it, and I say in solemn truth that no man can intelligently express an opinion concerning the dangers threatening our interests in the American Isthmus, until he has studied this treaty, and all that diplomatic history which preceded, and which has grown out of it. But I must tell you in passing, what this treaty pledged. Beginning with a guarantee that neither England nor the United States will ever exercise for itself any exclusive control over a Nicaraguan ship canal, it forbids the erection of fortifications commanding it, as well as the occupation, colonization, or exercise of dominion over any part of Central America. It further excludes any use of protection afforded by either party to the Central American States for accomplishing such ends, or for securing commercial privileges not accorded on equal terms to the other. Immunity from blockade or capture of vessels in the canal in time of war, is provided for, although practically useless. Furthermore these two powers agree to protect the canal from seizure, unjust confiscation, and the like, when begun by a responsible corporation, on "fair and equitable terms." This clause has been fruitful of dissension, but we may be sure that the American interpretation will endure if we say that it shall, and that *joint* protection with England will not be allowed. Next it is affirmed that they will use their influence with the Central American States and peoples, possessing or claiming to possess jurisdiction over the canal route, for securing certain beneficent regulations, but it will be observed that here a second time, an indirect recognition of the independence and territorial pretensions of the Mosquito Coast is clearly made as well as a recognition of England's rela-

tion to it as protector.   It agreed further to protect the canal and keep
it forever open and free, a practical assumption of sovereignty over
Nicaragua herself, presumably for the good of the world's commerce;
to secure treaties with the Central American States for facilitating the
construction of the canal; to seek an international guarantee of neutrality of the Isthmus, a provision which our Department of State has
stoutly refused since to abide by, owing to the danger of foreign entanglements.   Finally it avows that not only a special object is sought
by the treaty, but the establishment of a general principle of protection
and neutrality over all routes, by canal or railroad, which may ever be
built across any part of the American Isthmus.   It is doubtful if such
an assumption of the dominance of the Anglo-Saxon race in the affairs
of this world has ever gained expression in a State paper before or
since.   It stands alone, a unique instrument, affirming openly that
the reign of the Anglo-Saxon giants is supreme, that at the bidding of
these United States and of Great Britain the whole earth must yield its
highways to their commerce, and that the rest of mankind may enjoy
equal privileges only through their gracious condescension.   And yet
the spirit of this utterance is noble.   Every nation, strong or weak, is
promised equality with those two powers which are mighty enough to
compel the observance of justice.   Commerce is to be freed more and
more from all restrictions, and the open highways of intercourse are to
be, not on the sea alone, but by every passage, from sea to sea, which
none may close to the free use of mankind under cover of selfish
sovereign power.   Such is the Clayton-Bulwer treaty, a document so full
of good that we can only wish it had been more wisely drawn, so that it
should stand as a new bill of rights bringing blessings to all mankind.
But it was sown with seeds of discord, which nearly ripened into war
during the decade of the fifties, when we may safely say nothing but
the outbreak of our domestic strife, prevented a clash of British and
American arms over this vexed Isthmian problem.   Out of it has grown
the Treaty of Managua, whereby England to this day retains the opportunity of intervention in the affairs of the Mosquito coast, which would
at once involve a renewal of her claims to control the eastern terminus
of the Nicaragua Canal.   It has even constituted part of Great Britain's
claim to recognition by our Government of her encroachments in Belize.
It has indeed seemed like a compact set up for the sole purpose of fur-
nishing pretexts for violation of its spirit, by a pretended fulfillment of
its letter.   It has lost vitality, and yet is not dead.   In some form its
principles will be perpetuated.   We cannot ignore them ourselves; we
cannot suffer others to disregard them.   The result of such attempts
would be confusion, and strife, and the crippling of the progress of the
world.

It is not the glorious Republic of the West, nor yet the earth-encir-

cling empire of Great Britain, that has determined the freedom and
. neutrality of the passage to the Indies; it is the outcome of the needs
of humanity, which no power can thwart. It is merely a circumstance,
wonderful, providential, that the power of the dominant race on earth
should have been politically divided at this epoch of the history of the
world, so that the struggle for existence by the Anglo-Saxon nations
should spread the principles of liberty, and limit the engines of progress
to doing the greatest good to the greatest number. And so the spirit
of greed, or self-help, if you will, in each, restrains the aggrandizing
tendencies of the other. We may if we choose declare the treaty dead.
The logic of the case is plain. We have the compact, authorized by
our Senate. No diplomatic representative of the government, no
Secretary of State, no President can change it. Only the power that
ratified it can alter a single word, or grant a single privilege in contra-
vention of its articles. When General Cass, for the sake of peace,
allowed encroachments in Belize, he overstepped his powers; when
Secretary Fish and President Hayes declined to allow a joint protectorate, they refused to abide by the solemn promise of our government.
England has violated the treaty, and so have we. We may declare it
void at our pleasure, and with abundant cause; but likewise may
England do the same. But it has not been abrogated. A disgraceful,
crippled piece of diplomatic rubbish, it still holds a place, dishonored
by its presence, among the honorable compacts of its sponsors. And
while it stays there it is a menace to our political safety, for upon this
famous treaty rests another, the Treaty of Managua, craftily framed by
England, to secure a foothold near the route of the canal, with a
possibility of establishing full control in future. History is making
this very day and hour upon this question, and it may ere long out-
strip all others in importance. To-day * you have read dispatches
saying that Great Britain has sent a warship to Bluefields, and that she
refuses to recognize the sovereignty of Nicaragua over the Mosquito
coast. What does this mean? By what right does England
interfere in this matter? Let us see! As boys we have all read
and wondered at the deeds of the buccaneers of old. I am only reviv-
ing old historical memories to tell you that these ancient scourges of the
Caribbean were organized under a sort of republican government; that
they even made terms with respectable powers; that England under
Cromwell made an alliance with them to capture the island of Jamaica
in 1655. You also know that these pirates made their chief rendezvous
in the lagoons about the famous Cape Gracias á Dios, and were
harbored and fed there by Mosquito Indians, whom the pirates in turn
corrupted by all the skill in wickedness known to them. But you

---

* November 28, 1894.

may not know that when these miscreants fled from the south sea over-land and came wasted and worn, forever crushed, to this same Cape Gracias á Dios in 1688, England hastened to fasten her grip upon this coast by crowning a native chieftain king, and formally establishing a protectorate over him and his dominions. It was not because this land was valuable in itself that England wished it. You should see it to understand, — you should sail as I have done day after day through a network of channels between coral islands, or back of these through a labyrinth of lagoons and bayous, and see naught but sand and jungle, and you would believe that it was not the land that England coveted, but the strategic position, near the ocean highways of commerce, near the entrance into the richest portion of Central America, with a safe retreat in sheltered harbors in a part of the world where these are rare. It was a foothold in the enemy's country, a new advantage in her endless feud with Spain. Things ran in this groove until 1744, when England sent a superintendent to govern the Mosquito Coast. This aroused the ire of Spain so that in the treaty of Paris of 1763 England was forced to recognize the claims of Spain, and demolish all fortifications on the Mosquito shore and other parts of Spanish territory. Fresh incursions followed in spite of this treaty so that a new one was signed in 1783 by which England agreed to abandon the Spanish continent. She still held on to the Mosquito Coast, claiming that it did not belong to the Spanish continent, but to the *American continent*, a subtlety extinguished by the supplementary treaty of 1786, whereby she explicitly renounced all dominion or control over this particular territory. But she still guided the actions of the native chiefs, or kings, through the medium of British traders. As soon, how-ever, as the Spanish colonies had cast off the yoke of Spain in 1821, England at once crowned a Mosquito half-breed as king, placed him under her protection, and then proceeded to make and unmake Mos-quito " kings " at the rate of one each year, until she found a willing and reliable puppet. Such was the political relation of England to the Mosquito Coast as we found it in 1850. But there is another side also. In the beginning, according to early British writers, the Mosquito coast extended from Cape Cameron, on the north shore of what is now Honduras, to Pearl Lagoon, thirty miles north of Bluefields, and 90 miles north of Greytown. Later the English invaded the territory of the Cookra Indians to the southward, and set up their puppet king — Mosquito " ally " as they called him — to rule at Bluefields. Once they sent Nelson to extend the Mosquito territory to the Rio San Juan del Norte, the route of any future Nicaragua Canal, but being repulsed they waited until our war with Mexico had extended our Pacific possessions, and at once they seized this river and its port of Greytown in the name of the Mosquito

" king." There are many here who remember how we drove them out, and set up a provisional government which endured until the status of this coast was determined by the treaty of Managua. It had been the supposition that the Clayton-Bulwer treaty was to terminate British connection with the Mosquito Indians. I am sorry to cast aspersions upon a generation of American statesmen now passed away, but such an interpretation can by no possible subversion of plain English be sustained. England was right in asserting that this treaty only confirmed her in her claims as protector. But at last she pretended to yield to our demands, and offered to carry out our views in a separate treaty with Nicaragua, now known as the treaty of Managua, signed in 1860. By this agreement she did relinquish the protectorate over Mosquitio to Nicaragua, setting apart a reservation for the Indians, who were accorded the right of local self-government, under the nominal sovereignty of Nicaragua, and she recognized the complete sovereignty of Nicaragua on certain conditions, over two strips of coast, one north of the reservation, and the other south of it, extending to and embracing the Rio San Juan del Norte. The condition limiting this cession was that the binding force of the treaty is dependent upon the faithful observance of each and all of its articles. Once when troubles arose over this convention, the matter was referred to the arbitration of the Emperor (1881), who took pains to emphasize the right of England to interfere for the protection of her former ward, the Mosquito Coast. Consequently an infraction of this treaty of Managua offers England an opportunity to abrogate it, and re-assume her old protectorate. This would, of course, revive the conditions obtaining anterior to the treaty, and although England was kept out of Greytown by force of arms, she claimed it as part of the Mosquito Coast, and she would so claim to-day. Thus she would be in actual control through a puppet king of the very route of the canal, and she could legally land troops, and blockade ports, in the effort to maintain this control arrogated by her ward. And it is with deep chagrin that we must in honesty confess that the Clayton-Bulwer treaty gives her a right to do these things. So, we have recently seen the Mosquito Coast torn by dissensions, and invaded by Nicaraguan troops, in violation of the treaty. England, however, was not hasty. The time was not ripe. There was still a chance that our Congress might pass a bill affecting the canal. Emissaries of the canal company were in England and it might be that British capital would invest in the enterprise, and that she might have an interest of her own in maintaining the *statu quo*. Señor Barrios was sent to London by Nicaragua to negotiate a settlement of the Mosquito question. He was kept waiting. Six weeks ago, even, he had not succeeded in gaining an audience with Lord Kimberly. Now, all at once, a British warship goes to

Bluefields, and we learn that the mission of Señor Barrios has failed. Interpret this as you please, but I tell you there is danger ahead, danger for you, and hardship for your children and grandchildren, and disgrace for your country, unless our government firmly and unflinchingly exercises that right to dictate how the political status of the Isthmus shall be determined, which it has always assumed, and which has always, with more or less grumbling, been accorded by the European powers.

It will be impossible for me to even touch upon that group of treaties, some now abrogated, others unratified, and others still very materially affecting the future of this enterprise, such as the Dickinson-Ayon treaty, and the treaties between Nicaragua on the one hand and Costa Rica on the other, with all the great foreign powers, each of which contains articles relating to a future canal. Neither have I time to explain the canal concessions, but you will find them liberal to capital, restricting the ownership of the canal to a private corporation, which, however, does not preclude government ownership of canal stock or bonds, and you will find the conditions of forfeiture of the concessions clearly stated, and fully in accord with common principles of equity and justice. But I must impress upon you the fact that these concessions do not require the company to be an American company, but it may be organized anywhere, or transfer its allegiance by reorganization elsewhere at will. The Maritime Canal Company of Nicaragua has, it is true, been chartered by our Congress, which charter does indeed require that the company's office shall be in New York, and that its President, Vice-Presidents, and a majority of its directors, shall be citizens and residents of the United States, but there is nothing to preclude the leasing of the rights under the concessions, or of the completed canal, to foreign capitalists, so that our control is not established beyond chance of loss. Would our people suffer this? Would they calmly witness such a sacrifice of privileges for which they have contended these fifty years? And yet the Maritime Canal Company is struggling to-day against an apathy which confounds our wise economists and financiers, and each day it is coming into narrower and more dangerous straits. Money it must have, but where shall it turn to find it? We know that bills have been introduced into Congress to provide for a guarantee of the Canal Company's bonds by the government to the amount of $100,000,000. There is no legal objection to it. It would involve no transfer of concessions. The government would merely acquire the rights of a mortgagee, if it were forced to redeem these bonds, and it would of course exercise at all times a closer supervision over the company than now through the control of a majority of the company's stock, held as security for the guarantee, and giving the government the choice of ten directors out of fifteen. It must be observed, moreover, that there is a distinct difference between such bonds and those which governments usually issue upon the national credit merely. This guarantee would make them practically government obligations; the honor of the nation would be pledged to their payment; but there would be a material basis beneath them; an actual property which would have become a source of enormous revenue before these bonds would mature. The canal itself will re-imburse the national treasury for any outlay on this account. This is no dreamer's vision. A tonnage of fully 8,000,000* tons *per annum* goes to-day from European ports, and the Atlantic ports of the United States, to destinations in the Pacific Ocean not reached so easily via Suez as by way of Nicaragua. By far, the larger part of this vast trade is carried on directly between Europe and the Pacific. Without exception this whole enormous tonnage would perforce pass through the Nicaragua Canal, because it would be the cheaper route. The average distance saved by the canal for the whole of this tonnage would be fully 6,000 miles. The greatest distance saved by the Suez Canal is 4,480 miles. The tolls on the Suez Canal are $1.80 a registered ton. It is proposed to charge $2.00 a ton for the use of the Nicaragua Canal,— only 20 cents more than at Suez for an added advantage in distance saved of nearly 2,000 miles. On the basis of existing commerce only, disregarding any increase as a result of canal facilities, disregarding also the inevitable development of trade between our own Atlantic and Pacific coasts, this would yield a gross revenue of $16,000,000 *per annum*. The cost of maintaining and operating the canal, deduced from experience at Suez and Sault Ste. Marie, has been estimated at $1,250,000 a year; but suppose it were as much as $3,000,000! This would leave a net income of $13,000,000, or more than 6 per cent, upon a capital of $200,000,000. Should the United States guarantee bonds to the amount even of $200,000,000, the interest at $3\frac{1}{2}$ per cent would be $7,000,000, leaving a surplus of $6,000,000, which would suffice to extinguish the debt in 33 years, not including interest on this sinking fund. In other words, if the bonds were to mature in 40 years, before that time the canal would have more than paid the principal and interest of the bonds,— even if commerce does not grow. To issue these bonds is indeed in a certain way discounting the future, but it is also laying tribute upon the commerce of the world, and adding just that much to the aggregate wealth of the United States. Whoever buys a bond will receive interest and principal out of funds which in the end are derived from all nations whose commerce is aided by

---

*Recent estimates by Elmer L. Corthell place the registered tonnage now ready to use a trans-isthmian route at 6,493,000 tons, equal to a cargo tonnage of 9,650,000 tons.

this waterway. The question then is one of simple expediency. But if the people will not sustain this undertaking, if the government repulses it, then the company is doomed to pass into alien hands. Foreign capital will not freely flow into a company organized to do a work of an international character, while it is confined to American management, but as soon as the foreign capital exceeds that invested by Americans we will see the company forced to surrender its American charter and organize abroad. and this means practical political control to protect the investment, just as has transpired at Suez. You will remember that I said it might be fortunate that our people had not rallied sooner to the building of this canal. I have become impressed with a firm belief that they were wiser than they knew. Scarcely will you find a man or woman in the land whose patriotic interest is not awakened by the very mention of the name Nicaragua. It suggests to each a personal duty as a loyal citizen. But press this duty as one demanding instant action, and what do you find? A multitude of vague doubts and fears! The spectre of Panama frightens the timid ones away; the hopeless fog of the Clayton-Bulwer treaty, whose thick darkness so few have penetrated, but which has obscured for tens of thousands any clear vision of our rights in Central America, restrains the prudent ones, fearful lest it should involve that dreaded evil, a vigorous foreign policy. They fear to offer encouragement to a company which may lead to international entanglements. Furthermore, a great corporation's business is nobody's business, so far as the average stockholder is concerned. The small investor is like the sand which the great winds drift into helpless heaps. He wields no power; the man at the helm heeds him not. The great ones do as they please. And when the corporation, like this one, may come at last before the erratic courts of international law, the plain, logical layman's mind recoils from it as a dangerous, uncertain thing. Who will protect his interests in the company? Even though rascals might hold the keys of the money chest, who will promise that they be safely jailed? If diplomatic quarrels should threaten, who will guarantee that the government will not compromise to their financial damage in the interests of peace? A government is for the protection of the nation. It is the creature of the people, and public opinion will not often permit it to plunge them into a disastrous war for the protection of a private corporation. even though it be of great national importance. But if the government should assume the burden of responsibility, then it becomes a national affair, sustained in the interests of all, involving the national honor. The rascals can be impeached, or voted out of office at the next election; if foreign powers intrigue against the enterprise the force of the whole people will stand as a unit to preserve our rights,— a tremendous force which no nation on earth would risk a trial with.

There is no plan so certain to insure a speedy building of the canal as this, nor any which will so surely prevent a renewal of diplomatic entanglements over Central America. With a treaty still in force which has been openly violated ; disgracefully contorted, until its whole fabric is a mass of wretched shreds ; with another treaty threatening the security of the canal concessions ; with other treaties guaranteeing that neutrality and protection which we claim as our exclusive right to guarantee ; it was only the part of wisdom for our people to withhold their enthusiastic furtherance of the enterprise until it should rest securely upon the moral support of the whole American nation, of every party, from ocean to ocean. This is only possible when the canal is identified with the government itself so that its future shall be free from all uncertainties and doubts. Then the resources and energy of America will carry it to completion.

But can we afford delays ; can we longer afford to remain indifferent to this enterprise? What would America say if her right to navigate the northern lakes were taken away ; if any one proposed to close the Sault Ste. Marie Canal through which passes a larger annual tonnage than uses Suez? Would you suffer a reduction of one-fifth of the total commerce of America? And yet that is exactly what would happen if the Great Lakes were barred against us, and the Sault Ste. Marie Canal were closed. Twenty-two per cent of the whole freight movement in the United States is borne upon those northern channels. The total foreign commerce of our country is 27,000,000 tons *per annum.* The freight carried on the Great Lakes alone exceeds that amount by half a million tons. And it is not only the lake region that is benefited by this waterway. There is an immense outlying zone of attraction. The influence of lower rates reaches just so far as freight might find a cheaper route by part rail and part water than by rail alone. And so we witnessed in Dakota an increase in the value of wheat to the farmer of seven cents per bushel and a decrease in the cost of coal of $2 per ton as soon as rail communication with Lake Superior was obtained. (Herein lies the advantage of a waterway : it lowers freight rates ; it regulates freight rates ; it increases the possibility of production at a profit ; it permits the introduction of goods from other parts ; it opens up new fields of industry which high rates would keep forever closed.) The cost of water transportation is so very small that an increase of several thousand miles may be easily offset by lower rates. The merchant, the farmer, confronts here no abstruse problem. Suppose you are located 800 miles east of San Francisco. You wish to ship the produce of your farm or mine to New York City. At nine-tenths of a cent per ton per mile this will cost you $19.80 per ton. If the Nicaragua Canal were open, and you should ship by way of San Francisco and this water route, your ton of cargo would cost $7.20 to the

Pacific coast, and thence to New York, at two-tenths of a cent per ton per mile, $9.81, making a total of $17.01 per ton. You would save $2.79 in spite of the immense distance of 5,700 miles, and very naturally you would ship by way of the canal. These rates are not merely assumed for illustration. The average freight rate of all the railroads of the United States is .941 c. per ton per mile, a little more than I assumed. The average rate by water on the Great Lakes is .135 c. per ton per mile, or 48 per cent less than the figures used in the illustration. As a matter of fact the average charges of the railroads west of the Great Lakes, outside of their zone of attraction, in that region of which 80 per cent would be influenced directly by the Nicaragua Canal, is considerably over one cent per ton per mile, while the charges of the four great lines which come within the zone of water competition to the East are less than three-fourths of a cent per ton per mile, the difference in freight rates between the East and the West being actually over 30 per cent. The building of the canal will force down rates throughout the whole western portion of the United States. It would be cheaper to ship goods from St. Louis to New York and thence by the canal to San Francisco than to ship direct by rail at the existing average rate, and vastly cheaper to ship via New Orleans. If one should attempt to calculate the increased production of the farm and mine, the augmented exchange of merchandise, the enlarged market for our manufactures, that will follow the building of this canal, we would be no better able to represent the vast figure to our minds than we are to fully comprehend the significance in added wealth and in brighter horizons on the sea of life for each and every one of us which lies in the fact that the freight carried on the Great Lakes in 1889 was 22,517,000,000 ton miles. We can no more grasp such figures than we can comprehend the distance to the stars, but they mean that millions of men are sending cheaply to the markets of the world the product of their toil, which otherwise they could not send at all; that they are building happy homes through a thousand blooming valleys which otherwise would still remain a desert, the haunts of wild beasts and savage Indians. I think you will agree with me that it is poor economy to wait; that we cannot afford to wait; and yet, my friends, those whom we have sent to Washington to provide for our welfare and our national growth, year after year have trifled with this question, have prepared voluminous reports upon it, but have *done* nothing. Our late Congress, after a disgraceful wrangle over the tariff, adjourned without attempting even to partly redeem itself by passing an act in favor of this canal. Meanwhile agents of the canal company went to Europe seeking capital, and we now hear that some measure of success has crowned their efforts; that the canal is in the way of being lost to us forever! Lost! unless we can at this coming session persuade Congress to do its duty; or in the end fight to regain it. That which we might have had by merely laying tribute on the commerce of the future, would in such case, cost us millions of dollars, and thousands of human lives. Do you say we need not fight? That we may simply suffer England to own it? Well, then, are you prepared to have your intercourse with the great West checked; to have your ships placed under disadvantages forever; to have England menace you on the south as well as hem you in on the north, and threaten you from bristling islands on the east and west? Has it never occurred to you that the Anglo-Saxon giants are dividing the power of the world between them, and that, call it by what name you choose, one will in the end be the commercial vassal of the other? (Do not Halifax, and Bermuda, and Jamaica, and Esquimault, signify anything to you?) And then, when you look into all those cannon mouths pointing grimly at you, are you willing to have other cannon mouths yawning upon every ship of yours that sails the southern seas? Can you not perceive that to protect our growing commerce we would then need a navy that would overawe the greatest maritime power the world has ever seen, and that we would need to enter into treaties with European nations to help us guarantee the neutrality of this waterway, and that in consequence our political heart would beat in unison with theirs, and that their troubles would become our troubles? Where, then, would be that isolated security which has been our boast and our blessing? Shall we lay up tribulation for the future by letting the Nicaragua Canal slip from us now? If you have a voice, raise it in protest. Use whatever influence you have, as individuals, or collectively, to make Congress know your sentiments and to compel, if possible, that something be done while it is yet time. It is not that we are jealous of England, nor that we are seeking aggrandizement as a nation, that we want this canal, but because we must guard against dangers and disaster. We ask not that the stars and stripes shall wave over any ramparts in Nicaragua, but that the spirit of American freedom shall brood over this waterway, guaranteeing its peaceful use to all the world (applause).

Mr. H. R. Whitmore then read the following paper, prepared by

CAPT. W. L. MERRY, OF SAN FRANCISCO, ON THE NICARAGUA CANAL.

A Convention meeting annually cannot expect to fully understand the many questions of policy, international obligations, concessionary rights by Government charters from three sovereign powers, and other equally important questions connected with the construction of the *Nicaragua Canal.* But some salient points can be profitably alluded to, as a very inadequate substitution for the months, aye, years of time devoted to these questions by Congress, notably by the United States Senate in Executive Session, and by the Executive Cabinet.

1st. *The present conditions absolutely necessitate construction by a Company.* The administration of President Arthur negotiated with the Republic of Nicaragua in 1884 a treaty for the construction of the canal by the United States Government *direct*, with certain conditions: The United States was to have a joint sovereignty with Nicaragua over two and one half miles on each side of the canal; to fortify its terminals, to occupy with military forces jointly with Nicaragua, and to form a treaty of perpetual alliance with that Republic; also a loan of $4,000,000 gold was to be made to Nicaragua. This *Zavalla-Frelinghuysen Treaty* (so called) was ratified by the Nicaragua Senate, and was before our Senate when President Cleveland took his seat on his first inauguration. He at once withdrew it from the Senate, and in declining to return it expressed himself thus:—

"Maintaining, as I do, the tenets of a line of presidents from Washington's day, which proscribe entangling alliances with foreign States, I do not favor the policy. * * * Therefore, I am unable to recommend a proposition involving paramount privileges of ownership or right outside of our own country, when coupled with absolute and unlimited engagements to defend the territorial integrity of the State where such interests lie. * * * While the general project of connecting the two oceans by means of a canal is to be encouraged, I am of opinion that any scheme to that end, to be considered with favor, should be free from the features alluded to."

Mr. Cleveland's opinion is known to be unchanged and while he is President such a treaty cannot receive his approval, even if Nicaragua would again run the risk of a diplomatic rebuff, which is doubtful, especially as European influences are adverse to such action. Mr. Cleveland does not directly allude to the *Clayton-Bulwer Treaty* with Great Britain, ratified in 1850; but he probably had it in mind, as the said treaty explicitly states that, whenever a canal or other method of communication between the oceans, in Nicaragua, Panama, or any part of Central America, is built, Great Britain and the United States shall *have exact and equal rights and control therein.* The Zavalla-Frelinghuysen Treaty was a direct violation of the Clayton-Bulwer Convention, and would become possibly one of the "entanglements" alluded to. It is true that Blaine and Freylinghuysen claimed, in correspondence with Lord Granville, the British Foreign Minister, that Great Britain had herself violated the "*quid pro quo*" in the Clayton-Bulwer Treaty, and that consequently we were no longer bound thereby. But the fact remains that it has not been abrogated, and it is idle to ignore it by spread-eagle American talk. Now, the Panama Railroad was completed in 1856, six years after the Clayton-Bulwer Treaty, by an American corporation, and our Government was bound by treaty with New Grenada (now the U. S. of Colombia) to defend and protect it, which it has done by repeated landing of armed forces, and Great Britain has never complained of any violation of the Clayton-Bulwer Treaty in consequence. We have a right to conclude that the Nicaragua Canal constructed in the same manner, will not be objected to by England, and thus the entanglements to which Mr. Cleveland alludes will, in this particular, be avoided. I have made it plain why Mr. Cleveland's policy demands a canal constructed, as at Panama, by an American company. But the U. S. can absolutely control that company and its revenues by fixing the conditions of government, and this the Senate and House bills both do, although the latter — commonly known as the "Geary bill" — is not as liberal as the Senate bill, and does not even pay back fully the pioneer investors, if interest is considered. But that the American people demand complete government control is a certainty, and no good citizen objects to it. I think I have proven that a vote for construction at this time, "without the intervention of a company," is a vote against the canal during the present term of Mr. Cleveland, and probably much longer, for another Zavalla-Frelinghuysen treaty may not be feasible at this time.

2d. *Delay in the matter is dangerous to American control.* European influences are at work to deprive us of it, and if we wait until Mr. Cleveland's term expires, we shall probably have lost control (which can now be had free), and may either have to buy it at an exhorbitant price, or, worse still, have to fight for it against a nation with naval forces much greater than ours.

I presume that no intelligent and patriotic American will favor the idea of foreign control over the canal except so far as it may be permitted by the Nicaraguan government, in a friendly way. The strategetic and political importance of American control has been demonstrated by many occurrences known to students of American history.

3d. We have not yet considered *construction by the American Company without Government aid or control*, and unavoidably with European capital, largely. The capital that builds the canal will control the interests of the country through which it passes, to a great extent. European capital will promote European commerce, and employ largely Europeans in the administration. Such conditions will greatly weaken our national prestige, while such construction will unavoidably make the canal cost much more by reason of interest during construction, discount on securities to be sold, and banker's commissions. On this increased cost, American commerce must largely pay an increased toll to make profits for the investors.

I have endeavored to prove that, under present conditions, the bills

now before Congress, with such amendments as the wisdom of Congress
may suggest, offer the only practicable method of construction; that
opposition thereto must either come from misguided friends or from
concealed enemies of the beneficent work.   Private interests do not
affect my views.   I have initiated the commercial support of the Nicaragua Canal on the Pacific coast, jointly with Hon. Warner Miller,
Admiral Ammen, T. L. Phelps, and a small number of patriotic Americans, throughout the United States.   I want to live to go through the
canal when completed and I respectfully present the conditions to the
Trans-Mississippi Congress in the interest of truth and of our country.
I desire to refer briefly to

The benefit of the Nicaragua Canal to the Mississippi Valley.   The
Nicaragua Canal will open the Pacific Ocean to the Gulf States, and
create new markets for the Mississippi Valley.   The products of India,
China and Japan will reach there direct through the canal, and find
distribution up the valley and in the Gulf States, competing with the
distribution of the same products eastward from the Pacific Coast.

Japan and China are now large consumers of cotton; the former
especially, having greatly increased her manufacturing capacity in
cotton fabrics during the last few years.   What American cotton Japan
now receives is mostly shipped *via* New York, the Canadian Pacific,
and the English line of steamships across the Pacific, connecting
therewith — of course at comparatively high freights.   This trade
would furnish the return cargoes from the Gulf ports to China and
Japan, through the canal.   In fact, it is not possible to correctly pre-
dict the volume of this trade, which promises a new market for the
cotton of the South.

The trade of Australia, New Zealand, the Hawaiian Republic and the
islands of the Pacific would also be largely developed with the Mississippi Valley; — a growing commerce, to which no limit can be set, and
largely with English-speaking communities.

The commerce of the west coasts of Central and South America will
also be largely drawn to Gulf ports of the United States, and St. Louis
will be as accessible to the South American west coast as is San
Francisco.

The Nicaragua Canal will, in fact, open a new world of commerce to
the Gulf States of our Union and to the great Mississippi Valley; a
commerce now in its infancy, largely with nations constantly increasing
in population and inhabiting regions unsurpassed in fertility and natural
resources.   The Southern States are powerful factors in legislation at
Washington, and the Pacific States and Territories have good reason to
ask their aid in obtaining the necessary legislation which will secure
"An American canal under American control."   Jointly, the two
sections should be able to do this alone, but, with no portion of the

Union adverse to the beneficent project, which will so greatly stimulate the commerce and industries of our country, legislation should be assured at the approaching session of Congress. For this reason I sincerely hope the Trans-Mississippi Congress will add its urgent demand to that of the Great West for prompt action on the Nicaragua Canal, under control of our Government and primarily for the benefit of our people (applause).

Mr. Whitmore also read the following by

PROF. SYLVESTER WATERHOUSE, OF WASHINGTON UNIVERSITY, ON THE NICARAGUA CANAL.

Mr. President and Members of the Trans-Mississippi Commercial Congress: The commerce of the world impatiently demands the construction of the Nicaragua Canal.

Trade is intolerant of obstructions. Everywhere enterprise is seeking shorter channels of communication. The recently proposed canals from Bordeaux to the Mediterranean, from the Gulf of Mexico across northern Florida to the Atlantic, from the Chesapeake Bay to Delaware Bay, from Buzzard's Bay to Cape Cod Bay, from Lake Ontario to Georgian Bay, from St. Paul to Lake Superior, from Lake Erie to the Ohio, from Michigan City across Indiana and Ohio to Toledo, from Chicago to the Mississippi, and from Puget Sound to Lake Washington show the aggressive activity with which commerce and public safety are searching for more direct lines of intercourse. One of these canals is now in process of excavation. There is every probability that two others will be constructed. The rest may never be built, but the very conception of these schemes of internal improvement indicates the alertness with which every means of securing mercantile ascendency is now explored. The waterways lately completed from the Gulf of Aegina to the Gulf of Corinth — from the Elbe to the Baltic — and from Manchester to the Mersey, will not materially change the channels of trade. The greatest saving in distance which any one of them effects is less than 700 miles. For comparatively small and almost exclusively local advantages, Germany and England spent upon these water-courses sums nearly equal to the estimated cost of the Nicaragua Canal. The short channel across the Isthmus of Corinth was not so expensive, but its construction imposed . upon the limited resources of Greece a burden relatively greater than those which the opulent builders of the Baltic and Manchester canals had to bear. But the benefits of the Nicaragua Canal would be world-wide. A waterway across Nicaragua would wholly change the course of trade between our eastern States and all the lands that border on the

Pacific. It would also largely divert the commerce between Europe and the Orient from its present channels. It would save in a voyage from New York to San Francisco a greater distance than the entire width of the Pacific Ocean from the Golden Gate to Shanghai. Though the Nicaragua Canal would promote the prosperity of all mankind, the United States would be its chief beneficiary. While Europeans are spending scores of millions upon improvements of minor utility, will the richest people on the globe decline to build a work of incalculable importance to their own safety and prosperity?' Are the subjects of monarchies quicker than the freemen of a democracy to foresee and adopt the means of self-improvement? Beyond all other forms of polity, republics profess to care for the interests of their members. Shall the empires of the old world be permitted to surpass the republics of the new in an intelligent provision for the well-being of their citizens?

But it is not the purpose of this address to restate the arguments in favor of the Nicaragua Canal. Its powerful aid as a means of naval defense and as a safeguard of our Pacific coast, its diversion of Oriental commerce from foreign shores to our own, its economy of time, distance, freights, insurance, and exposure to marine losses, its general promotion of American prosperity and its special development of the resources of our Pacific States, its speedy appreciation of the products of our western frontier to values greater than the cost of the canal, its freedom from ice blockades and uninterrupted availability at all seasons of the year, its efficacy in binding the States of our Union in a still stronger alliance of mutual interests, its active advancement of the commerce of the Mississippi Valley, the advantages which shorter lines of communication would give to the United States in its commerce with Pacific and Oriental lands, the facilities which it would afford for the protection of our coaling station at Oahu, the wonderfully favorable physical conditions and the absence of serious engineering difficulties, the generous concessions and friendly co-operation of Nicaragua and Costa Rica, the strategic importance of Lake Nicaragua and the detersive action of its fresh waters upon the incrusted keels of vessels, the fewness of the locks, the superabundance of water for the service of the canal and the security of its banks from erosion by the natural storage of sudden floods in Lakes Managua and Nicaragua, the advantage of having as a part of the shipway a lake and river so broad that two vessels could sail abreast more than three-quarters of the distance from gulf to ocean, the healthfulness of the Nicaraguan climate and the commercial assistance of prevalent winds, the best and safest form of a congressional sanction of the work, the limited liability and exemption from financial loss that would attend a loan of our national credit, the reduced cost and lower freights of a canal built under the auspices of the United States Government, the approval of this great work by presidents and statesmen without distinction of party, the relative cheapness of construction, the variety and vastness of the products which would seek markets through this waterway, the liberal profits which a patronage broad as the needs of an international commerce would insure, the imperative necessity of an American control of the canal, and the danger in the event of·tardy action by the United States of the construction of this shipway by some foreign power and of a management unfriendly to the interests of this country — each topic of this long array has been discussed by engineers and conventions, by Congress and the press.   The fulness of the discussion has exhausted all the main arguments in behalf of the Nicaragua Canal.

But recent events in the Orient suggest new reasons for the early completion of this waterway. A few years ago, in a difficulty with Japan which diplomacy failed to settle, American men-of-war were compelled to vindicate the rights of our countrymen. The utter and humiliating inability of their fleet to repel American warships startled the Japanese from their fancied security. The suggestions of their defeat were not unheeded. The Japanese were quick to recognize the causes of their weakness. In the costly school of experience, they learned a lesson fraught with momentous consequences. The chastisement led to a thorough reorganization of the naval and military systems of Japan. The government increased its armaments on land and sea, and for years has been carefully training its marines and soldiers in the tactics of Europe and America.

But China, with its inert attachment to old customs, has been less progressive. Its few reforms have been insincere and ineffective. The present war between Japan and China tests the merits of the two systems. Everywhere the forces of Japan, disciplined by modern methods and equipped with arms of precision, are victorious. Apparently the Chinese will be ingloriously vanquished. They, too, will learn the practical wisdom which disaster teaches. Their statesmen are astute, and they cannot fail to see that nothing but a renunciation of their ancient policies and an adoption of western reforms will preserve the integrity and honor of the Celestial Empire. Li Hung Shang is a far-sighted man. If the lethargy of his government had permitted, he would long ago have introduced modern improvements into China. The late defeats of Chinese armies will compel the Emperor to sanction innovations. Means for the rapid transportation of troops, munitions, and commissary stores are necessities of national defense. Railroads must and will be built. But railways are everywhere the pioneers of progress. In India they have been powerful factors in breaking down the barriers of caste, increasing the exchanges of trade, and introducing the methods of western civilization. They will produce similar results in China. The railroads, built with the original motive of imperial defense, will be mainly devoted to the service of commerce. The Chinese, taught by far severer reverses than those which revolutionized the military system of Japan, will extend their lines of railroad to every part of the Empire. The larger profits that will spring from the quickened activity of domestic industries will reconcile the people to the introduction of the hated innovation. A wider intercourse with mankind will tend to dispel native prejudices against foreigners, and the gratification of wants steadily becoming more civilized and diversified will cause a larger demand for imported commodities. It seems certain that, before many years, even the interior markets of China will be open to the commercial competition of the world. The foreign trade of 300,000,000 of people is a prize which all great maritime nations will struggle to win. A controlling interest in this commerce, to which the United States from its relative nearness to China seems justly entitled, will not be acquired without the keenest rivalry.

Alert sagacity and energetic enterprise are the qualities that win commercial empire. The careers of the foremost nations are brilliant illustrations of mercantile forecast. The vigor with which England seizes the remote advantages which its foresight perceives explains its splendid success. This very Nicaragua canal furnishes a signal example of English forethought. As soon as it was foreseen that, in the distant future, a shipway might possibly be built across Nicaragua, the British Government claimed a protectorate of the Mosquito king. As his petty domain lay at the mouth of the San Juan river, this act of usurpation distinctly contemplated an ultimate control of the proposed canal.

A disregard of rights is never a good precedent for our countrymen to follow, but the sagacity which this unjustifiable seizure shows is worthy of American imitation. If the United States should enforce the Monroe doctrine, Great Britain would soon have to abandon its pretensions to the territory of the Mosquito king. In its contest for mercantile supremacy the United States will have to contend with an active and well-organized competition. In such a struggle, only enterprise and the most effective facilities for the cheap and rapid transportation of freights can achieve success. Harbors on our Pacific coast are insufficient. The freightage of merchandise across the continent is too costly. Our Eastern seaports must be directly accessible by water. But a *direct* voyage from the Atlantic to China implies a strait across the Isthmus of Darien. By this route, the voyage from New York to Shanghai is 2700 miles shorter than that from Liverpool. In their competition for the trade of China, a saving in distance equal to the width of the Atlantic should insure an easy victory for American merchants. By the aid of a shorter line of communication, our countrymen ought to obtain at least a proportionate share of the enriching commerce of China.

The same arguments apply with still greater force to our mercantile relations with Japan, and the western States of South America. By the new waterway, the distance from these countries to our Atlantic seaboard is much less than that from China. The completion of the railway from Buenos Ayres to Valparaiso will connect an extensive system of South American railroads with a Pacific line of steamships. If, after the Nicaragua Canal has been finished, the United States does not control the trade of the western Spanish republics, its failure can only be ascribed to a culpable neglect of a great opportunity. The excess of our manufactured products must seek foreign markets. But these markets can hardly be found in Europe, for transatlantic lands, manufacturing far more than they need for domestic consumption, are dangerous rivals of the United States in all the marts of the world. But Japan, China, and South America have not yet become manufacturing countries. The products of their factories do not supply home wants. There seems to be no good reason why Americans should not, through the facilities which the Nicaragua Canal would afford, become masters of a large part of this vast trade. The profits of this commerce would in a very few years defray the entire cost of the canal. But trade is everywhere conservative. When once it has established its business relations, it is reluctant to change. If Europeans are the first to obtain a control of the larger markets which will soon be open in the far East, it will be difficult to dispossess them of their ascend-ency. American merchants ought to insist upon an immediate construction of the Nicaragua Canal, and to be ready, with shorter lines of communication, to avail themselves of the mercantile opportunities which the Corean war is destined to provide. Unless our countrymen equal Europeans in foresight and enterprise, they will never win the splendid prizes of Oriental and Spanish-American trade.

There is an industrial reason for an immediate prosecution of this great work. The United States has not yet recovered from the panic. The losses in the shrinkage of values are incalculable. There is not in all our land a home which has not felt the effects of the business depression. Tens of thousands of laborers are still out of employ-ment. A large part of the $100,000,000 which will be required to build the canal would be expended in buying American machinery and paying the wages of American workmen. The work of construc-tion would give employment to thousands of laborers and the outlay of millions would hasten the revival of our languishing industries.

The recent resumption of work upon the Panama canal shows that the colossal failure of Lesseps did not wholly dishearten French capitalists. There is a possibility that the project of the great engineer may yet be completed.   This is a contingency which the United States cannot regard with indifference.   With the exceptional enmity of Napoleon III., the relations between France and the United States have nobly exemplified the constancy of our international friendship. But, if there should be any interruption of this amity, the possession of the Panama canal by a hostile power would be full of danger to the United States.   A shipway open to the fleet of an enemy, but closed to American men-of-war, would imperil our national safety.   In the event of a war between Great Britain and France, the mistress of the seas might wrest from its Gallic rival the control of the Panama Canal.   The acquisition of a shorter waterway through which its navy could hasten to protect British Columbia, or to attack our Pacific States, would gratify a long cherished ambition of the English Government.   Americans would find it more difficult to repel the aggressiveness of the English than to sur- pass the enterprise of the French.   The United States will never interfere to prevent the completion of the Panama Canal.   Con- sequently its only means of securing a superiority of commercial and defensive advantages is the prompt construction of the Nicaragua Canal.   From its greater nearness to the United States, its larger capacity for the passage of ships, its better climate, and the steady sweep of winds favorable to sailing vessels, the Nicaragua Canal would be far more beneficial to our own country than the Panama Canal would be to France.   Alike for purposes of mercantile profit and naval defense, our Government ought quickly to anticipate its French rival in cutting a ship canal across the Isthmus of Darien.

The building of the Nicaragua Canal would quicken the indus- tries of the United States with the impulses of a greater pros- perity.   Agriculture, manufactures, and commerce would unitedly support a measure whose consummation would so greatly promote their own interests.   The alleged unfriendliness of the trans- continental railroads to the water route must be a misapprehension. An opposition so injurious to the future welfare of those lines would indicate a short-sighted policy.   But assuredly, the directors can not be so devoid of forecast as not to recognize fruitful sources of railroad prosperity.   They could hardly fail to see that the Nicaragua Canal would vastly enlarge the population and resources of our Pacific States.   The increased values of lumber, cereals, and fruits, would alone soon exceed the cost of the shipway.   The trade of our western coast is now large and far-reaching.   A striking proof of its extent is the fact that a merchant of Johannesburg has recently come to this country for the purpose of chartering a line of steamers to carry lum- ber from Puget Sound to Africa.   The new water route would not only widely extend the commerce of our Pacific States, but it would also create many unforeseen industries.   These novel forms of mer- cantile enterprise which great public improvements never fail to develop would enrich our Pacific commonwealths with still ampler resources. The greater traffic of larger and more opulent populations would increase the business of the trans-continental railroads. The great prosperity which the new waterway would cause would augment the overland freights. The directors of our inter-oceanic railroads ought, for the promotion of their own business interests, to be strong and active friends of the Nicaragua Canal.

The best fruits of civilization have ripened in the climates of liberty. The free enjoyment of every civic right and the un-controlled exercise of every talent are essential to the highest development of material prosperity and spiritual refinement. The institutions of our Republic are the freest on earth. Here the only checks upon popular liberty are the restraints which the people have themselves imposed. Only an enlightened patriotism can preserve our precious heritage of free institutions. There are no material agencies which more powerfully foster an intelligent loyalty than rail-roads and steamships. These great factors of civilization diffuse intelligence, extinguish sectional enmity, enlarge social intercourse, liberalize public sentiment, preserve our language from the corruption of local dialects, bind our States more intimately together with the strong ties of commercial interests, and furnish indispensable facilities for national defense. Every important extension of our system of intercommunication increases the means of public enlightenment and strengthens the foundations of civil order. The Nicaragua Canal would tend more effectively than any other single line of transit to unify the interests and multiply the defenses of the United States. It would, by a wider dissemination of knowledge and the spirit of free institutions, extend through Spanish America the sway of liberty regulated by law. The general enlightenment which constant intercourse would cause would help to insure, throughout the western hemisphere, the perma-nency of free institutions. In its broader relations, this shipway would foster the fellowship and brotherhood of mankind, teach the grand economies of international peace, and persuade estranged peoples to reconcile their differences by the rational process of arbitration. In their eagerness for commercial profit, our countrymen ought not to ignore the nobler benefits which the Nicaragua Canal would confer upon mankind. Its ethical services in behalf of universal peace and a higher civilization deserve a distinct recognition. The strong interests and friendships which spring from greater intimacy of commercial intercourse would tend to settle international disputes by the inexpen-sive and bloodless adjustments of peace, rather than by the costly and sanguinary decisions of war.

The arguments in favor of the Nicaragua Canal are irresistibly con-vincing. The people of the United States recognize the vast importance of this waterway as an outlet of commerce and as a means of defense.

Action has not been delayed by political controversies. Our chief magistrates and eminent statesmen have, irrespective of party lines, advocated this measure. What, then, is the cause of Congressional inaction? It is partly due to the late panic which withdrew capital from the use of enterprise, and partly to the timidity of Congress. But the revival of prosperity has released hoarded funds from captivity, and the public approval of the Nicaragua Canal has relieved representatives from their hesitancy to vote for a measure that might not be sanctioned by the people. Constituencies are ordinarily apprehensive of a too lavish use of public moneys, and congressmen, obedient to the popular will, are wont to advocate retrenchment. But there ought to be a just discrimination. No sagacious merchant would hesitate to invest more capital in his business, if he was confident that the outlay would insure larger profits. But, so far as foresight can discern, the Nicaragua Canal will bring to the United States returns immeasurably greater than the cost of its construction. The precautions which protect a loan of national credit would secure the United States' treasury from loss, but if our Government should assume the entire expense of building this shipway, the investment would, with the single exception of the purchase of Louisiana, be the most profitable transaction in the fiscal history of the United States. A present economy that prevents future wealth is financial folly. Public opinion ought to demand of Congress an immediate endorsement of an undertaking from which our country would derive such boundless benefits. Congressmen would not dare to disregard the authoritative instructions of their constituents. This convention should supplement its own insistence upon favorable legislation by an earnest appeal to the people of the United States to demand of the Government an official sanction of this great enterprise. Sagacious statesmanship, impatient of Congressional delays, will promptly provide an effective means of extending our commerce, developing our resources, and defending our coasts.

American genius, expending only a small portion of the illimitable wealth of the United States and wielding the resistless energies which man has subdued to his service, will soon channel a passageway from ocean to ocean.

The glory of success will be as lasting as the utility of the work.

A spirit grandly ambitious and wholly dauntless is the inspiration of great achievements. America ought to emulate the invincible persistence of Hercules. The government of the United States cannot assert its determination to secure a shorter course to the Orient in more fitting words than those which express the demigod's sublime defiance of failure: —

"Inveniam viam, aut faciam" (applause).

Adjourned until Friday morning.

FRIDAY MORNING SESSION.

November 30, 1894.

The meeting was called to order by President Cannon at 10 a. m., who announced that the first business in order would be the receipt of names of Vice-Presidents and members of the Executive Committee from various States and Territories.

Resolutions were introduced.

SENATOR JOHNSON: I desire to have the word " agriculture " struck out of the resolution on Hydraulic Mining, which reads as follows: —

Resolved, That this Congress heartily indorses the recommendation of the Miners' Convention recently held in San Francisco, regarding the construction of dams in the mutual interest of hydraulic mining, agriculture and navigation, and further urges upon Senators and Representatives the extension of similar provisions to other States and Territories where similar conditions may now or hereafter exist.

Now, Mr. Chairman, so much of that resolution as refers to agriculture has not been called to my attention, and I prefer to have that stricken out. I know what those dams are for and I have no objection to the resolution, but do not want to be hauled into giving that on the part of agriculture.

MR. BENJAMIN: I accept the amendment.

The word " agriculture " was then stricken out and the resolution adopted.

MR. WHITMORE: I would ask to have the floor for a moment as a matter of privilege. I have a resolution, prepared by Prof. Waterhouse of Washington University, which was to have been offered by ex-Gov. Francis of Missouri, who was appointed a delegate by the Merchant's Exchange and also by the Governor. Owing to sudden bereavement in his family, he is prevented from being present. I simply wish to read the resolution and submit it with a few explanatory remarks and ask that it be acted upon by the Congress direct, as it is now too late for it to be referred to the Committee on Resolutions.

Resolved, That the Trans-Mississippi Congress, advocating a diversification of our national industries, recognizing the great textile value of Ramie and its luxuriant growth in our Gulf States, and believing that recent improvements in mechanical and chemical processes of preparing the fiber will render the production of this useful staple a profitable domestic industry, recommend the cultivation of this plant to our southern States as a new and important source of textile wealth.

Professor Waterhouse of Washington University, who has given much time and study to this subject, has kindly furnished the following statement in regard to it:—

The great economic need of the South and Southwest is a diversification of their industries.

Ramie is one of the most valuable textile plants in the world. It grows in our Southern States with rank luxuriance. Its floss is stronger than silk, and almost as lustrous. It is alike suited to the demands of utility and of luxury — it can be woven into the most useful, or the most exquisitely ornamental fabrics. The plant needs a warm, moist soil. Under favorable conditions, it will produce three crops a season. In a semi-tropic climate, the equable and steady supplies of water which irrigation furnishes would foster its most luxuriant growth.

The demand for this fine and beautiful fiber is vastly greater than the present supply.

The only obstacle to the successful culture of Ramie in the United States has been the difficulty of preparing the fiber for the loom. But the improvements in mechanical and chemical processes of treatment which have been made within the last year justify the belief that the domestic growth of Ramie would now open a new source of wealth to our Southern States.

It is in view of these facts that the Trans-Mississippi Commercial Congress is asked to recommend to the planters of our Gulf States, New Mexico and Lower California, the cultivation of Ramie as a profitable means of diversifying their industries and increasing their textile resources.

The resolution was then adopted.

The report of the Committee on Territories was called for.

A number of resolutions were reported from the Committee on Resolutions, embodied in one report.

Mr. Bryan called for a division of the resolutions, so that a vote could be taken on the Territories first.

The questions were divided.

THE CHAIRMAN: It has been suggested that these resolutions be divided and that the two first resolutions be adopted. They are reported unanimously and there is no minority report against them; we can get them out of the way and then proceed to the discussion of the other resolutions.

The following resolutions were read as reported by the Committee and adopted:—

Resolved, That Congress be earnestly requested to pass an amendment to the "Carey Act," (which donates 1,000,000 acres of the arid lands to each State in which they are located) extending the provisions of that Act to the Territories.

Resolved, That we earnestly urge upon Congress at its coming session to pass Enabling Acts providing for the admission of Oklahoma, New Mexico and Arizona into the Union as States. The admission of these Territories into Statehood would greatly promote their material prosperity, add to the wealth and strength of the nation, and vest in the people of said Territories the powers of local self-government to which they are justly entitled.

The following resolution was submitted as the majority report of the Committee:

Resolved, That the alarming condition of affairs which exists in the Indian Territory is a constant menace to the peace and safety of the people of the surrounding States, an obstruction to interstate commerce, and a disgrace to our civilization. The tribal governments of that Territory have signally failed to observe the requirements of existing treaties with the United States, and to protect from robbery and violence the lives and property of the people. We believe, with the Dawes Commission, that the lands of the Five Tribes, now monopolized by the few, should be allotted in severalty to all the members of the Tribes, the tribal government abolished and the Indians made citizens of the United States. To this end we favor the prompt provision by Congress for a State and Territorial Government over the allotted lands, and complete court-jurisdiction, and the uniting of all, or a part, of said lands with Oklahoma in single Statehood.

The following minority report was then submitted and read:—

"The undersigned members of the Committee upon Resolutions respectfully report that they are unable to agree with the action of a majority of the committee upon the report of the sub-committee upon Territories, and as a minority report recommend the adoption of the substitute offered by the delegation from the Indian Territory in lieu of the second resolution offered by the sub-committee on Territories.

(Signed)　　　　　　G. B. DENISON,
FIELDING LEWIS,
Members Committee on Territories."

MINORITY REPORT — INDIAN TERRITORY.

WHEREAS: The fact that the Congress of the United States saw fit to provide by law for a Commission to treat with the Five Civilized Tribes of Indians for a change in the manner of holding the lands conveyed to them by the United States and for the abolition of the tribal governments now maintained by those tribes, and that said Commission has made its report in favor of radical changes; and,

WHEREAS: The correspondents of various newspapers have recently been sending to such papers highly sensational and largely untruthful reports of the conditions existing in the Indian Territory; and,

WHEREAS: We recognize the fact that the outside popular demand for a change from the present conditions, although largely based upon want of knowledge of the real situation, or upon belief in the statements that are actually without foundation, has grown so strong that it seems impossible to resist it; therefore, be it

Resolved by the Trans-Mississippi Commercial Congress:

First: That the wisest course that can be pursued in regard to the present Indian Territory is for the Congress of the United States to pass an Act increasing the number of judges in the Indian Territory, increasing the number of commissioners, and increasing their jurisdiction, and conferring upon the United States Court in the Indian Territory jurisdiction over all violations of law, and providing for a survey of the lands, and allotment among those entitled to share therein.

Second: That we believe the question of a Territorial Government or of Statehood should be deferred until after the allotment of the lands now held by the Five Civilized Tribes of Indians has been accomplished.

(Signed)

GIDEON MORGAN,
Chairman.

A DELEGATE (from Missouri): There is a great question upon the difference between these two reports, a great moral question for the people of this country to take into consideration, and they ought to take into consideration a broader scope than continuing that state of affairs. They can easily turn into a territorial condition, and the report simply means to step into that condition, so that the people of that country, and those who want to immigrate to that country, would be protected in their lives, and that the lives of passengers who travel through that country on the railroad and of innocent women and children will be safe. I favor the majority report.

MR. JOHNSON: I rise more to get information than anything else. It seems to me that the real bone of contention here is that the one side wish to add the territory known as the Indian Territory to Oklahoma, and have it admitted as a State, and that the Indians, the Five Tribes there, be made citizens. The other side oppose that. The people in the Indian Territory oppose being taken in as a State until those Indian Tribes have had their rights considered in the light of citizenship. Mr. President and gentlemen, that brings up a very important question. If that is done there rises the question of the right to fill the offices, and I do not doubt that those people down there in a general way are industrious people. But this has had a very brief consideration here, and I do not believe that this convention has the facts before them on which they can intelligently vote on that question at this time.

MR. HAILEY (of Indian Territory): Mr. Chairman, we have transferred to the U. S. Government over 90,000,000, acres of land that has built up this Mississippi Valley into the grand country that she is to day, and I am proud of it. We will be the last State that comes into the Union, and I say it is to the honor of this country that we should be granted one star in the constellation of stars that glitters in the flag of our country.

HON. SIDNEY CLARKE (of Oklahoma Territory):

Mr. President, and Gentlemen of the Trans-Mississippi Congress: I have been requested by the Committee on Resolutions to defend the majority report, and to present the conditions which exist in Oklahoma and the Indian Territory in connection with the demand for statehood. To those who are fully advised of the lamentable condition of affairs in the Indian Territory, the majority report needs no defense. The resolution of the majority covers the whole ground, by accurately presenting the facts, and demanding of Congress the proper remedies. Let me read it again in your hearing:—

" *Resolved*, That the alarming condition of affairs which exists in the Indian Territory is a constant menace to the peace and safety of the people of the surrounding States, an obstruction to interstate commerce and a disgrace to our civilization. The tribal governments of that territory have signally failed to observe the requirements of existing treaties with the United States, and to protect from robbery and violence the lives and property of the people. We believe, with the Dawes commission, that the lands of the Five Tribes, now monopolized by the few, should be allotted in severalty to all the members of the tribes, the tribal governments abolished and the Indians made citizens of the United States. And we favor the prompt provision by Congress for a State or Territorial government over the allotted lands, complete court jurisdiction, and the uniting of all or a part of said lands with Oklahoma in single Statehood."

The minority report pleads for delay in the establishment of civil government, and seeks to conceal the real condition of affairs in the Indian Territory — the reign of robbery and murder and blood — now prevailing there, and to abolish which the report of the majority asks the prompt intervention of Congress.

Mr. President, I shall deal only in facts. In advocating this report, I speak not only for the Committee on Resolutions but in behalf of the youngest and most populous of the Territories of the United States. If, in the time allotted me, I can give to this body a glimpse of a Territory born in a day, phenomenal in its growth, less than five years old, and now demanding and entitled to admission into the Union as a State, and of its peculiar relations to the Indian Territory, I shall be content. A new American commonwealth, thus speedily created, is an illustration of the energy and enterprise of the Anglo-Saxon race without a parallel in the history of civilization.

Oklahoma occupies a central position between the Mississippi river and the Rocky mountains. It has an average area of 36,352 square miles or 23,265,709 acres. This is 1,627,949 acres greater than the area of the State of Indiana. Should the present Indian Territory — the country of the Five Civilized Tribes — be united with Oklahoma in statehood, then the new State would have an area of 44,563,161 acres, 2,726,230 acres larger than the great State of Missouri. There are thirty States in the Union of less area than these two Territories combined, and twelve States have less area than Oklahoma alone. Nor are we lacking in population necessary for statehood. In Oklahoma, at the recent election, there were nearly 50,000 votes, showing that we have a population of 250,000. The Indian Territory has a population of not less than 250,000, exclusive of about 65,000 Indians and people of mixed and white blood connected with Indian tribes. Enumerated together, there is at this moment not less than 565,000 people living within the limits of the old Indian Territory, entitled to home rule, qualified for the responsibilities of statehood, and appealing to the Congress of the United States for prompt relief from exceptional and extraordinary conditions. Here is a population nearly twice as large as that of any territory heretofore admitted into the Union, and should Congress provide for admission as two States, then each would have a population equal to any Territory admitted, with two or three exceptions.

Why, sir, when this grand imperial commonwealth of Missouri entered the Union in 1821, she had but a trifle over 66,000 people. Now, after the lapse of nearly three-quarters of a century, with its grand history and unexampled progress; now that there has been built up within your borders this magnificent city, the center of the commerce and the civilization of the most fertile river valley on the face of the globe — the center of a vast empire of wealth and power; now that our government is strong and our free institutions are entrenched in the confidence of the mass of the people, north and south, east and west; now that the admission of Missouri has been followed by the admission of twenty States stretching from the great lakes to the Pacific ocean, there comes an appeal from the Territory of Oklahoma, that has four times the population Missouri had in 1821, inviting your aid in securing admission without delay into the sisterhood of sovereign States. Oklahoma can be joined with the Indian Territory and form a single State, as her geographical limits can be extended on the south, so as to include a portion or all of the Chickasaw Country. There is some diversity of opinion in Oklahoma as to the boundaries of the proposed State. Some of our people want to limit the State to the present boundaries of the Territory, reaching this conclusion through political considerations. But I think it safe to say that a large majority would prefer the boundaries of the old Indian Territory should be the boundaries of the new State, or if two States are to be formed that the Chickasaw country should be added to Oklahoma. Let me say here that the statehood movement in Oklahoma has been non-partisan from the first, and that now, more than ever before, men of all political parties are anxious for a deliverance from territorial conditions.

We appeal, therefore, Mr. President and gentlemen, to men of all political parties to favor our admission into the Union at the ensuing session of Congress, as suggested by the terms of the majority report. We appeal to every financial and commercial interest in all the States of the Mississippi valley to speak a good word in our behalf. We especially appeal to this great city and State, with which in the near future we shall be closely united in all the relations of trade, transportation and commerce, to instruct your Senators and Members of Congress, to vote for the admission of Oklahoma. By those who are familiar with the Territory of Oklahoma and particularly the magnitude of its agricultural and mineral resources, and the numerous elements of wealth and development within its borders, the justice of our demand for immediate statehood will be readily admitted. Look for a moment at our situation. Examine our geographical location and our convenient and natural relations to the trade of this city and to the States of the Mississippi Valley. Note if you please our rapid progress in the creation of taxable wealth and the consequent advantages to be derived from our trade and commerce. Large as it is to-day, it will be concentrated and increased with marvelous rapidity if Congress will give us statehood, and remove the fatal obstructions which now exist in the Indian Territory and which operate to paralyze and to destroy (applause).

The real value of taxable property in Oklahoma is not less than one hundred million dollars. Our cities and towns are growing rapidly, large are as of many million acres (as in the case of the Cherokee outlet), are settled in a single day, and the conveniences and necessities of life which it has taken many years to secure in all other territories, have been made available in Oklahoma in a few short months. There are now in operation in Oklahoma and the Indian Territory more than 1,500 miles of railroad. The two territories contain at least 2,000,000 head of range cattle and horses, a great proporion of which now escape taxation in the absence of civil government in the Indian Territory, and because of the inefficiency of territorial government in Oklahoma. Our soil is equal in fertility to that of Illinois, or of Missouri, or of Kansas, and the climate is salubrious and well adapted to the production of every variety of fruit, and of corn, wheat and cotton, and of all the crops common to that latitude. Surely we are entitled to home rule — to a State government — instead of being made the football of changing administrations and the prey of foreign officials!

By the census of 1890, the three territories of Utah, New Mexico and Arizona had a total population of only 421,118, or 153,882 less than the present population of the Indian Territory and Oklahoma, and only 171,118 more than Oklahoma has at the present time. I know of no citizen of Oklahoma but what believes that our neighbors on the west should have been clothed with the panoply of statehood long ago. And who does not now rejoice that Utah has at last secured justice at the hands of Congress, and who does not ardently hope for the prompt admission of New Mexico and Arizona at the coming session of Congress? Welcome, thrice welcome, say we to these three Territories into the family of sovereign States! Rich in mineral wealth, in gold and in silver — the money of the world — they may be crucified by the nation's financial policy of to-day, but they will rise to-morrow to emancipate the nation from its depression, and strip the moth and rust of an antiquated past from the financial standard of the future (applause).

It is for the interest of the people of the United States that our territorial system shall be promptly terminated. It was regarded by the early statesmen of the republic, by whom it was devised, as a temporary expedient, and now that population and development have possessed every portion of our great country, it is the part of wisdom to bury it out of sight forever. No political party should now oppose the admission of all the Territories as States. The petty interests of political partisans sink into insignificance compared with the magnificent results which follow the founding of new American commonwealths. With statehood comes the common school system, strengthened and perfected — the nursery of public intelligence and public virtue. With statehood comes the self-reliance without which neither communities or individuals can reach the full measure of prosperity. With statehood the obnoxious principle of taxation without representation is abolished, and every material, educational, moral and religious interest is made to conserve the common weal. It is of trifling consequence what the political complexion of the future States will be, compared with the legacy of wealth, intelligence and patriotism they will add to the common property of the nation, and woe to the political party that attempts to prevent their admission. There is no more glorious record in all our history than that which relates to the admission of new States into the Federal union, commencing with Vermont in 1791, and reaching up to the admission of Wyoming in 1890. In every instance where opposition was made to the admission of a Territory to statehood disaster has resulted to the opposing party.

Mr. President, I have spoken of the position of Oklahoma in its natural relations to the trade and commerce of the Mississippi valley, and to this great metropolis. But there is one obstruction which must be removed by congressional action before this trade can be safely and fully developed and the proper lines of transportation perfected. About 20,000,000 acres of land in the Indian Territory, lying directly between St. Louis and Oklahoma, is held in common by the Five Civilized Tribes. This land was originally intended for the exclusive occupancy of the Five Tribes. It was conveyed to them by the United States with this specific understanding. But these so-called Indians, a large proportion of whom are practically white people, have perverted the trust, a few designing men in each tribe have monopolized vast tracts of the best land, and in the absence of a Territorial or State government, a deplorable condition of affairs has ensued which, as stated in the majority report, is a disgrace to our civilization, and to the efficiency of the government of the United States. For nearly a year a commission appointed under an act of Congress has been attempting to negotiate with the Five Tribes for the abolition of tribal relations, the settlement of the Indians on lands in severalty on equal terms, and for the establishment of the usual forms of civil government. But the commission has utterly failed to accomplish anything. The tribal leaders, selfish beyond description in absorbing the land and money of the Tribes, absolutely refuse to treat with the commission, though they are confessedly powerless to preserve public order and to protect life and property. Let me quote only a sentence or two from the recent report of the commission to the President, descriptive of the situation. After enumerating the reasonable and just propositions submitted to the Indians, and stating how they have by various methods invited and induced at least 250,000 white people to come into the territory, "but few of whom might be called intruders," the report says:—

"These tribal governments have wholly perverted their high trust, and it is the plain duty of the United States to enforce the trust it has so created and recover for its original uses the domain and all the gains derived in the perversion of the trust, or discharge the trustees * * * The United States also granted to these Tribes the power of self-government, not in conflict with the constitution. They have demonstrated their incapacity to so govern themselves, and no higher duty can rest upon the government that granted this authority than to revoke it when it has so lamentably failed."

Mr. President, this report of the Dawes Commission — a commission composed of able and conservative men and only made after a long and careful investigation of existing conditions in the Indian Territory, is strictly true. Every interest of this great city, every interest of the States and Territories represented here, no less than the common welfare of the Five Tribes and of the whole nation, is jeopardized by such a deplorable condition of affairs. Large sections of the Indian Territory are at this moment dominated by desperadoes and robbers. Peaceable citizens residing in the Territory, railway trains, express companies, banks and private residences, are robbed almost daily by organized bands of criminals. If one band is killed or captured, another equally desperate springs up to take its place, and to perpetuate the awful record of crime and blood. All this has been fostered and made possible by the neglect of Congress to establish a government over that country, by including it within an organized Territory or State, and by denying to the 250,000 American citizens residing there, the power to establish the simplest police regulation for the suppression of crime, and the protection of life and property.

Let it be understood that in solving this problem, in asking Congress to lift this great population into statehood and prosperity — into a condition where they will have the power to protect themselves and establish good government, there is no proposition on the part of anybody to deprive the Indians of a single acre of land or a dollar's worth of property. But we do insist that Congress must now provide that law and order shall take the place of lawlessness and crime, that the reign of land monopoly and of conspirators and official rogues, now bold and supreme, shall be broken up, that the natural elements of trade and commerce shall be established and protected, and that this black spot on the map of the United States shall be wiped out forever. And in accomplishing this grand result, the real Indians of the Five Tribes, emancipated from the control of corrupt leaders and encouraged by the blessings and benefits and methods of our Christian civilization, will rejoice in their deliverance from the obstacles which have so long obstructed their progress to higher and better conditions. It is my personal belief that the best statesmanship in dealing with the problem would be, for Congress to promptly pass an Enabling Act at the ensuing session creating a single State out of all the old Indian Territory. But if Congress should be unwilling to promptly provide for single State-hood, then the Territory of Oklahoma as at present organized, with the Chickasaw country added on the south, should be admitted as a State at once, and the strong arm of the Federal law, carrying with it allotment of lands, abolition of tribal governments, the reformation of the courts, and destruction and death to desperate criminals, should be extended over the remaining Indian Territory (applause).

There is no doubt about the power of Congress to do this. It is in the interest of justice and civilization, and does not admit of delay. Speaking for the good people of Oklahoma of all parties and professions, and for those in the Indian Territory who are seeking relief from the condition described by Mr. Dawes and his associates, I appeal to you, gentlemen, to join us in our demand on Congress to enact the necessary legislation. May we not hope that the senators and representatives of the American people, will now regard the people of all the territories in a spirit of justice and patriotism, and that they will no longer hesitate to welcome Oklahoma, New Mexico and Arizona into the family of sovereign States? In rejecting the minority report, and in passing the report of the majority of the committee, this Trans-Mississippi Congress will voice in no uncertain terms a policy that will do justice to the Five Tribes, suppress the lawlessness and crime which now threaten their destruction, and place Oklahoma and the Indian Territory in their claims for statehood in a conspicuous position before the Congress of the United States (applause).

The majority report was then re-read.

The vote was then proceeded with upon the substitution of the minority report for the majority report.

A Delegate (from Missouri): Mr. Chairman, I would like to change my vote to 30 for Missouri.

The Chairman: That cannot be done unless that number are present. If there be only one member present he can only vote 10 votes.

The Delegate: We have in the neighborhood of 30 present.

Mr. Johnson called for the reading of the names of the delegation.

The Delegate: Mr. Chairman, I will make it 20 votes.

Mr. Johnson: I again call for the names, or let Missouri stand up.

The Missouri delegation rose and there were only five present.

The Chairman: As there are five members present, then you are entitled to fourteen votes.

Mr. Black: Mr. Chairman, I desire to appeal from the ruling of the Chair on the vote allowed to Missouri, for the reason that under the rules of this House, the ruling of the Chair was voted down. I made the same amendment myself and the rule was adopted that ten votes were all the votes allowed to each State or Territory, unless more than ten votes were present, and that the delegation vote the number of votes present up to thirty.

The Chairman: The Chair stands corrected. I remember that that was the understanding. Therefore, Missouri will record ten votes.

The substitute was lost

The question was then put on the motion to adopt the majority report, which was duly seconded and carried.

The Chairman: The Chair now begs to announce that the names · that were requested of the Vice-Presidents from the various States and of the members of the Executive Committee have not been reported, except in a few cases.

Mr. Whitmore: I wish to impress upon the minds of delegates the utmost importance of naming as members of the Executive Committee men who will take the most active interest in the work of the Congress, for upon them is largely dependent the delegations from the different States. The Vice-President may be a man of some high position. He has no work to do. It is an ornamental position and an honor, and therefore his eminence may be of some benefit; but on the Committee we want active, earnest, working men. I desire to call attention to the fact that no provision was made in our report day before yesterday for filling vacancies in the Executive Board. Being a member of the Executive Committee, I do not want to make a motion myself, but suggest that the Executive Committee have power to fill vacancies.

It was moved and seconded that the Executive Committee have power to fill vacancies.

The Chairman: The remarks of the Chairman of the Executive Committee are important. Utah has sent a large delegation here, and

I may say that it is due in the main to the Chairman of the Executive Committee.   He has impressed upon our people the necessity of having a strong delegation here.   One or two men on the Executive Committee in Utah took the matter in hand very zealously, and to this may be attributed that so large a delegation has come from that Territory, and I would strengthen his remarks and impress them as much as possible upon the minds of the delegates, that suitable, active men should be selected for these positions.

The motion, that the Executive Committee be authorized to fill vacancies, was then carried.

It was then

Resolved, That the Hon. Geo. Q. Cannon, the President of this Congress, and Hon. W. J. Bryan, Chairman of the Committee on Resolutions, be instructed to present to the Congress of the United States at its forthcoming session, and also to other proper bodies, the action of this Congress.

The special order of business, being the selection of a place of meeting for the next convention, was then called for, and the following communication was then read: —

To the Chairman of the Trans-Mississippi Commercial Congress.

Mr. President: The session of the Trans-Mississippi Commercial Congress is drawing to a close, and we are about to settle what city will be honored by securing the place for holding the next Trans-Mississippi Congress. As a representative citizen of Dubuque where I have spent my business life, I desire to say that it would be a pleasure to our city if we could secure the next meeting of the now permanent Trans-Mississippi Commercial Congress.

The city of Dubuque is one of the five great commercial, manufacturing, and enterprising cities on the Mississippi between St. Paul and New Orleans. It is only a short time ago that the Government torpedo boat " Erriceson " was launched in the Ice Harbor at Dubuque. In a few months the steamer " Windom," a revenue cutter, built for the Government, will be launched in the same harbor. Dubuque has four of the great railway systems centering in the city, reaching all points, north, south, east and west — the Burlington, the Illinois Central, Chicago, Milwaukee & St. Paul, and the Chicago Great Western railways. The city has several fine hotels, twenty miles of electric railway and is well lighted with electric lights. Dubuque could easily accommodate the six hundred people who have attended this convention as delegates. It would be hard to find a city that could extend courtesies, hospitalities and attention that the enterprising citizens and merchants of St. Louis have extended to this Congress and their many friends, but Dubuque, if selected as the next place of meeting of this Congress, will take St. Louis as its model and do everything in its power to show appreciation of the honor of having this Trans-Mississippi Commercial Congress meet within her doors.

BART E. LINEHAN.

The Secretary then read telegrams from the city of Portland, Oregon, inviting the convention to hold its next session there.

Mr. Buller (of Idaho): Mr. Chairman, while other nominations have been made at banquets, we thought it best to bring this matter up before the convention itself.

I think in considering the location of the next session, that there are many great questions that should be taken into consideration. We meet here to discuss the mining and irrigation questions and I believe if you locate the next session of the Congress within the borders of a State where these great questions have been made a success, all the people living within the jurisdiction of this district can learn more concerning these matters than they can if you locate it upon the shores of the Pacific Ocean every other year. Idaho is a wonderful State. We have beautiful valleys, ranging from 600 feet to 6,000 feet above sea level. Idaho has water ditches, upon which some of your river steamboats might ride. Idaho is a mining State, and if you come within the borders of that State, we will teach you the history of the silver dollar from the time it is found in the side of the mountain up to the time it is passed over some baker's counter in payment of the staff of life for some widow or some orphan. We have higher peaks — and if you climb to the summit you can even look down upon the roof of a Chicago business house. I am satisfied if you go there and stand upon the banks of the wonderful Snake River and cast your eye westward, just as the snow melts down before the noonday sun, all of the beautiful places that you have passed by will sink into the oblivion of forgetfulness.

Boise City is located where we have in the vicinity, the gold mine, the silver mine, the lead mine and the copper mine. We have magnificent hotels and are free to entertain you in true western style. We have opera houses which are sufficient to accommodate you all. There you will be met by your ex-President McConnell, who will bid you a hearty welcome with outstretched arms, and I am satisfied that if you come within our borders and meet our great boys and be introduced to our noble mothers and look upon our sweethearts, you will never regret coming within the State of Idaho to hold your next session of the Congress. With this slight and modest intimation of a small part of the great pleasures we have in store for you, I take great pleasure in nominating Boise City as the place for holding the next convention (applause).

Mr. Black: Mr. President, as I take it, this question of selecting a point at which our next congress will meet is more a subject to look at from a business standpoint than from an oratorical standpoint. I am satisfied that this congress is a congress of immense influence — that it could be made of absolute influence all over the entire Trans-Mississippi country. I come from the far Northwest corner of that country, and I am free to say, until the matter was called to my attention by President Whitmore through his letters and circulars, I was unacquainted with the vast import of it. I tried to get a delegation to come to this convention. It was found that no one in our locality knew anything about it. They had never heard of it. It had the reputation of being a crank convention. I have been here. I know that no such accusation could be laid against it, therefore I say that the location of the next meeting should be at a point near where a former congress has never been held, because when that congress meets in a community and those who live in that community have an opportunity of seeing what the congress is, it educates them. As I understand the matter, congresses have been held at Omaha, Galveston, New Orleans, Denver, Ogden, San Francisco and this, the seventh, at St. Louis, and each and every section of the country has had the convention, except the far Northwest. I believe that nothing would excite the interest of the people of the Northwest more than to hold this convention in one of the great cities of Oregon or Washington. That, as a business reason, I think, exceeds any other reason you could have. It is true that Idaho is in the Northwest, but Idaho is near to the great State of Utah, and has already received the benefit of a congress held in the West within a few hundred miles of them. For that reason I say this congress should be held at Portland. Another and very important reason; — this Congress, when it convenes, has a large or small number of delegates according to the expense with which the delegates get there. I do not know how many delegates in this hall are railroad men personally. This is my second trip from ocean to ocean and I have learned in that time that if I am going to the Atlantic coast, they have terminal rates. If I am going to the Pacific coast they have terminal rates to San Francisco, Portland, Seattle, Tacoma and even many of the smaller cities, and you can visit any of those places all for the same price. It is a matter of great importance to the people of this Trans-Mississippi region that when they go West they go where they can see all of it for the same price. When they go to Portland they can buy a ticket over the Canadian Pacific, thence South through Puget Sound, seeing a body of water the like of which exists nowhere in the world except in the Mediterranean Sea — and I think not even in the Mediterranean — seeing all of California and returning home for the same money. That is not true of Boise City. That is a second reason that will bring many more men to the next meeting of this convention if it is held in Portland. The third reason is the capacity of the city where we desire to hold it. We all know what St. Louis is. We do not think that we are going to beat St. Louis. St. Louis has done us proud, but we still insist that Portland is a city capable of taking care of all who come there. It has hotel accommodations for nearly 8,000. It has opera houses as well as

Boise City. We do not claim that Portland is the only city able to accommodate the convention, but we do claim that Portland is a city fit to accommodate it. For these reasons, I can say that the State of Washington most heartly indorses the invitation given by Portland for the convention to hold its next meeting there, and its 10 votes will be cast for Portland (applause).

Mr. Johnson: Mr. Chairman, I have not any favors to give nor to ask, nor has the State of Colorado, nor has its delegation. But the last meeting of this Congress was on the Pacific coast, held at the extreme western boundary of the Trans-Mississippi country. This convention is upon the Mississippi river, the eastern boundary of the Trans-Mississippi country, and I submit to this convention that it is just a little bit unjust to us to take the next convention back upon the Pacific coast again. That while it is a great pleasure to visit the Pacific coast for the eastern people, while it is a great pleasure for the Pacific coast people to visit the East, it is sometimes best to meet on middle-ground, or apparently middle-ground. Boise City is to some extent a place between the two extremes, and since the two extremes have had the convention, Colorado seconds the selection of Boise City (applause).

An invitation was then given by Mr. Savage of Kansas to hold the next meeting in the city of Topeka.

Mr. Bryan then read a telegram from the Mayor of Omaha, Neb., inviting the convention to hold its next meeting there.

Mr. Bryan: Mr. Chairman, it is not necessary for a city as well known as Omaha to be spoken of in eulogistic terms. Nebraska speaks for herself. You all know her, because you have to travel through Nebraska to get to any part of the Northwestern country, and we invite this Trans-Mississippi Congress to hold its next session in Omaha. So far as railroad rates are concerned, the Missouri river rates are based upon the distance from the Missouri river, and Omaha is one of the great cities, and we can afford to offer all the inducements in the way of rates that any city can offer. It is near the Eastern part of this Trans-Mississippi region. We are as near to the Dakotas, Minnesota, Kansas, Missouri and several States south, as any of those western States. The convention has been meeting on the Pacific coast and on the Gulf of Mexico. It is now meeting down here in the southeastern part of the territory. It met the last time at San Francisco and the year before at Ogden. It seems to me it is only natural that it shall now come up into our section of the country. One reason why I am specially anxious to have it come up to Nebraska is, that Nebraska has been equally divided on every question that has come before this body. I want you to come up there and help bring them all over to our side. If you could have this convention there once, the people of Nebraska would be a unit in favor of those questions upon which this section of the country is divided (applause).

Gov. PRINCE: Mr. President, I do not rise to name a place or to second a nomination, but simply to state the reasons which will actuate me in casting my vote. The question, it seems to me, is whether we are to select a place which would be the pleasantest place to go to, where we might enjoy ourselves the most, or to go to the locality where we can do the most good and have the most influence. Now, this body holds no legislative powers, and it cannot carry into effect anything it adopts. It can simply influence public opinion — that is all. Now, the public opinion that it is desirable that the western sentiment should influence, is the public opinion of the East. I think the nearer we can get to the community that it is desired to influence, and where it is necessary that we shall secure co-operative votes, in order to carry into effect our desires, the better. I should be very glad, if it were possible, if a meeting like this could have been held in the city of New York. Just suppose this body could have been set down in the middle of the city of New York and hold its sessions there and present its arguments there and hold these debates there. They would have had ten times the effect upon the community. It seems to me that by going very far West, we fritter away our influence. There is no place I would rather go to than to Portland or Boise City, but I do believe that we would practically lose a year and the influence of this organization, by taking the organization there. I think we should get near to the communities we wish to influence, and for that reason I shall vote for the place that is nearest East (applause).

SENATOR JOHNSTON: In my judgment, this congress is more a congress for solidifying the western mind than it is for proselyting in the East. The only way in the world that this congress will ever amount to anything, do any good to the people west of the Mississippi river, is by presenting a united front. We might go to New York and meet there a thousand times and not half the people would know we had been there. But there are differences of opinion among ourselves. The only way to accomplish anything in Congress is to go there with friends to back us up, and we must go there with a solidified front in order to do anything. It is also a school of education to us western people, to us clod-hoppers who have been out here for 45 years. We want to get together and rub off the rough edges. There is no place in the world whose education is so badly needed at this time as among the western people, and I am in favor of going to the Pacific coast with this congress and educating the people there. They know just as much as the rest of us, but they have not had the pleasure of our company up there in Portland. We could have more influence with them. Let us go up there and solidify this western sentiment (applause).

A DELEGATE (from Iowa): Iowa seconds the invitation to Dubuque. Notwithstanding she is so badly handicapped by the eloquent gentlemen from the Pacific coast and other places, Iowa is amply able to entertain you. She will provide lots of water — the only liquid which she manufactures. If she fails to present any of the liquids which have been presented in St. Louis, we will make a requisition on St. Louis and bring it there. We do not expect to win this battle, nevertheless we present the invitation just as cordially. If you want a central point, I think the recommendation has some merit. Minnesota is our near neighbor, and while speaking on this subject I want to informally say that I think it would have been well for this Trans-Mississippi Congress, although a little in opposition to its name, to have included the States bordering east of the Mississippi river which are interested in this question just as much as we are, viz., Illinois and Wisconsin. Minnesota borders on both sides of the Mississippi river. She is represented here, leaving out Wisconsin and Illinois. Illinois presents more front on the Mississippi river than any other State, and she is interested in all the vital questions that have been presented in this congress, and if it be possible for this convention to stretch their representation and take Illinois and Wisconsin in with them, I think it ought to be done.

The delegation from Utah then seconded the nomination of Boise City.

Mr. Butterfield of Oregon then addressed the convention in behalf of the city of Portland.

The vote was then taken and resulted in the selection of the city of Omaha on the second ballot.

The nomination of the city of Omaha was then made unanimous.

MR. BRYAN: Mr. Chairman, I want to thank the members of the congress for making this selection and to assure them that we will try and approach as near as we can to the hospitality shown by St. Louis.

MR. CLARKE: Mr. Chairman, I rise to a question of privilege. I hold a resolution unanimously adopted by the Committee on Resolutions. I am informed that the copy of the resolution has been lost and it is not in the possession of the Secretary. I sent the resolution to the Chair and asked that it be read and I appeal to the members whether or not they sustain what I have said.

The following resolution was then read and adopted:—

" *Resolved,* That we favor the cession of the non-mineral arid lands to the States and Territories in which they are situated, and that we favor the control by such States and Territories of the local waters for irrigation."

Mr. Bryan then offered the following, which was adopted:—

" *Resolved,* That the thanks of this Congress are hereby extended to its presidents, H. R. Whitmore and Hon. George Q. Cannon for the fair and impartial manner in which they have performed the duties of presiding officers of this Congress, and also to Messrs. Butterfield, Morgan and Edwards, the Secretaries, and to Charles Freeman Johnson, the official stenographer, for the prompt and efficient discharge of their respective duties at this meeting."

Ex-Gov. Prince then offered the following resolution, which was adopted:—

"*Resolved*, That the thanks of this Congress are hereby extended to the representatives of the press for the fair and accurate reports of the proceedings and the aid they have afforded in giving wide publicity to the acts and debates of the congress."

At this juncture a number of resolutions were offered, motions to adjourn *sine die* were made and considerable confusion prevailed.

Gov. PRINCE: Mr. Chairman, I have been trying to get in a resolution here, but owing to the confusion I have put it in my pocket. I have an announcement to make with regard to the Irrigation Convention at Albuquerque, and there is plenty of business yet to be done.

A DELEGATE: There are several resolutions here that have been held over until this afternoon.

MR. BRYAN: My attention has been called to the fact that there are several resolutions reported favorably and not yet acted upon. I therefore withdraw my motion to adjourn *sine die* and move that we adjourn until half-past two this afternoon.

This motion was carried, and the Congress adjourned.

FRIDAY AFTERNOON SESSION.

The meeting was called to order at 2:30 p. m.

THE CHAIRMAN: The time having arrived for the convening of the Congress, we will now have an address by Mr. John F. Cahill of St. Louis, on the "Commercial Possibilities of Western Waterways."

MR. JOHN F. CAHILL: *Delegates to the Trans-Mississippi Commercial Congress:* It was stated by your worthy retiring President at the opening of this Congress, that a local commercial body, composed of 3,000 members, represented only one-half of one per cent of this city's population, while the delegates appointed by our city's Chief Executive represented the remaining ninety-nine per cent. The former body has accredited to this Congress forty-two delegates, while the city proper has but ten; so that the basis of representation — the fundamental principle of our institutions — is so largely out of proportion — so recklessly ignored in this case — that a delegate who, like myself, is charged with the temporary representation of ninety-nine per cent of his fellow-citizens of St. Louis, must feel no small degree of embarrassment in accepting such a responsibility.

But it is the theme, and not the instrument, it is the sentiment of our *whole people*, and not the multiplied voice of a small minority, that should prevail in a great intellectual conclave of this character, convened to promote the nation's welfare by carrying into effect the motto that Missouri has borne on her shield for three-quarters of a century, that " the welfare of the people must be the supreme law."

In afflictions of the human system, the best physician is he who can accurately diagnose the disease, remove the cause with the least depletion, and vitalize the physical powers by equalizing and vigorizing the circulation.

An earnest and intelligent attempt to discover the causes of disorder is the first step in the road to remedial results.

The main purpose of this Congress is to discover, discuss and endeavor to alleviate, if we cannot cure, the evils that afflict our country. Many of the distinguished members of this Congress are studious specialists who have devoted time and means to the investigation of the evils with which the people of their respective localities are burdened, with the view of presenting them to the National Congress and justly insisting on their removal.

We who dwell on the banks of the nation's greatest highway, sympathize with the people of Colorado, Washington, Idaho, Montana and Wyoming because of their present inability to utilize the great treasures that lie in their silver bearing mountains; with the people of Kansas, Nebraska, Texas, Iowa, Minnesota, Arkansas and golden California, because of the depression in the prices of their splendid crops and the high cost of transporting them to the markets of the world; and with the young and vigorous people of Utah, New Mexico, Arizona, Oklahoma and the Indian Territory for their laudable ambition for equality, as sisters, in the grand galaxy of sovereign States; and we can all join in one sympathetic effusion when we come to consider how grossly neglected have been our God-given birthright — the free waterways of the West — and their outlet and extension to the seas of the world — the Nicaragua canal. I would like to dwell on this latter subject if the time allotted me would permit, but, as its benefits and vast advantages to the people of the U. S. have already been ably presented, I can only add a God-speed to this great work that should be taken up and carried to speedy completion by our own government in the interests of its commercial power and national security.

The Transportation Possibilities of Western Waterways is the special subject to which I will now ask your attention. As editor of a bi-lingual journal for 17 years, devoted to the cultivation of our commerce with the republics of Latin America, as consular representative of some of these interests during the same period of time, as one who had the honor of giving inception to the Pan-American Congress and the doctrine of inter-American reciprocity when Jas. G. Blaine held the portfolio of State in 1881, as an American who has resided among, and dealt with, these Southern republican neighbors of ours for nearly 30 years, I ask you to consider whether such credentials may not entitle my statements to credence in the impartial judgment of this great Congress of Western intelligence, patriotism and enterprise.

The voice of this mighty valley is for tonnage — cheap tonnage to bear away the excess of productions of the farm, the factory, the forest and the mine to foreign parts, and bring back such products as we need in exchange. These broad acres, that seldom fail to yield a generous harvest, must be worked up to further capacity. To do this, ample reward must be given the tiller of the soil for his labor, and to the miner, manufacturer and merchant for their industry and enterprise.

The cereals and staples that abound in this magnificent domain, which we call the Mississippi Valley, must bring remunerative prices and encourage the farmer to sow more generously. Next only in importance to the financial question is that of transportation. No matter how low the prices or how poor the crops, experience teaches that there is no corresponding changeability in the cost of transportation, domestic or foreign.

The cost of carrying a bale of cotton, to-day, from its field of production in the Trans-Mississippi region of the Southwest to New York is $5.50, or more than $1.00 per 100 lbs., and at a time when the market price of the staple is less than 6 cts. per pound. From St. Louis to the city of Mexico, for example, the cost on general merchandise by rail, or rail and water, averages $40.00 per ton or $2.00 per 100 pounds. These exhorbitant rates have driven away from the West the trade that could be built up with the countries of Latin America under more favorable conditions of transportation. The Latin Americans can have goods delivered from almost any of the European ports, 4,000 miles distant, for $15 to $16 per ton; — hence we can never hope for this trade in the Mississippi valley unless our waterways are utilized.

One of the chief duties of the hour is to make an end of antiquated systems that are inadequate for the necessities of to-day and adopt new and better appliances in the machinery of commerce that will cut down, to at least one-half the present charges, the cost of transportation to and from the great centers of the West and South. Adhesion to old ideas and systems in marine construction is one of the main causes of our present troubles. While on land we, of the West, have contributed our share in supplying the country with intelligence and inventions, we are still in the kindergarten of navigation where the instruments of commercial power are to be found. Because of the fact that we have not learned how to use the free waterways and have substituted for them, almost exclusively, the costly railways, we are now paying the penalty. Because of our unwisdom in this respect, we have in this rich Trans-Mississippi region scores of thousands of men who are deprived of work and the means of supporting their families — men who tramp the country in vain for a chance to earn their bread — while thousands of them, broken, discouraged and demoralized, are compelled to become the desperate nucleus of revolutionary forces that are a constant menace to our free institutions.

When in 1803 the genius of Thomas Jefferson broke the chain that confined our young republic to the slopes of the Alleghenies and gave us this magnificent empire we proudly style the Mississippi Valley, it could never have entered into the mind of the author of our political Magna Charta that we could not work out our own commercial independence, or that such a mighty system of inland waterways, embracing some 20,000 miles, of which the Mississippi is the central artery, would have remained practically neglected and abandoned for nearly one hundred years, to be supplanted by a gigantic system of expensive railway monopolies that have continued to absorb the economic life-blood of the people of this republic and dominate its legislation.

We can feed the world from this valley while enricihng ourselves if our representatives at Washington insist, unitedly, upon what is to-day, the true panacea for our general depression in trade.

In ten or twelve years the government has frittered away about $12,000,000 on the Mississippi, and a large part of this has gone to maintain corps of engineers, clerical adjuncts, commissioners, etc., while the condition of the river remains so little improved that the lightest draft-boats are stranded on the bars between this city and Cairo during the low water season. Large and liberal appropriations by Congress in the improvement of the Mississippi and its chief affluents should be demanded by our western representatives, so that this long neglected work may be continued without interruption and a minimum depth, of not less than ten feet, is secured and maintained between St. Louis and the sea at all seasons.

This work would give employment to labor, encourage the farmer, the artisan and the merchant, and open the way for a development of commerce between the Trans-Mississippi region and the outside world that would add hundreds of millions annually to the wealth of these great and growing States. But while this work is pending we have it in our power to utilize the genius of invention and assist nature by the application of art, in a new and ingenious device in naval construction. While despairing, in our long wait, of the great river ever being sufficiently deepened, for ocean-going vessels, we have undertaken to solve the problem and, at the same time, to save millions to the government, by *shallowing the ship.* The commercial instrument I refer to is born of the conditions of the great rivers of the West and is specially adapted to the commercial demands of to-day.

Before closing I desire to call the attention of this Congress to an invention in marine construction that had its origin in this city and is specially designed for and adapted to the present conditions of the Mississippi. The invention is known as the "Lucas Ship," and consists of a combination of principles that constitute an ocean-going steamer with the light draft and large carrying capacity of a river steamboat.

Some of the best naval architects and ship-building experts of the country have given their indorsement to this new type of river and ocean craft, and plans have been made for the construction of a ship of 3,200 tons of the following dimensions: Length 230 ft., beam 40 ft., depth 18 ft., net freight capacity 1,200 tons on 7 ft. and 2,000 tons on 9 ft. of water.

The vessel is to be supplied with an adjustable keel, in three sections, that can be dropped to any required depth when in the ocean and raised to a level with the bottom of the hull when navigating shallow waters. Ordinary ocean vessels of this size and tonnage require 20 or more feet of water and are, therefore, unable to ascend the Mississippi or other rivers similarly conditioned, or to navigate shoal waters. There are numerous rivers, inlets and shoal waters all along the gulf-coast of Mexico, where this type of vessel could be profitably and effectively used in carrying the products of our industries to those neighboring markets and returning direct to our wharves with cargoes of coffee and other tropical products without transfer, re-handling, delay or damage to goods. The cost of transporting freight by this new system would be considerably less than one-half the present charges, as it would involve no rail transportation, the cost of which is $2\frac{1}{2}$ cents per ton per mile, while all water transportation is only 4 mills per ton per mile. Such a vessel is admirably adapted, not only for ocean service, but for service on the rivers of South and Central America, which are the chief avenues of transportation in those countries. A company was organized to promote this enterprise, a few years ago, but the adverse financial conditions of the country intervened to prevent the enterprise from securing the means to build the first ship. It attracted wide attention because of its being pregnant with the promise of converting every interior river town in the west *into a seaport,* for all practical purposes; and it received the indorsement of numerous naval experts and commercial organizations throughout the country, among which was the National Board of Trade at its last session at Washington, D. C.

In view of the importance of this invention I will offer the following resolution and request for it the favorable action of this convention : —

WHEREAS, The question of cheap transportation lies at the base of commercial prosperity, and,

WHEREAS, The Mississippi River and its tributaries constitute the national highway to the sea and afford to the people of the United States more than 20,000 miles of free water tranportation by which they can send their products to, and receive their supplies from, the markets of the world; and

WHEREAS, The invention of a vessel especially designed and adapted for the navigation of those inland water-courses, as well as the ocean, having been critically examined and approved by competent naval experts and engineers as entirely practicable and calculated to do away with the transfer and re-handling of freight and the expenses and delays incidental thereto, therefore

Resolved, That the *Trans-Mississippi Commercial Congress* recognizes in the Lucas ship project the promise of a solution of one of the great commercial problems of the age, viz.: cheap and direct all-water transportation to and from the markets of the world, and recommends this enterprise to the special consideration of our representatives in congress, at Washington, to the end that an appropriation be granted to test the merit of the invention.

The resolution was referred to the Committee on Resolutions.

Gov. PRINCE: A few days ago we passed a resolution favoring the use of American products in the U. S. Navy. Mr. Black of Washington State is going to Washington, and he takes great interest in this subject. I therefore offer the following resolution :—

Resolved, That Mr. A. L. Black, of the State of Washington, be hereby appointed to present to the Honorable, the Secretary of the Navy, the resolution of the Congress favoring the use of American products in the U. S. Navy.

Adopted.

Gov. PRINCE: While I am on the floor, I desire to perform a duty, which I have postponed, of announcing the Irrigation convention to take place in the City of Albuquerque, N. M., and extending an invitation to all members of the Congress to be present at that time. It is the National convention on that subject — the adjournment of the one which took place this year in Denver. It will be the occasion of a great deal of interest to all of us who live in the different portions of New Mexico. We propose to have side trips to other portions of the Territory and will endeavor in every way to make your stay pleasant. We extend this invitation heartily in the name of the people of New Mexico.

It was then announced that the Executive Committee would meet immediately after the adjournment of the Congress in the room of the Committee on Resolutions in the front of the building.

Resolutions were then introduced asking the indorsement of the congress of the resolutions adopted by the International Deep Water Association convention recently held in Toronto.

Mr. Smith (of Iowa): At this convention in Toronto delegates were present from every province of Canada and from 15 States of the United States. They desire to have the channel deepened from the great lakes of Superior and Michigan, so that products can be shipped from the lakes to Liverpool. We desire to have a court established by mutual consent of the British Government and the Government of the United States to hear and determine this question. We want cheap transportation from the headwaters of the Mississippi river, to increase the power of the Mississippi river, that the products of the North may be carried to the South, and the products of the South carried to the North. These are the objects sought to be indorsed by this convention. It goes to the very meat and marrow of cheap transportation. This matter has received the indorsement of more than 26,000,000 people of the United States and the people of Canada, and I come as a special delegate from that body to this body and ask your indorsement. I trust no gentleman here will raise his voice against it, because it will help the people of the United States. I ask unanimous consent for the indorsement of this resolution by this convention.

Mr. Castle: It is growing very late in our session and this appears to be a very important matter. I understood that it was reported unfavorably by the sub-committee.

Mr. Smith: No, sir; it was reported favorably.

It was then moved and seconded that the matter be referred to the Executive Committee, to be reported upon at a future time.

Mr. Whitmore: The gentleman understands that that committee can make no report to this session of the Congress.

This motion was then carried.

Mr. Black: Mr. Chairman, we are about to adjourn. The work done between now and the next congress will decide largely what the character and personnel of the congress will be. Personally, I am very much in favor of newspapers and I believe that it would do more to excite interest in the next congress than anything else, if we could have some sort of an organ run in the interest of this congress — that it would be a matter of great importance to this congress and do much toward making the next session of this congress a successful session. I, as a member of the Executive Committee, would not feel justified in voting at a meeting of the Executive Committee on a proposition of this kind, unless this congress in session shall so empower us to do, and I, therefore, move the adoption of the following resolution:—

Resolved, That we favor the publication of a periodical in the interest of the Trans-Mississippi Commercial Congress, and refer the matter to the Executive Committee, with power to act.

This motion was seconded and unanimously carried.

PRESIDENT CANNON: Before we adjourn I wish to say that I think our friend and efficient stenographer, Mr. Charles F. Johnson, deserves many thanks from this congress for his close attention, the diligence and zeal and fidelity with which he has attended not only to his duty here, but in keeping the run of the business. I feel myself that we are under many obligations to him, and I am personally, for his attention. I wish to repeat my sense of obligation to him since I have been in the Chair.

EX-GOVERNOR PRINCE: We are greatly indebted for the success of this congress and our pleasant sojourn in this city to the Merchants' Exchange of St. Louis, the largest commercial body west of the Mississippi, as well as to the various organizations which have extended to us a like invitation. I desire to offer the following resolution:—

Resolved, That the Trans-Mississippi Commercial Congress hereby expresses its grateful appreciation of the public spirit, generosity and efficient action of the Merchants Exchange and other Business Organizations of St. Louis, as shown in the ample provision and convenient arrangements which they have made for the requirements and the entertainment of the Congress, and of the courtesy and generous hospitality which has been extended by the citizens of St. Louis both collectively and individually to the delegates.

Adopted.

MR. BLACK: Each State should report two Executive Committeemen, one for one year and one for two years. There has been no report made except as to who are Executive Committeemen, but they do not state who are intended for one year and who for the two-year term. It might save trouble if we have it at this time.

The names of the Vice-Presidents and Executive Committeemen were then read so far as reported.

MR. FISK: Mr. Chairman, I learn that the resolution on the sugar bounty was adopted by the Committee on Resolutions. If there is any member here, I would like to be set right if that is not so. I am unable to learn that it has ever reached the Secretary's desk and been passed upon by this congress, and I would like permission to read that and have it considered. I am told by members of the Committee that it was adopted in full Committee and that it never reached the Clerk's desk, and I will now read it:—

WHEREAS, The United States imports 1,600,000, tons of sugar yearly for which it pays $150,000,000; and,

WHEREAS, The tariff laws of 1890 provided that a bounty of 2 cents per pound should be paid for all sugar manufactured in the United States until the year 1905 and that foreign sugar come in free; and,

WHEREAS, By reason of this low treaty stipulations were entered into with the sugar producing countries to the south of us whereby their ports were open to the free entry of many of our farm products; and,

WHEREAS, By the terms of the bounty, our citizens' were induced to make large investments in sugar plants and long time contracts, and,

WHEREAS, The repeal of this bounty has closed the ports of these countries to the free entry of our products, to the detriment of the agricultural classes and to the great injury to those who were, by the terms of the law, induced to make large investments and enter into long time contracts; therefore, be it

Resolved, That Congress be requested to restore the bounty as it existed in the tariff law of 1890.

MR. SAVAGE (of Kansas): Mr. Chairman, two days ago, when this congress had full delegations present, a resolution was introduced to pay the farmer a small bounty on staple products shipped out of this country. It was ascertained at that time that the sentiment of this meeting was against it and it was referred, to come up at our next regular meeting. Now, to-day, at this moment, we have in attendance not over one-eighth of the delegates; they have gone home and it seems to me unfair for the congress at this time to pass that resolution when seven-eighths of the members have gone. It will not be a fair expression of this congress, and I move you it be referred to the Executive Committee to pass on at our next regular meeting at Omaha.

MR. MARSHALL: Mr. Chairman, I was Secretary of the Committee on Resolutions, and I think the gentleman is mistaken in his statement. That resolution was never approved by the Committee on Resolutions. We never got it. It was referred to a sub-committee. That sub-committee killed it. We have never reported it back to the convention. There are at least fifty resolutions that went to the different sub-committees and they never came back to the House. We never reported favorably on that resolution.

THE CHAIRMAN: The only ground upon which it can be introduced or entertained, is a supposition that the Committee on Resolutions adopted it. If that is not the case, of course it has no standing. It cannot be entertained now.

MR. CRAIG: Would it not be quite parliamentary to bring that resolution upon its merits and let this congress pass upon it? I move now that it be placed in the immediate position of being passed upon.

THE CHAIRMAN: There is a resolution already taking precedence of that, that this resolution be referred to the Executive Committee.

This motion was seconded and carried.

M. J. DONOVAN (of California): Mr. President, I have a resolution that I would like to introduce, that I think is in the interest of the Trans-Mississippi Congress. With your permission I will read it from my place on the floor.

"*Resolved,* That the Executive Committee be authorized by a two-thirds vote when in session, or two-thirds of the members signing a paper indorsing the same, to perform any work that may in their judgment further the action or suggestions of this congress in the Congress of the United States.

My reason for offering that, gentlemen, is this: the committee will not meet for a year, or ten months at least. There have been many important things passed by this congress, and it seems to me that it is but meet and proper and just that the executive body of this congress, the only thing that lives after we adjourn, may have the power and right to do things, to adopt necessary resolutions and take necessary measures to have the suggestions and the deeds of this congress placed properly before the Congress of the United States, and follow up to that ultimate success that we all of us desire.

This motion was duly seconded and carried.

MR. WHITMORE: One of the members of the Executive Committee has called attention to the fact that considerable work has been laid out by the Committee, which may make it necessary to raise some funds. An announcement of the new plan of organization will be sent to all delegates, and we desire them to make an endeavor to see that the funds for the organization are forthcoming from the commercial organizations of their respective States.

A motion was made that the congress adjourn *sine die.*

PRESIDENT CANNON: Before adjourning, the Chair desires to express thanks to the Congress for the courtesies extended to him and to congratulate the Congress on the harmony of its proceedings and the solidity with which it attended to its business. In accordance with the motion which has been made, this Trans-Mississippi Congress now stands adjourned, to meet at Omaha at the call of the Executive Committee.

RESOLUTIONS

ADOPTED BY

The Trans-Mississippi Commercial Congress

AT ITS SEVENTH SESSION,

HELD AT

ST. LOUIS, NOVEMBER 26TH–30TH, 1894.

NICARAGUA CANAL.

Resolved, That the Trans-Mississippi Commercial Congress respectfully and urgently requests legislative action on behalf of the prompt construction of the Nicaragua Canal under the control and supervision of the Government of the United States.

WEST INDIES AND SOUTH AMERICA — Extension of Trade.

Resolved, That this convention recommend the encouragement by Congress of more extended trade relations with the West Indies and with the Republics of South America, in so far as such relations can be extended by friendly legislation.

AMERICAN RAILWAYS, TRANS-PACIFIC STEAMSHIPS AND PACIFIC COAST CITIES — Discrimination against.

Resolved, That the Congress of the United States be requested to investigate the alleged discrimination against American railways, American Trans-Pacific steamships and American Pacific Coast cities by the privilege given to United States consuls outside of the United States to pass goods to the points of destination without appraisement or inspection.

AMERICAN PRODUCTS — Use in the U. S. Navy.

Resolved, That we approve the true American ideas of the Hon. H. A. Herbert, Sec'y of the Navy, in fostering and using American as distinguished from foreign supplies, and we do further recommend that a departmental order or proper legislation be made that will insure the use of American coal and American products in the United States Navy where the same can be done without material loss to the Government.

Mississippi River Commission — Approval of Work of.

Resolved, That we approve of the experiments made by the Mississippi River Commission for the removal of obstructions by the use of dredges and portable jetties in order that that plan may be thoroughly tested.

Alaska — Laws.

Resolved, That this Congress, representing the interests of the great West, do most earnestly petition the Congress of the United States to pass such laws as will insure to the inhabitants of the Territory of Alaska protection to landed interests, a proper administration of law and order throughout the territory, and the extension of mail facilities into the Yukon river district, to Northwestern Alaska and Fish river districts. To carry out this resolution we earnestly ask that a commission be appointed at the next session of Congress, of which the governor of the Territory shall be an *ex-officio* member, whose duty it shall be to visit the different sections of the Territory and to render a report to Congress; and that such recommendation take due form of law by appropriate legislation.

Duluth Harbor — Appropriation.

Resolved, That, in view of the great agricultural resources of the northern part of the great Trans-Mississippi regions, Congress should appropriate sufficient money to increase the depth of the water in the harbor of Duluth from sixteen feet, its present depth, to twenty feet, the Government standard.

Hennepin Canal — Appropriation.

Resolved, That the Illinois and Mississippi Canal, known as the Hennepin, and connecting the Mississippi river and the lakes, should receive a sufficient appropriation annually from Congress to speedily finish the work.

Texas Coast — Deep Water Appropriations.

Resolved, That this convention through its Secretary request all members of the United States Congress from the Trans-Mississippi States to favor liberal appropriations for deep water on the Texas coast.

Classification of Mineral Lands in Northern Pacific Land Grant.

Resolved, That the members of the Senate and House of the United States Congress, from the several Trans-Mississippi States, be requested by this Congress to give their hearty support to House bill No. 3,476 (which having passed the House is now in the hands of the Senate Committee on Public Lands), providing for the examination and classification, as to their mineral character, of the lands on the odd numbered sections, within the limits of the grant to the Northern Pacific Railroad, in the States of Montana and Idaho; and to assist in passing similar bills, in aid of the other mining States and Territories, in which are vast quantities of mineral lands, still unpatented, on the odd-numbered sections, within the limits of the railroad grants.

HYDRAULIC MINING.

Resolved, That this Congress heartily indorses the recommendation of the Miners' Convention, recently held in San Francisco, regarding the urgency of the appropriation for the construction of dams in the mutual interest of hydraulic mining and navigation, and further urges upon Senators and Representatives the extension of similar provisions to other States and Territories where similar conditions may now or hereafter exist.

MINING SCHOOLS — Support of.

Resolved, That Senators and Representatives be urgently solicited to secure the passage of an amendment to the bill passed by the National Congress at its last session, providing that proceeds of the sale of public lands to an amount not exceeding $12,000, in each State designated in said bill, shall annually be applied to the support of Mining Schools and Mining Investigations, extending the application of said bill to all the Territories in which mining is an important industry.

MINING LAWS — Amendment to Sec. 2,335 U. S. Mining Act.

Resolved, That the members of Congress of the Trans-Mississippi States be requested to aid in securing the following amendment to the United States Mining Act, to wit, to add to section 2,335 the following words:—

PROVIDED, That all applicants for patent for lands upon which a mineral location has been made and notice of such location recorded, must, except when otherwise in this act provided, give to such mineral claimant notice of said application, in writing, if possible, or otherwise by notice of publication in a newspaper, published in the county wherein such lands are situated, at least once a week for sixty days.

AND PROVIDED FURTHER, That any contest arising from the character of the land as mineral or non-mineral, shall, upon the application of any party in interest, and within ninety days from the service of such notice, in writing or last day of such newspaper publication, be referred to a court of competent jurisdiction for determination; and suit by either party shall be commenced within thirty days after such reference has been made; and upon the filing of a certified copy of the final judgment, as determined by the procedure of the State in which the trial is had, patent shall issue accordingly.

SILVER.

WHEREAS, An appreciating money standard impairs all contracts, bankrupts enterprises, makes idle money profitable by increasing its purchasing power and suspends productive forces of our people; and

WHEREAS, The spoliation consequent upon the outlawry of silver in the interest of the creditor class, by constantly increasing the value of gold, is undermining all industrial society, therefore,

Resolved, That we demand the immediate restoration of the free and unlimited coinage of gold and silver at the present ratio of sixteen to one, without waiting for the aid or consent of any other nation on earth.

CURRENCY.

Resolved, That in direct opposition to the plan known as the Baltimore plan, the sense of this convention is that all issues of paper money should be by the general Government.

Resolved, That it is the sense of this Congress that the pending proposition for a reformation of our paper currency is one that in our judgment would create additional and perhaps insurmountable difficulties to the return to bimetallism, and that we are opposed to the same.

That in any currency reform acted upon we demand that a constituent part thereof shall be the remonetization of silver, or that it shall be of such a character as to be no impediment to our return to bimetallism as it existed prior to 1873.

DEEP WATER HARBOR AT SAN PEDRO, CALIFORNIA.

WHEREAS, Upon the completion of the Nicaragua Canal, a deep water harbor on the southern coast of California is indispensable to the commercial and naval necessities of the country, there being no adequate harbor facilities between San Diego and San Francisco, a distance of six hundred miles of sea coast; and,

WHEREAS, The United States Government, through its corps of army engineers, has, by its several boards in exhaustive reports unanimously selected San Pedro Harbor as the most eligible site for such deep water harbor, and the only practicable harbor of refuge between the points Dume and Capistrano, as required by Act of Congress; and,

WHEREAS, There is an interior harbor at San Pedro, which has been improved by the Government under direction of its engineer corps, and which has a dock frontage of more than two miles in extent,

THEREFORE, *Be it Resolved by this Trans-Mississippi Congress*, That the Congress of the United States at its coming session be urged to provide for the construction of this deep water harbor at San Pedro as already determined by the several Acts of Congress, and in accordance with the several recommendations of the Boards of United States Army Engineers (as shown by Executive Documents Nos. 39 and 41 of the Fifty-Second Congress, first and second sessions), and that the further improvement of the interior harbor at San Pedro be earnestly recommended.

UPPER MISSISSIPPI RIVER IMPROVEMENT.

Resolved, That this Congress urge such continuous appropriation by the Government for the improvement of the Upper Mississippi River as shall maintain the present improvements intact, and add such new ones as shall be needed, including dredging and jetties so far as practicable.

RAMIE — Its Cultivation.

Resolved, That the Trans-Mississippi Commercial Congress, advocating a diversification of our national industries, recognizing the great textile value of Ramie and its luxuriant growth in our Gulf States, and believing that recent improvements in mechanical and chemical processes of preparing the fibre will render the production of this useful staple a profitable domestic industry, recommend the cultivation of this plant to our Southern States as a new and important source of textile wealth.

OAKLAND HARBOR — Improvement of.

Resolved, That we recognize the injury that has been done to the City of Oakland and its commercial interests by the long delay in completing the improvement of its harbor, and we urge upon the Congress of the United States, not only on economic grounds, but also because of its imperative necessity, that an appropriation sufficient to finish the work be at once made, and that Oakland be also made a port of delivery.

CALIFORNIA RIVERS AND HYDRAULIC MINING.

WHEREAS, The Sacramento and San Joaquin rivers, the great waterways of California, are threatened with destruction by debris from hydraulic mining; and

WHEREAS, The filling of the channels of these rivers by such debris causes immense injury to adjacent farming lands; and

WHEREAS, Discontinuances of such mining prevents the output of large quantities of gold and the community suffers from lack of the money which should be made of that gold; and

WHEREAS, The National Government can cope with these conflicting conditions; now therefore be it

Resolved, As the sense of this Congress that the Government of the United States should make sufficient appropriations for, and cause to be done such work of impounding mining debris as may permit hydraulic mining without its causing injury to the navigable waters of this State and to adjacent lands, and should provide necessary appropriations for improving and maintaining the navigation of such streams.

FARRALONE CABLE.

WHEREAS, The Farralone Islands are situated West of the entrance to San Francisco Harbor, about twenty-eight (28) miles, and are the only guardians and watchmen of the entrance to the Golden Gate; and

WHEREAS, The commercial interests of the city and harbor at San Francisco require cable connection between the Farralone Light House, Weather Bureau and the United States Signal Station;

Resolved, That Congress be urgently requested to make provision for the introduction of a bill to provide for an appropriation for the construction of a United States Submarine Cable from a point on the mainland adjacent to San Francisco Harbor, to the Farralone Islands.

HAWAIIAN CABLE.

WHEREAS, The history of the Hawaiian Islands shows that their civilization and development are the result of the energy and progress of the United States to such an extent that they are to-day pre-eminently an American colony, and that they depend for their future progress and for the maintenance of their civilization upon their connection with this country; and

WHEREAS, The commerce of Hawaii is almost exclusively with the Pacific Coast States of the United States, and large investments of capital belonging to United States citizens have been made from time to time in the Hawaiian Islands;

Resolved, That this Trans-Mississippi Congress respectfully calls the attention of all United States Congressman and Senators to the imperative necessity of the immediate construction of a Submarine Cable between a point on the Pacific Coast of the United States and the Hawaiian Islands.

CAREY BILL — Extension to Territories.

Resolved, That Congress be earnestly requested to pass an Amendment to the Carey Act (which donates 1,000,000 acres of the arid lands to each State in which they are located), extending the provisions of that Act to the Territories.

Territories — Enabling Acts.

Resolved, That we earnestly urge upon Congress at its coming session to pass Enabling Acts providing for the admission of Oklahoma, New Mexico and Arizona into the Union as States. The admission of these Territories into Statehood would greatly promote their material prosperity, add to the wealth and strength of the Nation, and vest in the people of said Territories, the powers of local self-government to which they are justly entitled.

Indian Territory — Territorial or State Government with Oklahoma.

Resolved, That the alarming condition of affairs which exists in the Indian Territory is a constant menace to the peace and safety of the people of the surrounding States, an obstruction to interstate commerce, and a disgrace to our civilization. The tribal governments of that Territory have signally failed to observe the requirements of existing treaties with the United States, and to protect from robbery and violence the lives and property of the people. We believe with the Dawes Commission, that the lands of the Five Tribes, now monopolized by the few, should be allotted in severalty to all the members of the tribes, the tribal governments abolished, and the Indians made citizens of the United States. To this end we favor the prompt provision by Congress for a State and Territorial government over the allotted lands, complete court jurisdiction, and the uniting of all, or a part of said lands with Oklahoma in a single Statehood.

Non-Mineral Lands — Cession to States and Territories.

Resolved, That we favor the cession of the non-mineral arid lands to the several States and Territories in which they are situated, and that we favor the control by said States and Territories of the local waters for irrigation.

Uncompahgre and Uintah Indian Commissions.

Whereas, By Act of Congress, dated August 16, 1894, the Executive Department of the United States was authorized to appoint commissioners to negotiate with the Indians on the Uncompahgre and Uintah reservations in Utah, with a view to the opening of said reservations to settlement by home-seekers, and

Whereas, The delay in putting said Act in operation is detrimental to the development and progress of the Trans-Mississippi region,

Now, Therefore, Be it Resolved, That this Trans-Mississippi Commercial Congress hereby urges upon the Executive Department of the National Government the necessity of immediate action in accordance with said Act of August 16, 1894.

NATIONAL GRANGE — Committee of Five to Attend.

WHEREAS, The National Grange Patrons of Husbandry, representing the largest body of organized farmers of the United States, with organizations and membership in nearly every State in the Union, in a spirit of equity has, by resolution, decided to call a conference of the leading industries for the purpose of considering the Tariff and Monetary questions; therefore, be it

Resolved, That the Trans-Mississippi Congress assembled at St. Louis, Mo., does hereby appoint a committee of five to be selected by the Chairman of this convention to attend the said Conference.

MISSOURI RIVER COMMISSION.

WHEREAS, The Congress of the United States did at its last session appropriate various sums for the protection of valuable property and to prevent the destruction of long established lines of interstate traffic communication by the ravages of the Missouri river, and,

WHEREAS, The sum of $35,000 was appropriated for the protection of property and to prevent the destruction of the bridge connecting the States of Missouri and Kansas at the city of Atchison, which bridge has been for many years a highway for interstate commerce, and,

WHEREAS, The expenditure of these appropriations has been committed to the care of the Missouri River Commission, which body fails to perform the trust imposed upon it;

Therefore, Be it resolved, That this Congress request the United States Senators and Representatives in Congress from the Trans-Mississippi States to secure speedy action by said Missouri River Commission, and

Resolved, That a copy of these resolutions be transmitted to the Senators and Representatives and the Honorable Secretary of War.

PUGET SOUND — Defense of.

Resolved, That the Congress of the United States is urgently requested to take immediate steps for the adequate defense of Puget Sound by means of war vessels regularly stationed there and by suitable fortifications on the shore.

EXECUTIVE COMMITTEE TO ACT DURING INTERIM.

Resolved, That the Executive Committee be authorized by a two-thirds vote when in session, or by two-thirds of the members signing a paper indorsing the same, to perform any work that may, in their judgment, further the action or suggestions of this Congress in the Congress of the United States.

PUBLICATION OF A PERIODICAL.

Resolved, That we favor the publication of a periodical in the interest of the Trans-Mississippi Commercial Congress, and refer the matter to the Executive Committee, with power to act.

A. L. BLACK — To Proceed to Washington.

Resolved, That Mr. A. L. Black, of the State of Washington, be hereby appointed to present to the Honorable, the Secretary of the Navy, the resolution of the Congress favoring the use of American products in the U. S. Navy.

ACTIONS OF THE CONGRESS — Presentation to U. S. Congress.

Resolved, That the President of this Congress, the Hon. George Q. Cannon and the Hon. W. J. Bryan, Chairman of the Committee on Resolutions, be instructed to present to the Congress of the United States, at its forthcoming session, and other proper bodies, the various actions of this Congress.

THANKS — To the Press.

Resolved, That the thanks of this Congress are hereby extended to the representatives of the Press for the full and accurate reports of the proceedings, and the aid they have afforded in giving wide publicity to the acts and debates of the Congress.

THANKS — To Officers.

Resolved, That the thanks of this Congress are hereby extended to its Presidents, H. R. Whitmore and Hon. Geo. Q. Cannon, for the fair and impartial manner in which they have performed the duties of presiding officer, and also to Messrs. Butterfield, Morgan and Edwards, the Secretaries, and to Mr. Chas. F. Johnson, the official stenographer, for the prompt and efficient discharge of their respective duties.

THANKS —. To the Business Organizations and Citizens of St. Louis.

Resolved, That the Trans-Mississippi Commercial Congress hereby expresses its grateful appreciation of the public spirit, generosity and efficient action of the Merchant's Exchange, and other business organizations of St. Louis, as shown in the ample provision and convenient arrangements which they have made for the requirements of the Congress, and of the courtesy and generous hospitality which has been extended by the citizens of St. Louis, both collectively and individually, to the delegates.

INDEX.